RELENTLESS

DEAN KOONTZ

.

RELE

A Novel

NTLESS

Bantam Books

Copyright © 2009 by Dean Koontz

Published in the United States by Bantam Books, an imprint of The Random House Publishing Group, a division of Random House, Inc., New York.

A signed, limited edition has been privately printed by Charnel House. Charnelhouse.com

BANTAM BOOKS and the rooster colophon are registered trademarks of Random House, Inc.

Library of Congress Cataloging-in-Publication Data
Koontz, Dean R. (Dean Ray), 1945–
    Relentless / Dean Koontz. —1st ed.
        p.   cm.
    ISBN 978-0-553-80714-1
1. Novelists—Fiction.   2. Critics—Fiction.   I. Title.
    PS3561.O55R45 2009
    813'.54—dc22   2009009866

Printed in the United States of America on acid-free paper

www.bantamdell.com

9   8   7   6   5   4   3   2   1

First Edition

Text design and title page art by Virginia Norey

To Gerda
for everything

Trifles make the sum of life.
—Charles Dickens, *David Copperfield*

The issue is clear. It is between light and darkness,
and everyone must choose his side.
—G. K. Chesterton

All men are tragic. . . . All men are comic. . . . Every man
is important if he loses his life; and every man is funny if
he loses his hat.
—G. K. Chesterton, *Charles Dickens*

Part One

Penny Boom Says Let It Go

Chapter 1

This is a thing I've learned: Even with a gun to my head, I am capable of being convulsed with laughter. I am not sure what this extreme capacity for mirth says about me. You'll have to decide for yourself.

Beginning one night when I was six years old and for twenty-seven years thereafter, good luck was my constant companion. The guardian angel watching over me had done a superb job.

As a reward for his excellent stewardship of my life, perhaps my angel—let's call him Ralph—was granted a sabbatical. Perhaps he was reassigned. *Something* sure happened to him for a while during my thirty-fourth year, when darkness found us.

In the days when Ralph was diligently on the job, I met and courted Penny Boom. I was twenty-four and she was twenty-three.

Women as beautiful as Penny previously looked through me. Oh, occasionally they looked at me, but as though I reminded them of something they had seen once in a book of exotic fungi, something they had never expected—or wished—to see in real life.

She was also too smart and too witty and too graceful to waste her time with a guy like me, so I can only assume that a supernatural power coerced her into marrying me. In my mind's eye, I see Ralph kneeling beside Penny's bed while she slept, whispering, "He's the one for you, he's the one for you, no matter how absurd that concept may seem at this moment, he really is the one for you."

We were married more than three years when she gave birth to Milo, who is fortunate to have his mother's blue eyes and black hair.

Our preferred name for our son was Alexander. Penny's mother, Clotilda—who is named Nancy on her birth certificate—threatened that if we did not call him Milo, she would blow her brains out.

Penny's father, Grimbald—whose parents named him Larry— insisted that he would not clean up after such a suicide, and neither Penny nor I had the stomach for the job. So Alexander became Milo.

I am told that the family's surname really is Boom and that they come from a long line of Dutch merchants. When I ask what commodity his ancestors sold, Grimbald becomes solemn and evasive, and Clotilda pretends that she is deaf.

My name is Cullen Greenwich—pronounced *gren-itch,* like the town in Connecticut. Since I was a little boy, most people have called me Cubby.

When I first dated Penny, her mom tried calling me Hildebrand, but I would have none of it.

Hildebrand is from the Old German, and means "battle torch" or "battle sword." Clotilda is fond of power names, except in the case of our son, when she was prepared to self-destruct if we didn't give him a name that meant "beloved and gentle."

Our friend and internist, Dr. Jubal Frost, who delivered Milo, swears that the boy never cried at birth, that he was born smiling. In fact, Jubal says our infant softly hummed a tune, on and off, in the delivery room.

Although I was present at the birth, I have no memory of Milo's musical performance because I fainted. Penny does not remember it either, because, although conscious, she was distracted by the postpartum hemorrhaging that had caused me to pass out.

I do not doubt Jubal Frost's story. Milo has always been full of surprises. For good reason, his nickname is Spooky.

On his third birthday, Milo declared, "We're gonna rescue a doggy."

Penny and I assumed he was acting out something he had seen on TV, but he was a preschooler on a mission. He climbed onto a kitchen chair, plucked the car keys from the Peg–Board, and hurried out to the garage as if to set off in search of an endangered canine.

We took the keys away from him, but for more than an hour, he followed us around chanting, "We're gonna rescue a doggy," until to save our sanity, we decided to drive him to a pet shop and redirect his canine enthusiasm toward a gerbil or a turtle, or both.

En route, he said, "We're almost to the doggy." Half a block later, he pointed to a sign—ANIMAL SHELTER. We assumed wrongly that it was the silhouette of a German shepherd that caught his attention, not the words on the sign. "In there, Daddy."

Scores of forlorn dogs occupied cages, but Milo walked directly to the middle of the center row in the kennel and said, "This one."

She was a fifty-pound two-year-old Australian shepherd mix with a shaggy black-and-white coat, one eye blue and the other gray. She had no collie in her, but Milo named her Lassie.

Penny and I loved her the moment we saw her. Somewhere a gerbil and a turtle would remain in need of a home.

In the next three years, we never heard a single bark from the dog. We wondered whether our Lassie, following the example of the original, would at last bark if Milo fell down an abandoned well or became trapped in a burning barn, or whether she would instead try to alert us to our boy's circumstances by employing urgent pantomime.

Until Milo was six and Lassie was five, our lives were not only free of calamity but also without much inconvenience. Our fortunes changed with the publication of my sixth novel, *One O'Clock Jump*.

My first five had been bestsellers. Way to go, Angel Ralph.

Penny Boom, of course, is *the* Penny Boom, the acclaimed writer and illustrator of children's books. They are brilliant, funny books.

More than for her dazzling beauty, more than for her quick mind, more than for her great good heart, I fell in love with her for her sense of humor. If she ever lost her sense of humor, I would have to dump her. Then I'd kill myself because I couldn't live without her.

The name on her birth certificate is Brunhild, which means someone who is armored for the fight. By the time she was five, she insisted on being called Penny.

At the start of World War Waxx, as we came to call it, Penny and Milo and Lassie and I lived in a fine stone-and-stucco house, under the benediction of graceful phoenix palms, in Southern California. We didn't have an ocean view, but didn't need one, for we were focused on one another and on our books.

Because we'd seen our share of Batman movies, we knew that Evil with a capital *E* stalked the world, but we never expected that it would suddenly, intently turn its attention to our happy household or that this evil would be drawn to us by a book I had written.

Having done a twenty-city tour for each of my previous novels, I persuaded my publisher to spare me that ordeal for *One O'Clock Jump*.

Consequently, on publication day, a Tuesday in early November, I got up at three o'clock in the morning to brew a pot of coffee and to repair to my first-floor study. Unshaven, in pajamas, I undertook a series of thirty radio interviews, conducted by telephone, between

4:00 and 9:30 A.M., which began with morning shows on the East Coast.

Radio hosts, both talk-jocks and traditional tune-spinners, do better interviews than TV types. Rare is the TV interviewer who has read your book, but eight of ten radio hosts will have read it.

Radio folks are brighter and funnier, too—and often quite humble. I don't know why this last should be true, except perhaps the greater fame of facial recognition, which comes with regular television exposure, encourages pridefulness that ripens into arrogance.

After five hours on radio, I felt as though I might vomit if I heard myself say again the words *One O'Clock Jump*. I could see the day coming when, if I was required to do much publicity for a new book, I would write it but not allow its publication until I died.

If you have never been in the public eye, flogging your work like a carnival barker pitching a freak show to the crowd, this publish-only-after-death pledge may seem extreme. But protracted self-promotion drains something essential from the soul, and after one of these sessions, you need weeks to recover and to decide that one day it might be all right to like yourself again.

The danger in writing but not publishing was that my agent, Hudson "Hud" Jacklight, receiving no commissions, would wait only until three unpublished works had been completed before having me killed to free up the manuscripts for marketing.

And if I knew Hud as well as I thought I did, he would not arrange for a clean shot to the back of the head. He would want me to be tortured and dismembered in such a flamboyant fashion that he could make a rich deal for one of his true-crime clients to write a book about my murder.

If no publisher would pay a suitably immense advance for a book about an unsolved killing, Hud would have someone framed for it. Most likely Penny, Milo, and Lassie.

Anyway, after the thirtieth interview, I rose from my office chair and, reeling in self-disgust, made my way to the kitchen. My intention was to eat such an unhealthy breakfast that my guilt over the cholesterol content would distract me from the embarrassment of all the self-promotion.

Dependable Penny had delayed her breakfast so she could eat with me and hear all of the incredibly witty things I wished I had said in those thirty interviews. In contrast to my tousled hair, unshaven face, and badly rumpled pajamas, she wore a crisp white blouse and lemon-yellow slacks, and as usual her skin *glowed* as though it were translucent and she were lit from inside.

As I entered the room, she was serving blueberry pancakes, and I said, "You look scrumptious. I could pour maple syrup on you and eat you alive."

"Cannibalism," Milo warned me, "is a crime."

"It's not a worldwide crime," I told him. "Some places it's a culinary preference."

"It's a crime," he insisted.

Between his fifth and sixth birthdays, Milo had decided on a career in law enforcement. He said that too many people were lawless and that the world was run by thugs. He was going to grow up and do something about it.

Lots of kids want to be policemen. Milo intended to become the director of the FBI *and* the secretary of defense, so that he would be empowered to dispense justice to evildoers both at home and abroad.

Here on the brink of World War Waxx, Milo perched on a dinette chair, elevated by a thick foam pillow because he was diminutive for his age. Blue block letters on his white T-shirt spelled COURAGE.

Later, the word on his chest would seem like an omen.

Having finished his breakfast long ago, my bright-eyed son was nursing a glass of chocolate milk and reading a comic book. He could read at college level, though his interests were not those of either a six-year-old or a frat boy.

"What trash is this?" I asked, picking up the comic.

"Dostoyevsky," he said.

Frowning at the cover illustration, I wondered, "How can they condense *Crime and Punishment* into a comic book?"

Penny said, "It comes as a boxed set of thirty-six double-thick issues. He's on number seven."

Returning the comic to Milo, I said, "Maybe the question should be—*why* would they condense *Crime and Punishment* into a comic book?"

"Raskolnikov," Milo solemnly informed me, tapping a page of the illustrated classic with one finger, "is a totally confused guy."

"That makes two of us," I said.

I sat at the table, picked up a squeeze bottle of liquid butter, and hosed my pancakes.

"Trying to bury the shame of self-promotion under cholesterol guilt?" Penny asked.

"Exactly."

From across the dinette, Lassie watched me butter the flapjacks. She is not permitted to sit *at* the table with us; however, because she refuses to live entirely at dog level, she is allowed a chair at a four-foot remove, where she can observe and feel part of the family at mealtimes.

For such a cute dog, she is often surprisingly hard to read. She has a poker face. She was not drooling. She rarely did. She was less obsessed with food than were most dogs.

Instead, she cocked her head and studied me as if she were an anthropologist and I were a member of a primitive tribe engaged in an inscrutable ritual.

Maybe she was amazed that I proved capable of operating as complex a device as squeeze-bottle butter with a flip-up nozzle. I have a reputation for incompetence with tools and machines.

For instance, I am no longer permitted to change a punctured tire. In the event of a flat, I am required to call the automobile club and get out of their way when they arrive.

I will not explain why this is the case, because it's not a particularly interesting story. Besides, when I got to the part about the monkey dressed in a band uniform, you would think I was making up the whole thing, even though my insurance agent could confirm the truth of every detail.

God gave me a talent for storytelling. He didn't think I would also need to have the skill to repair a jet engine or build a nuclear reactor from scratch. Who am I to second-guess God? Although . . . it would be nice to be able to use a hammer or a screwdriver at least once without a subsequent trip to the hospital emergency room.

Anyway, just as I raised the first bite of butter-drenched pancakes to my mouth, the telephone rang.

"Third line," Penny said.

The third is my direct business line, given only to my editors, publishers, agents, and attorneys.

I put down the still-laden fork, got up, and snared the wall phone on the fourth ring, before the call went to voice mail.

Olivia Cosima, my editor, said, "Cubby, you're a trouper. I hear from publicity, the radio interviews were brilliant."

"If brilliant means I made a fool of myself slightly less often than I expected to, then they were brilliant."

"Every writer now and then makes a fool of himself, dear. What's unique about you is—you've never made a total *ass* of yourself."

"I'm working on it."

"Listen, sweetheart, I just e-mailed you three major reviews that appeared this morning. Read the one by Shearman Waxx first."

I held my breath. Waxx was the senior critic for the nation's premier newspaper. He was feared, therefore revered. He had not reviewed any of my previous novels.

Because I didn't subscribe to that newspaper, I had never read Waxx. Nevertheless, I knew he was the most influential book critic in the country.

"And?" I asked.

Olivia said, "Why don't you read it first, and then we'll talk."

"Uh-oh."

"He favors boring minimalism, Cubby. The qualities he dislikes in your work are the very things readers hunger for. So it's really a selling review."

"Uh-oh."

"Call me after you've read it. And the other two, which are both wonderful. They more than compensate for Waxx."

When I turned away from the telephone, Penny was sitting at the table, holding her knife and fork not as if they were dining utensils but as if they were weapons. Having heard my side of the conversation with my editor, she had sensed a threat to her family, and she was as armored for the fight as the Brunhild whom she had once been.

"What?" she asked.

"Shearman Waxx reviewed my book."

"Is that all?"

"He didn't like it."

"Who gives a flying"—she glanced at Milo before finishing her question with a nonsense word instead of a vulgarity—"furnal."

"What's a flying furnal?" Milo asked.

"A kind of squirrel," I said, fully aware that my gifted son's intellectual genius lay in fields other than biology.

Penny said, "I thought the book was terrific, and I'm the most honest critic you're ever going to have."

"Yeah, but a couple hundred thousand people read his reviews."

"Nobody reads his reviews but geeky aficionados of snarkiness."

"You mean it has wings?" Milo asked.

I frowned at him. "Does what have wings?"

"The flying furnal."

"No. It has air bladders."

"Do yourself a favor," Penny advised. "Don't read the review."

"If I don't read it, I won't know what he said."

"Precisely."

"What do you mean—air bladders?" Milo asked.

I said, "Inflatable sacs under its skin."

"Has any review, good or bad, ever changed the way you write?" Penny asked.

"Of course not. I've got a spine."

"So there's nothing to be gained from reading this one."

Milo said, "It doesn't fly. What it must do—it must just float."

"It can fly," I insisted.

"But air bladders, no wings—it's a squirrel blimp," Milo said.

"Blimps fly," I said. "They have an engine and a big propeller behind the passenger gondola."

Milo saw the weakness of my contention: "Squirrels don't have engines."

"No, but once it inflates its bladders, the furnal kicks its hind feet very fast, like a swimmer, and propels itself forward."

Lassie remained poker-faced, but I knew that she had not been convinced by my lecture on the biology of the flying furnal.

Milo wasn't buying it either. "Mom, he's doing it again. Dad's lying."

"He's not lying," Penny assured him. "He's exercising the strong and limber imagination of a fine novelist."

"Yeah? What's the difference from lying?"

As if curious about her mistress's reply, Lassie leaned forward in her chair and cocked her head toward Penny.

"Lies hurt people," Penny explained. "Imagination makes life more fun."

"Like right now," I said, "I'm imagining Shearman Waxx being attacked and killed by a flying furnal with rabies."

"Let it go," Penny advised.

"I told Olivia I'd call her back after I read the review."

"Don't read it," Penny warned.

"I promised Olivia I'd call her."

Mouth full of pancake, Penny shook her head ruefully.

"I'm a big boy," I said. "This kind of thing doesn't get to me. I have to read it. But don't worry—I'll laugh it off."

I returned to my study and switched on the computer.

Rather than scroll through Olivia's e-mail on the screen, I printed out her opening comment and the three reviews.

First, I read the one from *USA Today,* and then the one from the *Washington Post.* They were raves, and they fortified me.

With professional detachment, I read Shearman Waxx's review.

The syphilitic swine.

Chapter 2

In New York, my editor, Olivia Cosima, had delayed going to lunch until I called her.

Slumped in my office chair, bare feet propped on my desk, I said, "Olivia, this Waxx guy doesn't understand my book is in part a comic novel."

"No, dear, he doesn't. And you should be grateful for that, because if he realized it was funny, he would have said that it failed as a comic novel."

"He thinks a solid metaphor is 'ponderous prose.'"

"He's a product of the modern university, Cubby. Figures of speech are considered oppressive."

"Oppressive? Who do they oppress?"

"Those who don't understand them."

"What—I'm supposed to write to please the ignorant?"

"He wouldn't put it that way, dear."

Staring at my bare feet, I decided that my toes were ugly. Whatever inspired Penny to marry me, it hadn't been my feet.

"But, Olivia, this review is full of errors—character details, plot points. I counted eleven. He calls my female lead Joyce when her name is Judith."

"That was one we all missed, dear."

"Missed?"

"The publicity letter that accompanied each reviewer's advance-reading copy mistakenly referred to her as Joyce."

"I proofread that letter. I approved it."

"Yes, dear. So did I. Probably six of us proofed and okayed it, and we all missed the Joyce thing. It happens."

I felt stupid. Humiliated. Unprofessional.

Then my mind cleared: "Wait, wait. He's reviewing the book, not the publicity letter that went with it. In the book, it's Judith."

"Do you know the British writer J. G. Ballard?"

"Yes, of course. He's wonderful."

"He reviewed books for—I think it was *The Times* of London. Years after he stopped reviewing, he said he'd had a policy of giving only good reviews to books he didn't have time to read. Would that every-one were so fair."

After a silence for reflection on her words, I said, "Are you saying Shearman Waxx might not have read *One O'Clock Jump*?"

"Sometimes you're so naïve, I want to pinch your cute pink cheeks," Olivia said. "Dear, I'm sure he skimmed parts of it, and perhaps an assistant read the whole thing."

"But that's . . . that's . . . dishonest."

"You've had an easy ascent, Cubby, your first book a major best-seller. You don't realize that the literary community has a few charm-ing little islands, but they're floating in a huge cesspool."

My insteps were as ugly as my toes. Swinging my feet off the desk, hiding them under my chair, I said, "His syntax isn't good."

Olivia said, "Yes, I often take a red pencil to his reviews."

"Have you ever sent one to him—corrected?"

"I am not insane, dear."

"I meant anonymously."

"I like my face as it's currently arranged."

"How can he be considered the premier critic in the country?"

"He's respected in the literary community."

"Why?"

"Because he's vicious, dear. People fear him."

"Fear isn't respect."

"In our community, it's close enough."

"Olivia, what should I do?"

"Do? Do nothing. You've always received ninety percent good reviews, and you will this time. The book is strong. It will sell."

"But this rankles. The injustice."

"Injustice is hyperbole, Cubby. It's not as if you've been packed off to a gulag."

"Well, it's frustrating."

After a silence, she said, "You aren't thinking of responding to him, are you? That would be a terrible mistake, Cubby."

"I know."

"You would only look like a defensive whiner."

"It's just that he made so many mistakes. And his syntax is so bad. I could really eviscerate him."

"Dear, the man can't be eviscerated because he has no viscera. He's a walking colon. If you cut him open, you only end up covered in crap."

By the time I returned to the kitchen, Milo and Lassie were no longer there, and Penny had finished eating. She stood at the sink, rinsing her plate before putting it in the dishwasher.

Now that they were cold and glistening with milky liquid butter, my pancakes looked as unappetizing as the deflated air bladders of a flying furnal. No longer hungry, I decided to skip breakfast.

Turning from the sink, drying her hands on a towel, Penny said, "So you read the review?"

"But he didn't read my book. Maybe he skimmed it. He's got so much wrong."

"What did Olivia think?"

"She says he's a walking colon."

"You shouldn't have let him into your head, Cubby. But now that he's in there, flush him out."

"I will."

She put her arms around me. "You're a sweet, talented man, and I love you."

Holding her tight, I said, "Don't look at my feet."

"What's wrong with your feet?"

"Everything. I should never go barefoot. Let's have dinner at Roxie's, celebrate publication day."

"That's my boy. You went off the track for a bit, but now you're on it again."

"Maybe I am."

"Let it go. Remember what Gilbert said."

She was an admirer of the late G. K. Chesterton, the English writer, and she made me an admirer of his, as well.

"'Nothing,'" she quoted, "'can do a man harm unless he fears it.' There's no reason to fear a weasel like Shearman Waxx."

"If I had shaved, brushed my teeth, and didn't have sour-coffee breath, I'd kiss you so hard."

Pinching my lower lip between her thumb and forefinger, and pulling it into a pout, she said, "I'll be around when you've cleaned up your act."

In the first-floor hallway, heading toward the stairs, I passed the open door of my study and saw Milo and Lassie sitting side by side in my office chair, boosted by a sofa pillow. This was a Norman Rockwell moment for the twenty-first century: a boy and his dog surfing the Internet.

Stepping behind the chair, I saw on the monitor an aerial view of a seaside house with an orange barrel-tile roof.

"What's that?" I asked.

Milo said, "Google Earth. I googled the guy, where he lives."

"What guy?"

"The Waxx guy."

When *I* was six years old, my technological prowess amounted to helping my buddy Ned Lufferman build a tin-can rocket powered by firecrackers that he stole from his big brother's Fourth of July stash. Ned lost the little finger on his left hand, and I was rushed to the hospital with a second-degree burn on the nose. There was also some concern that my eyebrows would not grow back, but they did.

Milo clicked the mouse, and a street view of the Waxx property replaced the aerial shot.

With cream-colored walls and terra-cotta window surrounds, the Spanish Mediterranean residence was both handsome and romantic. Twin forty-foot magnolias canopied the front yard, and red bougainvillea all but concealed the flanking property walls.

"I thought he was in New York," I said.

"No," said Milo. "Laguna Beach."

Barring heavy traffic, Laguna lay only twenty minutes away.

In this e-mail age, Waxx could live as far from his publisher as I lived from mine, yet meet his weekly deadlines. His presence in the vicinity was a surprise, though surely nothing but a coincidence.

Nevertheless, I was pricked by either intuition or imagination, and through me bled a cold premonition that the critic's proximity to me might be more significant than it seemed.

"Did you read the review?" I asked Milo.

"No. Mom told you—let it go. She's smart about this stuff."

"What stuff?"

"Most stuff."

"So if you didn't read the review, why did you google him?"

"It was Lassie's idea."

The dog turned her head to look back and up at me.

"Shearman Waxx is an enema," Milo informed me.

As I gently rubbed my thumbs behind Lassie's ears, I said, "While that may be true, it's not a nice thing to say."

"Wasn't me who said it."

Milo's small hands moved cat-quick from mouse to keyboard to mouse. He bailed from the current website and went to an online encyclopedia, to the biographical entry on Shearman Waxx.

Leaning over my son, I read aloud the first sentence on the screen: "'Shearman Thorndike Waxx, award-winning critic and author of three enormously successful college textbooks on creative writing, is something of an enema.'"

Milo said, "See?"

"It's an error," I explained. "They meant to write *enigma*."

"Enigma? I know what that is."

"A mystery, something obscure and puzzling."

"Yeah. Like Grandma Clotilda."

I continued reading: "'Waxx declines honorary doctorates and other awards requiring his attendance at any pubic event.'"

"What's a pubic event?" Milo asked.

"The word should be *public*." Scanning the screen, I said, "According to this, there's only one known photograph of Waxx."

"He's really, really old," said Milo.

"He is? How old?"

"He was born in 1868."

"They probably mean *1968*."

"Do real-book 'cyclopedias make so many mistakes?"

"No."

"Could we buy a real-book 'cyclopedia?"

"Absolutely."

"So when will we get Waxx?" Milo asked.

"What do you mean—get him?"

"Vengeance," Milo said, and Lassie growled softly. "When will we make him sorry he messed with you, Dad?"

Dismayed that Milo could read my anger so clearly and that it inspired him to talk of vengeance, I moved from behind his chair to his side, and with the mouse I clicked out of the encyclopedia.

"Revenge isn't a good thing, Milo." I switched off the computer. "Besides, Mr. Waxx was only doing what he's paid to do."

"What is he paid to do?"

"Read a book and tell his audience whether he liked it or not."

"Can't his audience read?"

"Yes, but they're busy, and they have so many books to choose from, so they trust his judgment."

"Why do they trust his judgment?"

"I have no idea."

The phone on my desk rang. The third line.

When I answered, Hud Jacklight, my literary agent, said, "The Waxx review. Great thing. You've arrived, Cubster."

"What do you mean—I've arrived? Hud, he gutted me."

Milo rolled his eyes and whispered to Lassie, "It's the Honker."

Because he doesn't understand children, Hud thinks they love it when he pinches their noses—their ears, their chins—while making a loud honking noise.

"Doesn't matter," Hud assured me. "It's a Waxx review. You've arrived. He takes you seriously. That's big."

Breaking her characteristic silence, Lassie issued a low growl while staring at the phone in my hand.

"Hud," I said, "apparently he didn't even read the book."

"Irrelevant. It's coverage. Coverage sells. You're a Waxx author now. That matters. A Waxx author. That's huge."

Although Hud pretends to read each of my novels, I know that he has never read any of them. He praises them without mentioning a plot point or a character.

Sometimes he selects a manuscript page at random and raves about the writing in a sentence or a paragraph. He reads it aloud over the telephone, as if my prose will sound fresh and limpid and magical to me by virtue of being delivered in his insistent cadences, but his voice is less that of a Shakespearean actor than that of a livestock auctioneer. By emphasizing the wrong words, he often reveals that he has no understanding of the context of the passage with which he has chosen to hector me.

"A Waxx author. Proud of you, Cubman. Celebrate tonight. You earned it."

"This is nothing to celebrate, Hud."

"Get a good wine. On me. Keep the receipt. I'll reimburse."

"Even Lassie thinks this review requires vengeance rather than celebration."

"A hundred-dollar bottle. Or eighty. There's good stuff at sixty. Wait. You said vengeance?"

"Milo said it and Lassie agreed. I explained it was a bad idea."

"Don't respond to Waxx."

"I won't."

"Don't respond, Cubman."

"I won't. I said I won't."

"Bad move. Very bad move."

"I'm already over it."

Milo had switched on the computer and returned to Google Earth, to the aerial photograph of the critic's house.

Leaning forward in the office chair, Lassie sniffed as though, even through an electronic medium, she could detect Waxx's infernal scent.

"Think positive," Hud Jacklight encouraged me. "You're a Waxx author now. You're *literary*."

"I'm so impressed with myself."

"Great exposure. A Waxx author forever."

"Forever?"

"From now on. He'll review every book. You caught his eye. He's committed to you."

"Forever is a long time."

"Other writers would kill for this. To be recognized. At the highest level."

"I wouldn't kill for it," I assured him.

"Because you've already got it. What a day. A Waxx author. My client. This is so good. Better than Metamucil."

The fiber-supplement reference was not a joke. Hud Jacklight had no sense of humor.

Humorless, without scruples, not much of a reader, Hud had been the most successful literary agent in the country for two decades. This said less about Hud than it did about the publishing industry.

"A Waxx author," Hud gushed again. "Incredible. Fabulous. Son. Of. A. Gun."

"It's November," I said in a perky voice, "but, gee, it feels like spring."

――――――――――

Before Penny and I left for Roxie's Bistro that evening, I had received calls from my publisher, my audio publisher, my film agent, and three friends, regarding the Waxx review. All of them said in various ways the same thing that Penny had advised: *Let it go.*

When Vivian Norby, Milo's baby-sitter, arrived, she said as she stepped into the foyer, "Saw the review, Cubby. He's an ignorant egg-sucker. Don't pay him any mind."

"I've already let it go," I assured her.

"If you want me to sit down with him and have a talk, I will."

That was an intriguing concept. "What would you say to him?"

"Same thing I say to every kid too big for his britches. I'd lay out the rules of polite society and make it clear that I know how to enforce them."

Vivian was fiftyish, solid but not fat, steely-eyed but warm-hearted, as confident as a grizzly bear but feminine. Her husband, a former marine and homicide detective—now deceased—had never won an arm-wrestling contest with her.

As usual, she wore pink: pink sneakers with yellow laces, a pink skirt, and a pink-and-cream sweater. Her dangling earrings featured silver kittens climbing silver chains.

"I'm sure you could make him properly contrite," I said.

"You just give me his address."

"I would—except I'm not dwelling on what he said. I've already let it go."

"If you change your mind, just call."

After closing the door behind her, she took my arm as if this were her house and she were welcoming a guest, and she escorted me out of the foyer, into the living room, almost lifting me onto my toes as we went. Shoulders back, formidable bosom raised, Vivian moved as forcefully as an icebreaker cracking through arctic seas.

Three years previous, she had been sitting for the Jameson kids on Lamplighter Way when two masked thugs attempted a home-invasion robbery. The first intruder—who turned out to be a disgruntled former employee of Bob Jameson's—wound up with a broken nose, split lips, four cracked teeth, two crushed fingers, a fractured knee, and a puncture in his right buttock.

Vivian suffered a broken fingernail.

The second thug, who fared worse than the first, developed such a disabling fear of fifty-something women who wore pink that in court, when the prosecutor showed up one day wearing a neck scarf of that fateful color, the accused began to sob uncontrollably and had to be carried out of the courthouse on a stretcher, by paramedics.

In the living room, Vivian let go of me and put her cloth carryall beside the armchair in which she would spend the evening.

"Your book is wonderful, Cubby." She had read an advance copy. "I may not be as educated as a certain hoity-toity critic, but I know truth when I see it. Your book is full of truth."

"Thank you, Vivian."

"Now where is Prince Milo?"

"In his room, building some kind of radio to communicate with extraterrestrials."

"The time machine didn't work out?"

"Not yet."

"Is Lassie with him?"

"She's never anywhere else," I said.

"I'll go give him a tickle."

"Penny and I are having dinner at Roxie's. If Milo makes contact with space aliens, it's okay to call us."

I followed Vivian out of the living room and watched as she ascended the stairs with a majesty only slightly less awesome than the looming presence of the mother ship in *Close Encounters of the Third Kind*.

When I entered the kitchen, Penny was fixing a Post-it to the refrigerator door, providing heating instructions for the lasagna that would be Milo's dinner.

"Vivian," I reported, "has assumed command of the premises."

Penny said, "Thank God we found her. I never worry about Milo when Vivian's here."

"Me neither. But I'm worried about *her*. Milo's tinkering again."

"Vivian will be fine. Milo only blew something up that once, and it was an accident."

"He could accidentally blow something up again."

She frowned at me, a disapproving expression with which I was familiar. Even then she looked scrumptious enough that I would have eaten her alive had we been in a country that mandated compassionate tolerance for cannibals.

"Never," she said. "Milo learns from his mistakes."

As I followed her through the connecting door between the kitchen and the garage, I said, "Is that a slighting remark about my experiences with fireworks?"

"How many times have you burned off your eyebrows?"

"Once. The other three times, I just singed them."

Regarding me over the roof of the car, she raised her eyebrows. Their pristine condition mocked me.

"You singed them so well," she said, "the smell of burning hair blanketed the entire neighborhood."

"Anyway, the last time was more than five years ago."

"So you're overdue for a repeat performance," she said, and got into the car.

Settling behind the steering wheel, I protested: "On the contrary. As any behavioral psychologist will tell you, if you can go five years without repeating the same mistake, you'll never make it again."

"I wish I had a behavioral psychologist here right now."

"You think he'd contradict me, but he wouldn't. They call it the five-year rule."

As I started the engine, Penny used the remote control to raise the garage door. "Wait until it's all the way up before you drive through it."

"I never drove *forward* through a garage door," I reminded her. "I reversed through it once, which is a whole different thing."

"Maybe. But considering it happened less than five years ago, I'm not taking any chances."

"You know, for someone whose parents call themselves Clotilda and Grimbald, you're remarkably funny."

"I would have to be, wouldn't I? Don't run down the mailbox."

"I will if I want."

We were having a fine time. The evening ahead was full of promise: good food, wine, laughter, and love.

Soon, however, Fate would bring me to a cliff. Although I would see the precipice before me, I would nevertheless step into thin air, taking not merely a pratfall but a plunge.

Chapter 3

In Newport Beach, on Balboa Peninsula, in a building near one of the town's two piers, Roxie's Bistro has low lighting, medium-Deco decor, and high culinary standards.

Most restaurants these days are as noisy as a drum-and-cymbal factory invaded by two hundred chimpanzees intent on committing percussion. Those establishments eschew sound-suppressing designs and materials under the pretense that cacophony gives the patrons a sense of being in a hip, happening place.

In truth, such restaurants seek and attract a type of customer whose very existence, in such numbers, proves our civilization is dying: boisterous and free-spending egotists taught since infancy that self-esteem matters more than knowledge, that manners and etiquette are merely tools of oppression. They like the sound of their own braying, and they seem to be convinced that the louder they are, the more desperately every onlooker wants to be in their clique.

Roxie's Bistro offered, instead, quiet intimacy. The murmur of conversation sometimes rose, though never became distracting. Combined with the soft silvery clink of flatware and an occasional surge of laughter, these voices made a pleasing music from the news of the day, gossip, and stories of times past.

Penny and I talked about publishing, politics, pickles, art, Milo, dogs in general, Lassie in particular, fleas, Flaubert, Florida, alliteration, ice dancing, Scrooge McDuck, the role of dark matter in the universe, and tofu, among other things.

In the golden glow of recessed lighting and in the flicker of candles in faceted amber-glass cups, radiant Penny looked like a beautiful queen, and I probably resembled Rumpelstiltskin scheming to take her next-born child. At least my ugly feet were hidden in socks and shoes.

After we finished our entrées but before we ordered dessert, Penny went to the lavatory.

Seeing me alone at the table, Hamal Sarkissian stopped by to keep me company.

Roxie Sarkissian had established the restaurant fifteen years earlier and was the award-winning chef. Although charming, she seldom ventured out from the kitchen.

Hamal, her husband, was the ideal frontman. He liked people, had an irresistible smile, and was diplomatic enough to soothe and win over the most unreasonable customer.

Standing by the table, he regarded me not with his trademark smile but instead with grave concern. "Is everything okay, Cubby?"

"Fabulous dinner," I assured him. "Perfect. As always."

Still solemn, he said, "Are you going on tour for the new book?"

"No. I needed a break this time."

"Don't worry about him, what he says."

Perplexed, I asked, "Worry about who, what?"

"He's a strange man, the critic."

"Oh. So ... you saw the Shearman Waxx review, huh?"

"Two paragraphs. Then I spit on his column and turned the page."

"It doesn't faze me. I've already let it go."

"He's a strange man. He always makes his reservation in the name Edmund Wilson."

Surprised, surveying the room, I said, "He comes here?"

"Seldom dinner. More often lunch."

"How about that."

"He's always alone, pays cash."

"You're sure it's him? Nobody seems to know what he looks like."

"Twice he was short of cash," Hamal said. "He used a credit card. Shearman Waxx. He's a very strange man."

"Well, rest assured, if he had a reservation for tonight and I were to run into him, there wouldn't be a scene. Criticism doesn't bother me."

"In fact, he has a twelve-thirty lunch reservation tomorrow," said Hamal.

"Criticism comes with the territory."

"He's a damned strange man."

"A review is only one person's opinion."

Hamal said, "He creeps me out a little."

"I've already let it go. You know what it's like. The restaurant gets a bad review—*c'est la vie*. You just keep on keepin' on."

"We've never had a bad review," Hamal said.

Embarrassed by the assumption I had made, I said, "Why would you? This place is perfection."

"Do you get many bad reviews?"

"I don't keep track. Maybe ten percent aren't good. Maybe twelve percent. My third book—that was like fourteen percent. I don't dwell on the negative. Ninety percent good reviews is gratifying."

"Eighty-six percent," said Hamal.

"That was only for my third book. Some critics didn't think the dwarf was necessary."

"I like dwarfs. I have a cousin in Armenia, he's a dwarf."

"Even if you use a dwarf as your hero, you have to call him a 'little person.' The word *dwarf* just incenses some critics."

"This critic of yours, he always reminds me of my cousin."

"You mean Shearman Waxx is a dwarf?"

"No. He's about five feet eight. But he's stumpy."

The front door opened, a party of four entered, and Hamal went to greet them.

A moment later, Penny returned from the lavatory. Settling in her chair, she said, "I'm going to finish this delightful wine before deciding on dessert."

"That reminds me—Hud wants to buy our wine this evening. He says send him the receipt."

"That would be wasting a perfectly good stamp."

"He might pay for half the bottle. He sent us champagne that time."

"It wasn't champagne. It was sparkling cider. Anyway, why would he suddenly want to buy our wine?"

"To celebrate the Waxx review."

"The man is criminally obtuse."

"He's not that bad. Just clueless."

"I don't like how he's always pushing to be my agent, too."

"He negotiates killer deals," I said.

"But he doesn't know squat about children's books."

"He has to know something. He was a child at one time."

"I doubt that very much. I said something about Dr. Seuss once, and Hud thought I was talking about a *physician*."

"A misunderstanding. He was concerned about you."

"I mention Dr. Seuss and somehow Hud gets the idea I've got a terminal disease."

Being defense attorney for Hud Jacklight is a thankless job. I gave it up.

Penny said, "He happened to have lunch in the same restaurant as my editor, so he asked her—does she know how long I've got to live. The man is a total—"

"Flying furnal?" I suggested.

"I wish a furnal would fly up his—"

"Buckaboody?" I suggested, inventing a word of my own.

"Exactly," Penny said. "This wine is lovely. I'm not going to ruin the memory of it by having to pester Hud for reimbursement."

As far as I can remember, in ten years I had never kept secret from Penny anything that occurred in my daily life. At that moment, I could not have explained why I failed to share with her that Shearman Waxx sometimes ate at Roxie's Bistro. Later, I figured it out.

"Are you thinking about the Waxx review again?" she asked.

"No. Not exactly. Maybe a little. Sort of."

"Let it go," she said.

"I am. I'm letting it go."

"No. You're dwelling on it. Distract yourself."

"With what?"

"With life. Take me home and make love to me."

"I thought we were getting dessert."

"Aren't I sweet enough for you?"

"There it is," I said.

"What?"

"That crooked little smile you get sometimes. I love that crooked little smile."

"Then take me home and do something with it, big boy."

Chapter 4

Having gotten up at three in the morning to do thirty radio interviews, I had no difficulty falling asleep that Tuesday night.

I endured one of my lost-and-alone dreams. Sometimes it is set in a deserted department store, sometimes in a vacant amusement park or in a train terminal where no trains depart and none arrive.

This time, I roamed a vast and dimly lighted library, where the shelves soared high overhead. The intersecting aisles were not perpendicular to one another, but serpentine, as if reflecting the manner in which one area of knowledge can lead circuitously and unexpectedly to a seemingly unrelated field of inquiry.

This library of the slumbering mind was buried in a silence as solid and as sinuous as the drifted sands of Egypt. No step I took produced a sound.

The wandering passageways were catacombs without the mummified remains, harboring instead lives and the work of lifetimes set down on paper, bound with glue and signature thread.

As always in a lost-and-alone dream, I remained anxious but not afraid. I proceeded in expectation of a momentous discovery, a thing of wonder and delight, although the possibility of terror remained.

When the dream is in a labyrinthine train station, the silence is sometimes broken by footsteps that lure me before they fade. In a department store, I hear a faraway feminine laugh that draws me from kitchenware through bed-and-bath and down a frozen escalator.

In this library, the thrall of silence allowed a single crisp sound now and then, as if someone in an adjacent aisle was paging through a book. Searching, I found neither a patron nor a librarian.

An urgency gripped me. I walked faster, ran, turned a corner into what might have been a reading alcove. Instead of armchairs, the space offered a bed, and in it slept Penny, alone. The covers on my side of the bed were undisturbed, as though I had never rested there.

Alarmed at the sight of her alone, I sensed in her solitude an omen of some event that I dared not contemplate.

I approached the bed—and woke in it, beside her, where I had not been lying in the dream. Gone were the nautilus spirals of books, replaced by darkness and the pale geometry of curtained windows.

Penny's soft rhythmic breathing was a mooring to which I could tether myself in the gloom; her respiration should have settled me but did not. I continued to feel adrift, and anxious.

Wanting something, not knowing what I wanted, I eased out of bed and, barefoot in pajamas, left the master suite.

Moonlight through skylights frosted the longer run of the L-shaped upstairs hallway. Passing a thus twice-silvered mirror, I glanced at my reflection, which appeared as diaphanous as a ghost.

I was awake but felt still dreambound. This venue, though it was my own house, seemed more sinister than the deserted library or than the department store haunted by an elusive laughing spirit.

My rising anxiety focused on Milo. I hurried the length of the main hall and turned right into the darker short arm.

From the gap between the threshold and the bottom of Milo's bedroom door, a fan of radiance continuously fluttered between a sapphire-blue intensity and an icy gunmetal blue, not the light of fire or television but suggesting mortal danger nonetheless.

We have a policy of knocking, but I opened the door without announcing myself—and was relieved to find Milo safe and asleep.

The dimmer switch on the bedside lamp had been dialed down to an approximation of candlelight. He lay supine, head raised on a pillow. Behind his closed eyelids, rapid eye movement signified dream sleep.

With him lay Lassie, her chin resting on his abdomen. She was as awake as any guardian charged with a sacred task. She rolled her eyes to watch me without moving her head.

On the U-shaped desk, intermingling clouds of color—each a shade of blue—billowed in slow motion across the computer monitor, like a kaleidoscope with amorphous forms instead of geometric shapes.

I had never seen such a screen saver. Because Milo's computer had no Internet access, this couldn't have been downloaded from the Web.

The Internet is more a force for evil than for good. It offers the worst of humankind absolute license and anonymity—and numerous addictive pursuits over which to become obsessive. Kids are having innocence and willpower—if not free will itself—stolen from them.

When Milo wanted to go online, he had to use my computer or Penny's. We have installed serious site-blocking software.

The wing of the desk to the left of the computer was covered with circuit boards, carefully labeled microchips in small plastic bags, a disassembled alphanumeric keypad, a disassembled radio, dozens of arcane items I had purchased for him at RadioShack and elsewhere, and a scattering of miniature tools.

I had no idea what my boy might be creating with any of those things. However, I trusted him to obey the rules and to avoid doing anything that might electrocute him, burn down the house, or transport him to the Jurassic Era with no way of getting back to us.

In movies, raising a prodigy is always an exhilarating and uplifting journey to triumphant accomplishment. In reality, it is also exhausting and even sometimes terrifying.

I suppose that would not be true if his genius expressed itself as a talent for the piano and for musical composition. Even Mozart couldn't play the piano with such brilliance that it would explode and kill bystanders with ivory shrapnel.

Unfortunately—or fortunately, as only time would tell—Milo's talent was for theoretical and applied mathematics, also theoretical and applied physics, with a deep intuitive understanding of magnetic and electromagnetic fields.

This we were told by the experts who studied and tested Milo for two weeks. I have only a dim idea of what their assessment means.

For a while we hired graduate students to tutor him, but they tended only to inhibit his learning. He is a classic autodidact, self-motivated, and already in possession of his high-school GED.

I am as proud of the little guy as I am intimidated. Given his brainpower, he'll probably never be interested in having me teach him a pastime as boring as baseball. Which is all right, I guess, because I've always been rotten at sports.

The wing of the desk to the right of the computer held a large tablet open to a working drawing of some device requiring an array of microprocessors, instruction caches, data caches, bus connections, and other more mysterious items—all linked by a bewildering maze of circuit traces.

If microsoldering was required, neither Milo nor I would be permitted to do it. Such work must be left to Penny. She has, after all, the steady hands of an artist, the emotional maturity that Milo lacks, and a mechanical competence of which I can only dream.

The ever-changing forms on the monitor, like a churning mass of blue protoplasm, had begun to seem ominous to me, as if this were a living thing that, by applying pressure, might crack the screen and surge into the room. I wanted to switch off the computer, but I did not. Milo had left it on not inadvertently but for some reason.

At the bed once more, I gazed at him for a while in the low lamp-light. A beautiful child.

Although blessed with a vivid imagination, I could not begin to envision the topography of Milo's mindscape.

I worried about him a lot.

He had no friends his age because kids bored him. Penny, Lassie, Vivian Norby, Clotilda, Grimbald, and I were his social universe.

I hoped he could live as normally as his gifts would allow, but I felt inadequate to show him the way. I wanted my son to know much laughter and more love, to appreciate the grace of this world and the abiding mystery of it, to know the pleasure of small achievements, of trifles and of follies, to be always aware of the million wonderful little pictures in the big one, to be a humble master of his gift and not the servant of it. Because I could not imagine what it must be like to be him, I could not lead on every issue; much of the time, we would have to find our way together.

I loved him enough to endure any horror for him and to die that he might be spared.

No matter how much you care for another person, however, you can't guarantee him a happy life, not with love or money, not with sacrifice. You can only do your best—and pray for him.

I kissed Milo on the forehead without disturbing his sleep. Impulsively, I kissed Lassie on the head, as well. She seemed to be pleased by this affection, but I got some fur on my lips.

The bedside clock read 5:00 A.M. In seven and a half hours, the dog would be sitting in the living-room window seat, watching the street and wondering when I would return with her cherished companion— and Milo and I would be having lunch at Roxie's Bistro, spying on the nation's premier literary critic.

Chapter 5

At 12:10, the lunch crowd in Roxie's Bistro was slightly noisier than the dinner customers, but the ambience remained relaxing and conducive to quiet conversation.

Hamal Sarkissian seated us at a table for two at the back of the long rectangular room. He provided a booster pillow for Milo.

"Will you want wine with lunch?" Hamal asked the boy.

"A glass or two," Milo confirmed.

"I will have it for you in fifteen years," Hamal said.

I had told Penny that I was taking Milo to the library, to an electronics store to buy items he needed for his current project, and finally to lunch at Roxie's. All this was true. I don't lie to Penny.

I neglected, however, to tell her that at lunch I would get a glimpse of the elusive Shearman Waxx. This is deception by omission, and it is not admirable behavior.

Considering that I had no intention of either approaching the critic or speaking to him, I saw no harm in this small deception, no need to concern Penny or to have to listen to her admonition to "Let it go."

Only once before had I deceived her by omission. That previous instance involved an issue more serious than this one. At the start of our courtship, and now for ten years, I had carefully avoided revealing to her the key fact about myself, the most formative experience of my life, for it seemed to be a weight she should not have to carry.

Because Milo and I arrived before Waxx, I was not at risk of running a variation of my garage-door stunt, accidentally driving through the restaurant, killing the critic at his lunch, and thus being wrongly suspected of premeditated murder.

Having conspired with me earlier on the phone, Hamal pointed to a table at the midpoint of the restaurant. "He will be seated there, by the window. He always reads a book while he dines. You will know him. He is a strange man."

Earlier, on the Internet, I sought out the only known photograph of Shearman Waxx, which proved to be of no use. The image was as blurry as all those snapshots of Big Foot striding through woods and meadows.

When Hamal left us alone, Milo said, "What strange man?"

"Just a guy. A customer. Hamal thinks he's strange."

"Why?"

"He's got a third eye in his forehead."

Milo scoffed: "Nobody has an eye in his forehead."

"This guy does. And four nostrils in his nose."

"Yeah?" He was as gimlet-eyed as a homicide detective. "What kind of pet does he have—a flying furnal?"

"Two of them," I said. "He's taught them stunt flying."

While we studied our menus and enjoyed our lemony iced tea, in no hurry to order food, Milo and I discussed our favorite cookies, Saturday-morning cartoon shows, and whether extraterrestrials are more likely to visit Earth to enlighten us or to eat us. We talked about dogs in general, Lassie in particular, and anomalies of current flow in electromagnetic fields.

With the last subject, my half of the conversation consisted of so many grunts and snorts that I might have been the aforementioned Sasquatch.

Promptly at 12:30, a stumpy man carrying an attaché case entered the restaurant. Hamal escorted him to the previously specified window table.

To be fair, the guy appeared less stumpy than solid. Although perhaps half as wide as he was tall, Waxx was not overweight. He seemed to have the density of a lead brick.

His neck looked thick enough to support the stone head of an Aztec-temple god. His face was so at odds with the rest of the man that it might have been grafted to him by a clever surgeon: a wide smooth brow, bold and noble features, a strong chin—a face suitable for a coin from the Roman Empire.

He was about forty, certainly not 140, as the online encyclopedia claimed. His leonine hair had turned prematurely white.

In charcoal-gray slacks, an ash-gray hound's-tooth sport coat with leather elbow patches, a white shirt, and a red bow tie, he seemed to be part college professor and part professional wrestler, as though two men of those occupations had shared a teleportation chamber and— à la the movie *The Fly*—had discovered their atoms intermingled at the end of their trip.

From his attaché case, he withdrew a hardcover book and what appeared to be a stainless-steel torture device. He opened the book and fitted it into the jaws of this contraption, which held the volume open and at a slant for comfortable hands-free reading.

Evidently, the critic was a man of reliable habits. A waiter came to his table with a glass of white wine that he hadn't ordered.

Waxx nodded, seemed to utter a word or two, but did not glance up at his server, who at once departed.

He put on half-lens, horn-rimmed reading glasses and, after a sip of wine, turned his attention to the steel-entrapped book.

Because I did not want to be caught staring, I continued my conversation with Milo. I focused mostly on my son and glanced only occasionally toward the critic.

Before long, my spy mission began to seem absurd. Shearman Waxx might be a somewhat odd-looking package, but after the mystery of his appearance had been solved, nothing about him was compelling.

I did not intend to approach him or speak to him. Penny, Olivia Cosima, and even Hud Jacklight had been right to say that responding to an unfair review was generally a bad idea.

As the tables between ours and Waxx's filled with customers, my view of him became obstructed. By the time we finished our main course and ordered dessert, I lost interest in him.

After I paid the bill and tipped the waiter, as we were rising from the table to leave, Milo said, "I gotta pee, Dad."

The restrooms were at our end of the premises, off a short hall, and as we crossed the room, I glanced toward Waxx. I couldn't see his table clearly through the throng, but his chair stood empty. He must have finished lunch and left.

The sparkling-clean men's room featured one stall wide enough for a wheelchair, two urinals, and two sinks. Redolent of astringent pine-scented disinfectant, the air burned in my nostrils.

Someone occupied the stall, but Milo wasn't tall enough to use one of the urinals unassisted. After he unzipped his pants, fumbled in his fly, and produced himself, I clamped my hands around his waist and lifted him above the porcelain bowl.

"Ready," he said.

"Aim," I said.

"Fire," he said, and loosed a stream.

When Milo was more than half drained, the toilet flushed and the stall door opened.

I glanced sideways, saw Shearman Waxx not six feet from me, and as if my throat were the pinched neck of a balloon, I let out a thin "Eeee" in surprise.

In the restaurant, his table had been at such a distance from ours that I had not been able to see the color of his eyes. They were maroon.

Although I have thought about that moment often in the days since, I still do not know whether, startled, I turned toward the critic or whether Milo, held aloft in my hands, twisted around to see what had made me gasp. I suspect it was a little of both.

The boy's stream arced to the tile floor.

For a man as solid as a concrete battlement, Waxx proved to be agile. He danced adroitly backward, out of the splash zone, and his gray Hush Puppies remained entirely dry.

"Sorry, sorry, sorry," I chanted, and turned Milo toward the urinal.

Without a word, Waxx stepped over the puddle, went to one of the sinks, and began to wash his hands.

"He's a little guy," I said. "I have to lift him up."

Although Waxx did not respond, I imagined I could feel his gaze boring into my back as he watched me in the mirror above the sinks.

I knew that the more I apologized, the more it might seem that I had intended to use Milo like a squirt gun, but I couldn't shut up.

"Nothing like that ever happened before. If he'd nailed you, I would have paid the dry-cleaning bill."

Waxx pulled paper towels from the dispenser.

As he finished peeing, Milo giggled.

"He's a good kid," I assured Waxx. "He saved a dog from being euthanized."

The only sound was the rustle of paper as the critic dried his hands.

Although Milo could read at a college level, he was nonetheless a six-year-old boy. Six-year-old boys find nothing funnier than pee and fart jokes.

After giggling again, Milo said, "I shook and zipped, Dad. You can put me down."

A squeak of hinges revealed that Waxx had opened the door to the hallway.

Putting Milo on his feet, I turned toward the exit.

My hope was that Waxx had not recognized me from my book-jacket photograph.

The eminent critic was staring at me. He said one word, and then he departed.

He had recognized me, all right.

After using paper towels to mop up Milo's small puddle, I washed my hands at a sink. Then I lifted Milo so he could wash up, too.

"Almost sprinkled him," Milo said.

"That's nothing to be proud of. Stop giggling."

When we returned to the restaurant, Shearman Waxx sat once more at his table. The waiter was just serving the entrée.

Waxx did not look our way. He seemed determined to ignore us.

As we passed his table, I saw the device that imprisoned the book was clever but wicked-looking, as though the critic were holding the work—and its author—in bondage.

Outside, the November afternoon waited: mild, still, expectant. The unblemished sky curved to every horizon like an encompassing sphere of glass, containing not a single cloud or bird, or aircraft.

Along the street, the trees stood as motionless as the fake foliage in an airless diorama. No limb trembled, no leaf whispered.

No traffic passed. Milo and I were the only people in sight.

We might have been figures in a snow-globe paperweight, sans snow.

I wanted to look back at the restaurant, to see if Shearman Waxx watched us from his window seat. Restraining myself, I didn't turn, but instead walked Milo to the car.

During the drive home, I could not stop brooding about the single word the critic had spoken before he stepped out of the men's room. He transfixed me with those terrible maroon eyes and in a solemn baritone said, "Doom."

Chapter 6

That afternoon, while Penny finished a painting for her next children's book, while Milo and Lassie worked on a time machine or a death ray, or whatever it might be, I sat in an armchair in my study, reading "A Good Man Is Hard to Find" by Flannery O'Connor, a short story that I much admired.

One of the most disturbing pieces of fiction ever written, it remains as affecting on the tenth pass as on the first. This might have been my twentieth reading, but Miss O'Connor inspired in me a greater dread than ever before.

I did not understand why phantom spiders crawled the nape of my neck, why chills shivered through my bowels and stomach, why my palms grew damp and my fingers sometimes trembled when I turned a page—all to a degree that I had never experienced previously with this work of fiction or any other. Later, I figured it out.

After I finished the story and as I sat staring at the page, where the words blurred out of focus, a disquiet rose in me that had nothing to do with "A Good Man Is Hard to Find." I told myself that my uneasiness related to my career, to concern about what Waxx would write in his review of my *next* novel, which he seemed to have promised to savage when he spoke the word *doom* in a portentous tone.

But surely that could not be the entire cause of the nameless worry that crawled my mind. I had not yet finished my next novel. It would not be published for a year. At my request, my publisher would withhold an advance review copy from Waxx. We had time to devise a strategy to thwart him. Yet my current uneasiness seemed to anticipate a more immediate jeopardy.

Peripheral vision alerted me to movement. I raised my eyes from the page, turned my head toward the open study door, and saw Shearman Waxx pass by in the downstairs hall.

I do not recall rising from the armchair or letting the book of short stories fall from my hands. I seemed to have *imagined* myself onto my feet in a thousandth of a second.

Now erect, I couldn't imagine myself moving. Shock paralyzed me.

My heart continued to beat at the pace of a man reading in an armchair. Disbelief forestalled a sense of jeopardy.

O'Connor's story had cast over me a pall of apprehension. In that altered state, my mind must have played a trick on me, must have conjured an intruder where none existed.

This phantom Waxx had not even glanced at me, as certainly he would have if he had been real and had come here to confront me for whatever reason. Perhaps Penny passed by in the hall, and the limber imagination of a novelist remade her into the critic.

The possibility that I could mistake my luminous and slender Penny for the dour hulk of Shearman Waxx was so absurd that my disbelief dissolved. I broke my paralysis.

Suddenly my heart mimicked iron on turf, the frantic thud of racing horses' heels. I hurried to the open door, hesitated at the threshold, but then crossed it. The hallway was deserted.

Waxx had been headed toward the back of the house. I followed the shorter length of the hall to the kitchen, half expecting to find him selecting a blade from the knife drawer beside the cooktop.

Even as that image crossed my mind, I was embarrassed by my near hysteria. Shearman Waxx would surely disdain such melodrama in real life as much as he scorned it in fiction.

He lurked neither in the kitchen nor in the adjacent family room that flowed from it. One of the French doors to the back patio stood open, suggesting that he had departed by that exit.

Standing in the doorway, I surveyed the patio, the swimming pool, and the backyard. No sign of Waxx.

That eerie stillness had befallen the world again. The water in the pool lay as smooth as a sheet of glass.

While I had been reading, gunmetal clouds had armored the sky. They did not billow, neither did they churn, but looked as flat and motionless as a coat of paint.

Because we lived in the safest neighborhood of a low-crime community, we were in the habit of leaving our most-used doors unlocked during the day. That would change.

Bewildered by Waxx's intrusion, I closed the French door and engaged the deadbolt.

Abruptly, I realized that the critic might have done more than pass through the house. If he had left by the family room, he could have entered elsewhere—and could have done some kind of damage.

Engaged in strange science, Milo was upstairs in his bedroom with Lassie.

In her second-floor studio, Penny painted the wide-eyed, sharp-beaked owl that hunted the band of heroic mice in her current book.

Although the dog had not barked and though no one had cried out in pain or terror, my mind insisted on the most unlikely scenario, on bludgeoned heads and cut throats. Our modern world is, after all, full of flamboyant violence; as often as not, the evening news is as disturbing as any slasher film.

I climbed the back stairs two at a time.

Chapter 7

Milo's bedroom door stood open, and he sat at his desk, alive and beguiled by electronic gizmos that meant less to me than would ancient tablets of stone carved with runes.

On the desk, watching her master at work, sat Lassie. She looked up as I entered, but Milo did not.

"Did you see him?" I asked.

Milo, who can multitask better than a Cray supercomputer, stayed focused on the gizmos but said, "See who?"

"The man ... a guy wearing a red bow tie. Did he come in here?"

"You mean the man with three eyes and four nostrils?" he asked, revealing that perhaps he had been more aware of my spy game at the restaurant than I had realized.

"Yes, him," I confirmed. "Did he come in here?"

"Nope. We would have freaked if he did."

"Shout if you see him. I'll be right back."

The door to Penny's studio was closed. I flung it open, rushed inside, and found her at the easel.

So dimensional was the image of the villain owl that it seemed to be flying at me from out of the canvas, beak wide to rend and eyes hot for blood.

Certain that she knew the cause of my breathless entrance, Penny spoke before I could say a word: "Did the coffeemaker assault you or have you used the dishwasher again and flooded the kitchen?"

"Big problem," I said. "Milo. Come quick."

She put down her brush and hurried after me. When she saw Milo tinkering in peace and Lassie without hackles raised, Penny sighed with relief and said to me, "The punch line better be hilarious."

"Stay here with him. Brace the door with that chair when I leave."

"What? Why?"

"If someone asks you to open the door, even if it sounds like me, don't open it."

"Cubby—"

"Ask something only I would know—like where we went on our first date. He probably can't imitate my voice—I mean, he's not a comic-book supercriminal, for God's sake—but you never know."

"He who? What's wrong with you?"

"There was an intruder. I think he's gone, but I'm not sure."

Her eyes widened as might those of a mouse in the sudden shadow of a swooping owl. "Call 911."

"He's not that kind of intruder."

"There isn't any *other* kind."

"Besides, I might have imagined him."

"Did you see him or not?"

"I saw something."

"Then it's 911."

"I'm a public figure. The media will follow the cops, it'll be a publicity circus."

"Better than you dead."

"I'll be okay. Use the chair as a brace."

"Cubby—"

Stepping into the shorter of the two upstairs hallways, I pulled the
door shut. I waited until I heard the headrail of the straight-backed
chair knock against the knob as she jammed it into place.

Dependable Penny.

Reason argued that a renowned critic and textbook author like
Shearman Waxx was not likely to be a psychopath. Eccentric, yes, and
perhaps even weird. But not homicidal. Reason, in its true premodern
meaning, had served me well for many years.

Nevertheless, from a hall table, I seized a tall, heavy vase with a fat
bottom and a narrow neck. Flat-footed athlete that I am, I held it as I
would have held a tennis racket—awkwardly.

In addition to Milo's quarters, this back hall served two small guest
rooms, a bath, and a utility closet. Quickly, quietly, I opened doors,
searched, found no one.

As I turned toward the longer of the two second-floor hallways—
off which lay the master suite, Penny's studio, and another bedroom
that we used for storage—I heard a noise downstairs. The short-lived
clatter rose through the back stairwell, from the kitchen, and the
silence in its wake had an ominous quality.

Ceramic vase held high, as if I were a contestant in a Home and
Garden Television version of a reality show like *Survivor,* defending
my home with any available decorative item, I cautiously descended
the stairs.

Waxx wasn't in the kitchen or in the family room beyond. All
appeared to be in order.

The swinging door between the kitchen and the downstairs hall was closed. I didn't think it had been closed earlier.

As I eased open the door, I saw Waxx at the far end of the hallway, exiting my study on the right, crossing the foyer.

"Hey," I called to him. "What're you doing?"

He didn't reply or glance at me, but disappeared into the library.

Chapter 8

I considered calling 911, after all, but the nonchalance
with which Shearman Waxx toured our house began to seem more
weird than menacing. When Hamal Sarkissian called Waxx strange,
he most likely meant eccentric.

In his reviews he assaulted with words, but that did not mean he was
capable of real violence. In fact, the opposite was usually true: Those who
trafficked in hostile rhetoric might inspire others to commit crimes,
but they were usually cowards who would take no risk themselves.

Still armed with the vase, I followed the hallway to the foyer and
pursued Waxx into the library.

In some higher-end Southern California neighborhoods, a library
is considered as necessary as a kitchen, a symbol of the residents' refinement. About a third of these rooms contain no books.

In those instances, the shelves are filled with collections of bronze
figurines or ceramics. Or with DVDs. But the space is still referred to
as the library.

In another third, the books have been bought for their handsome bindings. They are meant to imply erudition, but a visitor's attempt to have a conversation about any title on display will inspire the host either to talk about the movie based on the book or to retreat to the bar to mix another drink.

Our library contained books we had read or intended to read, a desk, a sofa, two armchairs, and side tables, but it did not contain Shearman Waxx. Evidently he had gone through the door between the library and the living room.

As I stepped into that adjacent chamber, I saw movement beyond the double doors to the dining room. Waxx entered the china pantry that insulated the dining room from the kitchen, and the door swung shut behind him.

By the time I crossed the living room and half the dining room, I saw Waxx through a window. He was outside now, walking toward the front of the house.

When I dashed to the next window and rapped on a pane as he passed, the critic did not deign to look at me.

I put down the vase and hurried into the living room once more. Waxx was not running, just walking briskly, but he passed the windows before I could get to one of them to rap for his attention.

In the library, through a window that faced the street, I saw him crossing the front lawn toward a black Cadillac Escalade parked at the curb.

Library to foyer to front door, I said, "No, no, no. No you don't, you syntax-challenged sonofabitch."

As I came out of the house onto the stoop, I saw Waxx behind the wheel of the SUV.

Again the day was becalmed. The dead air felt thick, compressed under the flat leaden sky. In the gray light of late afternoon, the fronds of the phoenix palms hung as motionless as if they were cast iron.

Later, I could not recall hearing the engine of the Escalade. The SUV pulled slowly into the street and began to glide away like a ghost ship glimpsed cruising a strange sea.

On the lawn, a flock of large black crows appeared not to have been disturbed by the critic's passage. As I stepped from the stoop onto the walkway, the birds erupted from the grass in a tribulation of wings so great that my eardrums shivered.

Hoping to catch up with Waxx when he braked for the stop sign at the corner, I ran into the street. Without pause, he accelerated through the intersection, and pursuit was pointless.

The crows shrieked into the sullen sky, but were silenced by altitude, and as I returned to the house, a single black feather floated down past my face.

Stepping through the front door, I smelled a thin but repulsive metallic odor. In the hallway, the odor swelled into a stink. In the kitchen, it was a stench.

The Advantium oven was set on SPEED COOK at the highest power level. Tendrils of gray smoke slithered from the vent holes on the bottom of the unit.

I stooped down, switched it off, and peered through the view window. Within a cowl of pale smoke, fire flickered.

Deprived of oxygen, the flames quickly died out. I opened the door, waving away the fumes that plumed into my face.

In the oven, a silver frame held a five-by-seven photograph. The fabric-covered backing board had caught fire. The glass was cracked, and the photo under it was slightly discolored.

The frame should have been on the desk in my study. The photo was of Penny, Milo, Lassie, and me.

In the men's room at the restaurant, Waxx had said the word *doom* without punctuation. This business with the photo seemed to add an exclamation point.

Chapter 9

After walking the house to lock every window and door, after setting the security alarm, I felt safe enough to leave Milo in his room with Lassie, while Penny and I huddled at the kitchen table, at the center of which stood the damaged photo in the silver frame.

"So you knew Waxx would be there for lunch," she said. "But you didn't tell me. Why didn't you tell me?"

"I wondered about that at the time."

"Are you still wondering about it?"

"No, I've figured it out."

"Share with me."

"I didn't want you to talk me out of going."

"You knew better than to confront him."

She wasn't angry, just disappointed in me.

I wished that she would get angry instead.

"I didn't confront him," I assured her.

"Seems like *something* must have happened."

"I just wanted to get a look at him. He's so reclusive."

Her blue gaze is as direct as the aim of an experienced bird hunter in his blind, her double-barreled eyes tracking the truth. My determination always to meet her extraordinary gaze has made a better man of me over the years.

"So what does he look like?" she asked.

"Like a walking slab of concrete with white hair and a bow tie."

"What did you say to him?"

"I didn't approach him. I watched him from a distance. But then at the end of lunch, after I paid the check, Milo needed to pee."

"Is the pee germane to the story, or are you vamping to delay telling me about the confrontation with Waxx?"

"It's germane." I told her the rest of the tale.

Frowning, she said, "And Milo didn't sprinkle him?"

"No. Not even a drop."

"Waxx said 'Doom'? What do you think he meant by it?"

"At first I thought he meant he'll rip my next book even worse."

Indicating the framed photo that I had rescued from the oven, she said, "Now what do you think?"

"I don't know. This is crazy."

For a moment we sat in silence.

Night had fallen. Evidently, Penny distrusted the darkness at the windows as much as I did. She got up to shut the pleated shades.

I almost told her that she should stand to the side of the window when she pulled the cord. Backlit, she made an easy target.

Instead, I got up and dropped two of the shades.

She said, "I need a cookie."

"Before dinner? What if Milo sees you?"

"He already knows I'm a hypocrite when it comes to the cookie rules. He loves me anyway. You want one?"

"All right. I'll pour the milk."

In times of trouble, in times of stress, in times of doubt, in times when even a vague sense of misgiving overcomes her, Penny turns to the same mood elevator: cookies. I don't know why she doesn't weigh five hundred pounds.

She once said just being married to me burns up seven thousand calories a day. I pretended to believe she meant I was a total stud. I love to make her laugh.

At the table once more, with glasses of cold milk and chocolate-chip-pecan cookies as big as saucers, we restored our confidence.

"Most critics are principled," she said. "They love books. They have standards. They tend to be gentle people."

"This guy isn't one of them."

"Even the biased and mean ones—they don't generally wind up in prison for violent crimes. Words are their only weapons."

I said, "Remember Josh McGintry and the magazine?"

Josh is a friend and writer. His Catholicism is an implicit part of his novels.

Over the course of a year, he received a venomous hate letter once a week from an anti-Catholic bigot. He never responded to them.

When his new novel came out, the same hater reviewed it in a national weekly magazine for which he was a staff writer. The guy did not reveal his prejudice, but he mocked the book and Josh's entire career in an outrageously dishonest fashion.

Josh is married to Mary, and Mary said, "Let it go."

Women have been saying "Let it go" since human beings lived in caves; and men responded then pretty much as they respond today.

Instead of letting it go, Josh wrote the editor in chief of the magazine, copying him on the hate letters. The editor defended his staff writer and suggested Josh could have forged the correspondence.

Emboldened, the bigot wrote to Josh on magazine stationery. The envelopes were stamped with one of the magazine's postage meters.

When Josh copied the editor on this new evidence, he received no reply. But a year later, when his subsequent book was published, the review in the magazine was not written by the same man.

This vicious review was written by a *different* bigot, a friend of the first one, who began also to send hate letters to Josh.

Again, Mary told him to let it go. Josh listened to her this time, though ever since he'd been grinding his teeth in his sleep so assiduously that he needed to wear a soft-acrylic bite guard.

"Neither of those guys showed up at Josh's house," Penny said. "They prove my contention—their only weapons were words."

"So you don't think Waxx will come back?"

"If he were a true nut, wouldn't he have already shot you?"

"It would be nice to think so."

"Anyway, you can't report him to the cops. I didn't see him. Only you saw him. He'll deny having been here."

"It's just—the whole thing was so freaky."

"Clearly, he's arrogant and eccentric," she said. "Some little thing you said set him off."

"All I did was apologize for Milo nearly peeing on him."

"He misinterpreted something. So he's had his payback. Probably the worst he'll do now is trash every book you ever write."

"Swell." I locked eyes with her. "You really think it's over?"

She hesitated but then said, "Yes."

As a truth detector, her double-barreled gaze works both ways. When she did not blink, I knew she was being a straight shooter.

"Cubby, he thinks you were spying on him, you violated his personal space. So he violated yours. Now, sweetie, let it go."

I sighed. "I will. I'll let it go."

Penny's smile could power a small city.

Together, we prepared salads, ravioli, and meatballs. Milo never knew that we had indulged in cookies and milk before dinner. But I'm pretty sure Lassie, with her exceptional sense of smell, detected the truth on our breath, because her mismatched eyes said *guilty*.

Later that night, I had difficulty falling asleep. When at last I slept, I found myself in another lost-and-alone dream: the infinite library with the winding aisles.

I had been prowling those byways for a while, in anticipation of a momentous discovery, when a serpentine turn in the stacks brought me to a place where the shelves held no books. Displayed instead, in big jars sealed with corks and wax, was a collection of severed heads in preservative fluid.

From floor to ceiling, onward past another turn and another, men and women peered out of their glass ossuaries, eyes wide but fixed. None wore an expression of agony or horror. Instead, they appeared to be either astonished or contemplative.

These bodiless multitudes, breathless in formaldehyde, disturbed me for obvious reasons but also for a reason I could not identify. As I began to realize that I knew them—or at least some of them—my heart raced in rebellion against the pending revelation.

Suspecting that the way ahead would never bring me again to any books, but only to additional heads in jars, I turned back toward the true library out of which I had wandered. Although I hurried farther than I had come, I found only heads behind me.

I first recognized Charles Dickens, bearded behind a curve of glass, and then Truman Capote. Hemingway, F. Scott Fitzgerald, Robert Heinlein, Zane Grey, Raymond Chandler. The creator of Tarzan, Edgar Rice Burroughs. Virginia Woolf. Somerset Maugham. Mickey Spillane.

A premonition chilled mere anxiety into a colder fear: I knew that I would recognize my face in a jar. And when I met my dead eyes, I would cease to exist in either the dream or the waking world, but would forevermore be only a severed head drowned in formaldehyde.

As I tried to run out of the dream, I strove not to look at the jars, but my eyes were repeatedly drawn to them. When the lights went off, the darkness was a blessing until, as I blindly progressed, I heard Shearman Waxx speak nearby: "Doom."

With my breath caught in my throat, I sat up in bed, in a room as dark as the lightless maze of the nightmare library. For a moment, I half believed that Waxx had spoken not in the dream but here in the waking world.

I exhaled, inhaled, and oriented myself by the feel of the entangling sheets, by the residual smell of fabric softener, by the familiar faint whistle of forced air coming through the heating vent, by the palest blush of moonlight at the edges of the heavy draperies.

The room was blacker than it should have been. The green numbers on my digital clock were not lit. The clock on Penny's nightstand had been extinguished, as well.

The luminescent numerals of the alarm-system keypad should have been visible on the wall, only a few steps from my side of the bed. They were not glowing.

Furthermore, a tiny green indicator lamp should have confirmed that the system was powered. And a red indicator of the same size should have noted that the alarm was set on HOME mode, which meant that the motion detectors were not engaged but that all of the window and door circuits were activated to warn of any attempted intrusion. Neither the green nor the red was lit.

The power-company service had failed. Perhaps a drunk driver had sheared off a utility pole. A transformer might have blown up. Such interruptions were rare and usually short-lived, nothing to worry about.

As the last clouds of sleep lifted from my mind, I remembered that the security system included a backup battery that should keep it operative for three hours. And when the main power supply was cut off, as the system switched to battery, a recorded voice should announce "power failure" throughout the house.

Apparently, the battery had gone dead. The recorded voice had never spoken.

I cautioned myself not to leap to conclusions. Coincidence is seldom credible in a work of fiction, but it is a primary thread in the tapestry of real life. An accident at a power station was a more likely explanation than was the return of the bow-tied critic.

From somewhere in the pitch-black bedroom, Shearman Waxx said again, "Doom."

Chapter 10

The temptation was great to believe that I had passed from the dream of the library into a dream of blindness and had not yet come awake.

As a writer, I succeed by deceiving readers into accepting that the story I'm telling is as true as their lives, that what happens to my characters should intellectually and emotionally involve them no less than they should be concerned about their real-world neighbors. But I have never been good at *self*-deception.

I was awake, all right, and Waxx stood or crouched, or roamed, somewhere in the bedroom.

My first impulse was to scream like a little girl. Fortunately, I repressed the urge. Waxx was one of those critics with crocodile genes; he would find most delicious any prey that was saturated with the pheromones of fear.

My nightstand—like the one on the farther side of the bed—was an antique Chinese chest with numerous small drawers of different sizes. In the top drawer closest to me, I kept a flashlight, which allowed me to find my way to the bathroom at night without switching on a lamp and waking Penny.

Each evening, before going to bed, I pulled this drawer partway out of the nightstand, so I could get the flashlight without making a disturbance. I am an incompetent handyman but a considerate husband.

Now I groped in the darkness, found the open drawer, and reached into it. The flashlight wasn't there.

I knew I had not misplaced it earlier. Waxx must have removed it before he woke me.

Penny also kept a flashlight in a drawer of her nightstand. Most likely Waxx had confiscated that one, as well.

Evidently, he had a flashlight of his own, with which he had stealthily prowled the room as we slept. If I wanted one, I would have to take his away from him.

Although I fully understood the wisdom of owning a gun, I didn't keep one in the house. Penny had been raised in a virtual armory and had no objection to firearms. But I had a covenant with Death to spare others as once I had been spared.

I assumed Shearman Waxx possessed a gun—as well as a butcher knife, a switchblade, an axe, a chain saw, a power drill with an assortment of bits, and a wood chipper.

Within reach, I had a couple of pillows and a bedside lamp.

As far as I could tell, Penny still slept. I saw no value in waking her at once.

Until Waxx switched on his light and revealed his position, he and I were equally blind. Because I knew the bedroom so much better than he did, the darkness counted slightly to my advantage.

He had heard me sit up in bed and gasp for breath when I broke out of my dream. But the noises I'd made might as likely have been those of a man thrashing at the sheets and turning over in his troubled sleep.

The first *doom* seemed to me to have been spoken in the lightless aisles of the dream library, and Waxx could not be sure that I heard him say it the second time.

Letting out a soft groan, then murmuring wordlessly, I pretended to be negotiating a nightmare. Using this anxious muttering as cover, I eased off the bed and, falling silent, crouched beside it.

Breathing through my open mouth, I made no slightest sound. If I decided to move, I felt confident that my pajamas were too soft to betray me with a rustle.

Although silent to the intruder's ears, I was not quiet to my own. My heart knocked like a savage fist upon all the doors of my defenses, chasing out my expectations of civilization and letting in the fear of anarchy and barbaric violence.

If Waxx made subtle sounds, I was not certain that I could hear them above this inner drumming. The rhythmic pressure waves of hard-pumped blood raised surf sounds in the nautilus turns of my inner ears.

The longer Waxx waited to speak again, the more I wondered what his game might be. I had no doubt that he had come here to harm us. That he wanted first to terrorize us seemed obvious, as well. But his boldness, the risks he took, and his eerie patience in the dark gave me the impression that his purpose was more complex than the psychotic thrill of torment and murder.

Before he spoke again, and especially before he switched on a flashlight, I needed to put some distance between myself and the bed. He would expect to find me there, and when he did not, when his light revealed his position but not mine, I might be able to catch him off guard, rushing at him from the side or from behind as he initially regarded the tangle of abandoned sheets.

Crouched and barefoot, in a slow-motion shamble that required tension in every muscle and that tested balance, I ape-walked toward where I expected to find an armchair. It ought to be just to the right of that point on the wall where the alarm-system keypad should have been softly glowing.

Shoulders slumped, arms low, I let my fingertips slide lightly, soundlessly across the carpet. If a knee buckled or a muscle cramped, I could steady myself with my hands.

I feared making a sound less than I dreaded colliding with Waxx in the blackness. My strategy would then be worthless, though I would still surprise him and might be able to overpower him before he shot or stabbed me.

I am five feet eleven and in acceptable physical condition. But I did not delude myself that his formidable bulk would prove to be flab. He would be difficult to take down.

In retrospect, I realize that in my desperation, I thought I could plot the scene as if I were writing fiction. Suspense novels are not my genre. Fate had dropped me into a real-life tale of peril, however, and because I lacked tough-guy experience, I had fallen back on imagination and craftsmanship to sculpt this narrative toward a twist that would not leave me dead in an early chapter.

Blinded, I nevertheless found the armchair where I expected it would be, which gave me hope that I remained the protagonist and had not become a supporting character destined for a bloody end in Part 1.

Elsewhere in the room, his position impossible to fix from a single word, the critic said quietly, "Hack."

He might be describing what he intended to do to me with an axe or cleaver, but I suspected that instead the word was intended as an insult, a judgment of my writing skills.

Separating the first armchair from another was an art-deco sideboard. The highly lacquered amboina wood felt cool against my fingertips as I aped onward.

Our sleigh bed stood against the east wall of the room. Logic suggested that Waxx had positioned himself at the foot of the bed, where his flashlight, when he switched it on, could cover both me and Penny.

Now near the south wall, I hoped to circle to the west, where I most likely would be behind him when at last he revealed himself.

Wondering at Waxx's failure to take quick and deadly action after penetrating the house so effectively, I halted at the second armchair, suddenly fearful of proceeding. I began to suspect that I had missed something, that the implicit meaning of the moment was different from what I imagined it to be.

This happens often when writing fiction. Outlines are a waste of time. If you give your characters free will, they will grow in ways you never anticipated, and they will take the story places you could not have predicted, raising themes you might or might not have intended to explore. Characters shape events; events illuminate the characters. The people in a story begin as seeds, become buds, and blossom in ways that surprise the author, precisely as real people frequently surprise him with their intentions and capacities.

As I crouched by the second armchair, Shearman Waxx electrocuted me.

Chapter 11

Out of the darkness, something thrust against the nape of my neck—two metal pegs, positive and negative poles. Before I could flinch away, hot needles stitched the length of my spine and then sewed through every branch of my peripheral nervous system to toes, to fingertips, to scalp.

My eyes rolled back in my skull, dazzled by an inner vision of gold and crimson fireworks, and I dropped out of my crouch. Facedown on the carpet, I twitched as a puppeteer jerked on the threads that the needles had sewn through me.

The words that came from me were none that I intended, slurred and meaningless.

Although coherent speech eluded me, I clearly heard Penny, who had been awakened by my cry.

"Cubby?" The click-click of her lamp switch. "What's happening?"

I resisted the twitching, but spasmed all the more for my resistance.

Yet I marshalled the clarity of mind and tongue to tell her what seemed most important: "He can see in the dark."

The bronze hardware on her nightstand rattled as Penny jerked open drawers in search of the flashlight that Waxx had confiscated.

She let out a thin shriek, like the plaint a bird in flight might issue if pierced by an arrow. The hard knock of her fall suggested that she might have struck her head on furniture.

The physical effects of the shock faded quickly. The twitching diminished to a nervous trembling, which was not a consequence of extreme voltage but an expression of my terror at Penny's suffering.

From full collapse, I rose onto all fours, then to my knees, my mind a jigsaw-puzzle box full of fragmented thoughts from which I could not fit together a defensive tactic.

The word *Taser* sizzled into my mind. And Waxx Tasered me again.

I fell from my knees onto my right side. My skull rapped the floor. I bit my tongue, tasted blood.

For a moment, I thought Waxx was tearing at my pajama shirt, but the clawing hands were mine. I tried to close them into fists.

Stuttering Penny's name, infuriated by my inability to protect her, I tried to jackknife off my side, onto my knees. The post-shock spasms facilitated this change of position. Probing the darkness, I found an armchair, used it for support, got to my feet.

I cursed myself that I was not prepared for this—not for Waxx in particular, but for someone lethal in the night. I knew well the capacity for cruelty in the human heart.

A groan of convulsive misery came from Penny as she was Tasered a second time.

A homicidal rage, of which I would never have imagined myself capable, focused me. Murderous *fury* more than terror cracked the dam of adrenaline, flooding me with sudden strength, animal determination.

I moved unsteadily toward where I thought Penny might be.

As invisible as the wind—and like the wind revealed only by his effects—Waxx came in from my left side, stinging me in the neck. The shocks were no longer hot but as cold as driven sleet.

Although I struck him, it seemed to be a glancing blow. My legs buckled, and I knew I would not get another chance to hit him.

As I struggled to stay on my hands and knees, he bent down and Tasered me a fourth time, again on the nape of the neck.

I lay prone and shaking, a coiled snake of nausea flexing in my gut. My mouth flooded with saliva, and I thought I would vomit.

He Tasered me again before the previous shock had begun to wear off. I wondered if the effects were cumulative, if enough of them could fry the nerves, induce a stroke, cause death.

He spoke only one more word to me: "Scribbler."

For a while, I seemed to be floating in the blackness of deep space, the floor under me no longer a floor but a spiral galaxy slowly turning.

My sense of time had been temporarily short-circuited. When I discovered that I had the capacity to crawl, and in fact to rise to my feet, I did not know whether one minute or ten had passed since my last Tasering.

I was surprised to be alive. If, like a cat, I had nine lives, I had used up eight of them one night a long time ago.

The taste of blood remained from my bitten tongue, yet when I called Penny's name, my voice broke as if my mouth and throat were not only dry but desiccated.

She did not answer.

Chapter 12

Waxx must have taken Penny with him, to what purpose I could imagine, to what end I refused to consider.

One moment more of blindness was intolerable. Faint moonglow at the edges of the blackout draperies led me to the windows. I found the cord, revealed the glass, the night, the looming lunar face.

"Cubby?"

Either she had been unconscious when I called to her or she had not heard me because my voice was even weaker than I thought.

After the unrelieved gloom, the merest moonlight was sunshine to my eyes, and I saw her pulling herself to her feet at the dresser.

I went to her, speechless with gratitude. Her breath against my throat, the graceful curve of her back under my right hand, and the sweet smell of her hair were poetry that words could never equal.

She said the only thing worth saying: "Thank God."

On the nightstands, the digital clocks came back to life and began flashing to indicate that they needed to be reset.

The alarm keypad brightened. A yellow indicator light announced a functioning system, and a red bulb confirmed that it was armed.

The recorded voice that reported on status changes remained silent, as though the alarm had never been disabled.

Neither Penny nor I said "Milo," but we hurried to his room, switching on lights as we went.

As my hand closed on the knob, a growl rose from the far side of the door. Lassie greeted us with raised hackles and bared teeth. As if we were not the real Penny and Cubby but evil replicants, she continued to threaten violence if we crossed the threshold.

Dogs have a sense of shame, in fact stronger than most people do these days. Penny played to it, disappointment in her voice: "Growling at me but not one bark to warn us about that lunatic?"

Lassie stopped growling but continued to bare her teeth.

"Not one bark for the lunatic?" Penny repeated.

The dog's flews quivered with what seemed to be embarrassment and relaxed to cover her teeth. Her tail wagged tentatively.

I came to Lassie's defense: "She was ready to protect Milo. Good girl."

The boy lay in bed, snoring softly. He didn't wake when Lassie sprang onto the mattress and curled beside him.

"Stay here," I whispered. "I'll search the house."

Voice hushed but adamant, Penny said, "Not alone. Call the cops."

"It's all right. He's gone. I'm just making sure."

"Don't be ridiculous. Call the cops."

"And tell them what? Did you see Waxx?"

"No. But—"

"I didn't see him, either."

Her eyes narrowed. "He said something, a word."

"Three words. *Doom. Hack. Scribbler.*"

She bristled. "He called you a hack?"

"Yeah."

"He should die hard. Point is—you heard him speak at the restaurant."

"Only one word. I hardly know his voice."

"But you *know* this was him."

"Evidence, Penny. Isn't any."

She pointed to a pair of red marks on her left forearm, like two spider bites. "The Taser."

"That's not enough. That's nothing. How often did he sting you?"

"Twice. You?"

"Five, maybe six times."

"I'd like to castrate him."

"That doesn't sound like the creator of the Purple Bunny books."

"Call the cops," she insisted.

"He'll say we made it up, to get back at him for his review."

"He didn't review me. Why am I going to lie about him?"

"For me. That's what they'll say. You know the media—if you give them a stick, they love to knock you down."

I couldn't say there was an event in my past about which I never told her. If I made accusations about Waxx that he denied, tabloid TV would start digging. They probably wouldn't be able to learn who I had been, as a child, but I didn't want to test their skills.

I said, "Besides, I have a feeling like...he *wants* us to call the cops."

"Why would he want that?"

"Either he wants us to call them or he doesn't care if we do. This is so screwy. I haven't done anything to him. There's something about this we don't understand."

"I don't understand *any* of it," she declared.

"Exactly. Trust me on this. No cops just yet."

Leaving her with Milo and the dog, I searched the house, found no one. Nothing had been damaged. Everything seemed to be in order.

All the doors were locked, and the security chains were engaged. The window latches were secure. No panes had been broken.

Christmas was little more than six weeks away; but Waxx had not come down a chimney and had not departed through one. All the dampers were closed tight.

In the master bathroom, I stripped off my pajamas and quickly dressed. I retrieved my wristwatch from the vanity, where I had left it before retiring for the night. The time was 4:54 A.M.

Catching sight of myself in a mirror, I didn't like what I saw. Face pale and damp with sweat, skin gray and grainy around the eyes, lips bloodless, mouth tight and grim.

My eyes were especially disturbing. I didn't see myself in them. I saw someone I had once been.

When I returned to Milo's room, he still slept.

Lassie had gotten over her shame. From the bed, she stared at us imperiously and issued a long-suffering sigh, as though we were keeping her awake.

Penny said, "I'm gonna scream if I don't have a cookie."

―――――――――――――――――――――

Chapter 13

This time: oatmeal-raisin with macadamia nuts.

Penny was too agitated to sit at the table. She paced the kitchen as she nibbled the cookie.

"You want milk?" I asked.

"No. I want to blow up something."

"I'm having Scotch. Blow up what?"

"Not just a tree stump, that's for sure."

"We don't have any stumps. Just trees."

"Like a hotel. Something at least twenty stories."

"Is that satisfying—blowing up a hotel?"

"You're so *relaxed* afterward," she said.

"Then let's do it."

"We blew up a church once. That was just sad."

"I'm angry and scared. I don't need sad on top of that."

I sat on a stool, my back to the breakfast bar, and watched her pace as I sipped the Scotch. The whiskey was just a prop; what calmed and fortified me was watching Penny.

"Blowing things up," she said, "relieves stress better than cookies."

"Plus it's less fattening," I noted, "and doesn't lead to diabetes."

"I'm thinking maybe we've made a mistake not involving Milo in all that."

"I'm sure he'd enjoy blowing up buildings. What kid wouldn't? But what about the effect on his personality development?"

"I turned out okay, didn't I?" she asked.

"So far, you're the nicest abnormal person I know. But if the cookies stop working for you..."

Grimbald, her father, was a demolitions expert. In Las Vegas alone, he had brought down four old hotels to clear the land for bigger and glitzier enterprises. From the time Penny—then Brunhild—was five years old until she married me, he had taken her with him to watch his controlled blasts implode enormous structures.

On a DVD that her folks produced for us, we have TV-news footage of young Penny at numerous events, clapping her hands in delight, giggling, and mugging for the camera as, behind her, huge hotels and office buildings and apartment towers and sports stadiums collapsed into ruins. She looked adorable.

Grimbald and Clotilda titled the DVD *Memories,* and for the soundtrack they used Streisand singing "The Way We Were" as well as an old Perry Como tune, "Magic Moments." They got teary-eyed when they played it every Christmas.

"I've learned something about myself tonight," Penny said.

"Oh, good. Then it's all been worthwhile."

"I didn't know I could get this pissed off."

Penny dropped her half-eaten cookie in the kitchen sink.

"Uh-oh," I said.

With a spatula, she shoved the cookie into the drain. She turned on the cold water, and then she thumbed the garbage-disposal button.

In an instant, whirling steel obliterated the cookie, but she did not at once push the button again. She stared at the drain as the water spilled down through the churning blades.

I began to suspect that in the theater of her mind, she was feeding pieces of Shearman Waxx to the disposal.

After a minute, I raised my voice to be heard above the motor, the whistling blades, and the running water: "You're beginning to freak me out."

Shutting off the disposal and the water, she said, "I'm freaking myself out." She turned away from the sink. "How could he see in the dark?"

"Maybe night-vision goggles, the infrared spectrum."

"Sure, everybody has a pair of those lying around. So how could he take control of our alarm system?"

"Babe, remember when we got a car with a satellite-navigation system? The first day, I kept responding to the woman who was giving me directions because I thought she was talking to me live from orbit?"

"Okay, I'm asking the wrong guy. But you're the only guy I've got to ask."

As I started to reply, Penny put a finger to her lips, warning me to be silent.

Cocking my head, listening to the house, I wondered what she had heard.

She came to me, took my glass of Scotch, and put it on the counter.

Raising my eyebrows, I silently mouthed the question *What?*

She grabbed my hand, led me into the food pantry, closed the door behind us, and said sotto voce, "What if he can hear us?"

"How could he hear us?"

"Maybe he bugged the house."

"How could he have done that?"

"I don't know. How did he take control of our alarm system?"

"Let's not get totally paranoid," I said.

"Too late. Cubby, who is this guy?"

The standard online encyclopedia answer that had been adequate only a day earlier—*award-winning critic, author of three college textbooks, enema*—no longer seemed complete.

"After his weird walk-through yesterday," Penny said, "I told you it was over, he'd made his point. But it wasn't over. It still isn't."

"Maybe it is," I said with less conviction than a guy cowering in the rubble of a city only *half* destroyed by Godzilla.

"What does he want from us? What do you think?"

"I don't know. I can't figure how his head works."

Her eyes were no less lovely for being haunted. "He wants to destroy us, Cubby."

"He can't destroy us."

"Why can't he?" she asked.

"Our careers depend on talent and hard work—not just on a critic's opinions."

"Careers? I'm not talking about careers. You're in denial."

For some reason—maybe to avoid her gaze—I plucked a can of beets off a pantry shelf. Then I didn't know what to do with it.

"In the mood for beets?" she asked. When I returned the can to the shelf without comment, she said, "Cubby, he's going to kill us."

"I didn't do anything to him. Neither did Milo. You haven't even *seen* him yet."

"He has some reason. I don't much care what it is. I just know what he's going to do."

I found myself looking at a can of corn, but I didn't pick it up. "Let's be real. If he wanted to kill us, he could have done it tonight."

"He's sadistic. He wants to torment us, terrify us, totally dominate us—and then kill us."

I was surprised by the words that came from me: "I'm not a magnet for monsters."

"Cubby? What does that mean?"

I know Penny so well that her tone of voice told me precisely what expression now shaped her face: furrowed brow, eyes squinted in calculation, nose lifted as if to catch a scent, lips still parted in expectation after she had spoken—the quizzical look of an acutely perceptive woman who recognizes a moment of revelation hidden in the folds of a conversation.

"What does that mean?" she repeated.

Rather than lie to her, I said, "I think I should apologize."

"Are you talking to me or the corn?"

I dared to look at her, which was not easy considering what I said as I met her eyes: "I mean—apologize to Waxx."

"Like hell. You don't have anything to apologize for."

"For going to lunch just to get a look at him." I couldn't explain myself to her. For ten years, I deceived her by omission, and now was not the time to confess. "For violating his privacy."

Incredulous, she said, "It's a public restaurant. This is a *private* residence. You looked at him, he *Tasered* us."

"An apology can't do any harm."

"Yes, it can. An apology won't placate him. It'll encourage him. He'll *feed* on any concession. Apologizing to such a man—it's like baring your throat to a vampire."

Hard experience supported what she said, but it was experience that I had long repressed and on which I was loath to act.

"All right," I said. "So what do you think we should do?"

"Locks and alarms didn't stop him tonight. They won't stop him tomorrow night. This place isn't safe."

"I'll have the alarm company upgrade the system."

She shook her head. "That'll take days. And it won't matter. He's too clever for upgrades. We have to get to a safe place, where he can't find us."

"We can't run forever. I've got a book deadline."

"And, good golly," she said, "we haven't even *begun* to do our Christmas shopping."

"Well, I *do* have a deadline," I said defensively.

"I didn't say run forever. Just buy time to do some research."

"What research?"

"Shearman Waxx. Where does he come from? What's his story, his past, his associations?"

"He's an enigma."

She picked up the can of beets in which I had previously shown an interest. "Take the label off this can, the contents are a mystery—but only until you open it."

"I can open a can," I said, because we had an electric opener that required of me no mechanical skill.

"And if Waxx is this freaking weird with us," Penny said, "he has to have been totally bizarro with someone else, maybe with a lot of people, so at the very least we should be able to find someone to support our claim that he's harassing us."

I acquiesced. "All right. We'll get someplace safe, then we'll go on the hunt."

"Still no cops?"

"Not till we know more about Waxx. I don't want a media circus."

"Cops can be discreet."

"They'd have to talk to Waxx. He won't be discreet. Come on. I'll help you pack."

"I'd rather you took Lassie out to poop. Fix breakfast for Milo. Deal with your morning e-mails. I'll pack after I shower."

"I don't know why that can of shaving cream detonated in the suit-case. It didn't have anything to do with me."

"Nobody said that it did, sweetie. Not either time. I just pack faster than you do."

"Because I like to make the maximum use of space. You can take fewer suitcases if you don't waste a cubic inch."

She kissed me on the nose and quoted Chesterton: "'A man and a woman cannot live together without having against each other a kind of everlasting joke. Each has discovered that the other is not only a fool, but a great fool.'"

We drew on each other's strengths, but perhaps more important, we found our strength increased and our love enriched by being able to laugh at our own and at each other's weaknesses.

As Penny opened the pantry door, I suddenly *knew* that the critic would be there, armed with something wickedly sharp. I was wrong. We were alone.

The specifics of the premonition proved false, but the essence was fulfilled a short while later. Before we left the house, Shearman Waxx would escalate the terror and deal us a devastating blow.

Chapter 14

At 5:30 that Thursday morning, a full half hour before dawn, when I went upstairs to wake Milo, he was sitting at his desk, working with his computer.

On the back of his plain white pajamas, the word SEEK blazed in red block letters.

Lassie stood on top of the highboy, peering down at me.

"How did she get up there?" I asked.

His attention fixed on the computer, Milo said, "The usual way."

"Which is how?"

"Yeah."

"Milo?"

He did not respond.

Although the boy wasn't touching the keyboard, groups of numbers and symbols flickered across the screen. On closer inspection, I saw multiple lines of complex mathematical equations chasing one another so fast from left to right that I could make no sense of them.

In truth, I would not have been able to understand them at any speed. I'm grateful that Penny is willing to balance the checkbook and review bank statements every month.

The screen went blank, and Milo at once typed in a series of approximately thirty numbers and symbols that, as far as I was concerned, might as well have been ancient Egyptian hieroglyphics. When he finished typing, his entry remained on the monitor for a moment, but then blinked off. Once more, tiers of equations streamed across the computer without any further input from him.

"What's happening?" I asked.

Milo said, "Something."

"Something what?"

"Yeah."

When my son was at his most mystifying, when he turned so far inward that he seemed almost autistic in his detachment, I had always before been intrigued, enchanted by the single-minded concentration with which he chased an idea through the labyrinth of his mind, his eyes bright with the excitement of discovery.

Not until now had I found his contemplative disjunction from his surroundings to be disturbing. The atmosphere in the bedroom was ominous, and the hairs on the nape of my neck were raised by a power less ordinary than static electricity.

"Something's happening," I pressed. "Something what?"

He said, "Interesting."

On top of the highboy, Lassie wagged her tail. Her reliable canine instinct for menace seemed to detect nothing troubling in the moment.

I was probably reacting to Shearman Waxx's assault on us and to the fear of his return, not to Milo.

"Listen," I said, "we're going on a little trip."

"Trip," Milo said.

"We want to get out of here by seven-thirty."

Milo said, "Thirty."

"We'll have something quick for breakfast, cereal and toast, then you'll shower in the master bath because your mom will be in our bedroom packing, and she wants you to stay close to her."

Milo intently studied the screen.

"Hey, Spooky, did you hear what I said?"

"Cereal, toast, stay close to Mom."

"I'm going to feed Lassie and toilet her. You come to the kitchen."

"Cereal, toast, gimme a minute."

On top of the highboy, Lassie looked eager but trepidatious.

"It's too far for her to jump," I said.

"Too far," Milo agreed, still enraptured by the computer.

"How do I get her down?"

"However."

From the linen closet across the hall, I fetched a step stool. I stood on it and lifted the dog off the highboy.

She licked my chin gratefully, and then she jumped from my arms to the floor.

Downstairs, I needed about a minute to find the measuring cup, open her feed can, scoop up the kibble, and put it in her bowl—and she needed even less time to eat.

In the backyard, while she attended to both parts of her toilet, I swept the darkness with a flashlight beam, half expecting to find Shearman Waxx lurking behind a tree.

When the dog was finished, I used the flashlight to locate the poop, double-bag it, and drop it in one of the trash cans beside the garage.

As always, she watched me complete this task as if I were the most mystifying creature she had ever seen—and quite possibly mad.

"If you were the *real* Lassie," I said, "you'd be smart enough to bag your own poop."

I washed my hands at the kitchen sink, and as I dried them, Milo arrived. While I made and buttered the toast, he poured two bowls of cereal.

Although I would have preferred shredded wheat instead of Franken Berry in chocolate milk, I decided to think of this as a bonding experience.

Until Milo sat to eat, I had not noticed that he had brought his Game Boy.

"No games at the table," I reminded him.

"I'm not playing games, Dad."

"What else can you do with a Game Boy?"

"Something."

"Let me see."

He turned the device toward me. Equations, like those on his computer, streamed across the small screen.

"What's that?" I asked.

"Stuff," he said, holding the Game Boy in one hand and eating with the other.

"What is it? What's it mean?"

He said, "We'll see."

I suppose if Mozart's father was an ignoramus about music, the little genius would have found it frustrating to try to discuss his compositions with the old man—but still would have loved him.

When Milo and Lassie were safely upstairs in the master suite with Penny, I went to my study.

I almost dropped the pleated shades at all three windows. But dawn had come, and I doubted that Waxx would still be lingering.

I switched on my computer and checked my e-mail without freezing up the keyboard, without damaging the mouse, and without destroying the Internet. Because I spend so much of my life writing, a computer is one machine with which I've grown comfortable.

As I was responding to an e-mail from my British editor, the phone rang. Line 3. Caller ID told me only UNKNOWN, but I took the call anyway: "This is Cubby."

A man whose voice I did not recognize said, "Cullen Greenwich?"

"Yes, speaking."

The caller sounded anxious, harried: "A lot of people think I'm dead, but I'm not."

"Excuse me?"

"So many others are dead. Most days, I wish I were with them."

"Who is this?"

"John Clitherow."

I had never met the man or spoken with him on the phone, but I had corresponded with him, exchanging perhaps a dozen long letters. He had written novels that I much admired.

More than three years ago, he told his publisher he wished to cancel the remaining book on his contract. He intended never to write again. In publishing circles, the assumption was made that he had a terminal disease and wished to keep his struggle private. I wrote him again, but he did not reply. I'd heard that he and his family—his wife, Margaret, and two children—had moved somewhere in Europe.

"I shouldn't be talking to you on your land line," he said. "Too dangerous for me, maybe for you, too. Do you have a cell phone?"

I picked up my cell from the desk. "Yes."

"If you'll give me the number, I'll ring you back. That'll be safer for both of us. No matter who he is, what he is, he can't listen in as easily to a cellular call." When I hesitated, he said, "Your metaphors are damned well *not* ponderous."

That reference surely had to be to the Waxx review of *One O'Clock Jump.*

I gave him the cell-phone number, and after he repeated it, he said,

"I'll call you shortly. I just need to change locations. Give me ten minutes."

He hung up, and so did I.

After staring at the computer for a moment, hardly recognizing the words that I had so recently written to my British editor, I got up and closed the shades at all three windows.

Chapter 15

As I finished lowering the last window shade, my third line rang. According to the caller ID, my agent, Hud Jacklight, wished to speak to me.

Because of the timing, I assumed this call and Clitherow's were related, and I picked up.

"One word," Hud said. "Short stories."

"Those are two words."

"Best American. You know it?"

Disoriented, I said, "Know what?"

"Short stories. Best American. Of the year."

"Sure. *The Best American Short Stories*. It's an annual anthology."

"Every year. Different guest editor. Next year—you."

"I don't write short stories."

"Don't have to. You select. The contents."

"Hud, I don't have time to read a thousand short stories to find twenty good ones."

"Hire someone. To read. Everyone does. Winnow it down for you."

"That doesn't sound ethical."

"It's ethical. If nobody knows."

"Besides," I argued, "the guest editor is always someone who writes short stories."

"The publisher and me. We're pals. Trust me. Very prestigious."

"I don't want to do it, Hud."

"It's a literary thing. You're a Waxx author. Got to do literary things. Be part of the 'in' crowd."

"No. That's not me."

"It's you."

"It's *not* me."

"It's you. Trust me. I know you."

"Don't try to arrange it," I warned him. "I won't do it."

"You're up there now. One of the elite."

"No."

"You can be in the pantheon."

"I'm going to hang up now, Hud."

"The American literary pantheon."

"Good-bye, Hud."

"Wait, wait. So forget short stories. Think—the great one."

No matter how much you want to terminate a Hud Jacklight call, astonishment and horror and curiosity often compel you to keep listening.

"What great one?" I asked.

"Think *The Great Gatsby*."

"What about it?"

"Who was the guy? The author?"

"F. Scott Fitzgerald."

"Wasn't it Hemingway?"

"No. Fitzgerald."

"I guess you would know."

"Since I'm one of the elite."

"Exactly. I'll talk to them."

"Who?"

"His estate. You'll write it. The sequel."

"That's ridiculous."

"You can do it, Cubster. You're pure talent."

I could not believe that I heard myself bothering to say, "*The Great Gatsby* doesn't need a sequel."

"Everybody wants to know."

"Know what?"

"What happened next. To Gatsby."

"He's dead at the end of the book."

"Bring him back. Think of a way."

"I can't bring him back if he's dead."

"They're always bringing Dracula back."

"Dracula's a *vampire*."

"There's your twist. Gatsby's a vampire."

"Don't you dare call Fitzgerald's estate."

"You're at a golden moment, Cubbo."

"I hate *The Great Gatsby*," I lied.

"The pantheon. If you'll just go for it."

"I have to hang up now, Hud."

"We gotta exploit the moment."

"Maybe we don't have to."

"I'll keep thinking. About opportunities."

"I'm in pain here, Hud. I have to go."

"Pain? What pain? What's wrong?"

"I have to go. It's a prostate thing."

"Prostate? You're only forty."

"I'm thirty-four, Hud."

"Even worse. Hey. Not cancer. Is it?"

"No. Just an urgent need to pee."

"Thank God. I'll keep thinking."

"I know you will, Hud."

I hung up.

Usually, after such a call from Hud Jacklight, I raced to Penny to share the details. Sometimes, that was the end of the workday for both of us, regardless of the hour. We could not get focused again.

Hud negotiated exceptionally good deals for his clients. I won't say that was his saving grace, but it was my excuse.

With John Clitherow's promised call due at any moment, I was finally convinced of something I had suspected for a long time: God has a sense of humor, and because the world is wondrous, He expects us to find reasons to smile even on the darkest days.

Chapter 16

When the cell phone rang, the voice of Hud Jacklight still ricocheted through my mind, no doubt destroying brain cells the way free-radical molecules damaged body tissue and accelerated the aging process if you didn't have enough antioxidants in your diet.

John Clitherow said, "I'm calling you with a disposable phone. I don't dare have anything in my name anymore. I'll throw this away and use a different disposable as soon as I hang up. This will most likely be the only call I can make to you, so I'm pleading with you, Cullen, for God's sake, don't write me off as a crank."

"You're not a crank," I said. "You're a brilliant writer."

"I haven't written a word in over three years, and if five minutes from now I don't *sound* like a crank, then I'm doing a piss-poor job of getting the gravity of the situation across to you, because the truth is crazier than a rabid monkey on methamphetamine."

"I've had some experience of crazy truths," I said. "Go on."

"When Waxx's review of your new book appeared on Tuesday, I

didn't see it. I only read it a few hours ago. Been trying to get your number ever since. You didn't take his criticism to heart, I hope. It's the bile and vomit of an envious and ignorant man, the stench of which he thinks he has disguised with mordant wit, except that his mordancy is no sharper than a sledgehammer and his wit is not wit at all but the raillery of an intellectual fop, a popinjay who wheezes when he thinks he pops."

Survival instinct told me to trust John Clitherow. But though I needed to know what he had to tell me—and perhaps already knew— I was loath to hear it.

Therefore, in light of recent events, I remained wary, hesitant to say anything against Waxx, lest he be orchestrating this moment, sitting beside Clitherow and listening to my every word. Paranoia had become my default position.

I said only, "Well, he's entitled to his opinion."

"He has no opinions, not of a considered and analytic nature. He has an *agenda*," Clitherow said. "And the first thing you must *not* do is respond to him."

"My wife told me to let it go."

"A wise woman. But letting it go might not be enough."

"The thing is, I didn't exactly let it go."

Clitherow barely breathed two words in such a way that they were less an expression of dismay than a prayer for a hopeless cause: "Oh, God."

Obeying instinct, I told him about lunch at Roxie's Bistro the previous day—and the moment in the men's room.

When I informed him that the critic had spoken one word, he repeated it before I could. "Doom."

"How did you know?"

He became agitated and spoke faster, words spilling from him in anxious torrents: "Cullen, for three years, I've continued to read the bastard's reviews, missed only a few. He's as inelegant and as jejune when he praises books as he is when he drops his hammer on them. But what he says about your *One O'Clock Jump* is the first time he's been that vicious since he assaulted my last book, *Mr. Bluebird*. He uses several identical phrases in both reviews. He says of you, as he said of me, that you are 'an extremist of the naïve' and that you're incapable of understanding that humankind is 'a disease of the dust.' He said of us, separately, that we mistakenly believe 'it is easy to be solemn but hard to be frolicsome,' which indeed I do believe, and which I'm sure you believe, a belief supported by the fact that for every thousand solemn novels that thud into bookstores, there's just one that is both meaningful and frolicsome, that has a sense of wonder, that is astonished by the universe and life, that knows regardless of the vicissitudes of existence, we were born for freedom and for joy and for laughter. Cullen, there are another half dozen things he said of me that he says of you in the identical language, in the same tone of scorn and near outrage. And this makes me afraid for you, very afraid for you and everyone you love."

So rapidly and urgently had he spoken that while I followed all he said, I did not fully grasp the darker implications of his words or why, sentence by sentence, his anxiety curdled into anguish.

John Clitherow paused only to take a deep breath, and he resumed before I could ask a question: "I wrote Waxx's newspaper, a response to the review of my book. Wasn't an angry word in it. I kept it brief and humorous—and only noted a couple of the many errors of fact in his summary of the plot. Five days later, my wife and I came home from an evening at the theater. Laurel, the baby-sitter, was asleep on the sofa, and the kids were safe in bed. But after Laurel had gone home, I found my letter to Waxx's newspaper in my study. It was the original that I had mailed, now pinned to my desk by a knife. The blade of the knife was wet with blood. In the low lamplight, I had seen our cat sleeping on the office sofa, and now I saw the stain under her, and she was not sleeping. Right then the phone rang, and though the caller's ID was blocked, I took the call. He said only, 'Doom,' and hung up. I'd never heard his voice, but I knew it had to be Waxx."

Because I was on the cell, no phone cord tethered me to the desk, and I rose from the chair. Sitting, I could not draw a deep breath, for I felt as though a passive posture invited an attack. Movement was imperative, being ready to respond, being watchful.

"He's been here," I told Clitherow, "but I can't prove it."

I described Waxx's bold intrusion the previous afternoon, when he had toured the house with such nonchalance that it seemed as if he operated under the misapprehension that our home was a public establishment.

The note of anguish in Clitherow's voice phased into something colder, what seemed to me to be an icy despair. "Get out of there. Don't spend another night."

Pacing, I quickly told him about the critic's second visit, the Tasering in the lightless bedroom.

"Go now," he said. "Right now. Go somewhere you have no previous connection, somewhere he can't find you."

"That's more or less the plan. My wife must be almost finished packing. We—"

"*Now*," Clitherow insisted. "You can't prove he Tasered you. *I* can't prove he killed my mother and father, but he did."

The air seemed to have thickened, offering such resistance that I came to a halt.

"I can't prove he killed Margaret, my wife, but the sonofabitch did. He did. It was him."

As he spoke, I stepped out of my study, into the foyer, from which I could see the hallway that served all the ground-floor rooms.

"I can't prove he killed Emily and Sarah...." Clitherow's voice broke on *Emily* and faltered to a halt on *Sarah*.

He'd had two daughters. Both under the age of ten.

Although much journalism has become advocacy in our time, I read various sources of news for the challenge of sifting the facts from the deceit and the delusion. So many people close to a novelist as well known as John Clitherow could not have suffered untimely deaths without exciting the nose for blood that still can wake a beguiled reporter to recognize genuine injustice. But I had seen nothing about this storm of homicide that tore his life asunder and blew him into hiding.

If Waxx had visited our house only once, if I had not been Tasered, I might not have believed Clitherow's claims. His story was cogent, his narrative voice convincing; yet the high body count—and the consequent implication that Waxx was not merely a sociopath of epic proportions but instead virtually a fiend—was flamboyant in a way that his novels never were.

Recent events reminded me, however, that truth is paradoxical, that it is always stranger than fiction. We invent fiction either to distract ourselves from the world—and thus from the truth of things— or to explain the world to ourselves, but we cannot invent truth, which simply *is*. Truth, when we recognize it, always surprises us, which is why we so seldom choose to recognize it; we abhor profound surprises and prefer what is familiar, comfortable, undemanding, and pat.

I didn't know John well enough to feel his grief as sharply as perhaps I should have, or to grieve properly for him. I had never met him except through the mail, and I had not even seen photos of his wife and daughters.

Inhibiting grief, of course, my growing apprehension not only darkened my mind and heart but also inspired a physical agitation that drove me into the hallway—then to the sidelights flanking the front door, in expectation of seeing a black Cadillac Escalade in the street.

In lieu of pity, I felt a nervous sympathy for John, and when I tried—inadequately—to express my condolences, I did so with a commiseration as tender as compassion but more remote and hopeless.

I don't think he needed or wanted commiseration. He had lost too much to be able to take consolation from anyone's sympathy.

John listened only until he regained his composure. In a voice fractured but not shattered, he interrupted me, speaking with greater urgency than ever: "Waxx has resources that seem supernatural. You can't overestimate his capabilities. He doesn't give you breathing room. He keeps coming back and back, and back. He's relentless. Kill him if he gives you the opportunity, because killing him is your only chance. And don't think going to the cops will help. Funny things happen when you go to the cops about Waxx. Right now, for God's sake, just run. Buy yourself time. As soon as you can, abandon your car, don't use your credit cards or cell phone, don't give him any way to find you. Get out of there. Get the hell out of there. *Go!*"

He terminated the call.

I keyed in *69, with no expectation that he would answer but with the hope that this call-back function would display his number. If he did not discard his disposable phone in favor of another, as he said that he would, I might be able to reach him later, when we were safely away from the house.

He proved to be as cautious as he had urged me to be. He could not be reached by *69, and no number appeared on the screen of my cell phone.

Turning away from the front-door sidelight and the view of the street, heading toward the stairs, I shouted, "Penny! We gotta go!"

Her reply came from the ground floor, from the back of the house.

Off the kitchen, in the laundry room, I found her with a pile of luggage. She was pulling a big wheeled suitcase into the garage.

I grabbed two bags and followed her. "Something's happened, it's worse than we thought."

She didn't waste a precious second asking what the something might be, but instead muscled the suitcase into the back of the Ford Explorer.

In a crisis, she functioned more like a Boom than a Greenwich, very much the daughter of Grimbald and Clotilda, working quickly but calmly, confident that she would be well out of the zone of destruction when the end of the countdown came.

Other luggage had already been loaded. With the bags remaining in the laundry room, the cargo space of the SUV would be packed from end to end and side to side.

"We need to travel light," I said, as Penny headed back toward the laundry room. "What is all this?"

Materializing beside me as I shoved two more suitcases into the Explorer, Milo said, "Stuff."

"What stuff?"

"Important stuff."

"Your stuff?"

Suddenly cagey, he said, "Could be."

He wore black sneakers with red laces, black jeans, and a long-sleeved black T-shirt on the chest of which, in white block letters, was the word PURPOSE.

Already, Penny returned, pulling another trunk-size suitcase with wheels.

"Where's Lassie?" I asked as I hurried toward the laundry room.

"Backseat," Penny said.

I fetched the last two bags and brought them to the Explorer.

"There's one more thing upstairs," she said.

"No. Leave it."

"Can't. I'll be just a minute."

"Penny, wait—"

"You can close the tailgate." She dashed from the garage into the house.

Loading the last of the suitcases, I said to Milo, "Get in the backseat with Lassie."

"What's going on?"

"I told you. A little trip."

"Why the hurry?"

Closing the tailgate, I said, "Maybe we have a plane to catch."

"Do we have a plane to catch?"

Giving him a dose of his own inscrutability, I said, "Could be."

"Is it the Northern Hemisphere?" he asked.

"Is what?"

"Where we're going."

"What does it matter?" I asked.

"It matters."

"Get in the backseat, scout."

"I should ride shotgun."

"That's your mother's job."

"She doesn't have a shotgun."

"Neither do you."

"So let's draw straws."

"Can you kick someone's butt?" I asked.

"Whose butt?"

"Whoever's. I need a butt-kicker riding shotgun."

"Mom could kick anyone's butt."

"So get in the backseat."

"Guess I will."

"That's my boy."

"Northern Hemisphere is important."

Climbing into the car, he looked so small that I couldn't help thinking about Emily and Sarah Clitherow. The possibility of losing Milo pulled my nerves as taut as violin strings.

Penny seemed to be taking a long time. I began to feel that I had not properly conveyed to her the grim nature and importance of the new development or the greater urgency that it imposed on us.

The big garage door had not been raised. The side door remained locked. Milo would be as safe here as anywhere. Yet I was reluctant to leave him.

Penny had gone upstairs alone. At least Milo had Lassie.

"Stay put," I shouted to the boy, and I sprinted into the house.

As I strode through the laundry room, a telephone rang.

This shrill call tone was different from that of our house phone and that of the cell in my shirt pocket.

In the kitchen, I heard the unfamiliar ring again. It seemed to come from the utility closet that backed up to the laundry room.

The closet contained no phone—unless it belonged to someone hiding there.

Chapter 17

In the nearest corner stood a broom, and I seized it, judging that stiff bristles jammed in the eyes would be as effective as any thrust I might make with a knife, which in any case was not as near at hand as this more domestic weapon and would require a closer engagement with Waxx than I relished.

As the call tone shrilled a third time, I opened the utility-closet door, revealing a twelve-foot-deep, five-foot-wide space with a gas furnace against the back wall. Fluorescent light from the kitchen intruded far enough to confirm that no one crouched in wait for me.

Using the broom, I brushed up the light switch and stepped into the closet as the phone rang a fourth time.

A common gas furnace is to me a mystery of engineering no less complex than a 747 and no less intimidating than a nuclear reactor. My incompetence with mechanisms and machines, and my deep wariness of them, are exacerbated, in the case of a furnace, by the presence of pressurized gas lines.

Yet even I knew that the furnace had not come from the factory with a cell phone epoxied to the face of it, and that in fact no phone had been there previously.

Wires trailed from the phone to a curious construction on the floor, beside the furnace. This ominous assemblage included a digital clock displaying the correct time, several items that I might not have been able to identify even if I'd had time to study them, and what appeared to be a block of clay of the kind with which children played, gray and oily.

On the fifth ring, the display screen lit, and the phone somehow accepted the call. Then it produced—or received—a rapid series of varied tones that might have been a coded message.

On the digital clock, the time changed from the correct 7:03:20 A.M. to the incorrect 11:57:00 P.M.

Even I, ignorant of most things mechanical, knew that our best interests would not be served if we were still in the house when the clock displayed midnight three minutes hence.

Suffering no heroic delusion that I could safely dismantle this device, I backed out of the utility closet and threw down the broom. I raced up the back stairs, shouting for Penny.

As I reached the top of the stairs and stepped into the short arm of the L-shaped upstairs hall, Penny turned the corner from the longer hall that served her studio and the master suite. She carried an artist's portfolio large enough to hold several paintings of the size that she had lately been creating for *The Other Side of the Woods*, the book she would publish next autumn.

She said, "Cubby, a phone's ringing, but it's not ours."

Our house had two furnaces, one for each floor. When I pulled open the door of the nearby utility closet and switched on the light, a phone like the one downstairs answered itself; wired to another clay-brick package, it produced a series of varied tones that surely were coded instructions. A digital clock identical to the one in the first closet switched from the correct time to 11:57:30 P.M.

Two and a half minutes and counting.

In spite of her childhood and adolescent experience of colossal destruction, Penny made no attempt to disarm the device but hissed "Waxx" as if it were a curse word, and plunged down the back stairs, two at a time, and across the kitchen, with me so close behind that the toes of my shoes might have scuffed the heels of hers.

Bursting from the laundry room into the garage, she slapped a wall switch, and the roll-up door began to rise.

As I clambered in behind the steering wheel, Penny swung up into the passenger seat, tossed the Explorer keys to me, glanced in the back, and said, "Where's Milo?"

The dog sat in the backseat, ears pricked and alert, but the boy was gone.

Chapter 18

Shouting for Milo, Penny and I flew from the Explorer as if we had been ejected by a device installed by James Bond's favorite car customizer.

If the boy was in the garage, he apparently was in no condition to answer our calls. Penny hurried to search in, under, and around the sedan in the second parking stall, while I returned to the house.

I thought of John Clitherow. He had been Waxx's primary target, but the critic had first taken John's family.

The greatest punishment is not your own death but instead the loss of those you love. How much worse that loss must be if you have to live with the bitter knowledge that those who trusted and relied on you had been dealt early deaths as surrogates for you, punished for your offenses.

Waxx was not merely a homicidal sociopath but also, in the fullest sense, a terrorist.

In the doomed house, in the sparkling laundry room that would soon be filthy rubble, in the kitchen that momentarily would itself be cooked, in response to my ever more frantic shouts, Milo finally called out—"Yo, Dad!"—and entered at a run from the downstairs hall.

He carried Lassie's favorite toy, which we had inadvertently left behind: a plush purple bunny with huge startled eyes and floppy ears and a white puffball tail. It was cute, and it had a squeaker in its tummy, and the dog adored it, but it wasn't a toy worth dying for.

With more athletic grace than I had ever before exhibited, I scooped Milo off the kitchen floor and into my arms, swiveled toward the laundry room, and ran.

Giggling and exuberantly squeaking the bunny, Milo said, "What's happening?"

"The place is gonna blow," I said.

The squeaking alerted Penny. By the time we reached the garage, she stood by the open driver's door of the Explorer.

Her eyes were even wider than those of the startled rabbit. "No time to belt him in, Cubby, hold him in your lap!"

Even though the door had rolled all the way up and offered no obstacle, I felt relieved that she would be driving. Two facts—that the SUV had a reverse gear, that the back wall of the garage remained intact—seemed to tempt Fate too much for me to drive.

Milo had wanted to ride shotgun, and now he shared that position with me. He sat in my lap, and I wrapped both arms around him.

Folding his arms around the bunny and holding it against his chest, the boy said to the toy, "Don't worry. Dad won't let anything happen to us."

Geniuses, even six-year-old prodigies, don't believe that toys live any kind of life. Milo talked not to the rabbit, but reassured himself.

I had left the key in the ignition. When Penny tried to start the engine, she got from it a cough, a cough, a groan.

She glanced at me as I glanced at her, and we didn't need to be telepathic to know we shared the same thought: Waxx had sabotaged the vehicle.

Chapter 19

The stumpy, bow-tied, elbow-patched, Hush-Puppied, horn-rimmed-glasses-wearing, white-wine-sipping, pretentious, thick-necked, wide-assed intellectual fraud must have been in our house from at least midnight, planting explosives and tampering with the cars before at last venturing to our bedroom after four o'clock in the morning to torture us with a Taser.

For once, however, we had overestimated his capacity for villainy. On Penny's third try, the engine of the Explorer turned over, roared.

Pressing back hard in my seat, bracing my feet against the floorboard, I cradled Milo as best I could, expecting to be blown out of the garage as if from a circus cannon, in a plume of fire and debris.

But Penny sped the length of the driveway and braked only slightly to make a left turn into the street. Morning traffic had not yet appeared. She drove half a block before letting up on the accelerator and coasting toward the curb.

Since exiting the garage, I searched the day, expecting to see Waxx either in a parked car or standing at some vantage point along the street. He seemed to have decided against a ringside seat.

Penny looked at me. I nodded. She used the remaining momentum of the vehicle to turn crosswise in the street, where she came to a stop, angled back the way we had come.

A kind of masochistic need to know enraptured us.

Through the windshield, we had a view of the first house we ever owned. Slate roof. Stacked-stone and stucco walls. Imposing but not pretentious lines. Welcoming.

With us in residence, that house had known much laughter and love. Milo had been conceived there, and within those walls we had transformed ourselves from a couple into a family, which more than anything had been what Penny and I wanted; still wanted; would always want.

The first blast shook the street, rocked the Explorer, and fissured one corner of our house, casting off slate shingles, slabs of plaster, and a bright rain of shattered upstairs windowpanes.

Even as the shingles, the shed stucco, and the shards of glass became airborne, the second blast shuddered the entire structure, blew out first-floor windows, toppled a stone chimney toward the backyard, and distorted the shape of the garage.

Within me, distortions occurred as well: to my perception of my place in the world, to my expectations of social order and simple justice, to my vision of the future.

A third explosion followed in maybe three seconds, not as loud and sharp as the first two but even more profoundly destructive: a heavy *whump*, as if Satan had fired up a burner on the biggest gas stove in Hell. The house seemed to swell, then twist, then shrink, and in an instant was engulfed in flames from end to end, flames more blue than yellow, not orange at all, seething and insatiable, leaping eagerly to the forty-foot-wide crowns of the matched phoenix palms.

Before neighbors rushed into the street, Penny wheeled from the burning house and drove away.

I saw tears standing unshed in her eyes, and I could have cried or cursed, but I kept my silence as she kept hers.

We had gone perhaps a block when in my arms Milo said shakily, "We didn't blow up our house, did we?"

"No, we didn't," I said.

"Who blew it up?" he asked.

Penny said, "A man I want to have a talk with someday."

"A very bad man," I added.

"I think I know him," said Milo.

"I think you do."

"I really liked our house," Milo said. "Now all our stuff is burned up."

"Not all of it," I said. "We seem to have like three tons of it here in the Explorer."

"A house is just a house," Penny said. "Stuff is just stuff. All that matters is the three of us are together."

In the backseat, Lassie growled.

"The four of us," Penny corrected. "The four of us are nicer, smarter, and tougher than Shearman Waxx. We'll settle this, we'll set things right again."

That we were nicer than Waxx, not even Waxx himself would have denied. He did not seem to value niceness.

With Milo on our side, we were more intelligent than the critic, although not more cunning. Like Mozart, Einstein, and other brainiacs, Milo had every kind of smarts in abundance, except for the one most important in this instance: street smarts.

I did not have a clue why Penny thought we were *tougher* than Waxx. Because she did not say such things lightly, I credited the possibility that, in us, Waxx had met his match, as absurd as that concept might appear to be.

Of course, she didn't have all the information that I possessed. Events had unfolded so quickly that I'd had no opportunity to tell her about John Clitherow.

As I watched her repress her tears and find a reassuring smile for Milo, I dreaded having to tell her about John's murdered family. But I had only twice ever deceived her by omission, and the second time—withholding the fact that Waxx would be at lunch at Roxie's when I took Milo there—had been a mistake of epic proportions.

In 1933, G. K. Chesterton wrote, "The disintegration of rational society started in the drift from hearth and family; the solution must be a drift back."

I had a disturbing feeling that getting back to where we had been would require more than drifting. We would need to swim with all the strength and perseverance we possessed, and the journey was likely to be upstream all the way.

Part Two

I Am My Brothers' Reaper

Chapter 20

Even miles from our burning house, Penny repeatedly frowned at the rearview mirror.

"Someone following us?" I asked.

"No."

The lead-gray sky of the previous afternoon, which had looked as flat and uniform as a freshly painted surface, was deteriorating. Curls of clouds peeled back, revealing darker masses, and beards of mist hung like tattered cobwebs from a crumbling ceiling.

She glanced at the mirror again.

"Someone?" I asked.

"No."

"It makes me nervous, the way you keep checking the mirror."

In my lap, Milo said, "It makes *me* nervous the way you keep asking Mom is someone behind us."

When she frowned at the mirror again, I could not help asking: "Anything?"

"If I see something," she said, "I'll tell you."

"Even if you think it's nothing, it might be something," I said, "so if it's nothing or something, tell me either way."

"Good grief," said Milo.

"Okay," I admitted, "that didn't make any sense."

Barely escaping our house before it blew up had left us in a state of shock. But as writers and readers, Penny and I were drunk on words, and we needed conversation as much as we needed air and water. Not much short of death could shut us up. Even Milo, when he wasn't lost in an electromagnetic-field-theory reverie, could be garrulous. The shock of our loss did not reduce us to a brooding silence; in fact, the opposite was true.

In the Greenwich-Boom family, conversation was not just talk but also a way we helped one another heal from the abrasions and contusions of the day. We started with practicalities and progressed swiftly to absurdities, which was not surprising, considering our conversations expressed our philosophies and experiences.

Penny thought we would be staying at a hotel, but I nixed that. "They'll want a credit card, at least for ID. We don't want to be using our credit cards right now."

As she braked to a stop at a red traffic light, she said, "We don't? Why wouldn't we?"

"John Clitherow called while you were packing. He gave me some advice. Credit cards were part of it."

"Clitherow—the writer?"

"Yeah. He read the review. He has some experience of this...of Waxx."

"What experience?"

Because I didn't want to talk about the murder of Clitherow's family in front of Milo, I said, "John wants me to tell you his three favorite children's stories are *Dumbo,* Kate DiCamillo's *The Tale of Despereaux,* and your first Purple Bunny book."

"That's nice. But you said 'experience.' What's he know about Waxx?"

"John especially likes the funny physiology in those books."

In my usually savvy wife's defense: Having been Tasered, having seen her house blown up minutes earlier, she urgently wanted to hear anything that I might have learned about the critic, and she was not in a state of mind that allowed her to pick up on kid-evading code.

Holding Milo with one arm, I grimaced at Penny, tugged on my left ear, and pointed at the boy.

She looked at me as if I were suffering delayed spasms from the Tasering.

I said, "Dumbo, Despereaux, Pistachio," because the last was the name of her bunny character.

The driver behind us tapped his horn to encourage us to notice that the traffic light had turned green.

As she drove through the intersection, Penny said, "I guess I misunderstood. I thought he called about Waxx."

In my lap, Milo said, "The little elephant, the little mouse, and the little bunny all had really big ears."

"Did they?" I asked. "Hey, yes, they did. How about that?"

"Mom," the boy said, "Dad's trying to tell you that I'm little but I've got big ears, and there's something Mr. Clitherow told him that I guess I'm too young to hear."

"So what did he tell you?" Penny asked me.

I sighed in exasperation.

"Probably something really bloody, strange, and scary," Milo said. "Or a sex thing, 'cause from what I know about it, that's totally weird."

"How do you know anything about sex?" Penny asked.

"Collateral information. While I'm reading about other things."

"How much collateral information?"

"Not much," Milo said. "Relax. I'm not interested in it."

"You better not be interested in it."

"It's boring," Milo said.

"It's even more boring than it is weird," Penny assured him.

"It's not all *that* boring," I said.

Milo said, "I guess someday it finally won't bore me."

"Someday," Penny agreed, "but that's decades from now."

"I figure seven years," Milo said.

"When you've conquered the problem of time travel," Penny informed him, "*then* I'll let you date."

"I don't think time travel is possible," Milo said.

"Then I won't need to worry about having a daughter-in-law with two nose rings, a pierced tongue, seven tattoos, jeweled teeth, a shaved head, and attitude."

"Never bring home a girl with attitude," I advised Milo. "Your mother will just have to beat the crap out of her."

"I don't understand why we can't just go to a hotel," Penny said. "But if we can't—then where do we go? Maybe to my folks' place?"

"No. Somewhere Waxx is unlikely to look."

"What about Marty and Celine's place?"

Marty and Celine were good friends who lived only a mile from us. They had flown to Wyoming to take care of Celine's parents, who had been nearly killed in an avalanche.

Since Monday, Penny had been checking on their house once a day, taking in mail and newspapers, watering plants as needed.

"I feel a little funny about it," I said.

"Marty and Celine won't mind."

"I mean . . . I wonder if friends as close as Marty and Celine are too much of a connection to us. Clitherow seemed adamant that we had to drop off the radar."

"But if somehow Waxx could find out who our closest friends are," she said, "he'd still need time, a lot of time, to do it."

"Maybe he already knows," Milo said.

The boy's suggestion was the intellectual equivalent of a shock from a Taser.

In spite of what Clitherow had told me about the many similar phrases in the reviews of *Mr. Bluebird* and *One O'Clock Jump,* I had continued to operate under the assumption that John had become a target for destruction because of the letter he had written to Waxx's editor and that I had earned a promise of doom merely by conspiring to get a look at the great man in Roxie's Bistro.

Waxx's assaults on John and on us were no less psychotic but a great deal more logical, strategically and tactically, if we assumed that he had planned to kill us and our families *before* he published reviews of our novels. Harder to credit was that his violation of our house twice, the planting of sophisticated packages of explosives, and the Tasering were part of an *impromptu* response to the encounter in the bistro men's room, all within fourteen hours of Milo's brief misdirection of his stream.

I remembered what Clitherow had said about Waxx being less a critic with opinions than one with an agenda. Understanding that agenda would be key to survival.

"What about the Balboa sinkhole?" Penny said as she turned onto Pacific Coast Highway.

Marty was an architect and Celine was a Realtor, but they were primarily entrepreneurs. Over the years, they carefully acquired prime properties for the land value, tore down the existing houses, built new houses, and sold for a profit.

Usually they had two projects going at once, sometimes three. Fortunately, they foresaw the coming real-estate bust. By the time values began plummeting, they had only one project left to sell. Because it was a harborside house on Balboa Peninsula, because it had been on the market two years without an offer, and because they would make no profit from it, they called it the Balboa sinkhole.

When they left their keys with Penny before flying to Wyoming, they also left the keys to the peninsula house on the same ring, in the unlikely event that someone wanted to tour the place. Like many high-end homes, this one could be shown by appointment only and strictly to qualified buyers; therefore, no key was left on-site in a lockbox.

"Sounds plausible," I said. "Let's check it out."

Chapter 21

From the street, the Balboa sinkhole was a handsome contemporary structure faced in limestone, with two double garage doors.

A remote-control fob on the house key operated the roll-up doors. Penny parked in the only available space, beside three pickup trucks, all fully restored classics. Marty had a collection of these vehicles too large to fit in his own garage.

From the luggage in the Explorer, we took only two overnight bags for Penny and me, and one of the huge suitcases with wheels, nearly as big as a steamer trunk, which Milo insisted he needed.

Penny had the code to the alarm system.

In the house, Lassie scampered off to investigate every room, as any dog will when set loose in a new place.

The residence spanned two lots, and the side facing the harbor featured floor-to-ceiling glass. A private pier led to a boat slip that would accommodate at least a sixty-foot craft.

The view enchanted. Pleasure boats of all sizes plied the near and farther channels, though not as many as on a summer day.

A sleek white yacht motoring out to the Pacific, perhaps a 120-footer, filled me with envy, not of the owners' fortune, but of their carefree existence and of the freedom that the open sea offered them. Impossible to imagine that they would ever be stalked by a bow-tied psychopath or in fact by a lunatic favoring another kind of neckwear.

Because empty rooms are off-putting, the sinkhole had been professionally staged. This hadn't lured a buyer, but the furnishings made the house almost as cozy as our own.

While Penny, Milo, and Lassie settled in, I went out to cash a check for living money and to buy a disposable cell phone. We also needed sandwich fixings, snacks, and sodas to last a couple of days.

I was loath to leave them alone. But Penny insisted that Waxx had no way of knowing where we had gone.

A baseball cap made an adequate disguise for a quick shopping trip. Bestselling writers are not as widely recognized as actors. My hair is my most memorable feature. In articles about me, it has been described as "unruly" by the kinder journalists, although the cheap-shot artists have called it a "weird thatch" and a "convincing argument for shaved heads." A simple cap rendered me anonymous.

I drove one of Marty's classic trucks: a 1933 Ford V8, turquoise with bright yellow wire wheels. If I had not been worried about my wife and son being murdered, I would have felt so cool.

Midmorning, when I returned to our plush hideout, I found Penny in the huge kitchen, at the secretary, online with her laptop.

Because the house offered a few dazzling entertainment centers, including a home theater, cable service was maintained to allow the best possible demonstration of those features to potential buyers. Consequently, we had quick Internet access by cable.

In the vast family room to which the kitchen opened, Milo sat on the floor at a half-acre coffee table on which he had established *his* laptop and had linked it to an array of other devices, some of which he had designed and constructed from items I had purchased for him. A spiderweb of extension cords radiated to a series of wall plugs.

He looked like an elf who had forsaken his traditional magic spells and charms for techno wizardry. I trusted that he would not turn out to be a pint-size Frankenstein.

Earlier, Penny turned on one of three Sub-Zero refrigerators, in which I now stowed most of the food and beverages I had bought.

Focused on her computer, Penny said, "Did you know Shearman Waxx is an enema?"

"Yes. Milo informed me of that the day before yesterday."

"Same source says he was born in 1868."

"Wow, almost a decade before Edison invented the light bulb."

She said, "All his reviews from the past ten years are archived. Forcing terrorist suspects to read them aloud would be a form of torture more cruel than applying pliers to their genitals."

"It's the bad syntax," I said, pulling up a dinette chair to the secretary and sitting beside her.

"Partly. But it's also two other things. The butt-kissing factor is so high, when you're reading, you can hear his lips smacking."

"Whose butt is he kissing?"

"The literary Brahmins and whatever writer is the darling of the hour. The other thing is his seething hatred, which he disguises as a concern for quote 'cultural truths and societal evolution.'"

"What does he hate?"

"Everything before the twentieth century and most of everything thereafter. I'm still getting a handle on him."

Swiveling her chair toward me, taking her hands, lowering my voice to spare Milo from the story, I told Penny about my phone conversation with John Clitherow.

Her beautiful blue eyes, which were of a shade for which I had never found an adequate adjective, did not cloud or darken, or do any of the things that eyes are sometimes said to do in works of fiction. When I told her that Clitherow's parents had been murdered, however, I saw in the directness of her gaze, in the stopped-time steadiness of it, a solemnity more profound than I had ever seen before.

Upon hearing that Margaret Clitherow and her two daughters were likewise murdered, Penny closed her eyes. As I told her the rest of what I knew, I studied her pale lids, wondering if, when those two curtains raised, I would infer from her eyes fear or, worse, despair, or the steely resolve that would be more in character.

Without opening her eyes, she asked, "How did they die?"

"He didn't say. I'm going to research it."

"You're certain it was really Clitherow?"

"I've never heard his voice, but I'm sure it was him."

"It couldn't have been Waxx, another bit of terrorist theater?"

"No. This voice was different from what I know of Waxx's."

After a silence, she opened her eyes, which were as clear as ice water, and said, "The sonofabitch can't have Milo."

"He won't get any of us," I assured her. I wondered how I could deliver on such a promise, but I would not hesitate to die trying.

She squeezed my hands once, let go of them, and turned to her computer. "I want to read more of this bullshit, see if I can better understand the bull himself. Meanwhile...put on the alarm system."

Chapter 22

From the kitchen, I went into the adjoining family room to have a word with Milo.

On an overcast day like this, the polarized glass of the large triple-pane windows was not tinted. The house faced southeast, and on a bright morning, the glass would darken to control incoming sunlight without diminishing the view, which seemed no less spectacular now than in the moment when I had first seen it, during construction.

Sitting on the sectional sofa, overlooking Milo at his coffee-table workstation, I said, "You okay?"

"Pretty much."

"But not entirely."

He shrugged but kept his attention on the computer. "The house—that hurts."

"We'll get another house."

"I know. But it won't be the same."

"It'll be better," I promised.

"Maybe. I guess it could be."

On his computer screen, something that might have been a three-dimensional blueprint of an elaborate silo-like structure with numerous stacked chambers rotated to his command.

"What's that?" I asked.

"I'm not sure."

"Where did it come from?"

"That's what I'm trying to figure out."

After a silence, I said, "Do you think I'm an idiot?"

"No."

"Sooner or later," I told him, "every kid thinks his old man's an idiot."

Six-year-olds openly express affection. Most teenagers go through a period of sullen withdrawal or open hostility. Twenty-somethings have recovered from teenage hormonal madness, but have acquired a certain reserve.

Milo was chronologically six, intellectually twenty-something, and emotionally maybe ten or eleven. Expressions of affection at times embarrassed him but did not yet offend him.

Without looking away from the computer screen, he said, "I'm never gonna think you're an idiot."

"Just wait. You'll see."

"Never," he said, and chewed on his lower lip.

"Love you, Milo."

He nodded. "Yeah."

When I discovered I was chewing my lower lip, too, I changed the subject. "Where's Lassie?"

He pointed to a pair of cabinet doors to the right of the big plasma screen in the entertainment center.

"She's in the cabinet?" I asked.

"Yeah."

"Did you put her there?"

"No."

"Your mom didn't put her there."

"No."

"She got in there herself?"

"I think so. She likes it."

I went to the entertainment center and opened the cabinet doors to which Milo had pointed.

Lassie sat in the deep cabinet, facing out, grinning, wagging the tip of her tail.

"Why would she want to sit in a cabinet?" I asked Milo.

"I think she didn't like this thing."

"What thing?"

"This thing on the computer that I don't know what it is."

"So she hid from it in a cabinet?"

"I don't think she's hiding."

"Then what's she doing?"

"Maybe meditating," Milo said.

"Dogs don't meditate."

"Some do."

To Lassie, I said, "Come out of there. Come on, girl."

She would not move.

"Okay," I said, "I'm going to leave her in there, but I'm not going to close the doors on her."

"Whatever," Milo said.

Before I had crossed half the room, the stunning harbor view drew me once more to the windows.

Between the near and farther channels, scores of sailboats and motor cruisers were tied up at midwater moorings. To board and disembark, an owner needed a smaller craft to use as a tender.

Beyond the far shore of the harbor, hills rose to the Pacific Coast

Highway. Beyond the highway, other hills ascended, and over all, the sky loomed dramatic, bruised and swollen and scarred, and full of threat.

No one could know where we were, but prudence—and my paranoia—required that before twilight I would have to put down the motorized shades encapsulated in the first of the two air spaces in the triple-pane windows. After dark, the interior house lights would make clear targets of us to anyone on the seawall or aboard one of the boats in the harbor.

Behind me, at the entertainment center, the cabinet doors thumped shut.

When I looked back, Milo remained at his computer, but the dog was nowhere to be seen.

Chapter 23

In the study, which had no water view and which had been staged with furniture too contemporary for my taste, I sat in a steel-and-leather chair, at a steel-and-glass table that served as a desk.

Earlier, I had activated the disposable phone. It came with prepaid minutes, so I didn't have to give my name or a credit card.

Now I took a deep breath and phoned Penny's parents. Grimbald—formerly Larry—answered. "Boom."

"Hi, Grim, it's me, Cubby."

Grimbald had a formidable voice with a resonant timbre that made him sound like I imagined a hearty Viking would have sounded. "Hey, Cupcake," he called out to Clotilda, "it's our fair-haired boy, the famous writer."

"I'm not that famous, Grim."

"You're a damn sight more famous than me, in spite of the fact I've been blowing up stuff all my life."

"Listen, Grim, I wanted to get to you before you saw it on the news later today."

"You know we don't watch news, Cub. Last time we watched news, Cupcake shot the TV. Too damn expensive, buying TVs all the time."

"Well, someone else might see it and call you. So I wanted you to know we're all right. Penny, Milo, me, and Lassie—we all got out just fine, not a scratch."

"Got out of what?"

"The house. Our house blew up, Grim."

"Cupcake, they're all fine, but their house blew up." I could hear Clotilda in the background, and then Grimbald said, "Cupcake says isn't that ironic, considering your in-laws' profession. What the hell were you doing that your house blew up?"

"Nothing. They'll probably decide it was a gas-line leak."

"Not terrible damn likely."

"Grim, I'd like you to call the fire department, tell them you just heard about the explosion and you want them to know we weren't in the house, we're traveling in Florida, by car, a long road trip."

"Where are you in Florida? I've blown up a bunch of things down there."

"We aren't in Florida. That's just what I want you to tell them—to explain why we aren't there dealing with the aftermath."

After a hesitation, Grimbald said, "Cub, tell me you didn't blow up your own house."

"Of course I didn't. I'm not a criminal type, Grim. I don't do insurance scams."

"I didn't mean on purpose. I meant like maybe you were using the vacuum cleaner the wrong way or something."

"Even I can't blow up a house with a vacuum cleaner."

"Like if you thought you could use it to clean the burner rings on the gas furnace, but you didn't turn the furnace off—"

"It would never cross my mind to clean the burner rings."

"That's good. Because they don't need to be cleaned. Or maybe you thought you could use the portable barbecue indoors."

Staring down at my reflection in the glass tabletop, I thought my faint smile was a remarkable testament to the affection that I had developed for my in-laws over the years.

"Grim, I didn't blow up the place. Someone else blew it up, and he knew what he was doing, so I suspect the fire has been so intense that no clues are left, it'll look like a gas leak."

Astonished, he said, "You know people who'd want to blow up your house?"

"I think I know one."

"Who?"

"It's a complex story, Grim, and it's got a big you-must-be-pulling-my-chain factor, so I don't want to get into it now. I don't have time, I've got a lot on my plate right now."

"Are you in danger, Cub? Is Penny, Milo?"

"Yes, Grim, we are."

"Then you've got to go to the police."

"Not a good idea," I said. "I don't have a shred of proof. The cops couldn't do anything. Anyway, they wouldn't believe me. They might even suspect me of blowing up the house myself, like you did."

"I never thought you did it intentionally."

"Plus I'm a little bit of a celebrity. The story would be all over cable news, my face all over TV. Suddenly I'd be a lot more recognizable than I am now, and it would be harder—maybe impossible—for us to move around anonymously and hide out."

"It's so bad you've got to hide out?"

"Yeah. And another reason I called is—I don't think this guy will come after you, 'cause you're not *my* parents, you're Penny's folks, you're probably safe, but take some precautions."

"Don't worry about us, Cub. We're ready for anything."

"I know you are."

"We were ready for the country to fall apart back in the seventies, when the crazy government was running seventeen percent inflation and wrecking the economy. We were ready for the AIDS epidemic to wipe out civilization. Then Y2K, all the computers were supposed to crash and send off nuclear missiles. After 9/11, Cupcake and me were for sure ready for the crazy Islams, but they haven't showed up yet, either. Say . . . this isn't the Islams blew up your house, is it?"

"No, Grim, it isn't."

"You say precautions. Do we look out for anyone in particular?"

"He's about forty-one, white hair, stands five feet eight, built like a tank, may or may not be wearing a bow tie."

"He tries to come in here, he's toast. You should come here and hide out with us."

"I don't want to draw him to you guys."

"Hell, let's draw him, Cub. Let's lure him in and squash him like a bug."

"Maybe we will, Grim. When I know more about him. When I have a better handle on him than I do now."

"I like the way you sound, Cub. You sound together."

"Well, I might not be as together as I sound."

"Cupcake, she's always worried in a crisis you'd be useless."

"I won't hold that against her, Grim. I can see where she might get that idea."

"But me," he said, "I always suspected there's a secret you, and the secret you has the right stuff."

"I appreciate that."

"More than once, I've said to Cupcake, he can't be the milksop he seems to be, 'cause his books have a toughness in them."

"One more thing, Grim. You can't reach me by phone. I'm using a disposable, and it's probably the first of a series, until this thing is done. But Penny or I will check in from time to time."

"We won't miss a call. We'll be right here. I think for the duration, we'll go into lockdown. You know what that means?"

"Yes, I know."

"Remember what the Lord said."

"He said a lot of things, Grim."

"He doesn't want us harming the innocent, but he gave us 'the power to tread on serpents.' This man blows up your house, he sounds like a serpent to me. What do you think?"

"Definitely a serpent," I agreed.

"Then don't you hesitate to tread on him if you get a chance."

In the glass table, the image of my face was like a reflection in a pool of cloudy water, disturbing because its character remained indeterminate. It might have been the face of an earnest pilgrim or that of a fetal demon not yet born to his potential.

Chapter 24

Olivia Cosima, my editor in New York City, was still at lunch when I phoned. I left a voice mail preparing her for the news of our exploding home.

I also dictated a statement for Olivia to give to my publisher's publicity department, with which to respond to media inquiries.

Thankfully, Penny's editor was also at lunch, so I didn't have to answer any questions, and I left her a similar voice mail.

When I returned to the family room, Milo had taken a break from whatever arcane project he pursued on his computer. He stood at the glass wall, staring at the harbor.

Lassie had emerged from the cabinet. She stood at Milo's side, also gazing out of the floor-to-ceiling window.

Neither of them responded when I said that lunch would be in thirty minutes. They seemed to be entranced by the vista of harbor and hills.

In the kitchen, Penny remained at the secretary with her laptop.

"I made a complete list of the phrases Waxx used in your review and in John Clitherow's."

The list lay on the kitchen island. I picked it up from the black granite countertop.

Before I could begin to read, Penny said, "And I found another review... another novelist he savaged in a similar way, not exactly the same language but the same criticisms, and extremely vicious."

"Who's the writer?"

"Thomas Landulf."

"Vaguely familiar. But I've never read him."

"He published his first novel just fourteen months ago. *The Falconer and the Monk*." She consulted a notepad. "Waxx called it 'a triumphant example of idiot logic, an incandescent work of puerile nonsense that will be a shining beacon to perpetual juveniles and the terminally sentimental for generations to come.'"

"Better syntax than usual," I said, "but ouch."

"I wondered if Landulf wrote anything since, so I googled him."

Penny turned, glanced toward Milo at the family-room windows, then rose from her chair and came close to me.

Lowering her voice, she continued: "Eleven months ago, three months after the publication of his book, Tom Landulf tortured and killed his wife, tortured and killed his three-year-old daughter, and committed suicide."

Her piercing blue gaze had never been more compelling, and I was constrained to meet her eyes as long as she required.

"That's why the name rang a bell," I said. "Must have been a two-day sensation on the news, so I heard a little about it."

Because I am squeamish, my custom is to avoid watching or reading news about mass murders. More than a custom, it is a rule.

Penny said, "His wife, Jeanette, loved to play the piano. He cut off her ears. Then her fingers, one at a time."

The history of literature is replete with colorful monsters that come from netherworlds and other worlds and laboratories.

Penny said, "Photos he took while he dismembered her prove she was alive and conscious when he began. When eventually she passed out, it was from blood loss."

Vampires, werewolves, zombies, ravenous extraterrestrials, murderous poltergeists, abominations of nature, hideous creatures born of experiments gone wrong: None are real, all are projections, metaphors, an externalization of what lies within us.

"What he did to Melanie, the three-year-old, was unspeakable. I will never talk to you about it. Never. You'll have to read it yourself if you want to know. She was alive, too, through most of it."

The only monsters in this world are those who pass for human, who cast shadows and are reflected in mirrors, who smile and speak of compassion and shed convincing tears.

"When the wife and daughter were dead," Penny continued, "he drenched himself in gasoline and set himself on fire."

Eye to eye with her, I could not hear either of us breathing or a single motor in any of the three refrigerators, or a whisper of wind at any window, as if we were not as real as we supposed we were, but existed only on a plasma screen, characters in a film, watched by someone who, on a remote control, pressed the MUTE button.

Finally, Penny said, "The official conclusion of the police—two homicides and a suicide. What do you think?"

Because of the extreme sadistic nature of those crimes, I wanted to believe that the authorities had reached the correct conclusion, that Thomas Landulf had killed his wife and child, that the monster who could do such things no longer walked the world.

Penny's stare allowed no retreat from the truth.

"Most likely... not a suicide," I said. "And not two murders, but three."

"Most likely," she agreed. "And you know what I think? I think before the murders happened, Waxx must have been tormenting Landulf, like he's done with us."

"It's a good bet."

"So when he and his family are killed, why wouldn't the cops have wondered about Waxx?"

I reminded her, "Clitherow said funny things happen when you go to the cops about Waxx."

"When I first turned up Landulf, I thought *this* is what we go to the cops with. But then I realized..."

I nodded. "Yeah."

"...we really are alone. Who is he that he can't be touched?"

"Something as sadistic as the Landulfs...I have to wonder *what* is he?"

The slaughter of the Landulf family required reconsideration of Waxx and of the threat that he posed to us. By the hour, he appeared less professorial and more predatory, his refinement only a cloak to conceal deformities, his civilized demeanor a mask.

Chapter 25

Lacking an appetite, I nevertheless ate lunch. With the story of the Landulf murders so fresh in my mind, I should have found the food to be without taste, but it was delicious.

Perhaps even in Hell, the damned experience moments of grace, if only as a reminder that Hell is not the be-all.

After lunch, pleading exhaustion, Penny took a nap. Because she did not want to be in a bedroom, apart from us, she curled in the fetal position on a family-room sofa, facing the harbor, hoping the movement of the water and the gliding boats would lull her to sleep.

Milo returned to his computer and other gear on the coffee table. He sat with his back to the harbor.

By his side again, Lassie lay on her belly but with her head lifted, ears pricked, facing the windows. Perhaps the kiting seagulls and the occasional formations of brown pelicans intrigued her.

At the kitchen secretary, I used Penny's laptop to go online. I needed to learn more about how John Clitherow's family had died.

I dreaded discovering another multiple murder with details to freeze the marrow. What my search string led me to instead was a story without blood but no less disturbing.

According to press reports, Tony and Cora Clitherow, John's parents, had lived lakeside in Michigan. They rented a slip at a nearby marina, where they kept the *Time Out,* a Bluewater 563.

Exploring the company's website, I found photos of a craft like theirs. The low-profile, double-deck cruiser featured an upper helm station enclosed by a hard top and canvas walls. This sleek, handsome boat included a main cabin with galley and two staterooms with baths.

On that Thursday in late June, three summers previous, Tony and Cora had taken the *Time Out* for a day trip. With its amenities and range, the boat could overnight on water. But they had told the owner of the marina, Michael Hanrahan, they intended to return before dusk.

When they didn't dock by nightfall, Hanrahan was not concerned enough to report them missing. On a couple of prior occasions, they had made impromptu changes to their trip plans.

The next day, when the Coast Guard could not raise the *Time Out* by radio, a search was launched. At 4:10 in the afternoon, by its transponder signal, they found the boat adrift, five miles offshore.

Tony Clitherow sat belted in the chair at the upper helm station, naked and dead. The cause of death was not apparent.

A search of the vessel did not turn up Cora.

At the stern of the boat, a taut cable stretched from the gin pole into the water. With the windlass, they reeled in the line.

They pulled Cora from the lake as if she were a fish. She wore nothing but handcuffs. The windlass line entwined the chain between the cuffs and encircled her waist, secured to itself with carabiners.

She had been dragged through the water for many miles, no doubt at night when people aboard passing vessels would not see her.

Cora's challenge had been to avoid drowning as she cleaved face-down through the Bluewater's wake. Secured in such a way that she was unable to turn onto her back, she would have been repeatedly pulled under by turbulence, would have repeatedly broken the surface, striving always to keep her head up, gasping for breath.

Exhaustion defeated her. Although not a speedboat, the *Time Out* was capable of enough knots to make being towed through choppy water a punishing experience. Feathery bruises covered her body.

The continuous impact of the water or abrasive debris in it wore away her left eyelid. Both eyes were as frosted as etched glass.

An assessment of Tony's guilt would ordinarily depend on the coroner's report. But the autopsy proved inconclusive.

The quantity of alcohol in Tony's stomach and the percentage in his blood suggested that he could have died from alcohol poisoning. If he had been that drunk, however, he surely would have at some point vomited on the deck or on himself, which he had not done.

The homicide detective on the case, Warren Knowles, had resisted a determination that Clitherow killed his wife. Knowles argued that a tear at the corner of Tony's right nostril and a facial bruise raised the possibility he'd been restrained while a tube was fed through his nose and into his throat for the administration of alcohol by force.

In the opinion of the medical examiner, those injuries had more likely been sustained in a drunken fall or when Cora tried to fend off her husband as he sought to handcuff her.

Knowles also raised the possibility that the alcohol had been administered to cloak the true cause of death and that Tony might have been killed by an air embolism, a bubble that, injected into his bloodstream, traveled eventually to his brain. At a hearing, the detective spoke of a suspected needle puncture.

The medical examiner felt that associated injuries around the puncture, arguably sustained in an altercation with Cora, did not allow him to say with certainty that this was an injection site.

No determination of guilt had been made. The case file remained open, perhaps largely through the efforts of Detective Knowles.

Although John Clitherow claimed his wife, Margaret, and their two daughters, were also killed, I could find no mention of their deaths, by murder or otherwise. If John told me the truth—and I believed he did—he withheld something that would explain why their murders had gone unreported.

Reading about Tony and Cora further unnerved me. Grim scenarios played through my mind.

Agitated, I got up from the laptop and went to the glass wall in the family room, hoping the harbor panorama would soothe me.

The view had worked its magic on Penny. She slept soundly on the sofa, in what gray light the pregnant sky allowed.

Imagine that Tony had been entirely sober, with a gun to his head, and had been forced to pilot the boat while aware that his wife was being dragged and drowned in its wake.

Imagine that only *after* Cora's death was alcohol administered to Tony and an air bubble injected. Imagine his horror, his anguish, and the relief with which he might have accepted his own murder.

Imagination can be either a feathered or a scaly thing, flying to castles in the air or slithering down into a gelid darkness that suffocates all hope.

Many questions remained. How did Waxx board the boat and how did he depart? How did he overpower them and manage the awkward details of Cora's attachment to the windlass cable?

If even a thousand questions occurred to me, I would not begin to doubt that Waxx killed them, just as he mutilated Jeanette and Melanie Landulf while Thomas Landulf, their husband and father, was forced to watch before being set afire.

The signature of the murderer was the same for each crime: a singular cruelty, an incapacity for pity, a desire to humiliate as well as to kill the victims, and in each instance a determination to make the ultimate victim witness the suffering and degradation of whoever was murdered before him.

In a sudden flare of great dark wings, an immense blue heron, tall as a man, flew up from the nearer shore, glided low over water mottled taupe-zinc-cinder-slate, turning fully 360 degrees across the width of the nearer and smaller channel, before passing between the hulls of the vessels at the public moorings and dwindling across the farther channel toward the mainland.

Although I needed only an instant to identify the bird, my heart knocked as if I stood witness to something unearthly, to a creature as dark in its intentions as in its coloration.

My point of focus pulled back from the receding heron to the craft at the moorings. The standing rigging on the sailboats quivered in a light breeze. A man worked at some task on the deck of a sloop. Cabin lights glowed at the windows of a few of the motor cruisers.

The scene was a maritime pastoral, picturesque and potentially tranquilizing—and yet I felt uneasy.

My cell phone rang—not the disposable one that I had left on a kitchen counter, but the one in my shirt pocket, which was listed in my name. For reasons I did not fully understand, John Clitherow had warned me not to use it. I brought it with me, however, because it was the only number at which he could reach me if he decided he must speak to me again.

I answered the call, and Hud Jacklight said worriedly, "Cubby?"

"That's me."

"Are you alive?"

"Yes, I am, Hud."

"Your house. It blew up. You know?"

"I know. Listen, let me call you right back on another line."

I didn't wait for his reply, but terminated the call.

Because I did not want to wake Penny, who looked so peaceful on the nearby sofa, I left her and Milo in the family room with Lassie and retreated through the dining room to the living room, where the floor-to-ceiling glass presented a slightly different view of the harbor.

Chapter 26

Gazing at a picturesque and tranquil harborscape while talking to Hud Jacklight did not make his conversation seem more eloquent, more enlightened, or less absurd.

"You're alive? Really?" he asked.

"No. I'm speaking to you from"—I quoted Longfellow—"'the great world of light, that lies behind all human destinies.'"

After a moment of silence, he said, "You're scaring me, Cubbo."

"I don't want to do that, Hud. I'm fine. Penny and Milo and Lassie are fine. When the house blew, we were on the road."

"What road?"

"The open road, traveling."

"You were home. Yesterday."

"Now we're on the road doing book research. If anyone in the media calls you, don't talk to him. Refer him to my publisher's publicity department. I gave them a statement."

Beyond the window, in the dying breeze, queen palms trembled as if in delicious anticipation of rain. The moored boats rocked gently in the harbor's tamed swells. So lovely yet in some way... troubling.

"What about Penny?" Hud asked.

"I gave her publisher a statement, too."

"How's her agent?"

"Alma wasn't in the house when it blew, Hud. She's in New York."

"I mean the trauma. To Penny. Losing a house. Makes a woman think. For Penny, a turning point. Maybe it's time. For change."

Although he was in his seventh marriage, this might have been the first occasion in his life when Hud Jacklight tried to imagine what a woman thought about anything.

I punctured his swelling hope: "Penny thinks losing a house is enough change for a while."

"She said that?"

"In exactly those words."

"Well, I'm here. All I'm saying. I'm here."

"That's comforting to know, Hud."

High in the steadily blackening sky, a silent convulsion broke the string in an infinite necklace, and fat pearls fell through the day, bouncing on the slate patio, dimpling the water in the harbor, rattling gulls off the seawall to sheltered roosts.

"There's a bright side," Hud said. "To the house. Now that you're not dead."

"What would that be?"

"Human-interest angle. House blowing up. Loss. All the memories. Mementos. Gone. Oprah will want you. Every show will. Big sympathy thing. Gonna boost book sales."

The man working on the deck of the sloop hurried below as the raindrops shrank in size and settled into a steady drizzle.

He had been doing routine maintenance. Nothing more.

"Hud, I don't want people buying my book because they pity me."

"Why not?"

"For one thing, pride."

In anticipation of rain, harbor traffic had been diminishing. Now only a few craft were motoring to port along the waterways.

"Tough world, Cubaroo. Competitive. Dog-eat-dog. No writer can afford pride."

The weight of the rain had quelled the light breeze. All was still and silvered.

Hud continued: "Besides. It's a sin. Pride. Too proud to do *Oprah*. You know these things. Isn't it a sin?"

"If it's vanity, yes. If it's conceit, arrogance, yes, a sin. If it's self-esteem, maybe, probably. If it's self-respect, no."

"Kind of complex," said Hud.

"Everything is."

With the advent of the rain, the view of the harbor should have been even more relaxing. Rain washes the world clean, and the world needs cleansing. Yet as the drizzle added luster to most surfaces, my disquiet grew.

"Alma lost a client," Hud said. "Last week. Major client."

"Who was that?"

"Gwyneth Oppenheim."

"Hud, she didn't fire Alma. She died of cancer at eighty-six."

"Still not good. Losing clients. A bad sign."

My disquiet was probably residual emotion from being startled by the blue heron. Being Jacklighted didn't help.

I told him that Penny needed my assistance with something, not with her agent but with another matter, and I terminated the call.

Returning the cell phone to my pocket, studying the harbor as I moved, I left the living room for the dining room, and I paused at the windows there. The overhang kept the glass dry and clear.

The raw teak planks of the pier floor, gangway, and boat slip had darkened in the downpour from deep gray almost to black. The teak handrails were lacquered; wet with rain, they appeared to be jacketed in ice.

Stars folded into stripes, and from the limp red point of the neighbor's sodden flag, a thin stream of water unraveled to their pier deck.

Three large dark shapes undulated through the nearer channel, disappearing into the water only to reappear: a trio of sea lions.

Always, the eye sees more than the mind can comprehend, and we go through life self-blinded to much that lies before us. We want a simple world, but we live in a magnificently complex one, and rather than open ourselves to it, we perceive the world through filters that make it less daunting.

Complexity implies meaning. We are afraid of meaning.

I moved into the family room and stood behind the sofa on which Penny remained asleep, facing the harbor. The longer that you look at anything, the more you see, but not in this instance.

At the coffee table that went with the other furniture grouping, Milo's work still engrossed him.

He must have gotten up at some point because overhead lights were on.

Although a couple of hours remained until nightfall, the storm clouds and the rain had wrung down a faux twilight.

Pale on the window glass, room-light reflections made portions of the view ambiguous, feathered crisp edges, melded objects that in reality were distinct from one another.

From here, the harbor was not as visible to me as I was visible to anyone in the harbor.

Marty, architect and builder, once told me, in more technical detail than I could process, that each layer of glass in the triple-pane windows was specially processed in some way—laminated perhaps, involving nanotechnology of some kind. Also applied to both faces of each pane was a remarkable protective film. Consequently, this glass would not shatter and cause injury in an earthquake. Furthermore, were a madman or an incompetent burglar to seek entry to the house by smashing a window with a sledgehammer, he would need as much as five minutes to do so and, in the process, would have worn the edge off his lust for murder or larceny.

When the first high-powered rifle bullet pierced one of the windows, the sole sound was a hollow *pock!* The glass did not shatter; neither did it craze into the spirals and radials of a spiderweb. Except for a corona of short cracks, the hole looked as neat as that a power drill would make in a board.

I saw a small sparkling spray of tiny bits of glass even as I heard the *pock,* all but simultaneously saw the bullet hole, heard the spent round slap into something elsewhere in the room, but did not turn to see what had been hit.

Instead, I grabbed the sofa behind which I was standing and pulled it toward me, toppling it onto its back, dropping flat as I did so, and spilling a rudely awakened Penny onto the floor with me, where we were hidden from the shooter by the upended furniture.

"Gunfire," I told her, and she was clear-eyed and clearheaded by the time the second syllable passed my lips.

I looked toward Milo, who had been sitting on the floor at the coffee table, about twelve feet away, and saw him falling onto his side. For an instant, I thought he had been hit, but the lack of blood spatter confirmed a miss.

No sooner had the boy dropped for cover than, by a fraction of a second, another *pock* preceded the sound of a more violent impact, and the laptop on the coffee table blew apart.

Chapter 27

I cannot remember whether I was breathing like a marathon runner or was barely able to draw my breath, whether the sight of Milo in mortal danger sharpened my wits or dulled them. I know that although I was afraid, fear remained subordinate to a more intense emotion—call it horror—an abhorrence of the possibility that Milo might be killed, but coupled with horror was the energized despair that is desperation, which can make a cautious man reckless. In a crisis, the urge to act can rule the mind and heart, a mad dominion that favors the wrong action over no action at all, and I recall that forcing myself to hesitate and *think* took all the self-control I possessed.

We were on the ground floor, so the shooter didn't have to find a perch to angle down on us. He could be on the patio, on the private pier, on the seawall, on the upper deck of one of the boats at the public moorings.

Prostrate on the carpet, Milo presented a low profile, but he remained a target, highly vulnerable.

His eyes were squeezed shut, his face squinched, as though he were concentrating hard on wishing away the gunman. Right now he was not different ages physically, emotionally, and intellectually. At the moment, our brilliant little Milo was all six-year-old, and terrified.

No sign of Lassie. Maybe she retreated to the entertainment-center cabinet.

The patio had not been staged with outdoor furniture. The only obstructions between the shooter and the windows were the slender boles of four queen palms.

Getting behind furniture in the family room would make Milo more difficult to target with precision. But it would not make him safe.

Although Penny and I had the upturned seat of the sofa between us and the windows, I took no comfort in that barrier.

The shooter knew where we were hiding. The upholstered seat would not stop—would hardly slow—a high-powered rifle round. If he concentrated rapid fire on the bottom of the overturned sofa, one or both of us would be hit.

The window-piercing *pock* of a third round was followed by the crack of wood as the apron of the coffee table took the hit a few inches above our carpet-hugging son. Splinters prickled down on his head and back.

Cursing the gunman, Penny started crawling toward Milo.

Grabbing her by an ankle, I warned her not to abandon even the inadequate cover of the sofa. She tried to kick loose, and I held tight, desperate to gain a moment to think.

I wanted to go for Milo, shield him and move him, but if Penny and I were killed, Milo had less chance of surviving than he did even at this moment.

If he stayed flat and slithered, he could get behind furniture and then snake to the back of the room, putting ever more obstacles between himself and the gunman, and then make his way into the hall.

I needed to get his attention, but I remained reluctant to shout at him, for fear that, already terrified, he would be easily startled and would raise his head.

Suddenly Lassie appeared, ran to the boy, and stood over him. Even these circumstances could not knock a bark from her, but she began to lick her young master's left ear.

He opened his eyes, saw her, and reached up to pull her down out of the line of fire.

"No!" Penny kicked out of my grip and crawled toward Milo, intent on dragging him to safety but making of herself a target too easy to resist.

Chapter 28

Penny began on hands and knees but quickly rose into a crouch, leaving the cover of the sofa with perhaps no other intention than covering Milo with her body and taking a bullet for him.

For a moment, I froze.

Each of us is the sum of his experiences, not in the Freudian sense that we are victims of them, but in the sense that we rely on our experiences as the primary source of our wisdom, unless we are delusional and live by an ideology that refutes reality. At decision points in life, a sane person is guided by the lessons of his past.

Among other things, my past had taught me that the very fact of my existence is a cause for amazement and wonder, that we must seize life because we never know how much of it remains for us, that faith is the antidote to despair and that laughter is the music of faith.

But every lesson we learn from past experiences is not always the one we should have learned. One moment of my past had taught me that anger should always be watered down if not extinguished with humor, and I made no distinction between unworthy anger and the righteous kind. Anger is the father of violence, as well I knew, but I had not allowed myself to consider that wrath, when it is the product of pure indignation and untainted by ideology, is the father of justice and a necessary answer to evil.

The funny thing is, this awareness informed my fiction but not my life—until Shearman Waxx.

The bow-tied beast was my tormentor but also my teacher, for by the Taser attack and by the destruction of our house, he awakened the part of me that had been in this moral coma. And by shooting at Milo, he helped me to learn as a man what I already knew as a novelist: that wrath can lead to principled action *and* to principled violence.

If I'd had a gun, I would have gone out of the house to search for the source of the rifle fire, and would have tried to shoot Waxx dead before he shot me.

Lacking a firearm, I had no moral choice but to give in to the urge to act that suddenly ruled my mind and heart, whether it was a mad dominion or not. Because I was unarmed and helpless to defend my family in a rational way, my only choice was irrational action.

As Penny rose from her hands and knees, into a crouch, breaking cover, I stood upright, making the better target of myself. I bolted across the room, toward the corner where the entertainment-center wall engaged the view wall, passing in front of the windows.

My wrath was so intense that I half believed a bullet couldn't stop me, though I didn't turn directly toward the windows with the intention of catching one in my teeth.

I heard a round *pock* the glass, perhaps two, and prayed that I was the target.

At the corner, I flicked down the wall switch that activated the motorized shades encapsulated within the three-pane windows. Because of the damage to the glass, I worried they might get hung up before fully descending.

As the blinds came down, I turned my back to the windows to look for Penny and Milo.

Somehow, she had flipped the immense coffee table across Milo, positioning it between him and the windows, and she had stood it on end. They were behind it, hidden from the shooter, though from this end of the room I had a narrow view of them.

The table was well made, solid. Nevertheless, a single round had cracked the top, torn out a chunk of wood, and penetrated to the other side, fortunately without striking either mother or son.

As the window shades reached the halfway point and continued to descend, one thing became clear to me. In this attack, Waxx had one target—Milo.

He could have killed me three times as I passed in front of the windows. But he never took a shot when I was most exposed, not even as I stood motionless at the switch to watch the shades come down.

As Penny muscled the coffee table on end, she must have been such an easy target that Waxx could have blown out her brains. And only one shot had been fired at the table after she and Milo were behind it—no doubt because Waxx did not want to risk killing her instead of the boy.

The shades now covered three-quarters of the glass.

Penny rose warily from behind the table, but instructed Milo to remain on the floor.

Just as with John Clitherow and Thomas Landulf, the psychopath intended, before killing me, to take from me those I loved the most. Waxx imagined a specific order to my losses. Milo first. So I could witness Penny's anguish before she, too, was murdered.

I suspected he wanted to reduce me to despair, to the utter abandon-ment of hope, that I might accept my own murder gratefully, almost as a form of suicide. After seeing his wife and daughter brutalized, Landulf may well have pleaded to be killed. Although John Clitherow appeared to have taken extreme steps to stay alive, he told me that most days he yearned to join his family in death.

If one day I asked for death, I would be denying the value of life in general and the value of my life specifically, which would be as well a denial of the value of my writing. By begging death and receiving it, I would confirm Waxx's original criticism of my work.

The motorized shades reached the bottom of the glass wall.

Holding Milo close, Penny came out from behind the overturned table, and I hurried to her.

Because of his poor writing, I had judged Waxx an ineffective if influential critic, a curious eccentric. He was not eccentric but grotesque, demonic, not ineffective but a relentless murder machine, his mind a clockworks of meticulously calculated evil.

"Police," Penny said. "At least they can *stop* this."

I disagreed: "No. They won't get here in time."

Chapter 29

Denied Milo, Waxx would not shrug in resignation and leave. He would come into the house after the boy.

On the densely populated shores and islands of the harbor, houses stood close together. In this wealthy, peaceful community, gunfire would draw startled residents to their windows and their phones.

Already, we should have heard sirens. There were none.

Penny said, "After all that shooting, he's got to scram."

"No one heard it."

Wondering what to do, where to hide, I grabbed her free hand, drew her and Milo into the kitchen, intending to go from there into the downstairs hall.

Lacking wind and thunder, the storm had only rain for a voice, a susurration that could not mask rifle fire. The waterways were largely without traffic, free of engine noise.

The rifle must have been equipped with a sound suppressor. And in the rain, while cascades of breaking glass might have been heard, the *pock* of bullets penetrating shatterproof windows went unnoticed.

If Waxx had been cautious when positioning himself to shoot Milo, the dismal afternoon light and the skeins of rain would have made him all but invisible to anyone who stood at a window to enjoy the monochromatic beauty of the storm-bathed harbor.

Penny said, "The alarm system. There's a panic button."

Inset in a kitchen wall, a Crestron touch screen controlled the house systems: heating, cooling, music, security.

Under my fingertip, the panel brightened with options. I pressed SECURITY. The display changed. I pressed PANIC, which should have set off a loud alarm and also automatically dialed the police with a recorded message declaring an emergency at this address. Nothing happened.

Earlier, I had set the alarm. Now it was off.

I attempted to set it again. The system was down.

"The garage," I said, "the Explorer, out of here."

"No. He'll come in that way, to stop us leaving."

She was right.

"Back door, front door," I said.

"Then where? On foot, in the rain, with a dog?"

Lassie whined.

Snatching her purse from the secretary, Penny said, "Upstairs."

"There's no way out from there."

"*Upstairs,*" she urged, and I trusted her.

As Penny led us into the hallway, I realized that Milo was carrying one of the mysterious devices of his design that had been linked to his computer. It was the size of a bread box.

"Heavy?" I asked as I followed him.

"Yeah."

"Gimme."

"No."

"I won't break it."

"No."

A loud noise at the farther end of the hall might have been Waxx kicking open the door between the garage and house. Stepping out of sight into the foyer, I didn't glance back, so I didn't know if we had been seen.

Penny climbed the stairs, and Lassie scampered ahead of her.

By the time I followed Milo into the upstairs hall, Penny was quietly pulling a door shut. Farther along the hallway, she closed another door. She was giving Waxx places to search before he got to the room in which we actually took refuge, which was the third room on the right, into which she disappeared with Lassie at her heels.

Although I couldn't be certain, I thought I heard someone coming up the stairs behind us.

When Milo and I entered the third room, Penny closed that door as silently as she had closed the others, and she engaged a deadbolt.

If Waxx was prepared to shoot his way inside, a mere deadbolt would not long delay him.

We were in the master bedroom.

Paneled corner to corner in black marble, the wall opposite the bed featured a stunning contemporary fireplace.

On the hearth stood a handsome set of stainless-steel fireplace tools. The poker would have been an acceptable weapon—if Waxx had been armed with a Wiffle bat instead of a gun.

From her purse, Penny fished the ring of keys that Marty and Celine had given her. She selected an electronic key: a plastic wedge about as big as a corn chip.

Elsewhere on the second floor, Waxx kicked open a door.

The face of the fireplace mantel featured a ring motif carved in the marble. The center ring was the largest, and all the others were the same, smaller size.

Penny held the electronic key to the large ring. A code reader beeped, and to the left of the fireplace, a concealed door—one of the panels of marble—swung open on a pivot hinge. A light brightened automatically in the space beyond.

Years ago, during construction, Marty mentioned that the house would have a panic room, but he never said where it would be located. Evidently, he recently walked Penny through it in case she needed to show it to a qualified buyer.

Another crash, elsewhere on the second floor, sounded nearer than the first.

Lassie padded through the secret door as if she knew all about such things and was not in the least surprised or impressed, and Milo followed his dog.

As disrespectful of other people's property as ever we had known him, Waxx kicked the master-bedroom door, but it held.

"Hurry," Penny whispered as I stepped through the marble wall.

Beyond lay a windowless shaft and a spiral staircase. The steel landing and treads were covered with textured rubber to facilitate a quiet descent.

In the bedroom, Waxx kicked the door again.

Milo followed the dog down the winding stairs.

As I stepped after Milo and as Penny came onto the landing behind me, I didn't hear gunfire, although I heard what must have been the consequences of it: the hard crack of splintering wood, the metallic bark of bullet-scored metal. Waxx was shooting out the lock.

In spite of the rubberized treads, a silent descent was not possible. Our passage sent vibrations through the spiral structure, an insectile hum that echoed off the walls.

Glancing back, I saw Penny descending. The secret door was closed tight at the top. I hoped sufficient insulation would prevent the noise we made from being heard in the master bedroom.

But it might not matter if Waxx heard us. He wouldn't have an electronic key, wouldn't know where the door was hidden, and could not shoot his way through marble.

Perhaps I should have felt safe. Instead, I felt trapped.

Chapter 30

Because he needed both hands to carry the electronic device, Milo could not use the handrail. Watching him descend unsteadily in front of me, I worried that he would fall. Although the treads were sheathed in rubber, the spiral stairs were steep and tightly turned, and bones could easily be broken in a tumble.

"Come on," I said softly, "let me carry that, Milo."

"No."

"I promise not to use it. I won't turn it on."

"No."

"I don't even know what it is."

"I remember the vacuum cleaner."

"That could happen to anyone."

"Not to just anyone," he disagreed.

"It wasn't operator error. The vacuum malfunctioned."

"Who said?"

"I'm speculating."

"Lassie had nightmares for months."

"She's too sensitive. She needs to laugh at life more."

"Anyway," Milo said, "no more stairs."

At the bottom of the shaft stood a steel door. It could be opened only with the electronic key held close to a key-code reader.

Beyond the door lay the panic room: a fireproof fourteen-foot-square space with a dedicated phone line, a toilet closet, a sink, a bed, and two cases of bottled water.

I snatched up the phone. No dial tone.

"We aren't staying here," Penny said. "While he's searching upstairs, we're getting all the way out."

Another steel door offered a second exit from the panic room. When Penny opened it, we were confronted with what appeared to be a blank wall.

This was in fact a tightly fitted pocket door that rolled aside. Beyond lay a utility closet that contained the house's water softener and filtration system.

Penny led us around the equipment, cracked the door at the front of the closet, reconnoitered the way ahead, and revealed to us the garage that contained the three restored classic pickup trucks and our Explorer.

Milo said, "Cool," and I echoed his sentiment.

As boy and dog scrambled into the backseat, as I got in the front passenger seat, Penny settled behind the wheel. She handed me the house keys, from which dangled the fob that operated the garage doors.

"Top button, but don't press it until I tell you. The moment he hears the garage door going up, he'll come running."

Milo had buckled himself into his safety harness. I warned him to hold Lassie tight.

Penny released the emergency brake before starting the engine.

She switched on the windshield wipers. As she shifted into reverse, she gave me the go-ahead.

When I thought of Waxx hearing the distant rumble of the roll-up and setting out at a run, that barrier seemed to take forever to get out of our way.

My attention was fixed on the door between the garage and the house, which stood half open, as Waxx had left it. He would come that way, firing at us as he crossed the threshold.

The moment the door cleared the roof of our SUV, Penny peeled rubber backing out of the garage, down the short driveway.

The end of the peninsula had little traffic in the off-season. Penny counted on blind luck as she reversed without hesitation into the street and hung a hard left.

Had I been driving, executing the same maneuver at precisely the same time, we would have struck a car, a skateboarding teenager, someone in a wheelchair, and a nun.

As Penny made that left turn, the luggage in the cargo area re-arranged itself with much thumping and rattling, then thumped and rattled some more when she braked to a stop and shifted into drive, but no vehicles collided with us.

Beyond the open roll-up, Shearman Waxx had not appeared in the garage.

The tires spun on the slick pavement, Penny eased up on the accel-erator, the Explorer found traction, and we headed up-peninsula.

Just beyond the house, a grape-purple Maserati Quattroporte stood at the curb, engine idling and parking lights on.

As one of the most stylish cars in the world, it would have attracted my attention in any circumstances. I focused on the sleek Maserati now with special intensity because it seemed to me to be as sinister as it was beautiful.

Of course, after the events in the house, everything in view raised my suspicions. Every tree loomed ominously, as if it would collapse upon us. Behind every dark window at every house, a watcher seemed to lurk with malevolent intent. The sky menaced, the gray needles of rain stitched a portentous mood into the day, and the blacktop glistened like a serpent's scales.

As we passed the Maserati, I looked down at the driver's-side window from my higher position in the Explorer, and the man behind the wheel gazed up at me.

Heavy protruding jaws, wide crocodilian mouth and thin cruel lips, brutish nose in which the nostrils were as big as nickels, overhanging Frankenstein-monster brow, sunken eyes as pale as those of an albino, eyes that in the somber light of the storm appeared luminous, and overall an impression of tragic malformation: Here was a face met when opening a door or turning a corner in a fever dream, a face materializing from the shadows in the delirium tremens of a chronic alcoholic.

Chapter 31

We felt safer mobile than stationary. As we traveled a random route through the drenched afternoon, considering our options, my mind returned again and again to the deformed face.

Penny believed that rain streaming down my window and down the window of the Maserati had distorted the countenance. He was a man like any other, perhaps ugly, but not the grotesque individual that I—and my vivid imagination—had conspired with the rain to invent.

Her reasoning made sense, and for a while I elaborated on her theory. With all that we had so recently endured, the world had become an asylum; and when the mind dwelt in constant expectation of one new madness or another, it could conjure menace from the mundane, invoke a phantom assassin from an innocent shadow.

Besides, we had not been followed by the Maserati or by another vehicle. If such a pale-eyed ogre existed, it had no interest in us.

All boys are fascinated by the bizarre and the singular, that which is alone of its kind. Initially, Milo expressed keen interest in what he called the Maserati monster, but soon he retreated to his strangely high-functioning Game Boy and to whatever equations and three-dimensional blueprints currently obsessed him.

Concerned about his emotional condition, Penny and I assured him that we would keep him safe. Remarkably, however, he seemed to have incurred no trauma from being the target of a skilled rifleman.

I loved him without reservation but knew that I might never fully understand him, which was as poignant as any truth could be.

We had more urgent issues to consider than the Maserati driver. Not least was how Shearman Waxx had found us so quickly, mere hours after we had taken shelter in Marty and Celine's spec house.

I now accepted as fact Milo's suggestion that Waxx might have known our friends before he wrote his review of *One O'Clock Jump.* The critic researched us and prepared his assault perhaps even before I finished the novel.

Because of my past writing, I offended him so much, he deemed me to be deserving of not only a savage review but also death.

We were fortunate enough, however, to have many more friends than Marty and Celine. If Waxx planned our murders for months, he'd had sufficient time to learn who we saw socially; but the list was long enough that, once we fled our burning home, he would have needed a few days to discover with which of our friends we had taken refuge.

Instead, he had shown up less than eight hours later, armed and with a plan of attack. This suggested that we revealed our location by some action, requiring little or no detective work on his part.

"Clitherow warned you not to use credit cards," Penny said.

"And I didn't."

"But even if you did—how would Waxx know?"

"Maybe he's a genius hacker, he can break into the credit-card company's computer, monitor your activity, track your whereabouts."

"So he can breach security systems with impunity, he knows how to handle explosives, he's a good rifleman, and he's a world-class hacker. What the hell kind of book critic is this guy?"

"One who still needs to improve his syntax."

Preferring to avoid lonely roads and open spaces, we cruised business and residential streets. Much of Orange County is a megaplex of cities and suburbs, from which the orange groves and strawberry fields long ago disappeared.

"When you cashed a check earlier, what bank branch did you use?"

I said, "It was at the upper end of the peninsula."

"Could he somehow track that?"

"Wouldn't hacking a bank's records be harder than penetrating a credit-card company?"

"Both hard, the bank harder," Milo confirmed from the backseat.

His opinion sounded suspiciously authoritative, but we didn't worry that he was hacking bank computers. He had been born not only a prodigy but also with a tao, a sense of right and wrong, so strong that he never told us a lie. He could be evasive but not dishonest.

This is why he dreamed of being director of the FBI instead of attorney general. Considering some of the unsavory characters who had held the latter post, Milo didn't have the credentials for it.

"John Clitherow told me to abandon our car," I said. "We were in such a hurry to find a place to lie low, I thought as long as we kept the Explorer out of sight in Marty's garage..."

"Could there be a tracking device on it?"

"John just said Waxx's resources seem supernatural and we shouldn't underestimate his capabilities."

"You mean we gotta buy a new car?"

"There'll be a public record of the sale. I don't know how long it takes for that to show up on DMV records where some supernatural hacker might be able to find it."

Penny said, "What're we supposed to do—*steal* a car?"

"That would be wrong," Milo advised.

"I was being sarcastic, honey."

"I hope so," Milo said.

We rode in silence, and then Penny said, "Milo, I want you to understand something."

"What?" the boy asked.

"Your dad and I sound a little lost right now. We're not lost. We're thinking. We're not the kind of people who just take crap like this. My family blows up things. If your dad had a family, they'd blow up things, too. Your dad is smart, he's quick, and he's brave, which he proved today, proved forever. We're going to figure this out, and we're going to strike back, and we're going to make this Waxx sonofabitch regret he ever stepped into our lives."

"Vengeance," Milo said, as he had said to me in his room two days previously, when the review was published.

The word sounded less offensive now than it sounded then.

"Justice," Penny said. "Call it justice. One way or another, we're going to *crush* Shearman Waxx with a big damn load of justice."

I began to wish I'd spent the past ten years writing thrillers, because then perhaps I would know something useful about tracking devices, electronic surveillance, phone tapping, and techniques of evasion when pursued by psychopathic book critics.

In the storm-dimmed light, most drivers were using headlights, which inspired happier thoughts of the impending Christmas holiday by transforming the falling rain into tinsel streamers, the foaming gutter water into angel hair, and every puddle into collections of silver ornaments waiting to be hung on a tree.

"Hud called me on my cell phone," I said, "but I immediately called him back on the disposable. That couldn't have been how Waxx found us because he was already watching us then. He opened fire a couple minutes later."

"I thought you only had the disposable."

"No. I'm keeping my phone in case John Clitherow decides to contact me again."

"What did the Hud call about?"

"Heard our house blew up. Thought you might want to dump Alma, get a new agent."

"What's he trying to imply—that Alma blew it up?"

"No. But he seems to feel you should be worried that Alma's clients are dying on her."

"Gwyneth Oppenheim?"

"He wants you to think maybe Alma's good karma is past its expiration date."

"And now her clients are going to die like flies?"

"Should I invite him to your funeral?" I asked.

"No way, not the Honker," Milo said from the backseat, and Lassie issued a low growl.

After I pinched my nose and honked, I said, "He thinks a blown-up house could get me on *Oprah*."

"Well, that's a big step up from *Dancing with the Stars*."

"It was like three years ago he wanted me to do that, and I *still* haven't taken samba lessons. I am such an ungrateful client."

"Remember that dinner, I'd finished the first bunny book. He spent an hour arguing, Pistachio shouldn't be a *purple* rabbit?"

"He said purple on book jackets doesn't sell."

"He urged me to go green for the environmental crowd."

"And make the rabbit a kitten," I recalled.

"Pistachio, the green kitten. Except he said Pistachio wasn't a good name for marketing."

"Hey, I forgot that part. What name did he suggest?"

"Toot. Toot the green kitten."

"Toot. I guess that works if you're marketing narrowly to little kids who're cocaine addicts."

With a faint note of disapproval, Milo said, "Are you guys thinking how to get another car?"

"Yes we are, dear," Penny said. "We're multitrack thinkers."

"We already have a slew of ideas," I said. "We're carefully evaluating them before we decide what to do."

Milo said, "I have a pretty good idea."

Penny and I glanced at each other, and I said, "Yeah? What's that?"

"Well, but you're the parents, I'm just a kid. I should defer to you, hear your ideas first."

I said, "Nobody likes a wiseass, Milo. What's your idea?"

He had a good one. We decided to pursue his scheme before taking time to evaluate our slew of more complicated ideas.

Chapter 32

Penny dropped me off at a discount store and drove continuously through the surrounding neighborhood while I bought three
raincoats with hoods and long-handled flashlights. If the Explorer
contained a tracking device, we would not appear to have stopped
anywhere.

As I waited outside the store with my purchases, the SUV did not
quickly appear. Nausea overcame me, and fear. Then Penny returned.

From there we drove to the serviceway behind St. Gaetano's, the
church we attended. Penny stopped, and I hastily pulled our remaining
luggage from the back of the SUV and dumped it on the pavement.

She departed, and after trying a back door to the church and finding it locked, I walked around to the front of the building. In my long
black raincoat with hood, I suppose I appeared monkish. I climbed
the steps and entered by the main door.

As the true twilight replaced the false and as nine-to-fivers began to leave work, no services were under way at St. Gaetano's. Vespers would begin in half an hour, but at the moment the narthex and the nave were deserted.

At the back of the sanctuary, to the right of the altar, a door opened into the sacristy, where Father Tom daily prepared for Mass. The outside door of the sacristy brought me again to the serviceway where I had left our luggage in the rain.

I transferred the bags to a supply closet off the sacristy. There was a time, maybe prior to 1965, when they say you could leave unattended belongings almost anywhere and find them untouched when you returned. These days, a church is your only half-safe bet.

Vandals visit churches with increasing frequency, but thieves seldom do. Maybe the average thief worries that someone whose opinion he values might see him entering a house of worship and get the wrong idea, suspecting him of having gone over to the light side.

Earlier, in the car, I printed and signed a note to place on the luggage: DEAR FR. TOM, I'LL BE BACK FOR THIS STUFF SHORTLY. EXPLAIN LATER.

I hoped to retrieve the bags before anyone found them, making an explanation unnecessary. I didn't know the extent to which Waxx might expand his to-kill list to include people I told about him, so I half feared that involving Father Tom would make him a target.

Among other things, the closet contained a few rolls of paper towels. I took one, closed the door, and backed across the sacristy, blotting up the water that had dripped from my coat onto the floor, so no one else would open the closet to get towels to attend to the task. Outside, I dropped the towels, used and unused, in a trash can.

As twilight drowned and night swam down through the rain, I walked to the northwest corner of the church property, where two streets met.

After I waited about a minute, scanning the oncoming traffic, I spotted the Explorer approaching. In the gloom and the downpour, I could not clearly see the driver.

Blinking into the glare of the headlights, I suddenly *knew* that the vehicle would slow but not stop. And as it glided past the driver would be the Maserati monster.

When the Explorer pulled to the curb and I saw Penny behind the wheel, I shuddered with relief.

Some parts of the night were darker than others.

In the current economic mess, which politicians caused and which they insisted they could fix by imposing on us more suffering and unreason, many small businesses were destroyed. Previously thriving commercial centers, where entrepreneurs had stood in line to rent space, now had empty units not leasable at any price.

Beddlington Promenade had been a busy open-air shopping center. When the real-estate bubble burst, the property value dropped forty percent. The Promenade was losing tenants, hemorrhaging cash, and the highly leveraged owners let it go back to the bank.

Because the location remained superb, a retail specialist proposed to rescue the center. The bank wanted to finance this new owner in an arrangement that would have made it a partner.

Having seminationalized the bank, as it did many others, the government insisted on a say in its future operations. The Promenade deal would have been golden for the bank, but the federal regulators had a list of investments more appealing to the political class.

Beddlington Promenade closed. Vandals broke the windows at many of the empty stores, and sheets of plywood took the place of glass. Now Day-Glo graffiti covered the walls and seemed to throb in the dark, reminding me of cave paintings and of the crude symbols of barbaric languages.

The vast parking lot had once been graced with a geometric bosk of sizable trees, eighty to a hundred podocarpuses. With the failure of the Promenade, no effort was made to excavate these fine specimens and sell them. Over one summer, when the irrigation system was left off, the trees died.

Turning from the street, we entered this darker part of the night, and Penny parked under a bleakness of leafless and beseeching limbs.

We abandoned the Explorer and, with Lassie on a leash, walked two blocks to a bus stop.

Milo envied our black raincoats and profoundly disliked his bright yellow gear. "I look like a baby chicken."

I told him earlier that the store offered children's sizes only in yellow. Now I said, "Actually, you look more like a duckling."

"That makes me feel so much better."

"I'll bet if I squeeze your nose, it'll honk."

"Geese honk. Ducks quack."

"Let's see," I said.

Putting a protective hand over his nose, Milo said, "Mom, you've *got* to convince him to get a new agent."

When the bus arrived at the stop, the driver did not want Lassie aboard. A discreetly offered hundred-dollar bill changed her mind.

Penny and Milo sat side by side. I sat across the aisle with the wet dog on my lap.

Face surrounded by the hood, Penny looked like Audrey Hepburn in a movie about a saint.

Maybe the weather dampened spirits, but the other passengers were a somber lot. Only a few engaged in murmured conversations. Those at the window seats gazed out at the night or into the eyes of their reflections. The communal mood was that of people on their way to a forced-labor camp.

We traveled over four miles to reach our stop. From there we walked two and a half blocks to a Craftsman-style bungalow with a deep porch and a stained-glass window in the front door.

As can happen in parts of Southern California even in November, pink roses were blooming along the front walkway. Pink roses were also the motif of the stained-glass window.

We had called ahead and were expected. Vivian Norby answered the door before we could ring the bell.

She wore pink sneakers, a set of pink exercise sweats, and a bracelet of pink and blue beads. Her hair was tied up with a pink-and-blue scarf.

The gun in her right hand was big and not pink.

Chapter 33

The revolver had belonged to Vivian's late husband, the homicide detective, but as she welcomed us into the foyer, she grimly assured us that she knew how to use it and that she had no compunctions about plugging anyone who might have followed us with mischief in mind.

"We weren't followed," I said. "We took care not to be."

Holding the weapon down at her side, muzzle safely pointed at the floor, Vivian regarded me with motherly affection. "God love you, Cubby, you're a sweet man and a fine writer, but by nature you're a blithe spirit—"

Wincing, I disagreed: "Not blithe. Cheerful, generally cheerful, but not all the way to blithe."

"Blithe spirit," Vivian insisted. "You're a flaming optimist—"

"Not flaming," I said as I took off my raincoat. "Generally optimistic but not flaming."

She favored me with an expression of such motherly indulgence that I expected her to pinch my cheek. "You're a *blithe* spirit, a *flaming* optimist, and we'd want you no other way. But being the kind of man you are, you don't understand how infernally clever a truly wicked person can be. So we'll assume you *were* followed until time proves otherwise."

Frowning as Vivian closed the door, Penny said, "Okay, I told you on the phone we were in a spot of trouble. But how did you know it was the kind of trouble, you might need a gun?"

"Cop's-wife instinct," she said. "This morning your house blows up, fire so intense there's hardly ashes left. The news says you're in Florida doing book research when I know for a fact you're not. Then you call, trying not to sound scared, you need a little help. Hell's bells, my instinct would have told me to keep the Smith and Wesson handy even if I had been married to a *florist.*"

Lassie shook her coat, and water flew, and Penny said, "I'm so sorry, we're making a mess of your foyer."

"Heavens, Pen, it's only rain. Hang your coats on the hall tree. That towel on the floor is to dry the dog."

As I toweled Lassie, Milo struggled out of his hated slicker.

Vivian said, "How's the extraterrestrial radio coming along?"

Milo shrugged. "Better than the time machine."

"Have you talked to anyone on it yet? Or should I say any*thing*?"

"No," the boy said. "It's turning out to be something different from an interstellar communications device."

"How different?" Vivian asked.

"Very."

"It won't blow up the world, will it?"

"No. I stopped working on the thing that might have done that."

"Come on through to the kitchen," Vivian said. "I can tell you haven't had dinner, and you need it."

"We don't want to bother you," Penny said.

"I've got soup, I've got brisket and potatoes, I've got graham-cracker cream pie, and none of it's trouble at all. I always cook enough for four and freeze the leftovers."

As we went through the living room and dining room, I noticed that Vivian had closed all the draperies. In the kitchen, the blinds were drawn down to the windowsills. She was an apt conspirator.

Four places were set at the kitchen table. Fragrant steam rose from the pot of soup on the stove.

Vivian put the revolver on a counter and set a dish of cubed cooked chicken breast on the floor for Lassie.

As the dog gave her an adoring look, Vivian asked us what we would like to drink.

Opening a bottle of root beer for Milo, she said, "The critic is just as much a gibbering nutball as he is a hoity-toity snob, isn't he?"

Penny was no less startled than I. "Viv, we didn't say Shearman Waxx was our spot of trouble."

"I can add two plus two," Vivian said. "Besides, yesterday, long before your house blew up, I went online and started reading through the archives of his reviews."

"Why?" I wondered.

"I detested the man because of how unfair and vicious he was to you, Cubby, and I don't like detesting people. I wanted to give him a chance to prove he wasn't a complete rat. After I read about twenty of his reviews, I didn't detest him anymore. I *despised* him. And then I read ten more."

I said, "Maybe you shouldn't visit his newspaper's website, Viv. I don't know...but maybe he can track the e-mail addresses of people who go to his page, and right now he might be especially interested in people who stay there a long time."

Accepting a glass of milk from Vivian, Penny said, "My God, I spent hours in his archives this morning, after we got to the house on the peninsula."

"That's not how he found us," I assured her. "Maybe your e-mail address could lead to your home address, but not to the address of the Net port you used." To Vivian I said, "What's your e-mail name?"

"I hate people being anonymous on the Net," she said. "So I use Viv Norby."

"That would be enough. If he knows you're Milo's sitter or if he can find out, he could get your street address from a phone book."

"Stay away from his publisher's website," Penny urged.

"I'm not afraid of him," Vivian said.

"You should be," I told her.

"He's just a snotty pretend intellectual."

"Let's hope he's just pretend. The real intellectuals have spent a hundred years or more trying to destroy civilization, and they've made considerable progress."

Over dinner, Vivian wanted to know the full story, what Waxx had done to us and what actions we were going to take next.

Acting on the theory that the less she knew, the safer she would be, we had not intended to mention Waxx. But because her cop's-wife instinct told her that the destruction of our house was no accident and that Waxx must be somehow related to the incident, the equation had reversed. Less knowledge meant more danger for her, and the more she knew, the more cautious she would be.

When I got to the part about the brutal murders of John Clitherow's and Thomas Landulf's families, I hesitated, searching for euphemisms and metaphors that would allow me to inform Vivian without alarming Milo.

Into my hesitation, Milo said, "Sometimes, you forget I'm a kid but I'm also not. It isn't my primary field, but I'm interested in aberrant psychology. I *know* what kind of loons are out there, and I know the kind of crazy things they do, like cut off people's heads and stuff the mouths with severed genitalia."

Nonplussed, Penny and Vivian and I sat staring at Milo with our forks frozen halfway between our plates and mouths. Even Lassie, for whom our hostess had provided a chair at one remove from the rest of us, regarded her young master with a disconcerted expression.

I looked at Penny, and she shrugged, and I said, "Point taken, Milo," after which I held back none of the grisly details.

Judging by the gusto with which Milo ate dinner, at the end of which he demolished a piece of cream pie as big as his head, Waxx's monstrous crimes rattled him less than they rattled me.

Of course, my anxiety was higher than Milo's because my past had sharper claws than his did, and even after so many years of peace and happiness, memory could wound me anew.

Chapter 34

Vivian mostly used a Mustang, but she maintained her late husband's Mercury Mountaineer in good condition and drove it often enough to keep the oil viscous and the tires supple.

Because she was a cop's daughter and a cop's widow, I thought that she would press us to go to the police in spite of our lack of evidence, but she never did.

In her garage, as she gave me the keys to the SUV, she said, "There's something screwy about this. You see that, don't you?"

"It's everywhichway screwy, inside out, top to bottom," I said. "How do you mean?"

"This wing nut is clever, he's careful not to leave proof of his guilt—yet at the same time, he takes outrageous risks and acts as if, at the end of the day, he's untouchable and always will be."

Penny said, "It may just be the confidence of a narcissistic psychopath."

Vivian shook her head. "I smell something else. And it's some stink

I've smelled before, if I can remember when and where. Maybe you'd be smart not to go to the police until you have a stack of evidence taller than Milo."

"Why do you say that?"

"Don't know. Just a feeling. I'll brood on it."

Penny said, "Cubby suspects Waxx *wants* us to go to the police."

"Let's all brood on it," Vivian suggested. She offered me the big revolver. "I have a box of ammo for it, too."

"Keep it," I said. "You might need it."

"I have a 20-gauge pistol-grip shotgun. It'll stop any book critic ever born."

I almost said the book critic might not be the worst of it, but I hadn't told her about the deformed face glimpsed through the side window of the Maserati. Even I was beginning to think the ogre had been a figment of my imagination.

"Viv, we have a source of guns," Penny said. "We can get what we need. We'll be okay."

"I imagine the source would be Grimbald and Clotilda. You better be careful going to them. Waxx might expect that."

Vivian wanted to hug each of us, and each of us wanted to hug her, which resulted in such a rustle and flutter of raincoats that the echoes in the exposed rafters sounded like a colony of bats awakening to the idea of their nightly flight.

Vivian even picked up Lassie as if she were a mere Maltese and, holding her as she might cradle a baby, hugged the dog to her formidable bosom. "You folks . . . you're the family I never could have. Anything happens to any one of you, I'm not going to feel like pink for maybe the rest of my life."

That declaration resulted in another round of even longer and noisier hugs, with Vivian still holding Lassie and the dog licking our chins as we embraced with her between us. But at last we boarded the Mercury Mountaineer.

After pressing the switch to raise the garage door, Vivian returned to the driver's window of the SUV, tears pooled in her eyes. "Remember, if you get a different disposable phone, you call me right away with the number."

"I will. Right away."

First thing in the morning, she intended to buy a disposable of her own and call me with the number. We were taking the kind of precautions common to clandestine cells of revolutionaries.

We loved Vivian almost from the day we met her, but Penny and Milo and I were more emotional at this parting than any of us could have anticipated.

I backed the Mountaineer into the rain—then drove into the garage once more, put down the window, and said, "We meant to take Lassie."

Vivian looked at the dog cradled in her arms. "Mercy me." After she put Lassie in the backseat with Milo, she took advantage of this unexpected opportunity to say, "Maybe for a while, Cubby, not so blithe. Be an optimist but not a flaming optimist. For a while, expect the worst and make yourself mean enough to deal with it."

I nodded, put up the window, and reversed into the rain once more.

In the garage, Vivian waved at us until I shifted into drive and sped away.

Chapter 35

By the time we returned to St. Gaetano's, vespers must have concluded more than an hour earlier.

I worried that even as early as seven-thirty, the church might be locked. The benign days when houses of worship could be open around the clock without being vandalized were as far in the past as bell-bottom blue jeans, tie-dyed shirts, and psychedelic hats.

I dropped Penny near the front entrance. The rain suddenly intensified as she climbed the steps and tried the door. Unlocked.

As she went inside, I drove to the serviceway behind the church, parked but left the engine running. I got out, raised the tailgate.

The sacristy door opened. Penny braced it with a suitcase.

I went inside, and she said, "Somebody's in the choir storage room off the narthex. The door was open. I think it was Father Tom."

My note was where I had left it. Together, Penny and I quickly moved our belongings from the sacristy closet to the Mountaineer.

If I could avoid Father Tom, so much the better. Because I did not want to endanger him and also did not want to spend half an hour explaining the glimpse of Hell that our day had been, whatever story I told him would have to be at least incomplete if not a string of lies. I loathed having to lie to a priest, considering that by my calculation, I already was scheduled for 704 years in Purgatory.

When all the luggage was loaded in the SUV, I decided against testing our luck by blotting the rainwater from the sacristy floor, as I had done previously. I pulled the door shut, and we drove away.

Our destination was Boom World, as we called Grimbald and Clotilda's property, and our route from the church took us past Beddlington Promenade, the dark and deteriorating shopping center where earlier we abandoned our Explorer.

As we drove by, we had no difficulty seeing the SUV under the skeletal branches of the dead trees. It was illuminated by the headlights of the black Cadillac Escalade parked in front of it.

Penny said, "Didn't you tell me Waxx drove a black—"

"Yeah."

"Don't draw attention. Don't slow down."

"I'm not slowing down."

"Don't speed up."

"I won't."

"Don't hit anything."

"What about that red Honda?"

"What red Honda?"

"In the next lane."

"What about it?"

"Can I hit that?"

"Don't make me nuts, Cubby."

"It's harder to avoid being blithe than I thought it would be."

"Do you think he saw us?" she worried.

"No chance. He doesn't know what we're driving. And the rain. And there's a lot of traffic. We're just another fish in the school."

My personal cell phone rang, not the disposable.

Thinking *John Clitherow,* driving one-handed, risking a collision involving so many cars that it would set a world record, I fumbled the phone out of a raincoat pocket and took the call.

Shearman Waxx said, "Hack."

I heard myself saying, "Hoity-toity snob."

Disconcerted, he said, "Who is this?"

"Who do you think it is, you enema?"

"You think you're very cute."

"Actually, I have ugly feet."

"Already I found your SUV. Soon I will find you."

"Let's meet for lunch tomorrow."

"And I will cut out your boy's beating heart."

I didn't have a snappy comeback for that one.

"I will feed his heart, dripping, to your wife."

"Lousy syntax," I said lamely.

"Then I will, while you watch, cut out her heart."

Again, a perfect bon mot eluded me.

"And I will feed it to you."

He terminated the call.

I returned the phone to my pocket. I drove carefully with both hands, glad to have something to grip that would prevent them from trembling uncontrollably. After a moment, I glanced at Penny.

To the best of my recollection, I never before saw the whites of her eyes exposed all the way around her dazzling blue irises.

She said, "Hoity-toity snob? That was *him?*"

"It pretty much sounded like him."

"He saw us. He knows what we're driving now."

"No. The timing was coincidental."

"Then why did he call?"

"The usual ragging you get from a psychopathic killer."

"Ragging?"

"You know—all the gross stuff he's going to do to us."

After a hesitation, she said, "What gross stuff?"

Rolling my eyes to indicate Milo in the backseat, I said, "Dumbo, Despereaux, Pistachio."

Milo said, "Good grief."

"All right, all right. He says he'll cut out your heart and feed it to your mother. Are you both happy to know that? Mmmmm?"

"Don't worry, Milo," Penny said. "I absolutely won't eat it."

"What else did he say?" Milo asked.

"Then he'll cut out your mother's heart and feed it to me."

"This guy," Milo judged, "is a major sicko."

Lassie growled agreement.

We traveled several blocks in silence.

Some of the intersections featured pavement swales that were overflowing with swift-moving water. Passing through those rushing streams, the cars ahead of us sprouted white wings and seemed for a moment about to fly up into the storm.

Finally Penny said, "Not everything is a joke, Cubby."

"I know."

"We're in serious trouble."

"I know."

"But I have to say..."

I waited, then asked, "What?"

She laughed softly. "Hoity-toity snob."

"Well, he called me a hack again."

"He's not only a psychotic killer—he's also rude."

"He is very rude," I agreed. "I'd like to meet his mother."

"What would you say to his mother?"

"I would severely chastise her for poor parenting."

"Our Milo is never rude," Penny said.

"Because he's been properly raised."

"There was that one experiment that exploded," she said.

"Well, that's just the Boom side of him coming out. It's in his genes."

Behind us, Milo said, "This is so better."

"What is?" I asked.

"You guys—the way you are now."

"How are we now?"

"Not scared silent anymore. I like it this way."

I liked it better that way, too, and when I smiled at Penny, she smiled at me.

We would not have been smiling if we had known that eventually one of the three of us would be shot dead and that life would never be the same.

Chapter 36

At the eastern end of Orange County, many of the canyons are still home to more coyotes, bobcats, mountain lions, and deer than people. Carved into the foothills of the Santa Ana Mountains, some are mere ravines, others less narrow, all thick with trees and brush, a refuge for the contemplative, for those who dislike urban and suburban life, and for various eccentrics.

The serpentine, undulatory tossed-ribbon of a road unraveled as if it were the last feeble construction of the declining civilization that had built it. Huge California live oaks overhung the pavement, trunks and limbs char-black in our headlights.

The houses were well separated even at the civilized end of the road. They grew farther apart the deeper we penetrated the canyon, the name of which I will not provide, for reasons soon obvious.

With isolation came a different mood. Geological details seemed more dramatic, slopes steeper and rock formations more suggestive of violence. The woods thrust at us and the brush bristled aggressively, as though we had passed through a membrane, leaving benign Nature, entering a preternatural place in which a malevolent consciousness lived in the darkness, *was* the darkness, watched, and waited.

When I saw lamplit windows back among the trees, they no longer appeared warm and welcoming, but eerie and forbidding, as though the unseen structures were not houses but abattoirs, temples of torture, and fiery forges in which were cast images of strange gods.

The two-lane blacktop continued, but we turned onto a narrower gravel road that looped a few miles before rejoining the paved route. This one-lane track, which climbed the lower slopes of the canyon wall, was used largely by agents of the state forestry department.

Wet weeds swished against the sides of the Mountaineer, and some semitropical plant, with pale leaves as large as hands, slid its many palms across the passenger-side windows.

After some distance—for reasons soon obvious, I will not say how far—we came to a lay-by, where I could park alongside the track. When I switched off the engine and headlights, the darkness was as absolute as if we were in a windowless building. Only the drumming of the rain proved we remained outdoors.

The Boom house faced the paved road that we had departed. But we were not entering by the front door.

"We'll be eaten alive, going in this way," Milo predicted.

"No mountain lion will attack a group of people," Penny assured him. "They stalk what's smaller than they are—and what's alone."

"Lassie and me are smaller," Milo said, and the dog whined.

"But neither of you is alone," I said.

Milo was not a fan of wilderness. He embraced civilization and all its charms, regardless of its humongous carbon footprint.

Hoods up, with two flashlights, we got out into the rain, and I locked the Mountaineer.

Moving away from the gravel track, we waded through weeds and between trees until we came to a small low rock formation from which, in daylight, you could look down a gentle slope, through woods to the canyon floor, although not quite as far as the paved road.

Scattered nearby on the loamy floor of the forest, among ferns, were several stones, each a unique shape, but each weighing precisely 4.4 pounds. Any one of them was a functioning key.

I carried a stone to the rock formation and placed it precisely where Penny indicated with her flashlight.

We stepped back, off the lock slab, which would not move if either too little or too much weight was applied. After a moment, a five-by-six-foot horizontal portion of the formation pivoted along what seemed to be natural fissure lines, cast aside the 4.4-pound lock key, and stood on end: a trapdoor.

Although it appeared natural, the rock formation was man-made. Thirty-eight years previously, Grimbald, his intriguing father, his unique mother, his unusual brother Lenny, his irregular brother Lanny, his curious brother Lonny, his remarkable sister Lola, and his wondrous strange Uncle Bashir had joined with Clotilda and seven members of her uncommon and baffling family—all sixteen of them committed survivalists—to construct a combination home and end-of-the-world retreat prior to Grimbald and Clotilda's marriage, as a wedding gift.

You can think of this project as like an Amish barn-raising for newlyweds, except that none of these people was Amish, no barn was involved, they used power tools, they cussed sometimes, most of the construction was done in secret without building-department permits—and, if what we believe we know about the Amish is true, Grimbald and Clotilda began their married life with a great many more guns than did the couple for whom the barn was raised.

Although both Grimbald's and Clotilda's families are no more forthcoming than the great stone heads on Easter Island, although they have a high regard for subterfuge and hugger-mugger, they have hinted that they have come together to build similar retreats for one another in Northern California, Oregon, Nevada, and Montana.

Under the pivoting-rock trapdoor, our flashlights revealed a long narrow flight of concrete stairs and a stainless-steel handrail. Penny led, Milo followed with Lassie, and I brought up the rear, descending as if into a storm cellar.

Halfway down the stairs, we came to a one-foot-wide, eighteen-inch-high recess in the left-hand wall. A steel rod with a rubber hand-grip protruded from a slot in this recess. It was in the down position.

As Penny pushed the rod up, it made a ratcheting noise. I heard gears clicking somewhere.

Overhead, the rock trapdoor pivoted shut with a gasket-muffled thump. Without the inflowing air, the stairwell smelled of lime and wet dog.

After the end of the world, reliable electrical service will most likely not be available from the power company—nor, I might venture, will you be able to buy those delicious little chocolate-covered doughnuts that are currently to be found in any supermarket. Consequently, the three secret entrances to Boom World are opened and closed by a system of weights and counterweights riding on cables, controlled by hand-operated levers and wheels, a system so mechanically complex that I would rather die horribly in Armageddon than try to learn how to operate and maintain it.

At the bottom of the stairs was your standard impenetrable steel door. It looked not much different from the one protecting access to the panic room in Marty and Celine's peninsula house. The door had no keyhole; the lock-release levers were concealed in the floor drain.

The grid bars in the drain grate formed approximately half-inch square holes, except in each of the four corners, which featured a trio of larger openings. If you knew into which two corners to insert your fingers, you could lift the grate out of the way, exposing the drain and the hidden lock-release levers.

In the event that you inserted your fingers into the *wrong* holes, the grate would not release but would amputate your digits.

By the time my courtship of Penny matured to the inevitability of marriage, I had gotten to know her family, and I had on one occasion half-seriously wondered if, to protect their daughter from sexual predators, they had designed for her a wardrobe of cleverly booby-trapped clothing that would sever my hands at the wrists if I put them anywhere they had not been invited.

Taking every measure that might thwart Shearman Waxx, we had not called ahead to let Grimbald and Clotilda know we were coming. Therefore, even if we lifted the drain grate properly and correctly used the hidden levers to unlock the blast-resistant door, we would be at great risk crossing the threshold. The Booms were in lockdown mode, which meant additional lethal devices had been engaged in the hallway beyond this antechamber.

Beside the door, a capped pipe protruded from the wall. In the center of the two-inch-diameter cap was a pull-ring that connected to a taut, small-link chain inside the pipe. The pipe—and the chain—led into the main room of the shelter. When the near end of the chain was pulled, the far end swung a miniature brass hammer against a brass bell, producing a single loud, clear note.

With a series of pulls on the chain, Penny rang out her personal passcode. She waited ten seconds and rang the code again.

I could hear the notes echoing faintly through the pipe from a distant room of Boom World.

Half a minute later, mechanically triggered clockwork gears began to turn inside the steel barrier, retracting a series of bolts from the jamb. The door opened.

Penny confidently led the way across the threshold into the Hall of a Thousand Deaths.

Chapter 37

Grimbald and Clotilda actually called it the Hall of a Thousand Deaths, but they were exaggerating. In the walls of the seven-foot-high, fourteen-foot-long passageway were dark holes like the muzzles of pistols, spaced irregularly and at various heights. In each hole waited a spring-loaded steel rod, blunt on one end and as sharp as a pencil on the other. There were 180 of these lethal projectiles, not a thousand.

Mechanically rather than electrically controlled, the entire arsenal could be released in a single volley or in clusters of ten. The arming springs were so tightly wound and the rods so sharply pointed that Kevlar body armor would not protect a hostile intruder.

Electric bulbs brightened the hallway, but if the power failed, backup batteries would take over. The batteries could be recharged by Grimbald or Clotilda riding a stationary bike adapted as a generator.

To some people, survivalism is a hobby, to others a prudent philosophy. To my in-laws, survivalism was a religion.

At the farther end of the Hall of a Thousand Deaths stood a steel door, different from the first in that it had a porthole of bulletproof glass. This circle framed Grimbald's grinning face.

When he opened his door, he filled the doorway side to side, top to bottom. Six feet six, 250 pounds, barrel-chested, with a head larger than any haberdasher allowed for when producing a line of hats, with a jolly face as flexible as Silly Putty, Grimbald was an embodiment of many myths: a bit of Paul Bunyan, a little Santa Claus, a trace of Zeus, a measure of Mars, a pinch of Odin....

His bass voice lent an operatic quality to Grim's greeting: "Children! What a delightful surprise. Welcome to our stronghold."

As usual, he wore a vibrant Hawaiian shirt, khaki pants, and sneakers. The shirt presented an acre of lush palm trees silhouetted against a sunset; and one of his shoes could have carried the baby Moses down the river more safely than an ark of bulrushes.

Milo claimed to be afraid that Grandpa Grimbald—aka Grimpa—would step on him one day and not notice until, hours later, he realized that the icky stuff stuck to his shoe was squashed boy.

The name Grimbald comes from the Old High German word for "fierce" and from the Old English word for "bold." I had never seen him fierce, though certainly bold; I had no doubt that were you to attack him, he would have the ferocity to wring your neck till your head popped off.

In spite of Grimbald's formidable appearance and eccentricities—or perhaps because of them—adults found him charismatic, and kids found him irresistible. Milo loved his grandfather. Yellow raincoat flapping, he ran to the big man, allowing himself to be scooped off the floor and held in the crook of Grim's massive left arm, as if he were indeed no bigger than a baby chicken.

After accepting a kiss and bestowing one, Grimbald asked Milo, "Have you had another experiment blow up?"

"No, Grimpa. Not a one."

"That's too bad. Don't lose hope. Most things in life want to blow up, so it's just a matter of time."

Penny stood on her toes to kiss her father, and he bent down like Kong to Fay Wray. Then he rose a bit and, as I pulled back my raincoat hood, he kissed me on the forehead.

As Lassie jumped, jumped, jumped for Grimbald's attention, he caught her in midair by the scruff of the neck, kissed her cold nose, and gave her to Milo, holding both of them with ease.

We followed him through the door with the porthole, into the first of a series of subterranean chambers, a thirty-by-twenty-foot workshop, where he repaired the stronghold's mechanical systems.

He owned hundreds of hand tools, all of the highest quality. None were power tools because when civilization collapsed, he didn't want Clotilda to have to exhaust herself on the bicycle generator just to operate his drill and reciprocating saw.

Passing through the workshop, Penny and I took off our raincoats and hung them on wall hooks, but Milo remained ablaze in yellow.

The stronghold enjoyed electric lights, though after the end of the world, the Booms would rely on candles. They possessed thousands.

Beyond the workshop lay a large chamber stocked with enormous quantities of freeze-dried and canned food, also drums of seeds in case, after Armageddon, the earth eventually became farmable again.

Their bedroom was traditionally furnished, and the walls were brightened by poster-size photos of huge buildings in mid-collapse, structures that Grim and Clo had been paid to implode. The space was cozy, if claustrophobic due to the lack of windows.

They did not live in the stronghold 24/7. Above ground, they had a comfortable hacienda-style residence where they spent most of their time, except for those occasions when they flew off to far cities with their demolition team to create massive piles of rubble for substantial fees, which they referred to as having a blast, as in "We're having a blast in Dallas next Thursday."

They owned this above-ground house under a false name. They lived in it under another false name. A serious survivalist could disappear from the all-seeing eye of the state and move about like smoke, if he had to, before finally going underground.

Their official address was the small combination office and apartment in Anaheim, where a secretary who resembled the actress Judi Dench screened job offers to be sure the people who wanted a building blown up had both the authority and a legitimate reason to contract for the demolition.

Here in the canyon, they never spoke to their neighbors, which was no loss, considering that the nearest were at a distance and were an uncommunicative couple who, believing they had been twice taken against their will into spacecraft from a distant star, were hiding out from evil extraterrestrials.

Although they lived largely above ground, Grimbald and Clotilda went subterranean two or three days every month—what they called "in lockdown"—to stay in practice for the End of Days.

Because they seemed always to be finding excuses to go into emergency lockdowns in addition to the regularly scheduled ones—a scary declaration by the insane leader of Iran, a scary declaration by the benighted leader of the United States, and in this instance the destruction of our house—I suspected they preferred the bunker to the sunlit world but would feel *too* eccentric if they admitted it.

The main chamber, a combination living room and kitchen, offered armchairs, a sofa, wonderful stained-glass lamps, fantasy art that Penny—a homeschooled girl herself—had drawn as a teenager, and a sturdy knotty-pine dining table.

Their stronghold enjoyed an effective exhaust system that could separate a single source of smoke into seven wispy streams, dispersing them to different corners of the woods above, to avoid detection by roving bands of post-catastrophe barbarians or genetic-plague zombies, or whatever hellish beings might one day stalk the ruins of the world.

Consequently, Clotilda had the convenience of a wood-burning stove, on which she was cooking when we arrived. The fragrant air smelled of home fries, onions, and pot roast.

"Cupcake!" Grim called to her. "I didn't have to kill anyone, it was really the kids ringing the bell." .

Clotilda Boom—born Nancy, maiden name Farnham—was an Amazon: six feet three, broad shoulders, full bosom, strong arms, a spine as straight as a plumb line. Her thick mane of midnight hair, without a touch of gray, usually lay in intricate braids down her back, but now hung loose, great black curtains billowing around a striking face surprisingly beautiful considering that her features were bold enough for an Eskimo totem pole or the prow of a Viking longboat.

She wore laced boots that probably went to her knees, a long skirt of coarse gray material, a belt with a fang-bared serpent's head for a buckle, a man's blue denim shirt with the sleeves rolled up, and a silver pendant, an amulet in which she kept a lock of hair from the mane of a horse that had trampled to death a man who had tried but failed to rape her when she was fourteen.

Turning away from the stove, her face bright with sweat and with happiness at the sight of us, Clotilda said, "I *knew* you would come tonight when I saw the strange vein patterns in one of the basil leaves I put in the soup this afternoon."

I've known Clotilda for a decade, yet I can't say with certitude if her claim to the perceptions of a Gypsy seer is serious or tongue-in-cheek. Penny, who has known her mother longer than she has known *anyone,* is likewise unsure, which argues that Clo is playing a sly game, testing our gullibility, tolerance, and commitment to reason.

The name Clotilda comes from the Old German word that means "renowned in battle."

Clo threw her arms around Penny, lifted her off the floor, and kissed her two, three, four times. "Punkin', you're a slip of a thing, you aren't eating, you're going to wither away."

"I eat well, Mom," Penny assured her, waiting to be put down.

"You've gone off meat!" Clo declared. "Oh, girl, you've become a grazer!"

"No, Mom. I could never do that."

"Vegetarianism kills," Clo warned. "Your vital organs shrivel, your brain dims. Look in a mirror at your teeth. You have central incisors, lateral incisors, canines—all for the purpose of chewing meat. Vegetarianism is unnatural, it's not right, it's *creepy*."

"I eat plenty of meat," Penny assured her. "I eat it every chance I get. I *live* for meat."

"Eating it often isn't enough if you're eating small portions," Clo said, finally returning my wife to her feet.

Sometimes I find it hard to believe that Grimbald and Clotilda produced a daughter as petite, lithe, and comparatively demure as Penny. Two of the three proofs that she is their offspring—her hair as black as Clotilda's, her blue eyes the same shade as Grimbald's—do not convince. For me, the case is made by the fact that, in spite of her size, Penny is as tough and just as indomitable as the Booms.

Clotilda came to me as if she were a Valkyrie swooping down on a dying warrior to take possession of his soul, and I half feared she would sweep me off the floor and hold me in the crook of her arm.

She kissed my cheek. "Seeing you lifts my heart, Hildebrand."

"Likewise, Nancy."

"Ah, yes, yes, I forgot—you prefer Cubby."

"Since it's my name. You look wonderful, Clotilda."

"Every night before going to bed, I put a small silk bag full of thyme leaves under my pillow. You look very fit yourself."

To please her and forestall a lecture, I said, "I ate the better part of a cow last month."

"There is no *lesser* part of a cow. They are entirely delicious."

Turning from me, she descended upon Milo and clasped his head with both hands. Speaking in Gaelic between kisses, she smooched his brow, his eyes, his nose, his cheeks, each corner of his mouth, his chin. I believe it was some kind of blessing.

Next she plucked Lassie from the boy's embrace. Holding the dog at arm's length, laughing with delight, she turned rapidly in circles, her skirt flaring.

Were I to do anything of that kind, Lassie would either whimper with fear or bare her teeth and growl me to a stop. In Clotilda's hands, she grinned not with anxiety but with obvious pleasure, and her tail wagged, wagged, wagged.

Put on the floor, the dog tottered dizzily, but Clo remained in full control of herself and rushed back to the woodstove to tend to her cooking before anything burned.

"You'll stay for dinner," Grimbald declared.

Before we could reply, Clo said, "They already had dinner. I saw it in the basil leaf."

"Then while we're having dinner," Grimbald said, "you'll tell us more about the house blowing up, what you know of the method, how it looked as it fell, the debris pattern."

"They came for guns," Clo told him.

"Did you see that in the basil leaf?" I asked.

Pointing to the stone floor, Penny said, "I think she'll tell you that she read the pattern of the water drops that fell from Milo's raincoat."

"Exactly right, dear," said Clotilda, pointing a wooden spatula at her for emphasis. "*So*—you finally admit I have at least a little of the soothsayer's gift."

"What you have, Mom, is a gift for drama, for being enigmatical, and for caring."

"My daughter the skeptic. But I love you, too, dear."

At last putting down Milo, dropping to one knee, and helping the boy out of his raincoat, Grim said, "Guns? But I thought, Cub, you were against guns."

"I'm not against them for other people, Grim. But for me...I've just always had an aversion to them."

"And now?"

"I'm getting over it."

Chapter 38

From the main room of the stronghold, on your way to the armory, you pass through Penny's old bedroom. For fifteen years, since she moved out, her folks have left it exactly as it was throughout her childhood and most of her teen years, when she spent the monthly lockdowns underground with them.

Partly for sentimental reasons, they have not expanded the armory into her old quarters. They also hope that Penny and I will recognize the signs of impending Armageddon and will join them in this citadel of survivalism before a politician or a mad mullah, or a crazed dictator, or a group of angry utopians, or just the grinding work of the federal bureaucracy destroys civilization.

I don't rule out the possibility of one day taking shelter with them. Before I move in, however, I will *insist* that they remove from Penny's room the poster of Jon Bon Jovi naked to the waist, as I do not want to remind her that she has settled for much less than her teenage dreams.

The armory is next to the last major room in their subterranean complex. It contains a breathtaking array of weapons, as well as a supply of ammunition that would have lasted the defenders of the Alamo at least five years.

Of course, back when Penny was Brunhild, she was raised with guns. Although she had thus far deferred to my disinclination to own one, since our marriage she accompanied her parents twice a year to a shooting range, where they kept their marksmanship sharp.

I would have preferred to stay in the kitchen with Clotilda and Milo. But in defense of my family, if I truly did intend to overcome my aversion to firearms, I would have to look at one and even touch one sooner or later.

Penny and her father engaged in such technical discussions of the choices of weaponry available to us that although I tried hard to listen to them and to learn, I finally could make no more sense of their conversation than I could of the Gaelic with which Clotilda had blessed my son. Soon they managed to do what I would have thought impossible: They made guns seem less scary than boring.

I wandered out of the armory, into the final and largest chamber in the stronghold. Here lay the proof, if I had needed it, that Grim and Clo were not insane, that they were no worse than eccentric to the max.

Their survivalism was not just about the preservation of their lives in the event of universal destruction. They hoped as well to preserve the fundamental works of Western thought and art that had given the world—for a while—the only societies that believed every individual was born with a dignity and a God-given right to freedom that no one had the authority to deny or to abridge.

Books.

The classic works of Greek philosophy: Aristophanes...Aristotle, Plato...

The plays of Euripides. Plutarch on the lives of legendary and real Grecians and Romans. Herodotus on ancient history. Hippocrates on medicine. Euclid and Archimedes on geometry and math.

The masterpieces of the Middle Ages: Dante...Chaucer...Saint Thomas Aquinas...

From Shakespeare to Boswell's *Life of Johnson,* from Dickens to Dostoyevsky...

Of works published in the twentieth century, which produced more books than any other, they preserved fewer than a hundred titles. Conrad, bridging centuries with *Heart of Darkness.* Bellow... Churchill...Orwell...O'Connor...Pasternak...Waugh...

They kept three copies of each book. Two were carefully vacuum-sealed in plastic, using a kitchen appliance designed to package leftovers for the freezer, but the third copy remained accessible for their use.

I am led to believe that the rumored other family strongholds have libraries of their own, that perhaps some have collections of reproductions of the great art produced before the decline of the West, when the purposes of art were celebration and reflection instead of transgression and negation.

There are times when even extreme eccentricity is not abnormal but merely irregular, and there are even times when it is wisdom. All that seemed obsessive about the Booms' stronghold might on reconsideration be seen as prudent, and all that appeared selfish might be noble.

When I returned to the armory, Penny and Grimbald were closing a pair of metal attaché cases that contained the weapons and the ammunition that they had chosen for us.

Handing one of the cases to me, Grim said, "Penny can teach you gun safety and how to shoot. If I believed in reincarnation, I'd say she was Annie Oakley in a previous life."

My wife, the adorable gun nut.

Grim snapped thumb and middle finger. "Oh, right! And I've got those items Milo called me about."

For a disconcerting moment, I thought he meant that our boy had requested weapons of his own.

"No, no," said Grimbald. "A month ago he called me with a list of electronic items and highly specialized microchips."

"But I always get him what he wants."

Turning from us and lumbering deeper into the armory, like Thor trying to remember where he stored his latest batch of thunderbolts, Grim said, "Oh, you could never have gotten these things. They're embargoed."

"Embargoed by whom?"

"Government." He withdrew a small suitcase from a cabinet. "You have to have contacts in the black market."

"Why?"

Returning with the suitcase, Grimbald grinned and winked. "Well, let's just say these items have ... military applications."

Penny and I exchanged ten thousand words of concern in just a glance.

Grimbald wondered, "What's the nipper up to, anyway?"

"Something very different from an interstellar communications device," I said. "That's all we know."

"He's going to do something spectacular one day," Grimbald declared.

"We're half afraid of that," I said.

Chapter 39

When we returned to the kitchen, Milo was sitting on a stool while Clotilda, furiously cooking at the wood-burning stove, regaled him with what she had learned about the future from that morning's coffee grounds.

When Grim told Milo that the suitcase contained the forbidden electronics, Penny said, "I'm surprised you'd coerce your grandfather into committing a crime."

"Now, punkin,'" Grim admonished, "I've been buying illegal weapons most of my life. This stuff isn't weaponry. This is just a little favor for my only grandchild."

Clearly embarrassed, Milo said, "It's not that much of a crime, Mom. Besides, I'm not going to do anything wrong with the stuff."

"What *are* you going to do with it?" I asked.

"This cool thing."

"What thing?"

"It's the kind of thing you can't describe."

"Can't or won't?"

"It's the kind of thing you've got to experience," said Milo.

"When are we going to experience it?"

The boy shrugged. "Sometime."

Clotilda made a pitch to keep Milo with them in lockdown. "Your house blew up, you need guns. It's none of our business what's going on, but obviously you've got some problems, and he'll be safer here."

"Of course, it's your business, Mom," Penny said. "And I gave Dad a cut-to-the-chase version while we were in the armory." To me, she added, "Maybe we should leave Milo here."

Before I could respond, Milo spoke in a whisper that carried like a shout: "If you don't take me, you'll both be killed."

His blue eyes were even more compelling than his mother's. He stared at me, and then at Penny.

"You need me," he told his mother. "You don't know why yet, but you'll find out."

Again he turned his attention to me. His sweet face was that of a child, but his eyes were those of a grown man who had peered into the abyss and who was not afraid to gaze into it again.

Still in that remarkable hushed voice, he said, "I'm small, I'm young—and I'm so different. You've always respected that difference, and you've always trusted it. Trust me now. There's a reason I am the way I am, and there's a reason I was born to you. There's always a reason. We belong together."

Never had the nickname Spooky been better suited to him.

"All right?" I asked Penny.

She nodded. "All right."

When Milo smiled, I found his smile contagious.

Clotilda took one egg from a thatched-reed basket full of them and threw it on the floor. For a moment, she studied the splatter of white, yolk, and shell. "He's right. If you don't take him with you, we'll never see either of you again."

From his perch upon the stool, Milo surveyed the ruined egg, then grinned up at his grandfather. "Grandma's a hoot."

"She's a hoot and a half," Grimbald confirmed, and beamed with great affection at his bride. "I remember when I first saw her—such a radiant vision in the woods, on her knees, arms up to the elbows in a deer carcass."

A girlish blush suffused Clo's face as she was swept away by this romantic memory. "After you shoot it, gutting it in the woods saves a mess at home later. But there's always some danger that the blood smell will draw hungry critters. Your grandfather was standing in tree shadows, and when I looked up, I thought he must be a bear."

"She moved so fast, from carcass to rifle," Grim remembered, "that I almost became her second kill of the day."

Both he and Clo laughed, and she said, "But then he blurts out 'I have seen Diana, Roman goddess of the hunt and of the moon, here abroad in daylight and brighter than the sun.'"

"Grimpa really said that?" Milo asked.

"He really did. So I knew right then I either had to shoot him or marry him."

Having heard this story countless times before, Penny was less enchanted than Milo. "We've got a long way to go. Better get moving. Where's Lassie?"

"Probably in the potato bin," Milo guessed.

"I told you, sweetness, the bin's empty," Clotilda reminded him. "I forgot to fill it last month, and I used up the last for these home fries."

"That's why she'll be there, Grandma. It's a cool, dark, quiet place, and it smells good. Sometimes Lassie needs cool, dark, and quiet."

In the northwest corner of the kitchen, two bins were recessed in the stone floor, a pair of small concrete-walled vaults, one for pota-toes and the other for onions.

Clotilda, Penny, and I gathered around as Grimbald lifted the hinged wooden lid from the potato bin.

In the four-by-five-foot space, four feet below us, comfortably curled on a bed of empty potato sacks, Lassie looked up and yawned.

"The lid's heavy. How did she get in there?" Clotilda asked.

"The usual way," I said.

"And how is that?"

"I haven't a clue."

Chapter 40

With a destination that required a long drive, we set out from the Boom stronghold into a world of dark and rain and trouble.

I found the visit with Grim and Clo to be energizing, but the refreshment of mind and spirit faded soon after we were on the road.

Because Penny had gotten a two-hour nap at the peninsula house, she somewhat recovered from the sleep lost the previous night when Shearman Waxx Tasered us. Giving me the opportunity to have a snooze, she drove the first leg of our journey northward.

In the backseat, using a flashlight, Milo examined the items that his grandfather secured on the black market, while Lassie noisily sniffed them. He muttered excitedly to himself or perhaps to the dog.

The windshield wipers should have been as effective as the shiny pendant of a hypnotist. By the time we were on the freeway, the thrum of tires should have been a sedative.

In the best circumstances, however, I have difficulty sleeping in a moving vehicle. Arguably the primary shaping force of my life has been a curiosity about where I am going, not in a day or a week, but a curiosity about where ultimately I might be going. The forward motion of a car stirs in me this lifelong inquisitiveness, which is as much a yearning as it is a need to know, and mile by mile I grow more restless for revelation.

Eyes closed, I said to Penny, "Sometimes I worry about Milo. At the stronghold, I realized you had a childhood like his. Homeschooled. No friends your age. Your world limited to family, a kind of isolation. What were the negatives of a childhood like that?"

"None," she said without hesitation. "Growing up in a loving family, with parents who have a sense of humor and common sense and a sense of wonder—that's not isolation, that's a wonderful haven."

I loved the sound of her voice as much as the sight of her face. Eyes closed, I couldn't see her beauty, but I could hear it.

"More than a haven," she said. "It's a sanctuary, where you can decide who you are, what you think about the world, before the world *tells* you who you are and what you ought to think of it."

"You had your talent, writing and drawing, just like Milo has a talent for...something. Don't you wonder if less isolation and more experience in the early years might've made you a different artist?"

"One I wouldn't want to be. By the time I went to art school, all I wanted was better technique. I already had my own theories of art, so those of the most opinionated professors didn't corrupt me."

We rode in silence. Then I said, "What a magical world it is—folks like yours, living like they do, raising a wonder like you."

"I'm no more a wonder than anyone. And that's what makes the world magical. Every baby's a seed of wonder—that gets watered or it doesn't. As a kid, I loved going down into the stronghold. It was like something out of Tolkien, a hobbit's home."

I opened my eyes. The bracketing hills and the six-lane highway seemed not to await illumination by the headlights but to dissolve before those beams could reveal more. The pavement, other traffic, the guardrails, the landscape deliquesced into the solvent rain, and we appeared to be rushing always toward a brink and an abyss.

"Seventy percent of people in prison were raised without a dad in the home," she said. "I was lucky—I had a father and a half."

When I closed my eyes, the image of the melting world stayed with me, and carried me into sleep.

In my lost-and-alone dream, I walked a deserted highway that led through featureless salt flats, and not a single cloud graced the sky, and no currents moved the air nor did a single bird move through it, and no lines divided the blacktop into lanes, and the only salient detail was the blood trail that led toward a horizon that could not be clearly discerned.

The ringing of my cell phone woke me. It was my regular phone, not the disposable.

As I fished it from my shirt pocket, Penny said, "Should you?"

I hesitated, but then took the call.

John Clitherow—author of the Waxx-savaged *Mr. Bluebird* and writer on the run—said, "Cullen, I have to tell you how my wife and daughters died."

Chapter 41

"I have to tell you," John Clitherow repeated. "I have to."

Having slumped in sleep, I sat up straighter in the passenger seat, and saw that we were on a lonely stretch of highway with few lights visible on the flanking hills. Into the phone, I said, "I'm sorry for your losses. I did some research, I know about your folks. It's all so ... it's horrible."

The torment in his voice was thin, yet no less affecting for its thinness, just as the stropped edge of a knife is thin but cuts.

"Right after the Michigan police phoned me to say my parents' bodies had been found—the condition, such brutality—I told them about Waxx, the review, my dead cat. They did nothing with that, Cullen. *Nothing.* Why? And then Waxx called again. He just said 'Next?' and hung up. He was insane—and serious. He'd said 'doom,' now my folks were dead. But who's going to believe it ... fast enough to save the rest of my family? Not the cops. So I took Margaret, my wife, the two girls, we ran. I wanted them someplace secure before I went to the police again. We weren't followed. I *know* we weren't."

I heard him swallow hard, then swallow again.

When I glanced at Penny, she glanced at me. "Clitherow?" she asked, and I nodded.

"We drove over a hundred miles," he continued, "no destination, getting away from where he expected to find us. It was worse than fear, Cullen, it had nothing to do with intellect or imagination, it was undiluted *fright,* raw nerves. Fear can be controlled by an act of will, but I couldn't control what I was feeling. Then...a hundred miles made me feel better. God help me, I felt kind of safe."

The rain grew heavier and seemed to rush at us more urgently than before. Penny adjusted the wiper speed, and the blades arced faster, thumped louder.

John said, "We stopped at this nothing motel. A room with two queen-size beds. Not the kind of place we would have stayed before— which made it seem even safer, so anonymous. Margie and I could think things through there, decide what next. Emily and Sarah, our girls, only six and seven, didn't know their grandparents were murdered, but they were sensitive kids, they knew something was wrong."

The previous thin edge of pain in his voice had grown sharper, past distress now, short of anguish, but cutting ever deeper as he approached the recollection of his next loss.

"For the girls, Margie and I tried to pass the trip off as a vacation. Took them to a kid-friendly restaurant. Back at the motel, the girls went fast asleep in one of the beds, in spite of TV-news chatter. Margie wanted a hot shower. Closed the bathroom door so she wouldn't disturb the girls. I watched...I watched...the news."

A Peterbilt roared past the Mountaineer, traveling too fast for road conditions, flinging up a sheet of water from the puddled pavement. Cascades overwhelmed the wipers, and for too long we were blinded. All that might lie ahead vanished from view.

"I thought I'd see something on the news about my folks, but nothing. Then...Margie was a long time in the bathroom. I knocked, she didn't answer. I went in to see if she was okay, but she...she wasn't there."

John paused. His breathing was quick and shallow. Before it quickened further, he worked to control it.

Ordinarily, in weather this foul, I might have suggested to Penny that she pull off the highway and wait for the torrents to diminish. But stopping in this lonely night seemed like an invitation to Death, and I preferred hurtling half-blind into the downpour.

John continued: "The shower was running, stall door open. Her underwear, her robe on the floor. There was a double-hung frosted window. Bottom sash was up, curtains billowing. How could he have taken her so quietly, no struggle? I went out through the window. Behind the motel was a field, an endless field, far away a line of trees, all visible under a full moon, nobody out there, nobody."

Penny whispered my name, wanting to know something of what John was saying. I glanced at her but shook my head.

The sight of her flooded me with apprehension—that she would vanish like Margaret Clitherow, that she would turn a corner and not be there when an instant later I rounded the same corner, that she would walk from one room into another and be gone forever.

"The motel had three wings. I found my way around to the front," John recalled, "sure I'd see her being forced into a car. But the night was quiet. No one in sight. Only the desk clerk in the motel office, watching TV. Then I saw the door of our room standing open. I thought...I *knew*...I left the girls alone, now they were gone, too."

Another massive truck began to pass the Mountaineer, its array of running lights blurring as it cast up blinding sheets of water. Penny eased up on the accelerator to let the rig get past us more quickly, and I almost urged her to keep the pedal down.

"But in the motel room, the girls were asleep, just as I'd left them.

But on the second bed . . . sparkling on the bedspread . . . Margie's engagement ring, wedding band. I knew then she was dead or as good as dead. He wouldn't taunt me with the rings if she were nearby where I might find her. Explaining this to cops in a strange town—no chance. They'd think she walked out on me. The returned rings proved it. No abductor would return her rings. Waxx did it once, he could do it twice, the girls would be next. I had to think only of the girls."

Guilt twisted his voice. He believed he failed Margaret. Even if that was not true, he would always believe it.

I said, "Take your time. If it's too much now, you can call me later. Or not at all."

"No. I have to tell you. You don't understand. I *have* to tell you." He took a deep breath. "So I threw into the suitcases what little we'd taken out of them. Emily and Sarah were so sound asleep, they hardly stirred when I carried them out to our SUV and belted them in the backseat. When I drove away, no one followed us. But no one had followed us from home to the motel, not for a hundred miles."

"Credit card," I said, remembering the warnings he had given me.

"Yeah. I thought—the American Express I used at the motel. You see in movies, they can track you like that. But this wasn't the FBI. This was a half-baked book critic with no more resources for tracking someone than *I* have. So maybe he planted something on our SUV."

I said, "Some kind of transponder or something."

"So I found a residential neighborhood, cars parked at the curb, in driveways. I went looking for keys behind sun visors, under seats. Couldn't believe the risk I was taking. I was crazy with terror for the girls. I stole a Chrysler PT Cruiser, put our bags in it, moved the girls from our car. Emily grumbled, but I shushed her to sleep."

As Penny squinted through the smeary windshield, rain persisted, but suddenly the traffic washed away. Mirrors reflected the emptiness behind the Mountaineer. Ahead, no taillights were visible. Beyond the reach of headlights, the highway became a hidden vein in the wet flesh of the night, and we raced forward like an air-bubble embolism toward an unknown but inevitable moment of destruction.

"This was back east," John said. "We lived in New York State, but the hundred miles took us into Pennsylvania. In the PT Cruiser, I kept going south. My agent, Jerry Simons, lived in Manhattan but owned a four-acre retreat in Bucks County, spent weekends there in summer. Margie and I stayed once, for a week. Now, late September, I didn't know if Jerry was using the place. I called his cell phone, got him in New York, made up a story about needing isolation to finish my novel. The house was available. I knew where the spare key was hidden. The girls and I were there in three hours."

To this point, the tightly controlled emotion with which John Clitherow recounted these events suggested that I was the first to whom he had told the story in almost three years and that his need to unburden himself was acute. The urgency with which he spoke seemed to arise from a determination to share information that might spare me from losses like those he suffered.

When he arrived in memory at the house in Bucks County, however, his manner and his tone changed. His urgency abated, as did the note of guilt in his account. The distress that had been swelling toward anguish now shrank to a chilling insensibility, and his voice became flat, his cadence slow.

"I couldn't sleep that night in Bucks County. Sat in a bedroom armchair, watching over the girls, torn by grief and guilt and fear. I loathed myself, my helplessness. Self-hatred is exhausting. After dawn, I fell asleep in the chair. Woke and saw the girls were gone. Stumbled like a drunkard through the house, hunting them. Just before I found them in the family room, I heard them screaming."

The seeming indifference in Clitherow's voice didn't sound like stoicism, not like an intentional suppression of feeling. It was apathy, the consequence of reaching a tipping point. Having felt too much for too long, he was drained of feeling, of the desire to feel.

"In the living room, Emily and Sarah, still in their pajamas, ran toward me, weeping, screaming. I opened my arms, but they pushed away, eluded me. They ran into the kitchen, up the back stairs. And I saw they'd been watching television. And I saw on the screen...my wife, naked and chained to a wall. And she was still alive. And a man, face concealed by a hood, he was...he was...cutting her."

As I listened to John Clitherow, the cell phone grew damp and slippery in my hand. I held it tighter.

"And I didn't hear the girls screaming anymore," he continued. "I went upstairs to find them. And they weren't in the bedroom where they had slept, where I'd watched over them. And they weren't in the next room or the next. And they weren't downstairs. And they weren't in the backyard. They were gone. And I never found them."

Suddenly I wanted Penny to take the next exit, turn away from the place to which we were headed. We weren't detectives, we didn't know how to gather evidence and build a case. Besides, if we went where Waxx had been, if we probed his past, he was more likely to find us. The shadow of the predator is no place for the prey to hide.

John Clitherow droned through a nightmare that was no less terrifying for the flat tone of his voice: "And I went back into the family room where my wife was still on the TV. And he was still doing things to her. And on the floor in front of the TV were the pajamas my daughters were wearing when they ran screaming from the room, returned to me like my wife's rings were returned. I tried to take the DVD out of the player, there was no DVD. I changed channels. She was dying on all of them. And something happened to me then, I don't remember clearly, and I think I smashed the TV screen with a lamp. And I knew Jerry kept a gun in the house. And I searched and found it and loaded it with one round. I was going to kill myself."

I had not said anything to Clitherow in a while. Nothing I could say would make any difference. He didn't need to hear me speak to know that I was listening.

His voice sounded more lifeless than ever: "Maybe I didn't have the courage for suicide, or all the years I believed in the sanctity of life made suicide impossible. And gradually I started wanting to kill Waxx more than I wanted to die. So I put nine more cartridges in the gun. And I waited for him. And three days passed. And the phone rang. Waxx said just 'Porch.' And on the back porch I found a DVD."

Evidently Penny determined from my expression and my posture that I was in the thrall of an abhorrence so absolute that it nearly paralyzed me. My left hand was fisted on my thigh, and she closed her right hand tightly over it.

"And for a day I could not look at the DVD. And then I did. And my daughters were chained to a wall. And they must have been coached, promised mercy for cooperation, because they cried and pleaded to the camera, 'Daddy, don't hurt us again. Daddy, please let us go.' And then. And then they. And the horror began, and I turned it off. And the DVD was evidence, but evidence that falsely incriminated me."

Speeding into the cold rain, fast into the black night, we would eventually come head-on to a wall not of stone but of a solidified darkness, the iron-dense and perfect evil of Shearman Waxx.

"I don't know what he did with their remains. Since then I've stayed alive. Hoping to find him, kill him. Now I realize that was a delusion. He is untouchable, Cullen. He is the night itself."

John hesitated, and then wandered into an alley of depressive philosophy: "The innocent die, the wicked prosper. With a cunning ability to invert the truth, evil men claim to be noble, and people abandon reason, bow down to them, and accept all kinds of slavery."

Once a man with faith, with confidence in the common sense of the average man, Clitherow seemed surprised to hear himself speak those dismal words, for he inhaled sharply and after a pause returned to Waxx: "He's untouchable, relentless. Cullen, you think you escaped him. But he didn't want any of you to die in the house explosion. He wanted only to take it from you. If I hadn't phoned when I did, if I hadn't told you to get out, he would have called to warn you."

Implicit in that statement was the assumption that Waxx had been monitoring my phones, and not only knew that Clitherow had called but knew as well what he had told me.

"Cullen, he didn't want any of you to die in the explosion, because he breaks us down to ruins, step by step, not all at once. And now I am in the tower *de Paris* with—"

A noise both wretched and pitiable came through the phone line, and at first I thought that emotion had returned to Clitherow in a sudden stroke, that he was choking with grief.

A moment later, I realized this was more agony than anguish. It had been precipitated by a sound not made by the writer: a ripping noise, vicious and wet. I was listening to a man being murdered.

His phone dropped from his hand, clattered on the floor, did not disconnect. Briefly, his death throes issued from a distance.

But then came the thud-and-clump of a body falling. Perhaps his head was again close to the phone, because I heard him clearly. He seemed to be trying simultaneously to gasp for breath and to vomit.

I imagined that his throat had been slashed, that he was choking on his own blood.

I prayed for an end to his misery and at the same time hoped for one last gargled word, a revelation.

In mere seconds, Clitherow was finished and silent.

Earlier, when he became emotional and I suggested he call me back later or not at all, he said something that now had new meaning: *"I have to tell you. You don't understand. I have to tell you."*

He had not been surprised during the call by his murderer. They placed the call together. At the point of a knife, John Clitherow was forced to repeat the hideous story of his family's destruction both for my benefit and for his humiliation.

Before me, hard shatters of rain rattled off the windshield.

At some point after the calls that John made to me at our house earlier in the day, he fell into Waxx's hands. He used a disposable phone, but he called my listed number, not knowing that Waxx was already after me, and somehow that was his undoing.

We swept past a vehicle parked on the shoulder of the highway. I got only a rain-blurred glimpse of it, but I thought it was a black SUV. Not a Cadillac Escalade, surely not. Waxx couldn't be everywhere at once. No headlights appeared behind us in the side mirror.

Over the open phone line, from the scene of the murder, other noises arose: the killer in motion. He fumbled the phone when he picked it up. Then came his slow steady breathing.

Determined not to be the first to speak, I listened to him as he listened to me. My resolution did not hold, and although I knew who he must be, I said, "Who is this?"

His voice was low and gravelly, ripe with a false good humor that could not conceal the underlying menace: "Hello there, brother."

This was not Shearman Waxx, unless he was a man of many voices.

"Brother," he said, "are you with me?"

"I'm not your brother," I said.

"All men are my brothers," he assured me.

"Waxx? Is that you? Who are you?"

"I am my brothers' reaper," he said. His soft laugh was ugly.

I put down the passenger-door window, pressed END on my cell phone, and threw it into the night.

Chapter 42

Twenty minutes before midnight, Penny exited the inter-state at the first truck stop that appeared after I tossed away the phone. Bad weather put the long-haulers behind schedule, and they did not linger at the diner. The parking lot was mostly empty, and business slow.

She stopped under the shelter of one of several service islands, where ours was the sole vehicle at the pumps. We got out, leaving Milo and Lassie asleep in the backseat.

Neither of us thought it wise to run one of our credit cards through the scanner. Loath to leave her and Milo, I nevertheless hurried inside to put down the cash to get the pump unlocked.

The cashier was a good old boy with a plug of chaw tucked in his cheek, the kind who could talk the quills off a porcupine, and who was no doubt full of entertaining stories. He was great material for a novelist, but I was neither in Florida nor doing book research.

I pretended to be unable to speak English and invented a quasi-Slavic language of my own, which complicated communication enough to discourage him without insulting him. By the time I got back to the Mountaineer, Penny had the hose nozzle in the tank, and the numbers were spinning on the totalizers.

Beyond the service-island overhang, in the windless night, the rain came down in such straight skeins that the rigorous lines should have proved the law of gravity to any disbeliever, of which I'm sure there are multitudes, considering we live in an age of enthusiastic ignorance, when anything well-known for centuries is not only suspect but also considered worthy of being rejected in favor of a new theory more appealing to movie stars and deep-thinking rock musicians.

In spite of Milo's admonition that he was a kid but not a kid, I had not wanted him to hear about John Clitherow's brutal murder or what the writer had told me about the fate of his wife and two daughters. Now I gave Penny a condensed version but spared her none of the grim truth.

Although she didn't say my story had given her an appetite, she took the grisly details well, glancing worriedly at the backseat windows of the Mountaineer, in the direction of our sleeping son, only thirty or forty times.

She pumped all the gasoline we paid for and racked the hose in the nozzle boot, but we remained standing under the shelter, pale plumes of our breath smoking in the chilly air.

"So Waxx has a partner," she said, "a psycho best friend."

"And he sounds like a real peach, too."

"That explains why he was able to do so much, so fast."

"John Clitherow called him relentless. Easier to be relentless when you've got a posse."

"What the hell is this all about, Cubby? This morning, Clitherow told you Waxx was not just a critic with opinions but a critic with an agenda. *What* agenda?"

"I don't think he knew. It's just what he felt. But can a madman have an agenda that's anything else but mad? If we knew his agenda, we still wouldn't understand him or be able to deal more effectively with him. He'd still be nuts, and nutcases are unpredictable."

"I'm not so sure he's certifiably insane."

"Careful, sugar, or I'm going to think *you're* certifiable."

"Oh," she said, "he's freaking insane, all right, but he's pretty much one of the elite class that determines the rules of the culture, including who's certifiable and who's not. They don't lock themselves up. They carry the keys."

"Inmates in charge of the asylum, huh?"

"Are you going to pretend you haven't noticed?"

"Sounds like you're about ready to build our own stronghold."

"Don't think I haven't considered it."

"Listen, Penny, we've got to change plans now."

"Change what plans? Landulf?"

Thomas Landulf, the author of *The Falconer and the Monk,* who was reputed to have cruelly tortured and murdered his wife and daughter before setting himself afire, had lived and died in a small Northern California community not far from the Oregon border, a place called Smokeville. That's where we were currently headed.

In our desperation, the Landulf murders appeared to be the only place we could start building a case against Waxx. If Landulf had been well-liked in Smokeville, the locals might not buy the official story. They might know things that were never brought up at the inquest or reported in the media, things we might find worth knowing.

I said, "Clitherow is a lesson to us. He was safe. Then he tried to help us. By helping us, he gave Waxx a chance to get a new bead on him. If we start poking around up there in Smokeville, maybe Waxx or his buddy, the brother of all humanity, will hear about it."

The look she gave me was not one I would have photographed and kept forever in our book of fond memories.

"So what do you want to do instead?" she asked. "You want to go to Waxx's house in Laguna Beach, knock on the door, confront him?"

"No thanks, no way. I've seen *The Silence of the Lambs*. I know what happens to people who go into Mr. Gumb's house."

"So then what is your Plan B?"

I listened carefully, but I didn't hear myself saying anything. Only frosty plumes of breath came from my slack-jawed mouth.

"You just want to give up our lives and go on the run forever, like Clitherow?" she asked.

"No, no. I know that won't work. We Greenwiches, we're runners, but not the Booms."

"Damn right. Now more than ever, we have to go to Smokeville."

I stood there nodding stupidly, like one of those novelty dogs with a bobble head.

"Is this discussion over?" she asked.

"Well, I don't seem to be able to hold up my end of it, so I guess it's over."

"Good. We're maybe three hours south of San Francisco. You drive. It's my turn to catch some Z's."

I got behind the wheel. She settled in the shotgun position.

In the backseat, Milo was sleeping, and Lassie was sleeping but also farting. Fortunately, when she passed gas, the mutt produced a high flutelike note but no stink. Barkless, odorless, she seemed to strive always to give no offense.

As I followed the long entry ramp to the northbound lanes of the interstate, Penny said, "What was that last thing Clitherow said, the bit that didn't make sense, just before his throat was cut?"

"I think it was 'and now I'm in the tower *de Paris* with—' Then just gagging-wheezing noises."

"*De Paris.* 'Of Paris.' The Eiffel Tower? Was he calling you from Paris?"

"No. I don't think so. The knife was at his throat, he was done with the story they wanted him to tell me, he knew he was about to be cut—so maybe his mind snapped and he was just babbling."

"Did it sound like babble?"

"No," I admitted. "It was in that same terrible, flat tone of voice."

"Then it meant something," Penny said. "It meant something."

Chapter 43

I alone remained awake in the Mountaineer, unable to engage anyone in therapeutic conversation, and nothing relieved the solemn drum-drum-drumming of the rain except an occasional flute note from the musical dog.

My thoughts returned to John Clitherow's story of the murders of his wife and daughters. Waxx had wanted me to hear it directly from the doomed writer.

His purpose must be in part to demoralize me, to frighten me to the extent that fear ceased to motivate me and instead inhibited me from taking aggressive action in defense of myself and my family.

Remembering how I pressed Penny not to proceed to Smokeville, I realized with dismay how effective Waxx's strategy had already been.

Demoralization to the point of paralysis, however, was not his entire intent. Before killing John, Waxx had wanted to grind him down until he abandoned the view of life that had informed his books.

Embedded in that second intention was a clue to Waxx's agenda, the reason why—besides the thrill of murder—he wanted to kill John and Tom Landulf and me.

As I motored on through the night and rain, I became aware of Penny murmuring in what seemed to be a pleasant dream and of Milo snoring in the backseat—and just then Lassie orchestrated their noises into a serenade by adding a series of odorless toots.

This humble interval not only amused me but also struck me as immeasurably precious, one of those prosaic moments from which so much delight can be taken that the world *must* have been created as a place of joy. No machine universe, stupidly cranking onward, could produce moments of grace from such lowly material.

Here was why Waxx and men like him must not be allowed to achieve their ends. The world wasn't theirs. They could claim it only with the use of lies, intimidation, and violence. If we let them win, there would be no moments of grace, humble or glorious, ever again.

For most of my life, I had a covenant with Death to spare others as once I was spared, to be a man of peace. Such a covenant ceased to be noble and in fact became a shameful thing if it required that I not defend my life or the lives of the innocent.

Soon after dawn, we needed to find a lonely place where Penny could teach me rudimentary marksmanship.

Then, too, she would learn that early in our relationship, I deceived her by omission, and also deceived myself by pretending that withholding information from her was not a kind of lie, when indeed it could be nothing else.

She knew my parents died when I was six. She misunderstood that they perished in a car accident, and I allowed her misunderstanding to go uncorrected.

She knew that I had been raised thereafter by a wise and caring maiden aunt—Edith Greenwich—who had died of a swift-moving cancer when I was twenty.

Penny assumed that Aunt Edith must be my father's sister. I did not correct her assumption.

Gentle Edith, my mother's only sister, adopted me to ensure that I would not grow up as a figure of either pity or suspicion, bearing a notorious surname associated in the nation's mind with horror and extreme violence.

Because I had no living relatives except a couple of second cousins with whom I was not in contact, Penny also assumed that I came from a small family, the branches of which had withered away over the generations. I allowed that assumption to go uncorrected.

Once I had a brother, Phelim, who was six years my senior. The name Phelim is Irish and means "constantly good." As much as I can remember of him, he was true to his name, a kind brother.

My father's first name was Farrel, which is Celtic and means "valiant man." My most vivid memory of him proves that he was worthy of that designation.

My mother was Kirsten, which is a name from the Old English word meaning "church," which itself is derived from the Greek word meaning "of the Lord." After twenty-eight years, I recall most clearly three things about her: the beauty of her green eyes, the tenderness with which she treated me and Phelim, and her rich and contagious laugh.

My father had three brothers: Ewen, a name that is a Welsh form of John; Kenton, which derives from a Gaelic word for "handsome;" and Trahern, called Tray, which is Old Welsh meaning "strong as iron."

Of Ewen and Kenton, my father's older brothers, I remember too little. They were businessmen and, like my father, always working.

Trahern, the youngest of the four brothers, had a close-cropped stubble of blond hair, a two-inch livid scar slanting across his forehead, bloodshot blue eyes, chapped lips, sour breath, grime under his fingernails, and icy hands.

I vividly remember those things about him from that long-ago day in September, but I recall nothing about him from prior encounters. For me, he seems to have been reborn on that autumn evening, so new and singular that his past was washed out of time's record, much as a born-again man of faith will say that his sins were washed away in baptism, though Tray baptized himself that evening, not in water but in blood.

Tray's last name—also my father's, also mine back in that September—was Durant, which may ring a bell less loudly now than it did in the day when it was above the fold on all newspapers for weeks, in six-inch letters on the covers of the sleazier tabloids, and repeated like an evil mantra on TV news.

I opened the door to him.

Chapter 44

I am six years old. Every morning is a call to adventure. Every evening is a promise of mystery, especially this evening in mid-September.

The air is cool and the light is sharp, but by late afternoon, the edge wears off the sun, whereafter the day is blue and gold and magical during the drive out from the city.

Twilight distills blue into purple, reduces purple to crimson, by the time the family gathers for a celebration at the spacious farmhouse Uncle Ewen has bought and restored.

His forty-acre property by the river is not a working farm. A large freehold has been subdivided into smaller parcels.

The river runs red under the stain of sunset. Ripples, whorls, and lapping wavelets imply that exotic forms of life swarm under the surface.

My uncle has bought the place to have a weekend refuge from the city. As a man who plans ahead, he intends to retire to these fields and gentle hills in two decades.

In the dining-room fireplace, the andirons are brass griffins. They have wings and seem to be flying toward me, out of the fire.

My father, Ewen, and Kenton own a numismatics business. They buy and sell collectible antique coins as well as contemporary gold coins and bars desired for the protection they offer against inflation.

The brothers also have expanded into a proprietary line of gold and silver jewelry. They find good profits with every endeavor.

As I wander through the party, an unusual grandfather clock in the living room enchants me. Carved from mahogany, a monkey climbs the cabinet. His long arms, reaching up, encircle the face, while the fingers of his hands entwine above the twelve. His tail is the pendulum.

"Time is a monkey," Uncle Ewen tells me. "Full of mischief, unpredictable, quick as a cat, with a nasty bite."

At six, I have no idea what he means, but I like his words and their enigmatic quality.

Ewen, Kenton, and my father are the kind of men who view success as a reason to share. The entire family is lifted on their shoulders. Every employee is a relative, and enjoys a profit-sharing plan.

Only Tray is not part of the enterprise. He lacks the sense of responsibility for a position with his brothers. Besides, having no interest in real work, he would turn them down if made an offer.

Tray remains out of jail in spite of scrapes with the law. As will be discovered, he operates an illegal methamphetamine lab.

Ewen's housewarming draws all the family except Tray, who has not been invited, and my mother's sister, Edith, who lives nine hundred miles away.

Counting Ewen, his wife, Nora, and their daughter, Colleen, thirty-nine family members are present, including children.

An hour after sunset, Tray arrives unexpectedly. He is so estranged from the family that none of them has seen him in six months. No one imagines he knows about the gathering.

I am in the front hall when he knocks.

Through a moon-and-cloud pattern of clear and frosted leaded glass, I recognize Tray on the front porch. Seeing me, he puts his eye to the clear moon and winks.

I open the door to him.

"Cubby," he says, "clean up your act, kid. You've got a string of snot hangin' out of your nose."

When I wipe at my nose with a sleeve, he laughs, plants a damp icy palm against my face, and shoves me aside so hard I almost fall.

Closing the door, he brings the gun out from under his long coat: a compact, fully automatic rifle, essentially a short-barreled sub-machine gun capable of single-shot or continuous-fire action.

He grabs me by the hair and pulls me with him into the archway between hall and living room. Then he shoves me forward while he remains straddling the two spaces.

People see the weapon and shy back, but they do not at once try to flee, as though openly acknowledging the threat of violence will precipitate it.

The guests are distributed throughout the four main rooms of the lower floor, but Uncle Ewen happens to be in the living room when his errant younger brother appears.

"Hewey," Tray says, "how're they hangin'?"

Ewen remains cool. "What do you want, Tray? What do you need?"

"I don't know, Hewey. Maybe . . . two million in coin inventory?"

As it unfolds, Tray has heard a rumor—or has fantasized—about his brothers splitting their inventory between the walk-in safe at the shop and a secret safe in Ewen's newly restored farmhouse.

In truth, their inventory is only a fraction of what he imagines it to be, and the safe at the shop contains all their holdings.

Tray professes not to believe Ewen on either point. A short discussion ensues between them.

I cannot take my eyes off the gun. The weapon gleams like a magic object, like a sword once frozen in stone but pulled free, except the sorcery in this case is a dark variety.

Yet I do not realize that it might be used. The weapon is an object of wonder, magical because of its appearance alone, and does not need to function in order to cast a spell.

Because of the through-the-house music system and many lively conversations, the guests elsewhere do not hear the quiet drama in the living room. They do not remain out of the loop for long, because Tray soon makes some noise.

Kenton's sixteen-year-old daughter, my cousin Davena, stands beside an armchair.

After calling Ewen a liar, Tray says, "Hey, Davena, you're all grown up and pretty. When did that happen?"

Davena smiles nervously, not sure what to say. When she smiles, a dimple forms in her right cheek. Her ears are delicate and smooth, like blown glass.

Tray shoots her twice, and she falls dead over the footstool, her face in the carpet and covered by her hair, bottom in the air, skirt tossed up and panties revealed.

Although the word "dignity" is not in my vocabulary yet, I know this is wrong. I want to pull her skirt down, lay her on the floor, on her back, and smooth the hair away from her face.

Strangely, I do not think of her as dead, not right away. That is a recognition from which I rebel.

I do not want Davena to look foolish or clumsy, because she is in fact smart and graceful. No matter how much I feel that I should attend to her, arrange her in a more suitable fashion, I cannot move.

The gunfire draws shouts of surprise from other rooms.

Some people try to flee.

But Tray has come with two friends. They kick through the back door into the kitchen, through the side door into the dining room.

People scream, but the farmhouse is far from any neighbor.

My father, also in the living room, must realize the time for effective resistance is quickly fading. He seizes an eighteen-inch bronze statue of a farm boy and his dog, and rushes Tray, winding up the art work to swing it when he is close enough.

Tray shoots him in the face. And shoots him twice again as he lies dead on the floor.

I watch it happen, turn away.

Resorting to the magical thinking that children use to cope with trauma, I tell myself that my father will be okay until the ambulance arrives. The medics will rush him and Cousin Davena to the hospital, where both will be revived in the nick of time—revived, healed, home soon.

In the nick of time. The right thing always happens in the nick of time. Every storybook says so.

No one goes out through any window before the three gunmen have control of the residence.

They herd the family into the living room and dining room. They make everyone sit either on the furniture or on the floor.

Tray goes to work on Ewen again, demanding the location of the secret safe, the fortune in coins that does not exist.

Ewen offers to take Tray to the brothers' store and open that—the only—safe.

Tray thinks the risk is not worth taking when a Midas trove is hidden in this very house.

I am not listening to much of their argument, and I am so young, with the limited perceptions of an ordinary child, yet I sense Tray does not really believe in the secret treasure room. This is a story he invented to induce his buddies to come there with him.

In truth he has one and only one intention: to kill us all. Some atavistic part of my brain, afire with primitive wisdom older than I am, brings me finally to the recognition that two are dead and that others will be killed soon.

With Davena and my father murdered, the men who came with Tray have nothing to lose. As accomplices and kidnappers, they are already candidates for death sentences or life in prison.

Later, police will determine that Tray and the other two were amped on methamphetamine—and in a mood to make a sport of violence.

In frustration, Tray uses the butt of his weapon to smash Ewen's face, then shoots him in the stomach.

By this time, I am no longer turned away from what is happening. I am so afraid, but for some reason I feel that I must watch.

Tray no longer has any interest in the secret trove of inventory that he has known does not exist. He is Fate, and exhibiting the cold enthusiasm of a serpent going egg to egg in a henhouse, he moves deliberately from one seated relative to the next.

He greets each of them by name, sometimes calls them an ugly word or makes an obscene suggestion, sometimes offers a compliment. Regardless of what he says, he shoots each of them to death.

Two curious things happen in that farmhouse, and this is the first: Even after the initial deaths, there are enough people in the living room to rush Tray and overpower him before he can shoot them all, yet no one makes a move against him. They see him kill each of them in the order they are seated, and those still alive weep or beg, or sit in a silent daze, but they offer no resistance.

We see this occur on other occasions in the twenty-eight years since the Durant killings, but on that night it is a new phenomenon.

Are the victims so committed to a reasoned disbelief in the existence of Evil that, when face-to-face with its agent, they are incapable of acknowledging their error?

Or are they capable of recognizing Evil but unable to believe there is a power opposed to it that stands ready to give them the strength— and a reason—to survive?

Perhaps it is the nurtured narcissism of our age that leaves some unable to imagine their deaths even as the bullet is in the barrel.

This is the second curious thing that happens in that farmhouse: I survive. How I survive is easy to describe. *Why* I survive is beyond my ability to explain.

After watching Tray kill three more people where they sit, all fear lifts from me, and I know what I must do.

I do not run. I do not hide. Neither option crosses my mind.

First I go to my cousin Davena and restore her modesty by straightening her skirt. And that feels right.

As carefully as I can, I roll her off the footstool over which she has collapsed, and I get her onto her back. I smooth her hair away from her lovely face.

I say, "Good-bye."

My father's face is broken and fallen inward. Over the arm of a chair is Aunt Helen's shawl. I arrange it to drape my father's ruined countenance.

"Good-bye."

Tray proceeds through the room, killing people one by one, and I follow several deaths behind him, restoring where I can some small measure of dignity to the deceased.

A psychologist might say these are the actions of a boy in a dissociative state, but that is not correct. As I minister to the dead, I remain at all times aware of what I am doing, of where I am, and I know that the killings are proceeding beyond my control, in this room and subsequently in the next.

Not only has fear been lifted from me but also horror, and for the purpose of completing my task, I seem to have lost the capacity for repugnance. These are members of my family, and nothing about them in death can disgust me, just as nothing about them in life disgusted me.

To each, I say good-bye.

I am conveyed across the bar of grief, that I might do this service, and though the day will come when I will find myself on the harder side of that bar, for now I do not weep.

Cousin Carina, one week short of her twentieth birthday, sits on a chair with a cane back, head lolling against the wall. Before being shot, she lost control of her bladder. Her skirt is soaked, and her stockings.

As I move toward the sofa to get a camel-colored cashmere throw, with which to cover Carina's lap and legs, I step aside to let one of Tray's friends pass.

He is a pale man with a mustache. An ugly cold sore mars his lower lip. He is looking for women's purses.

While I arrange the cashmere throw to cover Carina properly— "Good-bye"—and while I examine the remaining victims to see if there is anything I can do to make them more presentable, the man with the cold sore rummages through the purses for money and takes the wallets from the dead men.

He does not speak to me, and I do not speak to him.

Tray enters and says to his friend, "I'm gonna see what shit they might have upstairs."

"Be quick about it, this is so goddamn off the rails," his friend replies. "Where's Clapper?"

"In the dining room, doin' what you're doin.'"

Having done what I can for the twenty dead in the living room, I proceed to the dining room to continue with my mission.

Tray's other friend, Clapper, is a large bearded man. On the dining table are gathered the purses and the wallets of the eighteen victims in this room. He is stripping out the folding money as he half mutters and half sings "Another One Bites the Dust," which had been a hit for Queen a couple of years earlier.

My brother, Phelim, who is twelve, sits on the floor in a corner, his back to the junction of walls. His legs are straight out in front of him, arms at his sides. Except for the hole in his throat, he looks peaceful. I cannot see anything to be done for him.

"Good-bye." I do not whisper the word but say it openly.

Apparently the people on the dining-room chairs were instructed to put their arms behind them and to hook them between horizontal backrails. They are not only sitting in their chairs but also hanging from them. This prevents the limp bodies from collapsing onto the floor.

My cousin Kipp's wife, Nicola, has been humiliated before being murdered. Her sweater has been pulled over her head, hiding her face, and her bra has been torn off.

I am an easily embarrassed boy. With great care not to touch her breasts, I work the sweater off her head and gingerly tug it down over what should not be exposed.

While I struggle with the sweater, Clapper finishes searching purses and wallets. Fists full of money, he goes to the living room.

He and the man with the cold sore are talking, but I am not interested in what they have to say to each other.

In the last chair, I find my mother.

I very much want to do some small thing for her.

After a moment, I see what it must be. She is proud of her dark glossy hair, but now it is tangled and disarranged, as if someone has seized it and twisted it to force her into the chair.

Among the purses on the table, I recognize hers. I take from it a comb, and I return to her.

Her face is lowered, chin on chest. As I am deciding how to hold her head to raise it, the more easily to comb her hair, Tray returns to the room from his search of the second floor.

He has his gun, which no longer seems magical, and I wait to see what he will do.

As he crosses the room toward me, I know that I should be afraid, but I am not.

He passes me, proceeds to Nicola, picks up her bra from the floor, and works it in his hand. Frowning, he stares down at her covered breasts.

Shreds of skin hang from his chapped lips, and he chews on them absentmindedly.

After a moment, he throws the bra aside and calls out "Clapper," as he goes into the living room.

I wait with my mother and the comb.

All three men return to stare at Nicola, at her sweater as it should be.

Raising his gun, warily but with some urgency, Clapper pushes through the swinging door into the kitchen.

The man with the cold sore disappears into the hall, and Tray into the living room.

I wait with my mother and the comb.

From overhead comes the sound of hurried footsteps. In the cellar, a door crashes open. For a minute or so, every corner of the house produces noises.

The three meet in the hall. I cannot hear what they are saying, or I choose not to hear, but judging by the tone of each voice, Tray is angry and the other two are alarmed.

Their voices and footsteps recede. A door opens, slams shut, and I am pretty sure it is the door with the frosted-glass clouds and the clear-glass moon through which Tray's eye once winked at me.

The house is quiet.

Outside, a car starts. I listen to the engine noise as it fades down the driveway.

I put a hand under my mother's chin and lift her head. I comb her beautiful hair.

When her hair is as it should be, I kiss her cheek. Every night, she tucks me into bed and kisses my cheek. Every night until now.

"Good-bye."

I ease her head down as it was. She appears to be slumped in sleep. She has gone to another place but still loves me, and though I am staying here, I still love her.

After returning the comb to her purse, I cannot imagine what comes next. I have done what I could to spare the dead embarrassment, and I am no longer needed.

Suddenly I am more exhausted than I have ever been. Climbing the stairs in search of a bed, I almost stop to sleep on the landing.

I forge on, however, and choose the bed in Colleen's room, onto which I climb without remembering to take off my shoes. Head on the pillow, I am too tired to worry about being scolded.

I wake during the night and see a frosted moon in the window. But it is far beyond the window, and it is real.

After using the bathroom across the hall, I return to Colleen's room and stand staring at her telephone. I have the feeling that I should call someone, but I do not know whom.

A few months earlier, my mother helped me to memorize our home-phone number, all ten digits, in case I am ever lost.

I am in Uncle Ewen's new house, so I am not lost. Strangely, however, I feel I am somewhere I do not belong, and I feel alone.

Deciding to call home, I pick up the phone. No dial tone.

I am not afraid. I am calm. I go to Uncle Ewen and Aunt Nora's bedroom. I try their phone, but it does not work, either.

Descending the stairs, I am overcome by an expectation of a big discovery, whether good or bad I do not know, but something *huge*. I hesitate on the landing, but then continue to descend.

The house is as silent as a soundless dream. Never before in the waking world have I encountered such stillness.

When I try the phone in the living room, it proves to be out of order, like the others.

Standing before the grandfather clock, I decide the monkey is not time, as Uncle Ewen said. Instead, the monkey is stealing time.

Previously, the creature's face was impish, its expression playful. Now it is a monkey from a different jungle. It seems to sneer, and in its eyes I see a threat that I cannot name.

Backing away from the clock, I think I hear a woman laughing in the dining room. Indeed, this is my mother's contagious laughter, but for once it does not inspire as much as a smile from me.

In the dining room, I do not hear the laughter anymore, and there is no phone to try.

The brass griffins still fly in the fireplace, but the logs they carried on their backs are ashes now, and embers.

Silence settles once more, and I am unable to hear the hinges on the swinging door or even my footsteps as I go into the kitchen.

The telephone on the wall beside the refrigerator is as useless as the previous three.

At a kitchen window, I stare into the moonlit night. No one is in the backyard, either.

They have all gone away.

I wander through the house, downstairs and upstairs, and down again, feeling lost and alone. Twice, I think I hear footsteps in the distance, but when I stand quite still and listen, I hear nothing.

Eventually, I am in Uncle Ewen's study for the third or fourth time. Previously, I did not notice the telephone.

Putting the receiver to my ear, I am surprised by a dial tone.

As I will later learn, the phone-service cable was cut outside the house. But in the interest of business security, because of his sensitive financial discussions conducted by phone, my uncle Ewen required an entirely separate, dedicated private line to serve his study, and that one was overlooked.

Using the keypad, I enter 1 plus the ten digits of our home number that I have memorized. It rings until the answering machine picks up. I hear Mother's recorded voice.

Following the beep, I can think of no message to leave. Although I have said nothing else, I say "Good-bye" before I hang up.

After further thought, I dial 911.

When the sheriff's-department operator answers, I say, "They all went away, and I'm alone here."

In response to her questions, I tell her my name, that I am six years old, that I am at Ewen Durant's house, and that I have been alone since before eight o'clock the previous evening.

According to Ewen's desk clock, it is now 4:32 in the morning.

Also on the desk is a framed photo of Aunt Nora, Cousin Colleen.

"I slept some, like two hours," I tell the operator, "but since before midnight, I been looking, nobody's here. I didn't take off my shoes before getting on Colleen's bed, so I'm probably in trouble."

She asks me if I know where they have gone, and I say no, and she tells me a deputy will come to help me, and I say thank you, and she says not to be afraid, and I say I am not afraid, just alone.

Leaving the house through the front door, I am surprised to see all the cars along the driveway. It leads down to the state highway, and a dozen vehicles stand one behind the other on the shoulder.

The night is mild and full of stars, with a smell of mown grass.

I watch moths gliding under the soft light in the porch ceiling, where one of the two bulbs is burned out. They make no sound.

I sit on the top porch step to wait.

I hear the approaching engine before I see the sheriff's-department cruiser far down on the highway. No siren, no flashing lights. It slows, turns onto the driveway, and comes to the head of the line of parked vehicles.

The deputy who gets out of the cruiser reminds me of the tall motorcycle cop on that TV show, *CHiPS,* and I know he will help me as soon as I see him.

I stand up as he approaches, and he says, "You must be Cubby," and I say, "Yes, sir," and he says, "So you're alone here," and I say, "Yes, sir," and he asks who all the vehicles belong to, and I say, "To my aunts and uncles and cousins. That one there is my dad's." He looks at all the house's lighted windows and asks where my folks are, and I say, "They're gone, sir," and he asks if I know where they've gone, and I say, "No, sir."

He follows me to the open front door, where he rings the bell, and when no one answers, he calls, "Anybody home?"

I figure policemen have to do things their way, by the rules, so I do not remind him that I am alone.

He asks me to show him the way, and I lead him through the open door with the clouds and the moon.

Just across the threshold, in the front hall, the deputy says, "Son? Cubby? Wait a minute."

I turn to look up at him. His face has changed, and not just because the light is brighter here.

"What's wrong?" I ask.

"Your shoes."

My sneakers are more red than white, and dark, and wet with blood. On the wood floor around me are bloody footprints.

With his right hand, the deputy draws his revolver, and with his left, he pulls me to his side and half behind him.

In three steps, he reaches the archway between the hall and the living room, and he says, "Oh, my God."

Looking past him, I see everyone dead, and now I remember what happened before I went to sleep in Colleen's room.

Soon many deputies and the sheriff himself are at the house, plus other people not in uniform, who seem as busy as the police.

The sheriff is a nice man, tall and older and with a belly, but he does not listen well.

I tell him that because I was not afraid, Tray and his friends could not see me. The sheriff says I must have found a hiding place.

I tell him that after I woke up in Colleen's room, I forgot what happened for a while. But because I was not afraid and because the dead people did not want to frighten me, I could not see them, just like Tray could not see me.

The authorities conclude I combed my mother's hair and restored the dignity of other victims *after* Tray and his buddies left.

But I know the truth. Most memories from early childhood fade or vanish altogether, but my memories of that night are as clear as if the event were only a week in the past.

I know how I survived. I do not know why.

That night and the next day, I do not cry. They say I am brave, but I am not. I am instead the recipient of a great mercy, because upon me was conferred a power of endurance, emotional and mental, that is far beyond my six years. It will remain with me until my name is changed, and will for the rest of my life seem unearned.

Months later, a court rules behind closed doors, and thereafter I am Cubby Greenwich, living with Aunt Edith in a new city.

That evening, at long last, the grief comes and the tears. The murderers are in their cells, the murdered in their graves. Tears can wash away all that has obstructed hope, and grief that does not break us will only make us stronger.

What psychological problems I experience for a couple of years are all related to these facts: I am the one who heard Tray knock; I am the first to see him on the front porch; I am the one at whom he winked through the clear moon, as if we were conspirators; I am the one who opened the door to him; I am the sole survivor.

I feel to a degree responsible and believe illogically that no one else would have opened the door to Tray.

Furthermore, for a long time I will not answer a door because of the irrational fear that others like Tray and his two friends will be drawn to me because they know I will always grant them entrance.

Sessions with a psychologist are unproductive.

Although she has little experience of children, my aunt Edith possesses the wisdom and patience to show me that guilt requires fault and that fault requires intention. She works, as well, on my irrational fear and convinces me in time that I have no reason to be afraid of a knock or a doorbell: *I am not a magnet for monsters.*

Like her sister, my mother, Edith loves to laugh, and from her I learn that laughter is our armor and our sword.

Years later, when I am twenty and Edith is on her deathbed, I tell her that I believe I was spared that night in September for a reason, for something of importance that I will one day be called upon to do. And Providence put me in her care because she was kind and wise enough to heal me and therefore prepare me for whatever task will be required of me. I tell her she is as good a soul as I have ever met or hope to meet, that she is an angel in the flesh, and that I will speak her name to God every night of my life before I go to sleep.

Chapter 45

Penny slept, Milo slept, and the dog sat looking out a window and sighing periodically as I drove north on the Golden Gate Bridge.

Halfway across the bay, the rain abruptly diminished, and by the time we reached the northern shore, I was able to turn off the windshield wipers.

More than an hour later, past Santa Rosa, at four o'clock in the morning, Milo woke, said he could go another hour without peeing, and rummaged quietly through his gear until the backseat brightened with an unusual pale blue light.

Hoping not to wake Penny, I asked softly, "What's that?"

"This thing," Milo said, matching my quiet tone.

"What thing?"

"This thing that makes it happen."

"Makes what happen?" I asked.

The dog sighed, probably with pity for me, and Milo said, "What nobody would believe could happen."

I said, "I might believe it could happen. Try me."

"Oh, man," Milo whispered, impressed by something he had just seen, "this is radical."

"I've got a strong and limber imagination," I reminded him.

"Not this limber."

"Come on, tell me."

"It's too complicated to tell," Milo said.

"I love complicated."

"Dad, you don't have the scientific background to understand."

"If you don't tell me, I'll turn on the radio."

"So turn on the radio."

"I'll find a fire-and-brimstone preacher station."

"Then I'll blow up the car."

"You won't blow up the car."

"Try me," Milo said.

"You wouldn't hurt your mother."

"I could blow up just the driver's seat."

"That's a fake-out. You can't blow up just the driver's seat."

"Try me."

"Come on, Milo. Driving hour after hour is boring. I need some mental stimulation."

"All right. Which came first—the chicken or the egg? Think about it."

"That's bogus. There's no answer. It's a paradox."

"There's an answer."

"So tell me the answer," I challenged.

"If I just tell you, that's no mental stimulation."

"I don't want to know about chickens and eggs."

The blue light pulsed in the backseat, and Milo said, "Wow."

"I want to know about the *thing* that makes it *happen*."

"Makes what happen?" Milo asked.

Fresh from her nap, Penny said, "Remind me—which one of you is the genius with the IQ they can't measure?"

"That would be Milo," I said modestly.

"Not from the evidence of this conversation," Penny said.

Milo said, "Ouch."

"She nailed you, dude," I said.

"And which of you," Penny asked, "needs to set an example of mature behavior?"

I said, "That would be Lassie."

"Good one, Dad." The blue light pulsed, Milo said, "Holy-moly," and he began muttering equations to himself.

"There he goes back into his cocoon," I said. "I almost broke him, almost learned about the thing that makes it happen what nobody would believe, then you woke up."

"Yeah, right. Which came first—the chicken or the egg?"

"Paradox. No answer."

"The answer is the egg—it's time for breakfast."

———

At another truck stop, after fueling the Mountaineer, we had breakfast in a window booth at dawn, as the first golden sunlight made visible on the big sheet of glass all the fly specks that a backdrop of night had concealed.

We had to leave Lassie alone in the SUV, but we parked where we could keep an eye on her while we ate. The dog could keep an eye on us, too. From a backseat window, she withered us with the dreaded Stare of Accusation.

After we brought her a grilled hamburger pattie to augment her kibble, we were heroes in her eyes once more.

California is a huge state, bigger than most countries. The drive from Boom World in Orange County to Smokeville was over 850 miles, and we still had at least five hours to go.

We could have flown north, but not with all the I'll-blow-up-the-car-if-I'm-not-allowed-to-take-it gear that Milo needed, not easily with Lassie, and not without showing up on a passenger list that the apparently omniscient Shearman Waxx would peruse within nanoseconds of our takeoff.

Having slept over four hours before breakfast, Penny took the wheel for the next leg of our journey.

I felt rumpled and grimy, my beard stubble itched, I already had acid-indigestion from my poblano-chile omelet, and I knew I would not sleep in the glare of daylight. Nevertheless, I told Penny, "When the highway comes back toward the coast, up where it gets lonely, wake me. We'll find an isolated spot, you can give me gun instruction."

Perhaps half a mile farther, I fell asleep.

When Penny woke me two and a half hours later, we were no longer on U.S. Highway 101. We followed a rutted, weedy dirt road with the sun at our back. Still stiff and dry from the heat of summer, the weeds bristled in front of us and lay broken in our wake. No one else had come this way since at least the previous spring.

The road descended through a pine woods to the coast. Waves broke onto a short slope of pearly sand. The sand feathered into a wide expanse of shingle: a deep bed of small waterworn stones and pebbles smoothed by centuries of tidal action.

Penny parked on the shingle, at a place where it was backstopped by a bluff.

When she switched off the engine, I said, "If you're worried that a gun is too complex a machine for me, that I'll shoot off my nose, I want you to know this is different now. I can do this."

"A shot-off nose, I can handle. Let's just not have anything like the vacuum-cleaner incident."

"I'm serious, Penny. I can do this."

She put a hand against my cheek. "I know you can, sweetie. You can do anything."

———

I didn't realize that before I learned to shoot, I had to learn how to stand, which involved not just the feet but the entire body through the arms to the position of the hands on the gun. Penny favored the Weaver stance for some situations, the Isosceles stance for others. All this was easier than learning how to waltz, but harder than I expected.

Milo and Lassie remained in the Mountaineer. I'm sure that Milo continued to be sufficiently engrossed in weird science that he paid no attention to the spectacle that I made of myself. But every time I glanced at the SUV, the dog was watching and appeared to be laughing.

The metal cases we brought from Boom World contained shoulder rigs for carrying our guns under jackets, spare magazines, ammo, and the same .45-caliber pistol for each of us: a Springfield Armory Super Tuned Champion, which is a customized stainless-steel version of the Colt Commander.

On this lonely part of the coast, the nearest house must have been at least five miles away. A light offshore wind would blow some of the sound of the gunfire to the sea.

The first twenty or thirty times that I squeezed the trigger, the pleadings and the screams of victims came back to me from that far September and seemed as real as the crack of the pistol and the crash of the surf breaking behind us.

At that time of year, the northern coast was cool, yet soon I stood sheathed in sweat. The mind is a trickster with an infinite repertoire, and mine transformed the odor of gunfire into Tray's sour breath precisely as it had been that long-ago September night.

Learning, I fired a hundred rounds of Federal Hydra-Shok .45 ACPs, and I would have needed five hundred if my instructor had not been so capable and so patient. At the end of the session, I was not a marksman by any standard, but I understood recoil and how to manage it. If events required close-range self-defense, I might not make a complete dead fool of myself.

We had used large-leafed plants on the bluff face as targets. Some marked for shredding were unscathed, although a satisfying percentage were now cole slaw.

As Penny showed me how to clean the gun, we sat together on a large rock where the shingle met the beach.

The time had come, and so I steeled myself and said, "You know I never lie to you."

"It goes both ways."

"I deceived you by omission when I told you I was taking Milo to Roxie's for lunch but failed to mention Waxx would be there."

"I made note of it in my little book of your crimes."

"I didn't know you kept a diary of my crimes."

"It's titled *His Transgressions and How He Will Pay*."

"Sounds kind of medieval."

"What can I say. I'm a very fourteenth-century girl."

The offshore breeze and the sun did not disarrange and parch her hair, but groomed it into greater beauty, as if Nature considered her its special child.

"Well," I said, "I hope you have some pages left in that diary."

"Another deception by omission or a flat-out lie?"

"The former. It goes all the way back to when we were dating. It's something...so dark I didn't want it hanging over you, over our life together. But now I think maybe I should have told you."

"Does it concern just a stripper or is there a llama involved?"

I took a deep breath, blew it out. "Aunt Edith not only raised me but also adopted me. My born name isn't Greenwich."

"Couldn't be Hitler, you're not that old. Anyway, it's Durant."

I could not have been more surprised if she had shot me. "How do you know that? How long have you known?"

Cleaning her pistol with the same expression of affection that brightened her face when she brushed Lassie's coat, Penny answered the second question first: "Since shortly after we were married."

Only one explanation occurred to me: "Grimbald. He wanted to find out everything about the man his daughter was marrying. He's the kind who would know a private detective."

"What kind is that? A Boom? But it wasn't Daddy. It was your aunt Edith."

I could not have been more surprised if, after having shot me once, she'd shot me again. "Edith died four years before we met."

"Cubby, when a good woman knows an important thing needs to be done, she won't let death prevent her from doing it."

Penny clearly enjoyed teasing me with this revelation, which I supposed was a good thing, since it must mean she wasn't angry.

"Edith suspected you might keep those events secret out of guilt or shame—or modesty. She knew the story revealed what a brave and decent boy you were."

"Not brave," I disagreed.

"Oh, yes. Very brave at six. And she thought it was a miracle that you were spared, *the way that you were spared*. She believed a wife should know her husband had some special destiny. So she wrote it all in a long letter, which she entrusted to her attorney."

"Johnson Leroy."

"Yes. He kept track of you at her request. When he learned of the marriage, he sent me her letter."

"And you never told me."

"She asked me not to tell you. She wanted you to have a chance to tell me of your own volition, sooner or later."

I had dreaded recounting the hideous details. Now, fourteen years after her death, Edith lifted that weight from me.

"She must have been quite wonderful," Penny said.

I nodded. "I think she was very like her sister. So...in a way, I didn't entirely lose my mother when I was six."

"I memorized the opening line of her letter. 'Dear nameless girl, I know that you have a kind heart and a good soul and a lovely laugh, because Cubby has chosen to spend his life with you, and Cubby values all the right things.'"

For a moment, I couldn't speak. Then: "I'd like to read that letter."

"I've saved it for you," she said. "And one day, for Milo."

"Oh, well, I don't know...."

"Of course you know," Penny said. "Eventually Milo should read it. If there was a miracle, let's not pretend we don't know why you were spared. Without you and me, there would be no Milo. And if I know one thing for sure, it's that someday, somehow, the world is going to be a better place because Milo's in it. Don't you think?"

I met her eyes, that double-barreled gaze of truth. "I think. Yeah. I think."

Finished cleaning her pistol, she said, "You know another thing I'm sure about?"

"If there's a big surprise in it, I can't handle another one."

"I'm sure, you'll never again have a problem with a tool or a machine. No more hammered thumbs, no vacuum-cleaner catastrophes."

"That'll take a second miracle."

"Because all that clumsiness was never anything but an elaborate excuse not to have a gun, not to learn how to use one."

"Where did you get your psychology degree?"

"The school of common sense. If you could turn the toasting of a slice of bread into a calamity, no one would ever want you to pick up a gun."

"Calamity is a pretty strong word."

"Kitchen-repair bill was three thousand bucks. And you are *not* a clumsy man. Consider your writing. Consider how you are in bed."

"I'm no Jon Bon Jovi."

"I'm no longer a schoolgirl with expectations as low as that. You learned the basics of guns today, and the world didn't end."

"The day's not over."

She kissed me. Her tongue was sweet.

"Aunt Edith was right about one thing," I said. "I sure do know how to pick 'em."

Watching from the Mountaineer, Lassie had laughed at me so much that she needed to pee.

Thereafter, Penny drove us off the shingle, to the dirt road, and back toward Highway 101.

"How did the gun thing go?" Milo asked.

"Your mother's still alive," I said.

"What about your feet?"

"I didn't shoot either of them."

"Triumph."

My disposable cell phone rang, and it was Vivian Norby. She had gotten a disposable of her own, and she gave me the number.

"How's it going?" Vivian asked.

"We haven't driven your Mountaineer off a cliff."

"You mean you've made Penny do all that driving herself?"

"I'm not going to let you sit Milo anymore. Obviously, he's a bad influence."

"Listen," Vivian said, "I've been on the Net doing research, and I've got some interesting news. I don't think Thomas Landulf was Waxx's only victim in Smokeville. There's maybe another one, his name is Henry Casas, and he's sort of alive."

Chapter 46

Smokeville was so picturesque that you kept looking for the gnomes and elfenfolk who constructed it.

The buildings on the main street and most of the houses were Victorian, with enough gingerbread to make any Modern Movement architect grind his teeth to dust.

This settlement of four thousand lay on lowlands just above the sea. Its western neighborhoods sloped down through cedars and hemlocks to the shore.

In the sea were magnificent rock towers, weathered into fanciful shapes, from which the wind, when at sufficient force, raised the voices of mournful oboes, of soft uilleann pipes and penny whistles yearning for Ireland.

Warburton Motor Court was a collection of quaint little cottages from the 1930s, shaded by the robes of immense deodar cedars like giant monks gathered for worship.

Cash in advance and the license-plate number of the Mountaineer bought us enough trust from the desk clerk that I was not asked to provide a credit card or a driver's license. I signed the register as Kenton Ewen, borrowing two of my lost uncles' first names.

Milo abandoned one trunk when we fled the peninsula house, but he had the bread-box thing he saved from that debacle, the items that Grimbald obtained, and a second trunk of oddities, curiosities, and incomprehensibles. He was eager to set up shop in the cramped living room of the cottage.

According to the address Vivian Norby obtained, Henry Casas lived within easy walking distance of Warburton Motor Court. Given his circumstances, we felt that I would have the best chance of seeing him if I went alone.

Penny and I were loath to split up, but we were now armed and less vulnerable than before. She remained with Milo and Lassie in the motor-court cottage.

Henry Casas's house was a splendid Victorian with a deep front porch and an Italianate double door with a stained-glass fanlight.

Two and a half years ago, Henry's mother moved to Smokeville from Atlanta, to run his house and to oversee his care.

The woman who answered the doorbell appeared to be in her mid-fifties. Her flawless skin, doe eyes, and petite frame suggested a delicate flower, but her hands were strong and marked by work, and there was about her an air of one who never shrank from a challenge.

"Good afternoon." She had a southern accent.

"Are you Mrs. Casas?"

"Henry's mother, yes."

"Mrs. Casas, my name is—"

"I know who you are, Mr. Greenwich. I can't for the life of me imagine why you're here, but it's a pleasure to welcome you."

She stepped back from the threshold and ushered me inside.

Although she assumed that I hoped to see her son, she took me first to the library, which had many books and no DVDs.

The most striking things in the room were two paintings by Henry. His talent was immense.

A narrative artist of real genius, his technique was meticulous. One work was egg tempera on a gesso foundation, the other a dry-brush watercolor. His sense of light, the clarity of his execution riveted the eye. Clearly, he was influenced by Andrew Wyeth, but his subjects were his own, as was the complexity of his intent.

Turning from the second painting, I went directly to the heart of the matter: "Mrs. Casas, was your son a friend of Thomas Landulf?"

She met my eyes no less directly than did Penny, and I saw that she had already decided to trust me. "Yes. They were good friends."

"Does Henry believe that Tom Landulf killed his wife and child, then set himself afire?"

"No, Mr. Greenwich, he does not."

"Please call me Cubby."

"Thank you, Cubby. I'm Arabella. Bella to friends."

"Does Henry wonder if his assailants may have been the same people who murdered the Landulfs?"

"He is certain of it. But the police consider the Landulf matter settled. And they have made no progress on Henry's case."

"Bella, the people who killed the Landulfs and brutalized your son—they're now trying to kill my family, and me."

"Then God help you, Cubby. And I'm sure Henry will want to help as well. I assume you want to see him."

"If it's not too great an imposition."

"Are you prepared for him? Do you know what was done to him?"

"Yes. But I would guess hearing about it isn't the same as seeing him firsthand."

"Not the same at all," she agreed. "The thing to remember is, he does not want pity or even sympathy. Especially not from someone he admires, like you."

I nodded. "I won't offend him."

"You may have heard a police theory that Henry solicited men in a gay bar and went somewhere with them, not realizing he had fallen into the hands of psychopaths."

"I hadn't heard that."

"Well, it isn't true. Henry is not gay, and neither were those who mutilated him. He was awakened in this house, taken from it in the middle of the night—and brought back two months later. Please wait here while I let him know you've come to visit."

Alone for the next ten minutes, I gave my mind and heart to the appreciation of the two paintings.

Henry Casas would do no more of his great work. At the age of thirty-six, he was blinded by the measured application of an acid. His hands were amputated at the wrists with surgical precision.

Perhaps because he had been known to speak so articulately about painting and culture, in resistance to certain ideological art, his tongue and his vocal cords were removed.

Now he lived without sight, without a sense of taste, without an easy means of communication, with no outlet for his talent, still this side of death but perhaps, on his worst days, wondering if he should take the final steps.

Chapter 47

A former first-floor drawing room had been converted into a combination bedroom, sitting room, and studio, with a wooden floor and no carpet.

Easels and art supplies suggested that somehow Henry still worked, though no paintings were in view.

Barefoot, in jeans and a flannel shirt, he sat in a wheeled office chair, at a computer, from which he turned toward us as we approached.

His glass eyes—actually plastic hemispheres—were attached to his ocular muscles and moved like real eyes, though he was blind.

He remained a handsome man, and nothing in his expression or his attitude suggested he felt defeated.

Mechanical hands, not prostheses meant to look like real hands but three-digit robotic devices, had been attached to the stumps of his wrists and evidently were operated by nerve impulses.

When I told him what a pleasure it was to meet him and spoke of my admiration for the paintings in the library, in such terms that I hoped he would know I was sincere, he listened with a smile.

In reply, he turned to the computer keyboard, and with one of his steel fingers, he began to type.

I could hardly imagine the laborious effort he had expended teaching himself to find the right keys without the assistance of eyes and with fingers that could not feel what they touched.

When he finished, I assumed I should step closer to read the words on the screen, but before I could move, he pressed a final key, and a synthesized computer voice spoke what he had written: *"I'm a crazed fan. Halfway through your new book. Splendid."*

Bella indicated a portable CD player and an audio edition of *One O'Clock Jump* on a table beside the sofa.

His mother had explained why I had come. He was willing to answer my questions, was in fact eager to help.

I told him about Shearman Waxx, a condensed version of what we had already endured at the critic's hands.

On the phone earlier, Vivian Norby had called Waxx not merely an enigma but more precisely a black hole. After hours of work on the Internet, she had been able to learn nothing more about him than we already knew.

Who were his parents? Where was he born? Where did he go to school? What jobs did he have before his first book on creative writing was adopted in so many universities and he was hired as a reviewer? Even questions of that fundamental nature could not be answered.

In frustration, wondering if Waxx might have written anything under a pseudonym, Vivian made search strings out of some Waxx-isms, favorite and unique expressions that were repeated in his reviews—and she was led to an art critic named Russell Bertrand, who was published regularly in the foremost art journal in the country.

Russell Bertrand excoriated some painters and sculptors as viciously as Waxx went after some writers. Not only were Waxxisms embedded in Bertrand's reviews, but his prose also proved to be burdened by Waxx's signature syntax.

When Vivian sought Bertrand's biography, she found that it was more spare than Waxx's bio, without even a home location to be found on Google Earth. Another black hole. Or the same one.

Next, Vivian searched Bertrand's review archives, looking for artists he savaged with particular enthusiasm, one of whom was Henry Casas in Smokeville, California.

Henry and Bella were encouraged by the headway we had made in our investigation, but I warned them to keep their expectations realistic. We were a long way from having any evidence that Waxx—alias Russell Bertrand—had committed crimes.

My hope that Henry might be able to describe his kidnapper was not fulfilled. He had been sedated through most of the period when he had been in captivity.

Speaking through his computer, he said one thing that rattled me: *"Not just one of them. During two months, I heard eight . . . ten voices. Maybe more."*

If his perceptions during captivity were not so drug-addled that they should be dismissed, then we had gone from a lone psycho to a pair of them—and now to an entire *organization*, which defied belief.

"One thing more," Henry said. *"Mother, show him."*

"Are you sure we should?" his mother asked.

Henry nodded vigorously.

"Come see," she said, and led me across the room to a pair of tall cabinets. From one of these, she withdrew a painting and held it for my consideration.

This work was not exquisite, as were those in the library. It lacked the clarity and the powerful, singular use of extreme light that exemplified the other pieces. The technique was far short of masterful, the images were not complex, and objects were not of the proper proportions. Yet you could see the same mind at work, the same creative sensibility.

I turned to Henry to ask how he had done this, and I saw that with his right foot, he held a brush, which now he manipulated with considerable finesse.

His determination and indomitable spirit were admirable, but that made no less tragic the fact that he remained a first-rate talent reduced to methods of execution that could never properly express the visions in his mind.

"He knows it can't approach the quality of what he did before," his mother said. "He has to use my eyes, my description of what he achieves with each brushstroke before he lays down the next one. But what he hopes, what I hope, is eventually he'll create more primitive expressions of his vision that will, in their own way, be wonderful. And if it never happens, it's worth the struggle. Every image he paints—it's spitting in the faces of those bastards. But no one must know. We don't want them coming back. If Henry finds a way to do work of a certain caliber—it'll be his legacy, shown after his death."

Her dedication to her son was no less impressive than Henry's dedication to exploring his talent under these worst imaginable conditions.

Putting away the painting and removing another from the same cabinet, Bella said, "His kidnappers and the people who worked on Henry when he was conscious—they were careful to keep their faces concealed. Only one went unmasked. Henry has struggled to produce that face, time and again, but I don't think it's of any value to you. It's not just the fact that he now lacks sufficient technique for portraiture. Clearly, the drugs on which they kept him affected his perceptions."

When she turned the painting toward me, I saw a countenance not well-rendered and not identical to what I had seen, but nonetheless I recognized the deformed individual in the Maserati.

Part Three

Zazu, Who's Who,
Here Dog, There Dog,
Doom, Zoom, Boom

Chapter 48

As long as I can remember, novelists and filmmakers and cult leaders have been depicting and predicting the end of the world by fire or ice, by asteroid or magnetic-pole shift, and they have always found a large audience for their visions.

In the hearts of modern men and women, there is an inescapable awareness that something is wrong with this slice of history they have inherited, that in spite of the towering cities and the mighty armies and the science-fiction technology made real, the moment is fragile, the foundation undermined.

During my walk from the Casases' house to the motor court where we were staying, in spite of my blithe spirit and flaming optimism and high standing in the Society of Great Fools, a sense of impending catastrophe impressed itself upon me.

But if disaster came, it would be the collapse of civilization, not the end of the world. This blue transparent sky, the sea, the shore, the land, the dark evergreens ever rising—all would endure, unaffected by human misery.

With its rich Victorian architecture and peaceful tree-lined streets, Smokeville served as a symbol of what the modern world had thrown away: the respect for tradition that can be rock under our feet; the certitude of our place in the universe and of our purpose, which allows peace of mind.

Fire, ice, asteroids, and pole shifts are bogeymen with which we distract ourselves from the real threat of our time. In an age when everyone invents his own truth, there is no community, only factions. Without community, there can be no consensus to resist the greedy, the envious, the power-mad narcissists who seize control and turn the institutions of civilization into a series of doom machines.

Have a nice day.

As I arrived at the motor court, I made an effort to spiff up my mood. Civilization wouldn't collapse. At worst, my sense of impending catastrophe meant that Penny, Milo, Lassie, and I were going to die. There. With a little attitude adjustment, I saved millions of lives.

Penny had closed the draperies. As I approached, I detected her at a window, peeking out between panels of fabric.

When she let me in, she declared, "I feel like a mouse."

"I was thinking some Chinese take-out."

With great earnestness, she said, "We're the mice, trying to get to the other side of the woods, like in my story, and Shearman Waxx is the owl, and I *know* the mice are the heroes, mice are *always* the heroes because they're little and cute, and you can't have cute little villains, but I gotta tell you, Cubby, I want to be the owl so bad, I want to swoop down on Waxx and snap him up in my beak and tear his guts out. Being mice *sucks*."

"So you missed me, huh?"

"Splitting up sucks. When are you going to the Landulf house?"

"It'll be dark in an hour, so now's not good. I want to wait until morning."

"We're going with you. We're not hiding here like mice."

"Were you standing at the window the whole time?"

"Not the whole time. I was working with the laptop, but after a while I got claustrophobia, then a little vertigo on top of the claustrophobia, then nausea on top of the vertigo. It wasn't as bad as that time we were stuck in the elevator with Hud Jacklight, but it was similar."

We had left Penny's laptop and Milo's at the peninsula house, but we still had mine.

"What were you doing with the laptop?"

"I was online, seeing what other painters Russell Bertrand might have savaged."

"This place is wired for Internet access?"

"Yeah. There's a little card about it on the desk. Government program to bring Internet access to cheap motels for the benefit of the traveling poor. This place isn't all that cheap."

"When Milo's head of the FBI, he can look into it."

"That's another thing," Penny said. "Milo has been freaking me out a little. He's being kind of . . . quirky."

"Not Milo."

The boy sat on the floor, his paraphernalia spread across half the cottage living room. A small strange tool, the purpose of which I could not guess, nestled like a pencil behind his right ear. Over his left ear hung several loops of ultrafine wire, apparently not because he was wiring himself into a version of Iron Man's superhero suit but because he wanted to keep the wire where he could find it when he needed it.

As he worked on a series of small objects that resembled crystal salt-and-pepper shakers, he kept up what sounded like a conversation with someone: "Yeah...I guess so.... Well, that requires a capacitor.... Oh, I see.... I wonder what megahertz.... Hey, thanks.... This is cool...."

I might have thought he was talking to his canine companion, but the dog was not at his side. When I checked the bedroom, she wasn't there, either.

Returning to the living room, I said, "Milo, where's Lassie?"

"Probably in a drawer."

"You put her in a drawer?"

"No. I'm just guessing."

"What drawer, where?"

He pointed to a knotty-pine chest. The lower two drawers were deep, the top three more shallow.

When I opened the bottom drawer, I found Lassie lying on her back, her hind legs spread wide, her forepaws tucked against her chest. She grinned, tongue lolling, and her tail swished around the interior of the drawer.

"How did this happen?" I asked Penny.

"I have no idea."

"You didn't put her in here?"

"Why would I put a dog in a drawer?"

"Well, she seems to like it."

"How on earth would I know she'd like it?"

"Relax. You didn't put her in here. I believe you."

I tried to coax Lassie out of the drawer, but she remained comfortably ensconced.

"There's something wrong with this dog," Penny decided.

"She's just a little eccentric."

"Maybe I can lure her out with those bacon biscuits she likes."

"Good idea."

Leaving the dog in the open drawer, I knelt on the floor beside Milo.

Evidently his mom had encouraged him to shower. He wore fresh clothes. Bold red letters on his white T-shirt spelled PERSIST.

His collection of custom T-shirts came from an ordinary mall shop. Periodically, he gave his mother a series of new words that he wanted to wear.

No, I can't explain it to you. Milo can't explain it to us, either. Our conversations about it have all been like this:

"Why do you have to wear words, Milo?"

"Names are important."

"These aren't names."

"Every word is a name."

"How do you figure?"

"Every word names an object, an action, a quality, a quantity, a condition...."

"So why are names important?"

"Nothing could be more important."

"But why?"

"Because nothing is if it isn't named."

Kneeling at his side in the cottage living room, I said, "I'm going to get take-out. What would you like?"

Fixated on his work, Milo said, "I'm not hungry."

When we stopped for lunch at a McDonald's in Eureka, he had been so absorbed by the strange displays on his Game Boy that he ate only half his cheeseburger and none of his fries.

"You've got to eat, Milo. I'm not going to let you sit here doing... whatever it is you're doing... if you don't eat."

"Pizza," he said. "Vegetarian with black olives."

"All right." I patted his shoulder. "And I promise never to tell your grandmother you ate vegetarian."

Grimacing, he said, "No. Grandma Clotilda—she'll read about it in her coffee grounds or something. Better add pepperoni."

On my walk to and from the Casas house, I had seen a pizza shop a block from the motor court. I called and placed an order.

Later, as I was about to leave, Milo said, "Dad, be really, really careful. Keep your eyes open. We're running out of time."

That declaration alarmed Penny. "What do you mean? Keep his eyes open for what?"

"Don't worry," I said. "I'll be back in ten minutes."

"You better be," Penny said. "Hear me clear, Cubby, you damn well better be."

I hugged her. "I love you, too."

Chapter 49

At Smokeville Pizzeria, no one tried to kill me.

Walking back to the cottage in the twilight, I learned why the town was named Smokeville. At certain conditions of temperature and humidity imbalance between the ocean and the shore, the sea gave up some of its substance, and the thirsty land drew the mist eastward so aggressively that it looked less like fog than like smoke harried by the heat of a fire behind it. Faux smoke seethed through the trees, the houses smoldered, and twilight dimmed behind the racing fumes.

Milo ate well, but not at the dinette table with us. He remained on the floor, engaged in his mysterious project. Lassie watched him from atop the television cabinet.

I told Penny about Henry Casas, his mother, Arabella, and the painfully tedious method by which he now painted.

She was as astonished as I had been that the impressionistic portrait of one of his tormentors should at once be recognizable as the deformed man in the Maserati. Most disturbing, however, was Henry's contention that he had been imprisoned and mutilated not by a lone psychopath or even two, but by an organization of many.

His hands and tongue were removed with clinical precision, under anesthesia, and he received competent postoperative care while being held against his will. Consequently, the organization, whatever its nature, included at least one good surgeon and others with medical knowledge.

I could not believe that a large group, including highly skilled health-care professionals, could come together to assist one another in their secret lives as serial killers. This was something else—and worse—than we had thought.

The more that we learned, the more the odds of our survival seemed poor.

Researching the artists whom Waxx had savaged under his pen name, Russell Bertrand, Penny had found another who seemed to have been a victim of more than the critic's words.

"Cleveland Pryor, a painter. He was found dead in a Dumpster in Chicago, where he lived."

His body was so tightly wound in so much barbed wire that he appeared almost mummified. According to the coroner's report, the wire had been cinched to Pryor while he had been alive.

"Cleveland never knew his father," Penny said. "His mother died when he was nineteen. Never married, no children, so at least he didn't have to see everyone he loved destroyed before Waxx murdered him."

In her research, she also discovered that some writers and artists of a new philosophical movement were relocating to Smokeville or were considering doing so. They hoped to establish a creative community.

Like Henry Casas and Tom Landulf, these people rejected both the nihilism and utopianism of our time and of the previous 150 years. They sought a future based not on the theories of one man or on one narrow ideology, but on the centuries of tradition and wisdom from which their civilization had grown.

"Which explains," I said, "why Waxx might have had two targets in the same small town."

"He probably has more," Penny said. "And...here *we* are."

———————⟶

Having gone to bed at nine o'clock, exhausted, I woke at 11:10 P.M. Before retiring, we switched off only one of the two nightstand lamps. Penny remained asleep beside me.

The cottage bedroom offered two double beds with mattresses that were no doubt provided free by a chiropractor in need of business. The second bed was empty.

Remembering John Clitherow's vanished daughters, I hurried out to the living room. Milo remained at work on the floor. He sat at the center of what seemed to be a much larger array of gadgets, gizmos, thingamajigs, and thingamadoodles than had been there previously.

My laptop rested on a footstool, and Milo gazed at the screen, on which streamed a mystifying video of complex but unidentifiable constructs.

"When are you coming to bed, kiddo?"

"Not yet."

"You need your sleep."

"Not really."

Lassie sat under a straightback chair. The legs and stretcher bars formed a cage around her. She barely fit in the cramped space, but she was grinning, her tail wagging.

As surely as Costello knew what Abbott would reply when asked "Who's on first?" I knew the answer when I asked, "Did you put the dog under the chair?"

"No," Milo said. "She did it to herself."

"That can't be comfortable."

I lifted the chair straight up, off the dog, and set it aside.

Lassie stood, shook herself, and cocked her head at me as if to say that I remained, in her view, by far the most curious part of this family.

Looking at the video on the laptop, I said, "What is that?"

"Structure," Milo said.

"Is there any point in my asking what structure?"

"No."

The image enlarged as the camera appeared to descend into it, much like a microscope probing a tissue sample at an ever-increasing power of magnification—and then a new pattern arose where the previous one had been.

"What's that?"

"Deeper structure."

"That's what I thought. Come to bed soon."

"Okay."

"Is that a sincere okay?"

"Okay."

At the doorway between the living room and bedroom, I glanced back. Milo raised one hand to the computer screen, as if he wanted to reach into the image of the deeper structure and feel it. The dog was caged under the chair again, and grinning.

———————>

When I woke at 1:22, Penny was asleep beside me, and Milo's bed remained empty.

I was at once aware of the whorls and pulses and radiating fingers of blue and red light that shimmered beyond the open door, as if someone had parked a police cruiser in the cottage.

When I entered the front room, I found that the entire ceiling had become a projection screen on which were displayed patterns more complex and dimensional than those that had been on the computer during my previous visit.

Two-dimensional versions of the images appeared as streaming video on the laptop screen. A cord led from the computer to a jerry-built device that projected them in 3-D onto the ceiling.

Milo lay on the floor, in a debris field of high-tech thingums and doohickeys and flumadiddles, staring at the spectacle overhead.

Movement drew my attention to the sofa. Lassie was lying there, on her back, also staring at the ceiling, all four legs kicking as if she were running through a meadow. She did not appear to be in distress, but perhaps in a state of rapture.

I sat on the floor beside Milo and said, "Structure?"

"Yeah. Even deeper than before."

"Structure of what?"

"Everything."

"Do you understand what you're looking at?"

"Yes."

I tried another tack: "Where is this coming from, Spooky?"

"Somewhere."

"From some Internet site?"

"No."

"From some government computer you hacked into?"

"No."

I pushed aside a few dofunnys and half a dozen something-or-others, and stretched out on my back beside my son. The visuals on the ceiling were awesome from this perspective.

"Did this turn out to be an interstellar communications device, after all?" I asked.

"No."

"Come on, is this stuff from an alien world?"

"No."

"Is it from the far future, a time transmission or something?"

"No."

"Can you say anything besides *no*?"

"Yes."

"I'm just doing what your T-shirt says. It says *persist*."

"You should go to bed, Dad. This is gonna be too much for you."

"Are you kidding? I do this stuff all the time. So now . . . what is this stuff we're doing?"

"I'm learning," Milo said.

"Am I learning, too?"

"I don't think so. You really should go to bed, Dad. If you keep watching this, it's going to get too scary for you."

"Oh, no. I'm enjoying it. Are you enjoying it, Milo?"

"It's amazing."

"It's like fireworks," I said, "without the risk of burning off your eyebrows."

On the sofa, the upside-down running dog issued what sounded like a whimper of delight.

"This is beautiful," I said. "Isn't it beautiful?"

"It's elegant," Milo said, "in seventy-seven ways."

"It's the most beautiful thing I've ever seen. Isn't it the most beautiful thing you've ever seen, Milo?"

"It's very beautiful, Dad."

"Isn't it? Isn't it beautiful, Milo?"

"Yes."

"It's so beautiful that it's getting a little ominous."

"Close your eyes, Dad. It's a good ominous, but you're not ready for it."

"Just a little ominous, Milo. And now . . . more than a little."

"I warned you it might get too scary for you."

"I don't scare easily, son. I was once trapped in an elevator for three hours with Hud Jacklight."

"Scary."

"I was so afraid your mother would rip his throat out. I didn't want your mother to end up in prison. I love your mother, Milo."

"I know, Dad."

"It's more beautiful by the second, but it's also more ominous. I feel like . . . when I'm looking into this, whatever it is, at the same time it's looking into me."

"Close your eyes, Dad, or you'll get very dizzy."

"Oh, no, I'm not dizzy at all. It's so strange and complex and ominously beautiful. Milo, do you feel like your skull is going to collapse?"

"No. I don't."

"I feel all this pressure, like the hull of a submarine at forty thousand feet, as if my skull might collapse like a popped balloon and squirt my brain out my ears."

Milo didn't say anything. On the sofa the dog whimpered with pleasure again, and farted.

I said, "This thing on the ceiling . . . it's getting alarmingly, dreadfully beautiful, Milo. Horribly, terrifyingly beautiful, and the whole room is spinning."

"I warned you about dizziness, Dad. If you don't close your eyes, nausea is next."

"Oh, no, I don't feel the least bit ill. Just anxious, you know, and alarmed, maybe even aghast. And humbled. This is very humbling, Milo. This is too beautiful for me."

"Close your eyes, Dad."

"This structure, whatever it is, it's too deep for me, Milo. It's like a thousand times too deep for me. Here comes the nausea."

I passed out before I could throw up.

Compared to me, Mozart's father had it *so* easy.

I woke on the living-room floor shortly after four o'clock in the morning, and my skull had not collapsed. Almost as good: I felt fresh and buoyant, with a sense of having experienced something transcendent, though I could not put into words what it had been.

In the light of a single lamp, the ceiling was blank, mere plaster and paint.

When I sat up, I discovered that Milo had packed away all his gear. Not a single item littered the cottage floor.

In the bedroom, Penny lay sleeping in one bed, Milo and Lassie in the other.

I stood watching them sleep.

In spite of where we were, how we had gotten here, and why we had come, I felt that at this moment of our lives, this place was exactly where we belonged. We were not drifting but rising, rising toward something right and of significance.

Everything that rises must converge. The ultimate convergence of man and maker requires the navigation of that final passage, death. At that moment, however, watching my family sleep, I was in the thrall of a quiet elation and was not thinking of death, though as it turned out, Death was thinking of me.

Chapter 50

In the morning light and stillness, the fog no longer mimicked smoke. Damp and chill, it barely eddied, stirring significantly only in the wake of the Mercury Mountaineer.

The vehicle was fully loaded. Although we paid for two nights at the motor court, we left nothing behind at the cottage. I wanted to be able to flee Smokeville and its environs, and make for the open highway without delay, if suddenly flight seemed essential.

Tom Landulf, whose first book had been published only fourteen months previously and who had died three months thereafter, had lived outside of Smokeville, along a winding state route, where houses were few, the sea beyond view, and the forest everywhere encroaching.

On the Internet, Penny found a recent magazine story about the case and its aftermath, in which a Realtor suggested the property might not sell for years. Potential buyers were reluctant to live in a place where extremely violent murders had occurred.

The house stood back from the road, cloaked in fog. We almost missed it. The Realtor's sign near the mailbox caught our attention.

I didn't want to park in the driveway. If a car pulled behind us, we might be boxed in even though we had four-wheel drive.

In front of the property, neither shoulder of the two-lane blacktop was wide enough to allow me to park off the pavement.

After continuing north on a gradual downslope for about three hundred yards, past a meadow only glimpsed between white curtains of mist, then past a length of bearded forest, I came to a wide lay-by on the right. I was able to get forty feet off the pavement, where the fog would shroud the vehicle from what little traffic might pass.

My intention was to go alone, but Penny responded as if I had proposed to strip naked and walk into a lion's den, while leaving her and Milo staked out as sacrificial lambs.

"I'm just going to go in there and prowl around," I said. "I can do that best alone. I don't even know what I'm looking for."

"We won't know what we're looking for, either," she said. "If the three of us don't know what we're looking for and we look for it together, we'll find it or we won't find it quicker than you would or wouldn't find it on your own."

"That sounded like something I would say."

"I know. We've been married too long."

"Look, Penny, the police have already been through the place. If there were anything to find, they would have found it."

"Then why did we come all the way to Smokeville?"

"To meet the locals who knew Landulf. The house is secondary."

"Then don't go in, and we'll all not go in together."

A back door opened, and we turned to look at Milo.

He said, "I'm going in, and I'm going to pretend you came with me, while you can sit here and pretend I stayed with you, so then we'll have gone in *and* not gone in together."

After telling Lassie to stay, he got out and closed the door.

I said, "He sure does have the Boom family hardheadedness."

"You mean the Boom family determination," Penny said.

We got out, locked the Mountaineer, and left Lassie to guard it. If she wanted to squeeze into the glove box, that was her business.

The fog seemed to penetrate my flesh and lick its cold tongues in my bone marrow.

Milo zipped up his quilted jacket. On the long-sleeved black T-shirt he wore under the jacket, white letters spelled FREEDOM.

Penny checked under her blue blazer and I reached under my corduroy sport coat to be sure that our shoulder rigs were snugged, pistols ready. Each of us had a spare magazine.

Nevertheless, I felt like a mouse. I think she did, too.

Because I didn't want to be seen approaching the former Landulf residence, we avoided the paved road. I led the way and Milo took middle position through the trees for about fifty yards, after which we came to the long meadow that gradually sloped toward the south, where we should find the house on the higher ground.

A vehicle went by on the road: engine noise and headlights. The fog prevented me from identifying category, make, or model.

In the drowned light, under the hundred-fathom weight of the threat that hung over us, trudging up the meadow, I felt like a deep-sea diver making his way toward a sunken ship, seeking something of value in the wreckage.

The house loomed out of the murk, a handsome Victorian wrapped by a veranda. A garage stood separate from it.

I intended to break a window, but Penny said, "Better knock."

"If there's anybody here, it's a ghost."

"Just to be safe—knock."

We climbed the front steps. Finding a doorbell, I rang it.

Just as I was about to turn away, a light came on behind the curtained glass panels that flanked the door.

"Uh-oh," Penny said.

The door was opened by a sixtyish man who looked as if he had hound dog in his heritage. His eyes were large and sad, and the bags under them would yield enough skin to make a pair of leather gloves. His jowls, dewlaps, and heavy slumped shoulders gave an impression of age and weariness. But he was a big guy with large hands. A second look suggested that he would be a formidable adversary in a fight.

"Can I help you folks?" he asked.

Having thought the house was deserted, I had prepared no story to use if someone answered the bell.

Now I heard myself saying, "Good morning, sir. If you have the time, we'd like to sit awhile and talk to you about Jesus."

"Well, son," he said, "I admire you spreading the word, but I've got a church I've gone to thirty years, no need to change."

I knew a good door-to-door evangelist would not give up easily, but I had no idea what one would say next, so I smiled and nodded and rolled my tongue around in my mouth, hoping it would find some words.

Penny said, "Excuse me, sir, but aren't you Sheriff Walbert?"

"I used to be, ma'am. Now I'm just Walbert, first name Truman."

"It was wrong what they did to you," said Penny.

"Well, ma'am, much of what people do to one another is wrong, and most of it's worse than what was done to me."

Disoriented more than I had been in the fog, I smiled at Penny as I imagined a door-to-door evangelist might smile at his evangelist wife when he wanted to know what the hell she was talking about.

Penny said to me, "That reading I was doing. Mr. Walbert was sheriff when Tom . . . when all that happened here. He hardly got into the investigation before the county evoked a 62-and-out rule."

"Sheriff before me," said Walbert, "didn't retire till he was 72. The rule was never enforced before. Fact is, if you'll pardon my cynicism, I'm not sure it existed before."

In the loop now, and reading in Penny's demeanor that Walbert might be an ally, I gave him a chance to declare himself by saying, "Terrible thing Thomas Landulf did."

"Well, I'd say it's a terrible thing whoever did it."

"But killing his own wife and daughter," I said with dismay.

"The true commandment is 'Thou shalt not murder.' It doesn't say 'kill' in the original language, because killing's a whole different thing from murder. Furthermore, Moses didn't provide us categories of murder, some worse than others. If you're going to go door-to-door for Jesus, Mr. Greenwich, you better learn-up a bit."

I winced at his use of my name, and said to Penny, "It's this hair. I should have put on a hat."

"Sheriff," she said, "I think we all know Tom Landulf didn't kill anyone, and didn't commit suicide. Your being here makes me think we all might benefit by swapping information."

"Better come in," Walbert said.

Penny and I took Milo into the house of murder, where the murdering was not yet finished.

Chapter 51

For Penny and me, Truman Walbert poured mugs of black coffee richer than most espressos I've tasted.

"I read your books, Mr. Greenwich, because Tom recommended them, and he was right." To Milo, he said, "Mr. Big, about what I can offer you is a Coke or orange juice."

Instead of being offended, Milo seemed to delight in his new name, and he asked for juice.

Walbert said, "Roberta Carillo, she's the real-estate lady has the listing, said I could stay here a month or two, nobody's lookin' to buy anyway. It's not I want to live here. But maybe living here, something about the case will click, or I'll find something in the house I overlooked before. Tom, Jeanette, Melanie—they were dear to me, like family. A cop gets a thick hide, but this case cuts deep."

Walbert had been eating breakfast before we arrived. As he talked, he stood by the sink with his plate, wiping up the last of an egg yolk with a half-slice of toast.

"From the start, I didn't buy the tableau. It wasn't a crime scene the way they happen, it was a staged tableau. The evidence was three murders, not two plus a suicide, but I only had the case five days before out of nowhere they retired me against my will."

"Who's they?"

"The county board of supervisors. Half of them are weasels, you can expect anything from them. But the others are fair folks, and I was surprised they made the action unanimous."

"Somebody wanted you off the case," Penny said.

"Has to be, somebody paid large to get that unanimous vote or put a big scare into some nice people. Reading the faces of the board members, I'd say it was both. They looked wide-eyed, white around the gills, like they were afraid, but also kinda smug, like they'd been scared into letting something really good be done for them."

"Who's sheriff now?" Penny asked.

"They raised Ned Judd from deputy to sheriff till next election. Ned's not a bad man, just not sharp enough to cut butter. He accepted the murder-suicide scenario. Now he avoids me out of shame, though he doesn't know it's shame, he thinks he's embarrassed for me."

As Walbert put his empty plate in the sink, I said, "You really think living here might bring some inspiration about the case?"

"Maybe. Truth told, I'm doing it largely to irritate and unnerve the county supervisors. If they think I turned up something, one or two will come squirming around to find out what, and they'll spill something useful, whether they realize they have or not."

The doorbell rang, and Penny asked, "Are you expecting someone?"

Frowning, Walbert said, "Nobody visits except Roberta, the real-estate lady, but she's not a morning kind of girl."

Penny and I exchanged a glance as Walbert replied.

I said, "Sheriff, the people who killed the Landulfs tried to kill us."

Halfway to the hall door, he stopped and gave me a look that would have scared the crap out of me if I'd been lying to him.

"It's true," Penny said. "They can't know we're right here. But maybe they have a way of knowing we've been in Smokeville."

The bell rang again.

Indicating a door between the kitchen and the dining room, he said to me, "Go that way into the living room, where you can hear me at the front door. Maybe you'll recognize a voice. Whoever it is, I'll let him jaw, but I won't let him in."

Milo stood near a window, beyond which lay the back porch. Penny drew him away from it, close to her.

As Walbert went into the hallway, I hurried through the dining room, into the living room. I stood to one side of the archway that led to the hall just aft of the foyer.

I heard Walbert open the door. "Good morning, fellas. What can I do for you?"

"Mr. Walbert," a man said, "we represent the Landulf estate, and we never gave Ms. Carillo approval to let you live here rent free."

"You have business cards?"

"My name is Booth, this is Mr. Oswald. We took the listing away from Ms. Carillo this morning."

"Are you attorneys? Usually you folks have cards."

"We want you to vacate the premises immediately," Booth said.

"If the issue is rent, I'm happy to pay."

"Too late for that," said Oswald. "You've got to go now."

"If you gentlemen will just wait on the porch, I'll call Roberta and confirm she's lost the listing."

One of the men spoke, but I couldn't make out what he said, and then I heard movement in the foyer. The front door closed.

Truman Walbert's silence alerted me to the danger better than anything he could have said. Silence from a man to whom talk came easily.

I drew the pistol from my shoulder holster, and in the quick of action, it felt as new and cumbersome to me as when I first held it on the beach, taking instruction from Penny. Shouldn't think about how to hold it, thinking made the fingers stiff, just let the hand conform to the grip.

"What's this room on the left?" Booth asked, his voice close.

"It's like a den," said Walbert.

They must be just beyond the living-room archway.

Oswald said, "Big old bear like you needs a den."

Shift my weight, a floorboard might betray me. No lights on in the living room, good, the hall light would throw my shadow behind me, not toward them. But I could hear my breathing, shallow and quick, a dog panting, not good, if they listened they would hear it too, as close as they were, the breath of life suddenly become the breath of death. Inhale and hold.

"You open the door, go first, *Sheriff*," Booth said, greasing the last word with a sneer.

Once committed, keep moving, no hesitation. Breathless, pistol in both hands and arms extended, I stepped into the archway.

Truman Walbert was at the den door, facing away from me. One of the men, probably Booth, held a gun to the sheriff's head, and his back was toward me.

Oswald stood behind Booth and Walbert, also presenting his back to me. He had a pistol in his right hand, a big damn thing, pointed at the floor.

Two steps brought me to Oswald. Forgetting everything I knew about the Weaver stance and the Isosceles stance with its several variations, I said "Drop it" on an explosive exhale, as I jammed my gun to the back of his head.

Oswald twitched and froze when the muzzle of the .45 Champion pressed cold against his skull.

Booth looked over his shoulder. Shaved head, gaunt hard face, mouth as tight as a soldered seam, thin nose with more bone than flesh, eyes narrowed to coin slots: a death-vending machine.

I thought we were stalemated, everyone would have to back off slowly, stand down from this impasse, but Booth believed otherwise. He shot Truman Walbert.

Plinking vegetation at a distance doesn't prepare you for the necessity of putting a bullet in a man's head at point-blank range. As a theoretical target, even from only two steps away, Oswald was entirely plausible to me, but when I was standing so close to him that I could smell his cologne and see the mole on the back of his neck, he was not just an easy target but also a man, a man different from me in many respects but certain to be like me in some ways. I hesitated to do to him what Booth had done to Walbert.

An obvious professional who read my inexperience in an instant, Booth swiveled toward me, pivoting like a dancer, his weapon coming around, even as the late sheriff went to his knees and began to topple sideways.

Oswald failed to throw down his pistol, not as impressed by a gun to his head as I would have been in his position. My heart hammered, the rush of blood loud in my ears, and I knew Oswald was thinking faster about all of this than I could, plotting faster than any writer who had ever penned a page, just as Booth was moving with animal ruthlessness, with cold certainty. Oswald turned his head to the right, as if trying to see me, even though the muzzle of the .45 gouged his scalp.

Booth had already rotated sideways to me, a narrow profile, his weapon rising into position. A fraction of a second before I would have been looking down the bore of the barrel, two shots thundered in the hallway, and bullets rocked him, neck and shoulder. He started his fall just as the sheriff fully landed.

At the far end of the hall: a curl of smoke in the air and a thrusting .45 and Penny in the Isosceles stance.

Oswald was bringing his pistol up not because he hoped to turn it back on me in some trick shot, but because he intended to bring down Penny, avenging Booth.

I shot him in the head.

Either Oswald pitched away from me or I shoved him in disgust, but as he went, he fired one shot reflexively before the gun dropped from his hand.

The round missed Penny and shattered chunks of wood from the frame of the kitchen doorway.

My ears were ringing, deafened by the gun blasts in the enclosed space, and I backed up against the wall next to the archway, needing something to lean against for a moment, keeping an eye on Booth, the only one who might still be alive, the other two with broken-melon heads.

Another house full of bodies, twenty-eight years down the time stream from the first, one good man dead but also two very bad ones, nobody invisible to anyone else, no miracle here, my covenant with Death revoked: Now anything could happen.

Thou shalt not murder, but killing is a whole different thing from murder. Self-defense isn't a transgression, defense of the innocent is required, they give medals for defense of the innocent. A brass taste filled my mouth, a hot-copper odor burned in my nose, and a gorge rose but I choked it down.

Booth remained sprawled and still on the floor, but Penny kept a two-hand grip on her pistol as she approached him. She kicked his weapon out of his reach, circled him, trying not to step in blood or on various scraps of tissue, and confirmed he was dead.

I holstered my pistol. My hand ached.

"Stay there, Milo," she shouted toward the kitchen. "We're all right. Just stay there."

My ears were still ringing, but I was no longer deaf when she came to me. We held each other.

"You okay?" I asked.

"No. I didn't want to do it, not that, not ever."

"Kill or be murdered," I said. "You did well, exactly what you should've done."

"You too. My God. I'm shaking head to foot, head to foot."

"I wasn't fast enough," I said.

"Fast enough," she disagreed. "Walbert was dead one way or the other, you couldn't change that. They came here to kill him. And then to lie in wait for us."

She must have been right, but I said, "How did they know we'd come here?"

"How do they know anything? Think about it later. We have to get out of here. Lock the front door, close any living-room draperies that might give someone a line of view through the archway into the hall. I'll wipe off the coffee mugs, anything we might have touched in the kitchen."

As she hurried along the hallway, I negotiated the remains of the three men, striving not to think about the nature of the wet debris, and went to the front door.

My sweat-damp fingers slipped on the deadbolt thumb-turn as I tried to twist it the wrong way. Then I engaged the lock and rubbed my sleeve over it to blur the thumbprint I might have left.

I half remembered that after Walbert admitted us, he closed the door. None of us touched the knob, but I rubbed it with my sleeve, anyway.

As the ringing in my ears subsided, I heard a sound rising outside. An approaching engine.

Sidelights flanked the front door. I lifted the edge of a lace curtain, and looked out.

A dark green sedan in the driveway, near the front porch, must have belonged to Booth and Oswald.

Looming out of the mist, a black Hummer appeared to be more of a war machine than one of the full-scale Humvees that were used by the military. It parked behind the sedan, towering over it, and the driver left the engine running, headlights and fog lights blazing.

Doors opened like spaceship portals, and three men stepped down and out of the huge vehicle. Even in the mist, I could see that one of them was Shearman Waxx.

We were up against an organization, all right, and it was not the National Society of Book and Art Critics.

Waxx was holding a cell phone to his left ear, and behind me in the hallway, a phone in one of Booth's pockets played a few bars of Rod Stewart's "Do Ya Think I'm Sexy?"

I turned away from the front door, executed some broken-field running to quick-step through the horror on the hallway floor, and raced toward the back of the house as Booth's phone rang again.

Chapter 52

In the kitchen, Penny was polishing a coffee mug with a dishtowel, and Milo used a paper towel to buff prints off his juice glass.

Maybe this was only my perception, subjective and not true, but Milo appeared to have changed in minutes, as if the events in the hall-way, which he could imagine without seeing, had been an immersion in a baptistery that bleached out a measure of his innocence and left in him a sediment of experience that could never be washed away.

When he looked at me, his beautiful blue eyes seemed to contain shadows that had never before veiled them. His face was pale, his lips paler, his hands dove-white, as if all the blood had rushed to his heart, to fortify it after the blow that it had taken as he stood listening to his parents kill and nearly be killed.

I wanted to sweep him off the floor, hug him tight, kiss him, and talk him through this terrible moment, but to do so would be to ensure his death and mine, so completely had our lives spiraled out of our control.

"Waxx is here," I said, "and he's not alone."

Penny dropped the dishtowel, put down the mug, drew her pistol, and I discovered my gun already in my hand, although I did not recall having withdrawn it from the holster as I raced along the hallway.

The doorbell rang.

The chimes conflicted with a final burst of "Do Ya Think I'm Sexy?" before Waxx's call went to voice mail.

Snatching open the back door, I said, "Not south across the meadow. They might spot us before we're hidden by the fog."

They preceded me onto the back porch, and I pulled the door shut behind us.

"Straight east," I urged, "across the backyard, find the forest. We'll stay in the trees around the meadow to the Mountaineer."

We were at the head of the porch steps when the sudden swelling roar of an engine froze us.

Around the south side of the house came the Hummer, speeding across the lawn, wide tires unfazed by the wet grass. That it was black like a hearse seemed appropriate.

Instead of turning right and parking athwart the porch steps, blocking our escape, the Hummer continued east without hesitation. Failing to glance our way, the driver had not seen us.

The enormous vehicle vanished into the morning fog, and its crisp beams diffused, becoming an unearthly glow, goblin light.

Apparently, he intended to park beyond view of the house so that if we came visiting, as they hoped, we would think the place deserted. They would move the sedan for the same reason.

Out in the murk, the Hummer stopped. The driver killed the engine and the lights.

If he meant to walk back to the house, we could no longer go east toward the woods because we would risk encountering him. The slam of the driver's door carried clearly in the moist air. He was returning on foot.

The only route left to us was north, away from the house, then west and across the state route, thereafter south and finally east across the road again to the Mountaineer.

I indicated north, and Penny nodded, and the three of us took one step off the porch before we heard the voices: two men, coming around the north side of the house, evidently to try the back door.

We could get out of sight quickly enough only if we retreated to the kitchen.

Understandably, Penny was averse to going into the house again, and she hesitated. In an instant, however, she realized we couldn't attempt to take these two men by surprise and shoot them dead because that still left one out front plus the driver, who would be alerted by gunfire. Our luck wouldn't hold through so many confrontations.

Besides, here in the open, we couldn't protect Milo from return fire if we drew any.

Crossing the porch, I feared the back door had locked when we closed it behind us, but that was not the case. Holding Milo's hand, Penny ducked inside, and I followed.

I almost closed the door and engaged the deadbolt. Instead, I left it ajar, suggesting we had successfully escaped by this route.

The second floor didn't appeal. We might go through a window, onto a porch roof, drop to a lawn, but doing so quietly and with Milo required the Fates to be in a better mood than lately possessed them.

When Penny opened an interior door, I glimpsed a steep flight of concrete stairs descending into gloom. This seemed to be the worst of all possible options.

Voices outside. Footfalls on the back-porch steps.

The cellar was no longer merely an option. It was the only place we could go.

I followed Milo and Penny onto the descending stairs and quietly closed the door behind us.

Chapter 53

The chamber below was not a black pit. A pale radiance suggested that part of the cellar was aboveground, with a few narrow windows near the ceiling.

Nevertheless, darkness dominated. If we tried to proceed in it, inevitably we would blunder into something and make a lot of noise.

At the top of the stairs, I felt the wall, found the switch, and risked the lights.

Penny and Milo hurried down the concrete steps.

As I followed them, I heard voices in the kitchen.

Stepping away from the bottom of the stairs, I counted three casement windows in the north wall and three in the south, which were the sides of the house lacking porches. Set just under the ceiling, these openings probably measured eighteen inches wide by a foot high. The windows were hinged and were primarily intended to provide periodic ventilation.

On this foggy morning, they admitted little light; and even Milo would have needed to be a circus contortionist to escape through one of them.

The fluorescent tubes on the ceiling provided inadequate light, leaving portions of the cellar in gray shadows, and a couple of them continuously blinked.

From overhead came an exclamation of surprise, followed by hurried footsteps. The bodies had been discovered in the downstairs hallway.

The open back door would suggest to Waxx and to his fellow booklovers that whoever shot Booth and Oswald had left the premises. But these were pros, and they would search the house to confirm that conclusion.

There were four of them. The search would go quickly.

Penny opened one of two doors and turned on a light, revealing an eight-foot-square chamber with a two-foot-square, hinged iron plate on one wall. In this coal room, from the days before the gas furnace, the wall plate had been raised to accommodate the delivery truck's chute. Black dust, permanently impressed into the walls, lent the air an anthracite odor.

The rusted iron plate hung on corroded hinges. If it could be opened at all, it would make more noise than rolling back the door on the tomb of a pharaoh dead two thousand years.

Upstairs, the voices and the footsteps had fallen silent. The cautious but swift search of the house had begun. Most likely, they would start at the top and work down.

As Penny closed the first door, I disengaged a deadbolt and opened the second. Beyond lay a flight of exterior stairs.

A pair of rain doors covered the steps, sloping at a twenty-degree angle from the house. They were secured by a hasp. Joining the hinged strap to the swivel eye, the padlock could be opened only with a key.

No way out.

As I closed and locked the door, leaving it the way I found it, Milo whispered, "Dad. Take this."

When I turned, I found him holding out to me a four-inch-long, cut-crystal bottle with a domed silver cap that lacked holes.

"What's this?"

"Used to be a saltshaker."

"What is it now?"

"It's a thing that does something. Don't try to take the cap off, it's glued tight. Keep it in a pocket. Don't lose it, don't lose it, don't lose it."

From the east end of the cellar, Penny stage-whispered, "Cubby, here."

She stood in front of the old coal furnace, which was not in use yet remained, perhaps because the great iron beast would be too much trouble to dismantle and remove, or perhaps because someone had a misguided idea about its historical value.

To the left of the coal furnace stood the current gas model, smaller but still sizable. To the right were a hulking 100-gallon hot-water tank and a water softener with a large rock-salt tank.

"The light's poor here," Penny said. "Not easy to tell there's more than two feet of space between this equipment and the wall."

One of the two nearest fluorescent bulbs blinked continually, further confusing the eye because the strobe effect made everything seem to quiver.

"There's no other hiding place," Penny said as Milo took another crystal saltshaker from a pocket of his quilted jacket and gave it to her. "Spooky, what's in this?"

"Quantum electrodynamic stuff."

I said, "Get behind the old furnace. There's another light switch by the outer door, I've got to turn off the fluorescents."

As I went to kill the lights, I heard Milo whispering urgently to his mother, "Don't try to take the cap off, it's glued tight. Keep it in a pocket. Don't lose it, don't lose it, don't lose it."

In the dark, I returned to Penny and Milo by feeling my way along the north wall to the northeast corner of the room, then along the east wall until I encountered the rock-salt tank and the water softener. I found the space behind it sufficiently accommodating, and I eased along until I was in back of the 100-gallon water heater.

"You there?" I whispered.

"Here," Penny replied from behind the old coal furnace.

As I settled gingerly into a crouch, my back to the wall, my knees against the platform on which the hot-water tank stood, Milo whispered, "Dad, what did you do with the thing?"

"What thing? Oh, yeah, the quantum thermonuclear saltshaker."

"Quantum electrodynamic," he corrected.

"It's in my right pants pocket."

"Don't lose it."

"What if it breaks?"

"It won't break."

"Well, it's crystal."

"Not really. Not anymore."

Penny said, "Ssshhhhh."

We sat in silence for almost a minute.

Then I said, "How do I use it?"

"You don't," Milo said.

"But what's it do?"

"Something."

"It's automatic?"

"My unit is the controller."

Sensing that Penny was about to shush us again, I fell silent.

The longer we waited in the dark, the more it seemed to me that we had done the wrong thing by hiding there.

I was holding my pistol, and I was sure Penny must be holding hers, but I still felt trapped and helpless.

If I voiced my doubt, Penny would ask what was Plan B. I didn't have one. I kept my mouth shut.

The lights came on.

Chapter 54

By tilting my head to the right, I could peer out through the narrow gap between the old furnace and the hot-water tank. I had a clear view of the coal-room door about thirty-five feet away.

Farther to my right, Penny and Milo were discernible in the shadows.

Because the cellar was mostly open and bare, with just a couple of stacks of crates and a line of support columns, the guy appeared at the coal room less than half a minute after the fluorescents came on.

From this distance and in the inadequate light, I couldn't see enough of him to provide a credible description. Suffice it to say that in terms of the physical qualities of long-ago movie stars, he was more like Lon Chaney Jr. than like either Bela Lugosi or Boris Karloff, and nothing whatsoever like Cary Grant.

He had a gun. I half expected that from now on everyone I met would have a gun, even if I lived for a hundred years.

He opened the coal-room door and, like they do in the movies, he went in low and fast, gun arm out, the weapon just below his line of vision, left hand finding the light switch in an instant, as if by instinct.

When the coal room proved to be deserted, he clicked off the lights in there and came out, noticeably more relaxed than when he had entered my field of vision. He looked as if he had decided that whoever killed Booth and Oswald was no longer in the house.

Leaning left to peer through the narrow gap between the hot-water tank and the water softener, I watched him as he moved more casually to the exterior door, disengaged the deadbolt, and peered up the steps at the underside of the padlocked rain doors.

From the farther end of the cellar, someone said, "Brock?"

"Over here," our hunter replied as he closed the exterior door.

Leaning right once more, I saw Brock come face-to-face with Shearman Waxx in front of the coal-room door.

Waxx had traded his hound's-tooth sport coat with leather elbow patches for a tan cardigan sweater. He still wore a red bow tie.

"Two clear bloody shoe prints, part of a third in the hallway," Waxx said. "Small feet, shape of the shoe—has to have been a woman."

"What woman?"

"It's got to be Greenwich's wife, the Boom woman."

"They've *already* been here?"

"And gone. Three mugs in the kitchen. One with warm coffee."

"Warm?"

"Plenty warm. The other two clean, one dry and sitting on a damp dishtowel, the other washed but still wet. They were having coffee with Walbert is what I think, when Rink and Shucker show up to whack him, and after it went down, they're wiping off any prints they left. And there's a clean glass on the counter, probably their weird little Einstein, and on the floor a few spilled drops of orange juice."

Brock said, "Waxx, you're telling me a kid's-book writer took out Rink and Shucker?"

"Either she did or Greenwich did, or they did it together."

Evidently, Rink and Shucker were the real names of Booth and Oswald.

"Sonofabitch, what kind of writers take down Rink and Shucker? We've been going through these people like...like..."

"Butter through a knife," Waxx said, heading back toward the stairs.

Following Waxx, Brock declared, "By now, I know writers, and writers are fun to play with, you do what you want to them, they don't *play back* at you."

"Her footprints in the hall were the thinnest film of blood," Waxx said, "should have dried in five minutes, but they're wet. So they slipped out the back after being here when we pulled up."

As their voices grew more difficult to hear, I rose behind the hot-water tank and slipped sideways, past the water softener and the rock-salt tank.

From behind the furnace, Penny whispered, "Cubby, no!"

I had to hear as much as possible. In the open, I could see Waxx and Brock more than halfway across the cellar, their backs to me.

Crouched but visible to them if they turned, I moved quickly past a support column—

"Where was their car?" Brock asked. "They didn't come in a car?"

—and I hid behind the first stack of crates.

"They came in a car," Waxx said. "Left it somewhere in the area—then to the house, came on foot. Soon as I realized the shoe prints are wet, I already called the sheriff to cooperate with roadblocks between here and Smokeville, and south before Titus Springs, only seven miles of road between."

They were nearly to the foot of the stairs. I risked exposure and followed them.

"So they're boxed?" Brock asked.

"Boxed and bagged."

I dropped low behind the second stack of crates.

Waxx said, "They have maybe a four-minute lead, not enough. The area, it's quarantined, we're coming in from both ends."

"Just our people or the sheriff's, too?"

"The sheriff is for the roadblocks only because he can set them up faster than we can. The rest is none of his business. *Our* people were killed. Nobody kills our people and gets away. Now it's war."

"How many houses in those seven miles?"

"Maybe twenty. We'll sweep them all."

They were on the stairs, voices diminishing.

"What about side roads?" Brock asked.

"None paved. All the dirt roads are dead ends."

I hurried to the bottom of the stairs, staying just out of their line of sight if they should glance back.

"Any vehicle not obviously one of ours gets stopped," Waxx said.

"What about Rink and the other two?"

"We'll haul them out later, torch the place so it looks like idiot kids did it. Right now, we need every man for the search."

I dared to ease into the stairwell, the better to hear them, as Brock asked, "Still have fun with them—or pop 'em on sight?"

Stepping off the stairs into the kitchen, Waxx said, "We want them alive. Zazu has taken a special interest in them."

Brock had reached the top of the steps. When he switched off the lights, I ascended through the gloom, low and monkeylike in his wake, and heard him say, "Zazu? They'll wish we'd tortured them and set them on fire."

He closed the door, and I was at it a moment later, listening.

In the kitchen, Waxx said, "I have a plane standing by in Eureka to fly them south."

"The fog should lift soon," Brock said. "That'll help us."

A door opened…closed, and during the few seconds between, I heard a big engine fast approaching the house.

Assuming both Waxx and Brock had left, I opened the stairhead door two inches and surveyed the kitchen.

Through the windows, I saw them standing outside, on the back-porch steps, with a third man.

From the east, out of the fog, the Hummer appeared. It stopped on the lawn near the three men. They boarded the vehicle, and it roared away with them.

When I switched on the cellar lights, Penny and Milo were at the foot of the stairs, having followed me as I pursued Waxx and Brock.

"Did you hear?" I asked.

"Everything until they went into the kitchen and closed the door," Penny said.

As they climbed toward me, I said, "When they catch us, they're going to take us to Eureka, where there's a plane waiting to fly us south."

"Where south?"

"That's all I know."

In the kitchen, she asked, "You hear anything more about Zazu?"

"No. I'm not sure I want to hear more. Anyway, they aren't going to catch us." I scooped Milo off the floor. "Spooky, I'm going to take you through the dining room, into the living room, to the foyer and up the stairs. Until we're on the stairs, I want you to keep your eyes closed, all right?"

"I can handle it, Dad."

"Keep your eyes closed."

"They're just dead people."

"If you don't keep your eyes tight shut, I'll throw away the whatchamacallit thermonuclear saltshaker."

"No, don't. We're really, really gonna need them, the way things are going."

"Then keep your eyes closed."

"All right."

Penny asked, "What's upstairs?"

"I have a thing to do. And so do you, down here. Go through the jacket and pants pockets of Rink and Shucker."

"Oh, crap."

"You'll like it better than what I'll be doing upstairs. We need their ID, anything about who they are. And car keys."

"I guess I did vow for better or worse."

"The fun has only begun." I gave her a quick kiss. "Meet us in the foyer in three minutes. We've got to move fast."

She yanked an entire roll of paper towels off a dispenser near the sink, and said to herself, "Plastic trash bags," as she started pulling open drawers.

"Eyes closed," I reminded Milo.

Chapter 55

In my arms, Milo tucked his face against my throat. I put one hand against the back of his head to keep him where he was. If he opened his eyes, I'd feel his lashes moving against my skin.

Through the dining room, across the living room, around the three bodies, to the stairs, ascending. "All right, scout."

He opened his eyes and lifted his head. "What're we gonna do upstairs?"

"A Bruce Willis thing."

"*Die Hard!*"

"A later Bruce Willis thing."

I put Milo down in the upstairs hall, and together we located the bedroom in which Truman Walbert had chosen to bunk.

In the attached bathroom, I rummaged through the vanity drawers in search of his shaving gear. Because of Walbert's heavy jowls and the deep lines in his hound-dog face, I doubted that he had used a straight razor, and I was relieved to find an electric, which would make this job go quicker.

Using the sideburn trimmer, I cut a swath from my forehead, across the top of my skull, and down the back.

Watching snakes of my strange hair spiral to the floor, Milo said, "Extreme."

"What if I said you're next?"

"Then I'd have to knock you flat."

"Totally flat, huh?"

"I wouldn't enjoy doing it."

"That's nice to know."

Milo said, "But a man's got to do what a man's got to do."

When nothing was left but short bristles, I switched from the trimmer to the standard shaver head and buzzed away the stubble.

"How do I look?" I asked.

"Slick."

"I'll take that as a compliment. Let's go."

Indicating the hair mounded like dead rats on the floor, Milo said, "Don't we have to clean up?"

"We're desperate fugitives. We live by our own rules."

"Cool."

At the top of the stairs, I lifted him into my arms and told him to close his eyes until further notice. I carried him down to the foyer.

In the hallway, around the three cadavers, Penny had laid a carpet of green-plastic trash bags to avoid getting more blood on the soles of her shoes. The scene wasn't from a conventional TV commercial, but it effectively sold the point that the product was versatile, its many uses limited only by the consumer's imagination.

Penny came into the foyer with a smaller white-plastic trash bag containing what she had harvested from the dead.

I thought of my uncle Tray's methamphetamine-amped buddies

gathering wallets and purses from the many victims in Uncle Ewen's farmhouse twenty-eight years earlier, and I wondered at the complex and often eerie patterns evident in every life.

Seeing the new me, Penny said with dismay, "Oh, no. Where's your wonderful weird thatch?"

"Crawling around on the bathroom floor. Turns out, it has a life of its own, tried to attack us. Car keys?"

She fished them out of the white trash bag.

I said, "You drive us back to pick up Lassie while I make a phone call."

Outside, when I got a closer look at the dull-green sedan in which Rink and Shucker had arrived, I said, "Looks like standard government-issued wheels."

A three-inch-square sticker had been applied to the inside of the lower left-hand corner of the windshield, facing out to be read by security scanners. At the bottom were a number and data in the form of a bar code.

The primary element of the overall-gray sticker was a white circle that enclosed a symbol: three muscular red arms radiating from the center, joined at the shoulder and forming a kind of wheel, each arm bent at the elbow, each hand fisted.

"It's a triskelion," Penny said. "I'd guess the fists symbolize power, red endorses violence, and the wheel form promises unstoppable momentum."

"So you think they don't work for the Bureau of Compassionate Day Care."

"They might."

I put Milo in the backseat and got in the front with Penny as she started the engine. "We have to abandon the Mountaineer. Besides Lassie, is there anything in it we've absolutely got to have?"

"One suitcase," she said. "I can grab it in ten seconds."

"Milo?" I asked.

"That sack of special stuff Grimpa got me. I haven't used most of it yet."

"What about the bread-box thing you wouldn't let me carry out of the house on the peninsula?"

"Oh, yeah. That for sure. That is monumentally *crucial*."

"Did I say you can open your eyes now?"

"I figured it out back on the porch."

"My little Einstein."

" '*Weird* little Einstein,' he called me," Milo remembered. "He wants to know weird, he should look in a mirror."

As Penny followed the driveway toward the state road, I keyed in Vivian Norby's disposable-cell number on *my* disposable cell and prayed she would pick up.

Since only I possessed her new number, Vivian answered with, "Cubby?"

"Viv, I'm so sorry about this, but the bad guys are going to have your Mountaineer soon."

"Are *you* all right?" she asked worriedly.

"I'm bald, but otherwise we're all fine."

"You remember I told you I smelled something funny about all this and that it was a stink I smelled before somewhere, sometime?"

"Yes, I do. I remember the stink conversation."

"Well, like twenty-five years ago, Wilfred worked for this police chief who took this homicide case away from him with a lame excuse."

Wilfred Norby was Vivian's deceased husband, the ex-marine and detective. The name Wilfred comes from two Old English words, *willa* and *frith*, which together mean "desire for peace."

"Turned out," Vivian continued, "the chief and a half dozen of his top staff were corrupt. They were doing business with a drug gang that committed the homicide Wilfred got pulled from. The stink is corruption in high places, Cubby. This isn't just some wingnut on your case. This is something bigger."

"We're on the same page, Viv. Listen, as soon as the bad guys have the Mountaineer, they'll be coming to you, and when they find out you're Milo's sitter, they'll know you gave it to us."

"Just let them try to get anything out of me."

"I don't want them to try. Viv, they were on us so fast in Smokeville, all that research you've been doing into Henry Casas and other artists must have triggered some alarm built into one website or another."

"I don't like these sonsofbitches," she said.

"They're not on my Christmas list, either. My point is, they might already figure you're helping us, they might show up there at any time."

"This is so invigorating," Vivian said.

"Viv, I am very sorry, but I think you better get out of there right away. Take whatever things you're most sentimental about, you'd hate to lose. Go to your bank, withdraw as much cash as you can, and be ready to make a big change."

"I wish Wilfred could be here for this."

"Go to the Boom Demolition office in Anaheim. The secretary's name is Golda Chenetta, she looks like Judi Dench. Tell her you need to talk to Grimbald, tell Grim I said to take you to the stronghold."

"What stronghold?"

"He'll know. Viv, hear me clear now. Time is of the essence."

"It always is. I'm already in motion. Kiss Prince Milo for me," she said, and terminated the call.

Penny drove off the paved route, into the lay-by where we had left the Mountaineer, which was still shrouded in mist.

"What if they're waiting here for us?" she suddenly worried.

"Then we're finished."

Chapter 56

As if it were a time machine returning from an earlier century, fading from the rational past into the insane present, the Mercury Mountaineer materialized out of the fog. No one from the Bureau of Compassionate Day Care lurked around the vehicle.

Penny killed the sedan headlights but left the engine running. "What exactly are you intending to do?"

"Let's get what we need from the Mountaineer, and then I'll fill you in."

Lassie was ecstatic to see us. She even favored me with a nuzzle equal to that she gave Milo and Penny. I suspected she wanted to lick my bald head.

Penny intended to put the suitcase in the trunk, but I stopped her. "Everything on the floor in front of the backseat."

When we transferred what little we were keeping from the SUV, we stood at the sedan while I sorted onto the hood those items that Penny had taken from Rink and Shucker.

In their wallets, I found each man had a California driver's license in his name. But each possessed a second driver's license, also with his photo, Rink's in the name Aldous Lipman, Shucker's in the name Fraser Parson.

"Nothing suspicious about that," I said.

"No, no, nothing. The poor men suffer from multiple-personality syndrome," said Penny.

Standing between us, Milo said, "Let me see," and I passed the four licenses down to him. "When I'm director of the FBI, these are the kind of guys who're gonna learn what justice means."

The two men carried laminated cards that featured only their photos, their names, and a triskelion that matched the one on the windshield sticker. I put Rink's in my shirt pocket.

Each of them also had a thin leather wallet, a simple one-fold that held a badge and a laminated credential, with photo, identifying him as an agent of the National Security Agency.

"You think that's real?" Penny asked.

"I'm not sure anything's what it appears to be anymore except you, me, and Milo."

"And Lassie," Milo said.

"She appears to be a dog, and she is," I acknowledged. "But sometimes I'm not sure a dog is all she is."

The becalmed sea of fog suddenly began to move, not because a breeze had sprung up, but because the thermal balance between land and sea had tipped in the opposite direction than it had tipped the previous twilight, when I had been walking from Smokeville Pizzeria to our cottage at the motor court.

The fog flowed from the evergreen forest, across the lay-by, pulled westward by a new tide. As it gained speed, it began again to look more like smoke than like mist. The entire world seemed to be smoldering, evidence of an unseen fire raging just below the surface of things.

"I think the fog helps us," I said. "So we better move before the day clears. Remember—Waxx told Brock that any car not obviously one of theirs is going to be stopped, not just at the roadblocks but wherever they encounter it."

She said, "But we've got one of their sedans, and the triskelion is on the windshield."

"They're looking for Cullen Greenwich, the writer, but he's got strange hair, and I don't have any hair at all. They're looking for a man, woman, and child traveling together, but I'm a man alone."

"Alone?" Penny said. "Where are the woman and child?"

"And the dog?" Milo added.

"You'll be riding in the trunk," I said. "Won't that be fun?"

Chapter 57

From the lay-by where we abandoned the Mountaineer, I turned south, away from the Landulf house and Smokeville.

Within moments, a sign announced TITUS SPRINGS—4 MILES. Waxx had told Brock that the southern roadblock was established this side of Titus Springs.

I traveled less than a quarter of a mile before I began to miss Penny, Milo, and Lassie. I wished that somebody else would have been available to drive, so I could be in the trunk with my family.

The road rose and fell through geography that might have struck me as grand and harmonious at another time but that seemed portentous now, and as full of pending violence as missiles in their launchers. Every unusual shadow was an augury to be interpreted, the westward-racing fog an omen of fast-approaching chaos, the suffocated morning light a presentiment of mortality. Cedars and hemlocks and pines stood on both sides of the pavement, like ranked armies waiting only for a trumpet blast to signal the start of an epic engagement.

A low growl behind me instantly—and irrationally—brought to mind the deformed face of the man in Henry Casas's painting, but when I glanced over my shoulder with alarm, I saw only our Lassie on the backseat.

I smiled, said "Good girl," and returned my attention to the roadway before realizing that Lassie in the backseat was no less astonishing than if the Maserati monster had been there.

Only a couple of minutes earlier, I had lifted the dog into the trunk of the sedan. I had closed the lid on her.

Certain that I must have imagined her impossible liberation, I glanced back once more. She grinned at me.

My confidence in the reliability of my senses was so shaken that when, five seconds later, I decided to check on her presence one more time, I tilted down the rearview mirror with the expectation that a figment of my imagination would cast no reflection. But she regarded me with cocked-head insouciance.

She had *not* jumped out of the trunk before the lid slammed. I would stake a fortune on that wager.

Behind me, Lassie again issued a long, low growl.

Having been saved by something like a miracle when I was six years old, I decided two things: first, that a refusal to accept this phenomenon was not merely healthy self-doubt but was instead cynical skepticism that was unworthy of me; second, that young Milo had some explaining to do.

The land was repaying its debt of fog to the sea with such dispatch that already I could see much farther than when I had left the lay-by.

Downhill, on the left, headlights stabbed across the roadway and then arced toward me as an SUV appeared between trees and turned onto the pavement from a narrow dirt road, heading north. As the vehicle approached, I saw that it was an Explorer.

Clearly, the driver was interested in me. As he came uphill, he rode closer and closer to the center line until he had edged a few inches into my lane.

Suspecting that Waxx's protocols for his current operation required agents to acknowledge one another when they crossed paths, I remained close to the center line, reduced speed, and rolled down the window in the driver's door.

In the lower corner of the windshield, on the driver's side of the Explorer, was a square decal of a size suspiciously like that on the windshield of my sedan, but I could not at first discern what it might be. As we closed on each other, however, I recognized the red triskelion, three fisted arms forming a wheel.

His window was open, too, and as we coasted past each other, the driver gave me a thumbs-up sign with his left hand.

He had a blocky head suitable for breaking boards in a martial-arts exhibition, the bulging jaws of someone who might pull nails out of lumber with his teeth, the nose of a pugilist who had let down his guard too often, and the eyes of a pit viper. The guy riding shotgun was not nearly so good-looking.

After the briefest hesitation, I returned the driver's thumbs-up sign with my left hand, and as we glided past each other, I sighed with relief, eased down on the accelerator, and rolled up my window.

In my side mirror, I thought I saw the Explorer come to a halt in the middle of the road.

After readjusting my rearview mirror to capture the back window, I confirmed that Blockhead had brought his vehicle to a full stop. He hung a left turn and fell in behind me.

Something about me had made them suspicious. Perhaps I was not supposed to respond to his thumbs-up with a thumbs-up of my own, but was instead supposed to make the okay sign or wiggle my pinkie, or thrust my middle finger at him.

I could try my best not to be paralyzed by the viciousness of these evil people-of-the-red-arms, and I could strive to accommodate myself to their singular lunacy, but it just wasn't right that they also expected me to play their game by some book of boy's-club rules that included code signs, countersigns, and secret handshakes.

Because I had been accelerating and they had been stopped to ponder why I had not replied to their thumbs-up with a bird whistle appropriate to the moment, I was a hundred yards ahead of them. Now they began to close fast.

If I tried to run, they would *know* that I was not a faithful attendee at the altar of their asylum, and I would never get through the roadblock alive.

I had the pistol, and I could make a valiant stand, but it was two against one, and I wouldn't get a chance to let Penny Annie Oakley out of the trunk to help me defend our little piece of the American dream.

In spite of my reputed flaming optimism, I concluded that we were screwed. Lassie's growling in the backseat seemed to confirm my judgment, and I heard myself chanting over and over a four-letter synonym for *poop*.

He closed to within fifty yards as I ransacked my brain for strategy. To forty yards...to thirty...to twenty. Ten.

Then an inexplicable but not unwelcome event occurred.

In my rearview mirror, I saw the southbound Explorer abruptly swing hard left, into the northbound lane, as though to avoid a collision with something that had bounded into the driver's path, such as a leaping deer, though there was no deer nor anything else from which he needed to swerve.

At risk of crashing into the trees that crowded close to the pavement, the driver braked hard and pulled the wheel to the right. Considering that he had been accelerating when he made his first sudden change of course and that he was on a downhill run, this maneuver proved too extreme, and the Explorer tipped precariously to port as it came back across the pavement toward the southbound lane.

Careening off the road just where an embankment rose, the driver turned hard left again, ran along the slope at an angle that was not sustainable, wrestled the SUV back onto the pavement, but then shot across the southbound lane into the northbound once more, this time listing wildly to starboard.

He seemed to have gone from sobriety to extreme inebriation in an instant, or perhaps they were transporting a beehive for some nefarious purpose and the wee critters suddenly erupted in a rage, mercilessly stinging Blockhead and his companion.

Rapt by this spectacle, I almost made a lethal error. Switching my attention back and forth between the road ahead and the mirrors, I braked gently and reduced my speed to compensate for the distraction.

Blockhead pulled his steering wheel too hard to the right again but also seemed to tramp on the accelerator when he wanted the brake. The heroic Explorer could endure no more, and it leaned disastrously toward port, went over, and completed a wonderfully destructive 360-degree roll.

Because we were on a downhill run and because gravity will always have its way, the Explorer didn't lose speed in its tumble but came on as fast as ever as it rolled again—directly toward me.

I might have squealed, I'm not sure, but I swung the sedan to the right, onto the shoulder, but found room to get only half the car off the pavement.

Half proved enough, and the Explorer tumbled past as it came out of its second roll and with great exuberance executed a third.

I braked to a full stop and sat transfixed by the sight of the SUV rolling again and again, and yet again, down the hill, scattering pieces of itself in its wake. Finally the vehicle tumbled off the farther side of the road, ricocheted off a tree, caromed off another tree, and knocked this way and that into the woods, as if Mother Nature had decided to have a game of pinball.

By the time the Explorer came to a stop, both occupants were most likely dead, but for sure neither of them would be dancing by Christmas.

I suppose a good Samaritan would have hurried to the crash site and provided tender care to the survivors, if any.

After I considered what these people had done to the Landulf and Clitherow families—and what they hoped to do to mine—I found myself driving past the scene with a clear conscience. And if I spent 705 years in Purgatory instead of 704—well, I would just have to cope.

I drove on for perhaps half a mile in a daze.

Only then did I realize that Lassie no longer occupied the back of the sedan. At some point during the death plunge of the SUV, she must have clambered into the front. She perched now in the passenger seat, riding shotgun, gazing at the highway ahead with keen interest.

Chapter 58

Less than five minutes after Blockhead and his nameless sidekick arrived at the pearly gates with résumés that made Saint Peter call for the celestial security guards, I topped another rise and looked down another slope at a roadblock formed by two sheriff's-department cars parked nose to nose.

Although frightened, I was not a fraction as terrified as when we were playing let's-shoot-each-other-in-the-head at the Landulf house. I had been through so much in the past seventy-two hours that I earned my good-scout medal for nerves of steel and was working on my titanium certification.

In fact, I have to admit that I got a cheap thrill from the fact that this police roadblock was in my honor. All my life, I had been a good boy, living by the rules: making my bed each morning, flossing my teeth twice a day, eating my vegetables dutifully.... When I was a lad and then a single young man, all those girls who liked bad boys—which, strangely enough, seemed to be most of them—thought of me as a boring nerd, or thought of me not at all. If they could see me now—head shaved, carrying an unregistered concealed weapon, driving a vehicle stolen from a federal agent—they would swoon, become giddy with desire, and perhaps even throw their panties at me as if I were a rock star.

In truth, of course, I remained a good boy, trying my best to do the right thing. In this inverted world of the twenty-first century, the authorities were the unprincipled thugs, and the armed fugitive in the stolen car was a churchgoing family man who had a dog named Lassie.

As we approached the roadblock, I worried that having a dog beside me would blow my cover, but I didn't want the sheriff's deputies to see me stop and put her in the trunk. Then I decided that a psychopathic agent for a psychopathic federal agency might well have a service dog to assist him in chasing down and savaging the innocent.

That scenario would have been more plausible if Lassie were a Doberman or a German shepherd, weighed a hundred pounds more than she did, and were foaming at the mouth with rabies. But she was what she was, and I came slowly to a stop at the barricade with every intention of claiming that beside me sat a canine as highly trained as a circus bear and a thousand times more dangerous.

The four men manning the roadblock were uniformed sheriff's-department deputies. They looked wholesome, earnest, and sane. Two of them were leaning against the back end of a patrol car, drinking coffee and chatting.

Earlier, in the cellar of the Landulf house, Shearman Waxx told Brock that because he needed every man under his command to conduct the search for us, the two roadblocks would be manned solely by sheriff's-department personnel, and for once he was not lying like a snake in Eden. No plainclothes goons were in sight.

I was prepared to flash Rink's badge and ID, held so that one of my fingers covered his face in the photo, but the deputy at the point position reacted to the triskelion on the windshield and waved me around the barricade without delay.

The shoulder of the road was wide here, with sufficient room on the right to squeeze past the patrol cars, once the two deputies with the coffee cups politely moved out of my way. I almost gave them a thumbs-up sign, but then decided that might get me shot. Instead I remained stone-faced and ignored them, as I imagined an arrogant fed might disdain members of a rural police force, whom he regarded as hicks.

Perhaps eighty feet beyond the roadblock, a man walked in the northbound lane. Although his back was to me, I recognized Shearman Waxx. Ahead of him, past a couple of stone pines, off the road in a rest stop with a graveled area for parking and two picnic tables on a grassy sward, stood the black Hummer.

He must have been recently conferring with the four deputies. If I had arrived at the barricade two minutes sooner, Waxx would have recognized Lassie. Then the dog, Milo, Penny, and I would have been on our way to a torture chamber and thereafter to a wood chipper.

My initial impulse was to run him down and then stand on the accelerator, racing into the misty morning with the hope that, before a sheriff's-department cruiser caught up with us, an alien ship from a faraway star would levitate us into its cargo hold and whisk us away to be studied.

Repressing that urge, I did something riskier than hit-and-run. As Waxx opened the driver's door and climbed into the Hummer, I drove into the rest area and parked twenty feet behind him, where the stone pines partially screened the sedan from the men at the roadblock.

I could discern his silhouette in the driver's seat. He was alone in the Hummer, having assigned the three other men at Landulf's house to the search for us.

On the night Tray Durant murdered my family, when spared from death, I was six years old. Now Milo, six years old, condemned by the order of Shearman Waxx, was mine to save or lose. Driven by intuition, we had come north less on the run than on the hunt for information that might empower us. In the mysterious roundness of all things, Waxx might here be delivered into my hands, as I had been delivered *from* the hands of Tray.

Lassie curled up on the passenger seat to take a nap, and I got out of the car, wiping my face with one hand as if I were weary from long hours of committing whatever monstrous crimes one of the people-of-the-red-arms committed on an average workday. Turning my back to the Hummer, I raised my arms high, stretched elaborately, and finally sauntered around to the back of the sedan.

When I opened the trunk, Penny said excitedly, incoherently, "Lassie, she was here— The lid closed— Panting in the dark— She was— Then she—"

"Later, later, later," I insisted, taking her by the arm as she clambered out of the trunk. "Crouch down, use the raised lid as cover, Waxx is sitting in the Hummer like twenty feet away."

Milo popped out of the trunk as if on a spring and huddled with his mother.

In perhaps twenty seconds or less, I told them what we were going to do.

Milo said, "Cool," and Penny said, "Oh, my God," and leaving the trunk lid raised, I walked around the sedan and headed for the Hummer.

Chapter 59

I approached the vehicle with my bald head down, as if brooding about a problem. I drew my pistol only as I reached the driver's door and yanked it open.

Evidently, Waxx hadn't been watching me, as I feared. Surprised, he looked up from a BlackBerry, on which he was composing a text message.

Jamming the muzzle of the .45 into his side, I said, "Believe me, one wrong move, and I'll kill you with great pleasure."

He switched off the BlackBerry and started to put it on the dashboard.

"No," I said, and held out my hand.

When he gave it to me, I threw it hard to the ground, stomped it twice, and kicked it away.

"Imagine there's a bomb strapped to you," I said, "and it's got such a delicate trigger mechanism, any quick move will blow you to Hell." I backed off a step. "Now get out."

He appeared calm, but fury teemed in his maroon eyes.

I expected him to throw himself at me and try to seize my gun, but maybe he was a guy who took chances only after he had already stacked the deck.

At any moment, someone could drive into the rest stop and see me apparently robbing a respectable-looking gentleman. The deputies at the roadblock were partially screened from us by the stone pines, but they were within hailing distance.

When Waxx was out of the Hummer, I said, "Open the back door."

He did as he was told—and was surprised again when Penny swung up and into the backseat through the opposite door and pulled it shut behind her.

As she covered him with her pistol, I pressed mine against his spine and said, "She's handled guns all her life. She shot Rink from thirty feet and put the first round through his carotid artery."

To Waxx, Penny said, "I want to kill you worse than Cubby does. Keep that in mind as you're getting in."

He climbed into the backseat beside her, and I closed the door after him.

Holstering the .45, I hurried around to the other side of the vehicle, where Milo waited with Lassie.

I opened the passenger door and boosted the boy into the front seat. Lassie allowed herself to be lifted onto his lap.

After closing the door, I went around to the back, where Penny had left the suitcase and where Milo had put down the sack of stuff that we took from the Mountaineer before abandoning it. I opened the tailgate and stowed our things.

The immense cargo space already contained a large black suitcase with stainless-steel fittings. The luggage intrigued me. It did not appear to be a bag that contained only a few clean shirts and changes of underwear, but this wasn't the time to explore its contents.

A moment later, I settled into the driver's seat. The key was in the ignition, and I started the engine.

The huge wraparound windshield not only provided an excellent view but also made me feel that I was less a driver than a pilot, and king of the road.

As we headed north, Waxx said, "You're all as dead as Rink and Shucker."

"Shut up, asshole," Penny said, not as the author of *The Other Side of the Woods* might have said it, not as either the mice or the owl in that story might have said it, but rather like Joe Pesci, playing a sociopath in a movie like *Goodfellas,* would have said it.

Milo's eyes were as round and as large as any owl's when he whispered, "Dad, did you hear that word?"

I said, "Which word do you mean—*shut* or *up?*"

The motto of Titus Springs was definitely not "If you can make it here, you can make it anywhere." According to the sign at the town limits, the population was 1,500, but that probably included the out-of-towners who had been abducted and locked in the basements of some of the community's more colorful citizens, to serve as unconventional pets or as blood sacrifices the next time the weather gods withheld rain for too long.

Because the town served as the commercial hub for a score of even smaller towns and surrounding rural residents, there were more shopping opportunities than I expected, including a large locally owned hardware store that sold everything from horseshoes to nail guns to cattle prods to curling irons, from calendars of scantily clad women holding a variety of tools to forty kinds of hammers.

They offered numerous styles and gauges of chain, which they sold by the foot off large drum dispensers. I bought twenty feet of a sturdy chain, a bolt cutter, eight padlocks keyed the same, a roll of wide duct tape, scissors, a package of cotton rags, and a blanket.

The clerk at the checkout was a gangly young man with a crane's neck, a large Adam's apple, a rat's-nest beard, yellow teeth, and Charles Manson eyes. After he rang up the items and before he hit the TOTAL key on the register, he said, "You want some chloroform with that?"

I stared at him a moment and then said, "What?"

Scratching his beard with long bony fingers, he said, "To make her easier to handle while you're chaining her down."

This time I was speechless.

He laughed and waved his hand dismissively. "Sorry, mister. Don't mind me. I've got the best sense of humor in the family. If I'm not careful, Uncle Frank's gonna pull me off the register and make me stockboy again."

"Oh," I said, forcing a smile, then a small laugh. "I see what you mean—chains, padlocks, duct tape. Pretty funny."

Suddenly deadpan again, he said, "So you want that chloroform or not?"

I half thought he would produce a bottle of the stuff if I asked for it. But I laughed again, said "Not," and he hit the TOTAL key.

The windows of the old church were boarded up, and weeds grew from cracks in the walkway and in the front steps.

The gravel parking lot behind the building was not visible from the highway out front, and it backed up to rolling fields with no other structures in sight.

Milo and Lassie remained in the front seat, but the rest of us got out of the Hummer.

At my instruction, Waxx put his wallet and the contents of his pockets in the empty hardware-store bag.

I ordered him to lie on his back, and he refused to complain about the gravel, though his eyes told the whole story of what he wanted to do to me, starting with the extraction of all my teeth using pliers and a ball-peen hammer.

As Penny stood aside from Waxx, covering him with her gun, I told her, "If you see some guy coming, he's barefoot and buck-toothed and carrying a banjo, wound him first and ask questions later."

"This place isn't all that *Deliverance*."

"Yeah? You didn't meet Uncle Frank's nephew, he's got the best sense of humor in the family."

With a length of chain and two padlocks, I fitted Shearman Waxx with shackles, allowing enough slack for him to shuffle but not to run.

Next, I shackled his hands together in front of him, not behind, and left a comfortable but cautious foot of chain between his wrists.

Previously, I transferred our gear from the cargo space to the backseat. Waxx's black suitcase stood on the ground by the Hummer.

Chained, he had some difficulty getting to his feet.

At last I assisted him, and he glared at me as if my assistance might be another reason to mutilate and murder me.

I made him lie faceup in the Hummer's cargo space, head toward the backseat.

Penny stood at the open tailgate, her pistol aimed at Waxx's crotch. As I worked, they got into a staring contest that neither of them would break.

Flip-up metal rings were recessed in the carpeted floor of the Hummer. Items could be secured to the rings to prevent them from shifting during transit.

With additional lengths of chain, I padlocked Waxx's wrist shackles to one of those anchors, his ankle shackles to another.

When that task was completed, Penny put her pistol away, and we opened the black bag with the stainless-steel fixtures.

In an aluminum case within the suitcase, we found a formidable pistol with two spare magazines, a screw-on sound suppressor, and a shoulder rig.

Penny fitted the silencer to the barrel, stepped away from the Hummer, and fired two shots at one of the boarded-up windows of the church. The cracking plywood made a lot more noise than the weapon.

"I'll take this," Penny said.

"You were made for each other."

The suitcase also contained a Taser and what we assumed must be instruments of torture: a scalpel, four nasty little thumbscrew clamps, a pair of needle-nose pliers, a culinary torch of the kind used to glaze crème brûlée, and an array of other toys for sadists, including a thick rubber bite guard to prevent the subject from chewing his tongue while convulsed with pain.

A pharmacy kit was stocked with a variety of drugs, several individually packaged hypodermic syringes, cotton balls, a bottle of isopropyl alcohol, and a length of rubber tubing to be used as a tourniquet.

After examining the drugs, Penny selected a sedative.

"This is going to make the drive a lot more pleasant for us."

She leaned in the back of the Hummer and asked Waxx how much of the sleeping drug she could safely administer to him, and how often.

"You could accidentally give me an embolism if you inject an air bubble with the sedative," he said.

"You mean like you did intentionally to John Clitherow's father on that boat?"

"You are so dead," he said.

Penny said, "If the time comes to kill you, I won't make it as easy as a needle."

Waxx hesitated, but then told her the proper dosage.

She crawled into the cargo space with him, used the tourniquet to help clarify a vein in his right arm, and swabbed the injection site with alcohol.

For the first time, Waxx showed a trace of anxiety. "Where are you taking me?"

From the open tailgate, I said, "Home."

"Before you do anything that goes . . . a step too far," Waxx said, "there's time to reach an understanding."

"We understand enough about you already," I said. "And you'll never understand us."

"But this isn't right."

"It's not a fair world."

"You've committed numerous felonies," Waxx said.

My laugh had a bitter quality that didn't sound like me. I said, "Freak."

His face flushed, and he said, "Hack."

Penny put him to sleep less permanently than she might have liked.

Chapter 60

We spent the long day driving south, Milo and Lassie in the backseat, Penny and I up front, spelling each other at the wheel. The Hummer rode well, and we made good time.

Waxx remained supine in the cargo space, covered in a blanket except for his face. When you couldn't see the chains, he looked as if he were having, by choice, a pleasant snooze.

When we got hungry, we stopped for take-out and ate while on the road.

Each time that Waxx came around enough to tell us how totally dead we were, Penny administered additional sedative.

Among the items taken from his pockets were a set of what most likely were house keys. From the key ring hung a remote-control fob much like the one that we had used to open the garage doors at the peninsula house.

In his wallet, Penny found a card with the house alarm-system codes and the phone number to call in the event of a false alarm.

More interesting were the four photos of the woman, portraits. In one, she appeared to be in her forties; another two might have been taken about a decade later; and in the fourth, she most likely had been sixty-something.

She was a handsome woman but not pretty. At first her face seemed severe, but after studying her long enough, you realized that her features were generous enough and that the impression of severity came from the way she presented herself.

Pulled back from her face, her hair was worn in a chignon, a tight roll that lay at the nape of her neck. It had been dark in her forties and fifties, later gray.

In all four photos, her lips were pressed together as though someone were trying to force a spoonful of bitter medicine upon her. The corners of her mouth puckered with tension. She appeared to be incapable of a smile.

Her wide-set eyes were blue but not warm like Penny's, tempered by striations of gray. In every instance, she glared at the camera as if she loathed posing for photographs, and I suspected that in her presence you could almost feel the iciness of that stare.

In the wallet, Penny also found a folded index card with a typed bit of commemorative verse titled "To Mother on Her 60th Birthday."

While I drove, she read it aloud with the lack of feeling that it merited: "Mother of life, Mother of death. Mother of all, you take my breath. Mother of all our tomorrows. Give us a world without sorrows. Love is the illusion of fools. Wisdom is the power that rules. Mother bring us all together. Change this world now and forever."

"Doesn't seem like it comes from a Hallmark card," I said.

Penny said, "It's signed—'Your obedient son, Shearman.'"

From the backseat, Milo piped: "I might have blown something up that one time, but I've never dropped a poetry bomb like that on you."

"And I'm grateful, Milo," Penny said.

"Is Mother the woman in the four photos?" I wondered.

"I'd bet both kidneys and a lung on it," Penny said.

———⟶

After we had eaten a late lunch of cheeseburgers while rolling steadily south, with Penny at the wheel, I said, "I'm not sure why we're afraid to talk about it."

"I'm not sure, either," Penny said.

"I mean, with all the horrible things we've learned and seen and been forced to do these last few days, this doesn't seem scary by comparison."

"And yet," Penny said, "I'm so afraid to bring it up that I'd almost rather talk about what these crazy red-arm bastards did to Henry Casas and Tom Landulf and the others."

"I know what you mean. I'd almost rather read Waxx's idiotic poem a hundred times than open the door on this."

"And yet what could we learn that would be terrible? For some time, she's been doing strange things, but she's still just a dog."

"And such a very cute dog," I said.

"An adorable dog. Remember the day we rescued her from the shelter? She stole our hearts in a minute."

"In an instant," I said. "On first sight."

Penny blotted her left palm on her jacket, then her right, and took a firmer grip on the steering wheel. "All right, here goes."

I closed my eyes and drew a deep breath. "Here goes."

To Milo in the backseat, Penny said, "Honey, Spooky, remember when we were in the trunk of the car with Lassie?"

"That was interesting, riding in the trunk," Milo said, "but I wouldn't want to do it again."

Penny said, "I had my arm around Lassie to keep her calm."

"You didn't need to do that, Mom. She's a supercalm dog by nature."

"The thing is, honey, one second Lassie was cuddled with me, and the next second she was . . . gone."

The boy said, "Well, it was dark in the trunk, so you don't know, like maybe she crawled off in a corner."

"The way we were crammed in that trunk, there was nowhere to crawl, Milo."

"Besides," I said, "suddenly she was in the backseat of the sedan."

Cagey Milo said, "You saw her?"

"She growled, and I looked back, and there she was."

"You're sure that was when she was supposed to be in the trunk and not earlier?"

"Milo," I said. "You and your mom were in the trunk at the time. I'm not confused about the circumstances."

"I see," said Milo.

"Furthermore," I pressed, "the next thing I know, she's in the front seat, beside me."

"Maybe you asked her to come up with you."

In as stern a voice as we ever took with him, Penny and I simultaneously said, "*Milo.*"

"This isn't easy," the boy said.

After a silence, Penny said, "We're listening."

"Mom, Dad, I don't want you to think I'm a screwup."

"We don't think you're a screwup," I assured him.

"Not yet maybe. But I did blow up that one thing, and now this."

"This what?"

"This thing with Lassie."

"And the thing would be—what?"

"Well, here's the way it is," Milo said. "You know I was working on the time-travel thing."

"Yes," Penny said, "and you decided time travel is impossible."

"That was after I made the vest."

"What vest?" Penny asked.

"The time vest. The time vest for Lassie. I was trying to send her one minute into the future."

"You were experimenting with Lassie?" Penny asked with a clear note of disapproval.

"She loves working with me. It couldn't hurt her."

"What if it accidentally sent her a *billion years* into the future and we never saw her again?"

"Couldn't happen. Time travel is impossible."

Penny said, "You didn't know that when you pushed the button."

"What button?"

"The dog time-vest button."

"It doesn't have a button. It's a sliding switch."

"*Milo.*"

"Okay, okay, what happened was she didn't disappear one minute into the future, instead she teleported from one side of my room to the other, so when I thought I made a time vest, I actually made a teleportation vest."

I opened my eyes.

Penny blotted her hands on her jacket again.

I cleared my throat.

Penny said, "You haven't used this teleportation vest yourself, have you?"

"No. There seems to be a weight limit for teleportation. It's a thing Lassie can do, but I'm like ten pounds too heavy."

"Don't you ever try to teleport yourself anywhere," Penny said adamantly. "Don't you *ever.*"

"Milo," I said, "for God's sake, you've seen Vincent Price in *The Fly.*"

"Well, that couldn't happen in real life, only the movies," he said defensively.

A quibble occurred to me. "Wait a minute. When Lassie was in the trunk of the car, she wasn't wearing any vest."

"Well, see, that's the thing."

"That's what thing?"

"The funny thing I can't figure."

"*Milo.*"

"After Lassie teleported a few times in the vest, she like didn't need the vest anymore to do it."

Penny realized that she had been pressing on the accelerator during the latter part of this conversation, and we were rocketing along the freeway at just over a hundred miles an hour. She allowed our speed to fall back to the posted limit.

"Let me get this straight," I said. "Lassie is now a dog who can teleport herself at will, anywhere she wants."

"Not anywhere," Milo said. "There seems to be a distance limit. She can teleport across the room. Or like from the car trunk to the backseat. Or like from the backseat to the front seat. Or like into a drawer or to the top of a cabinet. But she can't go more than maybe ten feet, fifteen feet, maybe twenty. She travels point to point instantaneously, but they're just little trips."

Penny and I were both silent for a while, but there must have been an unusual quality about my silence, because she said, "Cubby?"

"Huh?"

"What is it?"

"I think she can teleport farther than twenty feet."

"Where do you think she went? Did she bring a souvenir back from Hong Kong?"

Remembering how the pursuing Explorer had abruptly gone out

of control, as if the driver had been attacked by a swarm of bees, I said, "She ported from the sedan to the Explorer that was pursuing us. Those guys are chasing us, gaining, and suddenly a dog that was never in the vehicle is all over them, maybe in the driver's face, then on his back, then in the other guy's lap, growling and snarling and biting—"

"Lassie would never bite anyone," Penny said.

"Never," Milo agreed.

"She might have bitten these guys. They looked like people who needed to be bitten."

Penny said, "So did she realize the thugs in the Explorer were a threat to us, and she basically took them out—is that what you're telling me? Is that really what you're telling me?"

"Dogs," Milo said, "have been very protective of their human companions for thousands of years."

Lassie growled in agreement.

—————⟶

After a long period of thoughtful silence, with Penny still behind the wheel of the Hummer, I said, "Milo?"

"Yeah, Dad."

"The saltshakers."

"What saltshakers?"

"The ones you gave us in the cellar of the Landulf house."

"Oh, those aren't saltshakers anymore."

Penny said, "I'm not sure I'm prepared for this right now. We killed two men this morning, we've got Waxx chained to the floor in back, we've got a teleporting dog, so it's like, you know, enough is enough for one day."

Quite reasonably, I explained my position to her: "To avoid any unpleasant surprises, I'd just like to know if the saltshakers will send me to Mars or turn me into a wolf, or throw me into a parallel dimension where dinosaurs still rule the earth. I'm not asking the hour of my death or whether I'm going to spend the rest of my life in a people-of-the-red-arms prison, I don't want information that would make living unbearable. I just want to know what the saltshakers will do."

Penny Boom said, "Let it go."

"It's defensive knowledge. It's like, what if you were walking around with a butane lighter in your pocket, and you didn't know what it was, you thought maybe it was a breath freshener, so you stuck it in your mouth to get a squirt of mint, and you clicked it, and you set your tongue on fire."

"Let it go."

"Milo," I said.

"Yeah, Dad."

"Will the saltshaker send me to Mars?"

"It's not a saltshaker anymore."

"Whatever it is, will it send me to Mars?"

"No, that's not possible."

"Will it turn me into a wolf?"

"That's kind of a silly question."

"But will it turn me into a wolf?"

"Of course not."

"Will it throw me into a parallel dimension where dinosaurs still rule the earth?"

"I don't mean to be rude, Dad, but that's stupid. Won't happen even with the pepper shakers."

"You've got pepper shakers, too?"

"Let it go," said Penny.

"Let's stay with the saltshakers, Spooky."

"That's all we've got," he said, "except they aren't saltshakers anymore, like I keep saying."

"What are they supposed to do?"

"You mean when they were saltshakers or now?"

"Now. What will they do now?"

"This thing that's like nothing anyone would think could happen. You have to experience it to understand."

Penny said, "Cubby, if you don't let it go, I'm going to start screaming."

"You won't start screaming," I said.

"Yes, I will, and I'll want to stop, I really will want to stop, but I won't be able to stop, I'll scream insane things like 'butane breath freshener,' all day, all night, and then what are you going to do with me, are you going to take me back to Titus Springs and ask Frank the hardware guy's geeky nephew to lock me in his basement?"

Suddenly it seemed to me that I had been hectoring Milo and Penny much as Hud Jacklight often hectored me.

Mortified, I said, "You're right."

She regarded me with suspicion.

"No," I said, "you are, you're right. Sometimes it's best to just let it go. We've been through a lot today, and it's not over yet. We still have to deal with Waxx, and that's enough. Dealing with Waxx is all by itself too much."

In the backseat, Lassie yawned loudly, and Milo said, "Dad, it's just that if I tried to explain the science, it would sound like gobbledygook to you."

"I've let it go, Milo."

"If it makes you feel better, Dad, I can guarantee you the saltshaker won't set your tongue on fire."

"That's good to know, son."

"It won't freshen your breath, either."

As we were entering the Los Angeles area, the day wanted to move on toward Japan, and I let it go.

A short while later, the twilight wanted to follow the day, and I let it go.

Letting go of things greatly relaxed me. I felt that at last I was making progress and that one day I would be the same Cubby that I had always been, would hold fast to my best qualities, but would have become a Cubby who could let things go.

We were now drawing very close to the moment when one of the three of us would be shot dead, whereafter life would never be the same.

Chapter 61

The Shearman Waxx house looked exactly like it did on Google Earth: cream-colored walls, terra-cotta window surrounds, a handsome Spanish Mediterranean residence set behind forty-foot magnolias that canopied the front yard. At night, romantic landscape lighting made the place magical.

Larger than expected, set on a markedly more expansive property than was customary in crowded Laguna Beach, the Waxx residence suggested an owner who possessed wealth and power. Neither Penny nor I had the stomach to torture information out of Waxx. Here, more than anywhere else, we might find files and other records regarding his mission and the group symbolized by the triskelion.

At some point during the day, Waxx would surely have been missed and a search for him undertaken by his colleagues. But they would be expecting to find him somewhere in that northern county and would not imagine that he'd been kidnapped and taken home in a marathon twelve-hour drive.

Nevertheless, we cruised by the house a few times, looking for the trouble that might be looking for us. All seemed calm.

No lights shone at any of the windows.

Using the fob on his key ring, I opened one of the doors at the pair of double garages, and Penny drove the Hummer inside. I put the door down.

Having expected a security alarm to be triggered when we drove into the garage, I was ready to let myself quickly into the house with Waxx's keys and enter the disarming code that we had found in his wallet. But no alarm sounded.

The three of us, with dog, stood in the garage for a minute, very still, listening, waiting for someone to appear. No one came.

Waxx remained unconscious in his chains, and we decided to leave him in the Hummer while we completed a tour of the house. Once we had found his files or evidence of a safe, we might need to scare a few answers out of him.

I unlocked the door between garage and house. Penny and I, guns drawn, shepherded Milo along a hallway into a kitchen. We turned on lights as we went.

Evidently designed for frequent use by caterers, the enormous kitchen was not just industrial but also off-putting. The appliances were all stainless steel, as were the counters and the backsplashes and the cabinets. The autopsy theater in a morgue was not as cold-looking as this kitchen.

In room after room, the furniture was stark, the upholstery all in shades of black and silver, the carpets gray, and the artwork so modern that it appeared to have been painted by machines.

We entered a large room that lacked furniture and art. The black-granite floor, gray walls, and indirect cove lighting most likely had been intended to convey a serene mood, but instead the decor made me feel empty. If you were disposed to despair, this place would induce it in but a minute.

As if meditating or in communion with the darkness until we turned on the lights, the woman in Shearman Waxx's wallet photos stood in the center of the room.

She was older than in the latest photo, at least in her mid-seventies. She remained a handsome woman, although thinner than I had imagined, tall and storklike.

Wearing a well-tailored suit—long black skirt, gray jacket, gray blouse—and a simple but stunning diamond necklace, she took pride in her appearance.

If her eyes had not been open and so watchful, I would have thought she was a mummified corpse, preserved with painstaking care.

"What have you done with my Shearman?" she asked, and her voice was strong, commanding, her diction clipped.

"He's sedated, chained in a Hummer in the garage," I told her.

Looking from pistol to pistol, she said, "And have you come here to kill me?"

"We've come here for answers," Penny said. "You're Mrs. Waxx?"

"Waxx is a name I chose and made my own. It was not imposed on me. I never married. I didn't need a husband to have a son."

She began to walk toward us, and the nearer she came, the more that she unnerved me. She seemed to glide rather than take steps, as if she were a motorized automaton, not a real woman.

"When a thing wanes, it diminishes. When a thing waxes, it grows more intense, more powerful. Waxx is my work name, and I fulfill it."

"You are one weird lady," Milo said with childlike directness.

"What is that filthy animal doing in my house?"

Milo took offense: "Lassie isn't filthy. She's as clean as you are. And she can do things you could never do."

Lassie did not lower herself to growl at this scarecrow, but regarded her with canine contempt.

"Bite your tongue, boy. You should know to whom you're speaking.

My maiden name is Zazu Wane. In *Who's Who*, my long and enviable entry is rich with details of my compassion and my charity. But what I have done that truly matters, I have done as Zazu Waxx, and it's more than a nation full of your kind could ever hope to achieve."

"And what achievement would that be?" Penny asked.

"For fifty years, I have pioneered the new science of designing culture. I have *shaped* American and hence world culture through many billions of dollars of sub–rosa propaganda campaigns but also—and more effectively—through the application of techniques more often employed in espionage and warfare."

"Sounds like it keeps you busy," Penny said.

"Oh, terribly busy, my dear."

"Better stop there," I said as Zazu came within ten feet of us.

She halted but looked so full of tightly coiled energy that she might have been able to strike as quick as a snake and cross ten feet in an instant.

"Billions of dollars," Milo said. "Are you that rich?"

Staring down her long straight nose at the boy, as a bird might study a bug before eating it, Zazu Waxx said, "I have the unlimited resources of the federal treasury."

"Sounds better than my allowance."

"And unlike our foolish and inept intelligence agencies, I have kept us on an entirely black budget all these years."

She was clearly proud of her achievements, not to say arrogant, not to say megalomaniacal. But I didn't think she would tell us about all of this if she expected us to leave the house alive.

Light bloomed in the space beyond this meditation chamber, and a moment later, through a door on the far side of the room came the Maserati monster, unaware of us, mumbling to himself, his big hands worrying at each other. He was Shearman Waxx's size and physical type, but he shambled more than walked, and he was a hunchback.

Here, without the intervening rain of our first encounter, he struck me as less monstrous than tragic. His mumbling became audible, and revealed a tortured spirit: "Don't touch, don't touch the pretty things, you'll break them, you stupid boy, you clumsy boy, don't touch the pretty things."

"*You,*" Zazu said sharply.

The man halted and looked up, his fearsome face now fearful, his eyes deep pools of dread.

"What have you broken now?" she asked.

His mouth worked, but no words came out. Then he escaped the black-hole gravity with which Zazu commanded his attention, and he noticed us. "Zazu, they don't belong here, they don't, they don't." He began to wring his hands. "What's happened? What's wrong?"

The rough voice was that of the brutal murderer who slit John Clitherow's throat and who, on the phone with me, called himself the brother of all humanity.

He was a creature of two moods: a miscreation with a rotten purpose and a taste for violence; but apparently also an outsider, alone in the world, whose singularity sometimes made him insecure, uncertain, and fainthearted.

"They don't belong here, we have trouble, we have trouble."

Clearly perturbed, Zazu said, "Shut up or I will shut you up."

Her perturbation might mean that the hunchback's surprise matched her own, which she had striven to conceal. If indeed we surprised her, she was not as in control of the situation as she pretended to be.

She said, "They claim your father is chained in the Hummer in the garage."

Penny and I exchanged a glance. We both said, "Father?"

"They say," Zazu continued, "that he's alive. They may be lying about both issues." To us, she said, "You have the guns. So I must ask—may he go confirm what you have said before we discuss whatever it is you want?"

Without the key to all the padlocks, freeing Shearman Waxx might easily take half an hour with the proper tools.

"I want him back here in two minutes," I said, "or I'll have to shoot you dead."

Zazu did not like the ticking clock, perhaps because she thought the hunchback unreliable, but she knew there could be no better terms than this.

The stare she turned upon the hunchback made him cringe. His shoulders slumped further, and he hung his head, regarding her meekly from beneath the shelf of his heavy brow.

She said to him, "If you want to be allowed to do those things you so much like to do, be back here in two minutes."

"Yes, Zazu. I will, I will, Zazu. I understand. Don't I always do what you say?"

The hunchback hurried from the room, by way of the door through which we had entered.

Suddenly I remembered John Clitherow's curious last words to me: *And now I am in the tower* de Paris *with—*

John had been trying to warn me, without giving away his game, that should a horribly deformed man cross my path, I must not pity him or let him get too close. Victor Hugo's famous novel *Notre-Dame de Paris* was in English titled *The Hunchback of Notre Dame,* and the tower of course was the bell tower of that cathedral.

I directed Zazu to move between us and the door by which the hunchback had departed.

The creature's big-knuckled, thick-fingered hands would be so clumsy with a gun that he probably always chose a knife, as with Clitherow, but using Zazu as cover seemed right to me.

Returning to the subject of her vaunted achievements, Zazu said,

"The problem with culture is that it swings like a pendulum, driven by one theory for a while and then by a countertheory."

"That's the same way it is when you're working on the time-travel problem," Milo said.

For a moment, Zazu looked as if she might spit a stream of blinding venom at the boy.

But she was too eager to talk about herself to be sidetracked from her favorite subject: "My life's work is to stop the pendulum from swinging ever again and to maintain it along the arc on which the genius Rousseau set it moving more than two hundred years ago."

"They say I'm a kind of genius," Milo told her.

"You are the wrong kind of genius," Zazu informed him.

"Watch it, bitch," Penny warned.

"Rousseau was a madman," I said, "and an absolute monster to people in his personal life."

"Yes," said Zazu, "*you* would think so. Shelley, Marx, Freud, Nietzsche, Tolstoy, Bertrand Russell, Sartre—they were all monsters to the people in their personal lives, but that was of no importance when you consider their contributions to the world."

"All madmen to one degree or another," I said. "Geniuses, yes, and some of them fine artists. But madmen. And their contributions to the world were . . . irrationality, chaos, excuses for mass murder, despair."

"Not madmen," she said. "*Intellectuals.* They form the opinions of the elite ruling classes. Then artists and writers must, with their work, carry the message of their superiors to the masses. Which you have not done, Mr. Greenwich."

She went on in this vein for another minute, and I began to think she was vamping, stalling for time to think of a way to deal with us. We had indeed surprised her.

When he could get a word in, sweet Milo said, "Don't put down my dad. He's the best dad in the world—and *soooo* patient."

Ignoring Milo, Zazu Waxx said to me, "With your books, you are pushing the pendulum in the wrong direction, which is why you must be broken, made to renounce your heresy, and purged."

Gasping as if from exertion and also weeping, the hunchback returned to the room. In his right hand he clutched a butcher knife that dripped bright blood.

As flamboyant melodrama goes, it didn't get any better than this. But remember, truth is always paradoxical, and always much stranger than fiction.

As tall as she already was, Zazu straightened her shoulders and lifted her head, and became noticeably taller. "What have you done? You idiot, you disgusting lump, what have you done?"

"That was my only chance," said the son of Shearman. "He's never been helpless before. He'd never be helpless again. That was my only chance, and I took it, I took it, I took it."

The death of her son, Shearman, obviously enraged Zazu, but it seemed to be more of an intellectual than an emotional issue. "You cretin. He was a pioneer in the post-humanity movement. The way you were engineered from his sperm cells, you were destined to be the first of a super-race."

The weeping hunchback regarded her with bafflement. "But I'm not, Zazu."

"That wasn't Shearman's fault."

"But it wasn't my fault, Zazu."

"At least Shearman made the effort."

Zazu was so slim and her suit so well tailored that I would not have thought she could have been carrying a concealed weapon. Magically, it appeared in her hand. She shot the hunchback in the head and then shot me in the chest.

As I fell, I saw Penny shoot Zazu.

Chapter 62

Lying on my right side on the black-granite floor, I could see Zazu's crumpled form, which seemed to be all sticks and baling wire tangled in haute couture. Her blood looked as black as the granite on which she had fallen.

My vision rapidly faded, and when in seconds full blindness settled upon me, I heard Penny speaking my name. I was not able to reply, not able to say *I love you* or *good-bye*. I heard from Milo a terrible cry, and I tried to reach out to him, but I had no strength.

As my vision left me, in the same way so did my hearing, diminishing until the silence of a perfect vacuum took me one step farther from the world of sensual delights. I wanted one more time to hear their voices, her laughter and his giggle, but a veil had fallen between me and them, a veil more imposing than a stone wall.

The last smell I remember was the odor of my blood, which at first seemed repellent but then in some way became so sweet that it moved me to tears.

About then the strange thing began to happen. My sense of smell swiftly returned to me, as did my hearing, and then my vision. I saw Zazu's black blood spurt *into* her through her wounds, and she rose off the floor to a regal height once more. Her dropped gun flew back into her hand.

As I had fallen, so I rose to my feet again. The bullets that had torn through me now retreated from my flesh and raveled backward through the air to the muzzle of Zazu's pistol.

The hunchback, too, had been reborn, standing with the dripping butcher knife displayed as if it were a precious talisman. He spoke his announcement of murder backward, and reversed out of the room.

And then time flowed forward once more.

"Not madmen," Zazu said. "*Intellectuals.* They form the opinions of the elite..."

From the way that Penny and Milo looked at me, I knew that we three were the only people in the room who were conscious of what had happened. Even Lassie was clueless.

Because we were carrying the saltshakers that were no longer saltshakers.

"—carry the message of their superiors to the masses. Which you have not done, Mr. Greenwich."

Because Zazu went on in this vein for another minute, we had the power to guide events as they best served us.

I had been to the razor's edge of death, balanced between this world and the next, and now Penny and Milo looked more precious to me than ever before. My heart labored, and I had to struggle against a great tide of sentiment that would have disabled me.

We let Zazu babble until, as before, Milo said, "Don't put down my dad. He's the best dad in the world." This time, instead of adding "and *soooo* patient," the boy said, "and nobody's gonna kill him on my watch."

Ignoring Milo, Zazu Waxx said to me, "With your books, you are pushing the pendulum in the wrong direction, which is why you must be broken, made to renounce your heresy, and purged."

Gasping, weeping, the hunchback returned to the room with the dripping knife to announce the murder of Shearman Waxx.

Zazu straightened her shoulders, lifted her head. "What have you done? You idiot, you disgusting lump, what have you done?"

"That was my only chance," said the hunchback. "He's never been helpless before. He'd never be helpless again. That was my only chance, and I took it, I took it, I took it."

Zazu repeated her speech about Shearman being a pioneer in the post-humanity movement.

"Dad," Milo said. "The thing is, for some reason, you can't replay the same moment more than once."

"Okay."

Zazu finished addressing her grandchild: "You were destined to be the first of a super-race."

The weeping hunchback regarded her with bafflement. "But I'm not, Zazu."

"That wasn't Shearman's fault."

"But it wasn't my fault, Zazu."

"At least Shearman made the effort."

This time, expecting it, I saw her draw the pistol from under her beautifully tailored jacket.

She shot the hunchback in the head, and as she turned toward me, Penny and I shot her, oh, maybe twelve times.

Once more, Zazu collapsed onto the black-granite floor. She blinked at us in disbelief, as if we had done the impossible and killed an immortal.

Her last words were: "You can't escape. Twelve thousand of us...in the agency. The work...goes on...without me."

We, too, went on without her.

Penny and I spent a while just staring at Milo, until he became embarrassed, shrugged his shoulders, and said, "See why it would have been so hard to explain when you don't know the science? It's a thing you just have to experience."

Penny and I spent a while longer staring at each other.

Finally, she said, "You know, suddenly a teleporting dog doesn't seem like such a big deal. She's as cute as ever, and she's too smart to teleport into the middle of a forest fire or something."

My disposable cell phone rang. Only Vivian Norby had the number.

"Hello?" I said shakily.

Hud Jacklight rammed back into my world with his trademark insistence: "I've been trying all day. To reach you. Big news."

"Hud, how did you get this number?"

"Milo's baby-sitter. Had to twist her arm. Tough lady."

"Hud, I really can't talk now."

"Made a deal. For you, Cubbo."

"I'm going to hang up now, Hud."

"Wait, wait. Not *The Great Gatsby*."

"This again?"

"*The Old Man and the Sea*. The sequel."

Although she could not hear Hud's side of the conversation, Penny put her gun to my head and said, "Fire him."

"That one doesn't need a sequel, either."

"There's a shark in it."

"So what?"

"Not the old man. He doesn't come back. The shark. The shark comes back."

"Fire him," Penny warned me.

I started to laugh.

"It'll be the first. A series. Listen to you. You're so happy. I love happy clients."

"I mean it," Penny told me, her gun still to my head. "Fire him now, Cubby."

Hud said, "*Cullen Greenwich Presents. Sequels to Classics.* Big literary thing. You don't write them. Someone else does. You just put your name on 'em."

I was laughing so hard tears streamed down my face.

"Listen. *Ben-Hur.* The gladiator guy? Reincarnated. As a pro wrestler."

I tried to speak, but I couldn't. I was convulsed.

"*The Call of the Wild.* Jack London piece. This time an alien spaceship. Under the ice. Aliens possess the wolves."

Between gales of laughter, I said to Penny, "You...you do it."

"*Tarzan.* Not raised by apes. Not Africa. Alaska. Raised by polar bears."

Nearly hysterical, I passed the phone to Penny.

She took her gun away from my head, spared my life, and said, "Hud, you're fired," and turned off the phone.

"This place is creepy," Milo said. "Can we get out of here?"

I holstered my pistol, lifted him into my arms, and held him tight. The smell of his hair. The smoothness of his boyish cheeks. The fierceness with which he hugged me. I was alive.

In the garage, we didn't look in the cargo space of the Hummer. We took our things from the vehicle and walked away from the house.

"Should we maybe wipe our prints off the steering wheel and stuff?"

"No point," I said, the laughter having passed. "Police will never have a chance to investigate. The agency will clean it up."

Beyond the house, the sea broke on a beach with a sound like war machines or like the laughter of a crowd, depending on how you chose to hear it.

The night was cool, the moon was bright, and the stars went on forever.

Chapter 63

The scenery is stunning where we live now, but I will not describe it.

We reside in a modest house, but beneath it is a secret haven that the Boom family came together to construct.

On the same property, Vivian Norby has a cottage of her own.

I am no longer bald, but I do not look much like the writer whose photos were on my book jackets. Penny styles her hair in a different fashion, has made some other changes, and is lovelier than ever.

Penny, Milo, Lassie, and I use our real names when we are alone with one another, but the rest of the world knows us by names that we chose after much discussion.

Through a series of clever maneuvers involving foreign banks, Grimbald was able to spirit all of our savings out of the country before the people-of-the-red-arms realized we had escaped Shearman and Zazu. Because I'd enjoyed six bestsellers and because the Purple

Bunny books had been earning well for eight years, and because we live simply now, we are set for a long, long time.

Grim and Clo have retired from the building-demolition business and now live incognito in their canyon.

I write novels and put them away in a chest of drawers rather than send them to a publisher. I no longer must suffer the shame of excessive self-promotion.

This story of our encounters with Shearman Waxx and his fellow booklovers may be published by a foundation, staffed by courageous people who believe in the beauty of tradition, in the necessity of truth, in the need for reason in a world of irrational ideologies.

Penny writes books, illustrates them, and puts them away as well. We hope the world will want her work and mine one day—and will not require of us that we be executed for it.

We follow the news as much as we can tolerate it. We see the signs, the gathering clouds, the horror that could come upon the whole world.

In spite of all that we have seen and now know, we have not lost hope, neither has our hope been diminished. We have a dog that teleports. We know what matters in life and what does not. We have a son who will one day provide the means for the sane to reclaim civilization from those who value theories more than truth and utopian dreams more than people.

Shearman Waxx was not relentless. Evil itself may be relentless, I will grant you that, but love is relentless, too. Friendship is a relentless force. Family is a relentless force. Faith is a relentless force. The human spirit is relentless, and the human heart outlasts—and can defeat—even the most relentless force of all, which is time.

ABOUT THE AUTHOR

DEAN KOONTZ is the author of many #1 *New York Times* bestsellers. He lives in Southern California with his wife, Gerda, their golden retriever, Anna, and the enduring spirit of their golden, Trixie.

Correspondence for the author should be addressed to:

Dean Koontz
P.O. Box 9529
Newport Beach, California 92658